revolution

TOR TEEN BOOKS BY JENNA BLACK

Replica

Resistance

Revolution

JENNA BLACK

A TOM DOHERTY ASSOCIATES BOOK
NEW YORK

This is a work of fiction. All of the characters, organizations, and events portrayed in this novel are either products of the author's imagination or are used fictitiously.

REVOLUTION

A Tor Teen Book
Published by Tom Doherty Associates, LLC
175 Fifth Avenue
New York, NY 10010

www.tor-forge.com

The Library of Congress Cataloging-in-Publication Data is available upon request.

ISBN 978-0-7653-3373-5 (trade paperback)
ISBN 978-1-4668-0491-3 (e-book)

First Edition: November 2014

P1

In loving memory of Merle Arnold Clark

Revolution

CHAPTER ONE

"WE are so screwed," Bishop said as he rummaged through the cupboards in his apartment, tossing everything he could find onto the kitchen counter. The other members of their fledgling new resistance had all joined him in the kitchen, although Nate's eyes were glazed over in a manner that suggested he wasn't listening, maybe wasn't even seeing anything around him.

Nadia wished there was something she could do for him. But of course, there wasn't, not when he'd seen his father shot in the head only a few hours ago.

"Not the most helpful commentary," Dante said, but the bleak look on his face showed he wasn't any more optimistic.

Earlier this morning, Nate and Nadia had stormed the Paxco Headquarters Building, demanding to speak to the Chairman. Their plan had been to blackmail the Chairman into stepping down in favor of Nate, but nothing had turned out how they'd planned. Now the Chairman was dead, shot in the head by Dorothy, who claimed to be his daughter and would succeed him to the Chairmanship because she'd framed Nate and Nadia for the crime. They'd survived the encounter and made it back to Bishop's Basement apartment, but that was about the best that could be said for their grand plan.

"I'm just telling it like it is," Bishop said. "I told you I couldn't hide so many people in the Basement for long. And that was *before* I found out some psychotic sentient machine wants to kill you so she can take over the world."

Nadia wasn't entirely sure *what* Thea—and Dorothy, the empty-minded Replica she'd created so she could impersonate a human being—really wanted. To continue her gruesome research into the mind/body connection, sure. There was no question Thea was even now procuring prisoners and Basement-dwellers to vivisect for the "good of mankind." But there was more to it than that, and Nadia doubted Thea's ultimate goal had anything to do with the good of mankind.

Bishop closed the last cupboard and made a sweeping gesture at the pile of food lying on the counter. "Except for a year-old frozen dinner in the freezer, that's all I've got."

None of them had eaten since a meager "breakfast" of canned beef stew the day before, but hungry as she was, Nadia couldn't say the offerings held much appeal. She picked up a dented, rusty can of some artificial ham product whose main ingredient was soy. It was well past its expiration date. Not that she was in any position to turn her nose up at whatever Bishop had to offer.

"That's not very much for five people," Agnes ventured tentatively. There were a couple of bags of noodles, crushed almost into powder, as well as the "ham" and a can of green beans, but that was it.

Bishop nodded in agreement. "Even if security doesn't hunt us down, we'll end up starving to death."

Agnes frowned at him. "But the soup kitchens—"

"—require ID," Bishop interrupted. "If you don't have ID, then you have to buy food from your local 'grocer.'"

Nadia could hear the quotation marks around the term. "What do you mean when you say 'grocer'?" she asked.

"Assholes who sell crappy leftovers for profit. They force people in their territory to hand over some portion of their rations, then sell the rations to others who don't have ID. My landlord is one of them."

Technically, no one in the Basement was supposed to have a landlord—the housing was all state-funded—but Nadia had learned through Bishop that even in this relatively tame neighborhood, Basement predators abounded. No apartment came without a price tag, and if you couldn't pay in money, goods, or services, you had no choice but to sleep in the street.

"I can pick up food at the kitchens," Bishop continued. "I never gave up my ID when I went to work for Nate. But rations for one aren't going to keep five of us fed."

Nate roused himself from his stupor and blinked a few times, as if coming back from a long way away. "How many dollars do you have left?" he asked Bishop.

Bishop had stolen Nate's stash of dollars—the currency of choice in the Basement—when he'd been forced to flee for his life, and based on the shabby, unfurnished state of his apartment, it didn't look like he'd spent a whole lot of them. Then again, he'd had to go into deep hiding and had paid the Red Death, one of the gangs that ruled the heart of Debasement, to take him in. Nadia had no idea how much money that had cost, but she bet it was a lot.

"If we eat like we're all on a crash diet, I might have

enough dollars to keep us fed for a week. After that, we'd have to decide whether to spend the rest on food or shelter, 'cause we won't have enough for both."

Nadia chewed her lip anxiously. The odds of them all surviving that week didn't seem too good. Thea, in the person of her puppet Replica, Dorothy, had let Nate and Nadia go, but that had been a strategic decision and was meant to be temporary. Thea wanted them dead. She just didn't want it to happen on the record.

Of course, finding them in the Basement might be a little harder than Thea expected. It was a community of cutthroats, thieves, and drug lords, but it *was* a community, of sorts. The kind of community that didn't take well to Paxco security officers and could be stunningly uncooperative even in the face of bribes. And the lawlessness of the area would work to their advantage as well—there were no security cameras anywhere, and they could buy whatever they needed through back channels without ever having to go near places where they might be recognized by security officers or Employees. If they had money, that is.

"So we have one week to come up with a plan to kill Thea and set the record straight so I can be Chairman," Nate said. He was looking more alert by the minute as his fury kindled. He'd had mixed feelings about his father, at best. The man *had* killed the original Nate Hayes, after all, and had not only approved Thea's experiments but had enabled them. He'd been a cruel and ruthless leader, abusing his power whenever he felt like it. But he was still Nate's father, and his death had been a hard blow.

"That about sums it up," Bishop agreed as he pulled a dented, misshapen pot out from under a cupboard under the sink, filled it with water, and put it on the stove's smallest burner, one that was about one-fourth the size of the bottom of the pot.

Dante frowned at him. "Why don't you put it on a bigger burner?"

"This is the only one that works."

Nadia grimaced. She'd known the accommodations in the Basement weren't great, but she'd never realized just what kind of conditions Basement-dwellers lived in. The apartment was a hovel, the appliances ancient and barely functional, and the food had no doubt been on its way to the dump before it was commandeered for the soup kitchens.

Agnes cleared her throat, then spoke up in her tentative, little-girl voice. She was older than Nadia—she'd be turning eighteen in just a few days—but that voice of hers made her sound even younger and more vulnerable than she was.

"Realistically, we know we're not going to beat Thea in a week."

Nate glared at her so fiercely she recoiled. "The hell we won't!" he snapped.

Nadia was prepared to cut Nate a lot of slack after what had happened, but she wouldn't stand for him acting like a bully. "Cut it out, Nate! Having a temper tantrum isn't going to help anything."

Nate turned toward her, and for a moment she thought he was going to bite her head off. He'd always had a temper and had rarely tried to control it. But he'd matured a lot since the day he'd awakened in the Replication tank, and he reined himself back in.

"Sorry," he said, though his eyes still flashed. "But I don't think moaning about how doomed we are is going to help anything."

"I wasn't moaning," Agnes said, giving Nate a glare of her own. "I was being realistic."

"Which is spectacularly unhelpful right now," Nate retorted.

"How would you know how helpful it is when you won't let me finish?"

Nate looked taken aback by the sensible question, and Nadia had to fight off a smile. She wanted to flash Agnes a thumbs-up, but she didn't want to risk setting Nate off again. His self-control was shaky at best.

Bishop didn't bother to fight his smile. The pot of water had reached an anemic boil, and he started dumping the noodles into it. The water immediately turned a frothy, starchy white, the noodles so crushed Nadia suspected the end result would be more like a paste than a soup. When he reached for the can of "ham," Nadia looked away, thinking it might be easier to choke down the food if she didn't examine it too closely.

"As I was saying," Agnes said, when Nate kept his mouth shut, "it's not likely we can solve all our problems in a week, and as Bishop was saying, we can't stay hidden here indefinitely. Which means we have to go somewhere else."

"There *is* nowhere else," Nate said.

"There's Synchrony," Agnes countered.

Synchrony was loosely allied with Paxco, although Nadia had no idea what the current state of that alliance was. Up until last night, it had looked like they were on course for a very strong bond indeed, with Agnes due to sign a marriage agreement with Nate as soon as she turned eighteen. But now that Nate had supposedly assassinated his father and kidnapped Agnes, who knew what the relationship between the two states was? Chairman Belinski had to be frantic to find his daughter, but Thea was no doubt determined to make sure that didn't happen. Thea had to know that Nate and Nadia would have told their companions the whole truth, and that meant she would want them all dead as soon as possible.

"Synchrony?" Nate asked, as though he'd never heard of the place before.

"We'll be out of Thea's reach there," Agnes said. "My father can provide twenty-four-hour protection, and we wouldn't have to worry about starving to death or getting murdered by a mob of Basement-dwellers."

"And how exactly do you propose we get there?" Nate asked. "We can't just hop on a plane, even if we could afford it. We could steal a car to get us to the border, but how would we get across? I don't think the nice men with the machine guns will let us through. For all we know, they have orders to shoot us on sight."

Agnes stared at him with wide eyes and swallowed hard. "My father can have people waiting for us."

"On the Synchrony side of the border, sure," Nate agreed. "And that'll do us a lot of good when the Paxco border patrol arrests or shoots us on *this* side of the border."

Agnes raised her chin. "You think my father would be okay with Paxco forces arresting or shooting me? Synchrony may be small, but I don't think even Paxco wants to go to war against our military."

"That would be true if someone other than Thea were calling the shots for Paxco," Nadia said. "But it's hard to know just what Thea will do. Loss of human life doesn't bother her, and she might think disposing of all of us is worth the minor inconvenience of a war."

"But even if she's using Dorothy to usurp the Chairmanship," Nate argued, "the Chairman isn't all-powerful. She would need the board of directors' approval before she declared war, and I can't see—"

"But *she* wouldn't be the one doing it," Nadia said. "She doesn't need the board's permission to order the border patrol to shoot us on sight, and it's Chairman Belinski who would actually declare war."

"So we have my father send a delegation over the border into Paxco," Agnes said. "They meet us and escort us over the border. The border patrol wouldn't be able to shoot us without shooting the delegation, and that's something they won't be willing to do."

Nadia wasn't so sure about that. Thea might guess they'd head for Synchrony, and she'd no doubt have contingencies in place. All it would take was one person firing a gun, and all hell would break loose. It seemed likely the five of them would somehow get killed in the cross fire if something like that were to happen.

"What's more dangerous?" she mused out loud. "Trying to survive in the Basement with limited money, or trying to cross the border when Thea is almost certainly expecting us to try it?"

"Both choices suck ass," Bishop said.

"Will you quit with the language?" Nate asked peevishly, giving him a light punch on the arm.

Nadia rolled her eyes. She had long ago become immune to Bishop's language, and even Agnes seemed to be getting used to it, no longer flinching when he said one of those words that was not used in polite Executive society.

"It doesn't matter what language he uses," Nadia said. "He's right."

"Of course he's right," Agnes agreed. "The important question isn't what's more dangerous, it's what will serve us better if it works. And I don't think that choice is all that hard to make."

When she put it that way . . .

What good could possibly come from hiding in the Basement? Nadia and her friends would be powerless here, with no money or supporters. But if they could make it to Synchrony and cut some kind of deal with Chairman Belinski, they might be able to stop Thea from achieving whatever her end goal was. The idea of conspiring with a foreign Chairman, of potentially betraying her state to one, did not sit well in Nadia's stomach, but it seemed like the lesser of two evils.

"So," Nate said, "I guess we're going to Synchrony."

Agnes let out a breath of relief, her shoulders sagging. She had to know they had a lot of potentially lethal hurdles still to leap, but Nadia understood the appeal of the idea of going home.

"I'll have to call my father and see what I can arrange," she said, looking at Nate and raising an eyebrow. "You have a secure phone, right?"

Nate nodded and pulled a phone out of his pocket. Nadia's adrenaline suddenly spiked as she remembered something Dorothy had said during their confrontation earlier.

"How sure are we that the phone's secure?" she asked. "And that Chairman Belinski's phone is, too? Dorothy said she found one of the videos we made, which means she has feelers all over the net. What do you want to bet she can listen in on phone lines, too?"

Agnes gave the phone in her hand a doubtful look. Then she seemed to come to a decision and stood up a little straighter, her chin sticking out with a hint of stubbornness. "We can't get to Synchrony without taking risks. Even if Thea can listen in to the phone call and track its origins, at least we can tell my father what's *really* going on."

"Will he believe us?" Nadia asked. "I mean, I think it'll sound pretty damn crazy to someone who hasn't been wrapped up in it from the beginning."

"He'll believe *me*," Agnes said.

Nadia hoped it wasn't wishful thinking.

Agnes turned on the phone, quickly tapping in a number. She held the phone to her ear, then frowned and lowered it. "Nothing's happening."

Bishop made a little sound of disgust. "Because phone service is out. Happens all the time around here. It's not like anyone in power gives a shit whether we can use the phone or not. Could be days before they get around to fixing it."

Nadia met Nate's eyes, and she could see he was having the same thought as she. Thea knew their first move after this morning's fiasco would be to run to the Basement, the one place where they could escape the city's ubiquitous security cameras. Disabling the Basement's phone service was an obvious way to stop them from reaching out for help—or from telling anyone the truth about Dorothy.

"I guess if we want to call my father," Agnes said, "we'll have to go where there's service even if it means risking being spotted. I don't think we can afford to wait until service is restored. Assuming it ever is."

Apparently, Agnes's thoughts had traveled the same road.

"I don't know," Bishop said, frowning fiercely. "Could be exactly what Thea wants us to do. Maybe she's trying to flush us out, one way or another."

"It doesn't matter," Nadia said firmly. "I want us all to get out of this alive, but the most important thing of all is to get word out about Thea. She's gained a frightening amount of power, and she now has all of Paxco under her control. She *has* to be stopped, and contacting Chairman Belinski seems like the best way to stop her."

Synchrony was considered one of the less powerful states because it wasn't particularly wealthy. However, the reason it wasn't wealthy was that it spent so much of its money on its military, a military that was well trained and very well equipped. Powerful enough to defeat Thea's commandeered forces, if it came to that.

"So we're going on a road trip," Nate said, trying to sound casual and unconcerned.

"Let's wait until nightfall, at least," Bishop suggested. "We'll be harder to recognize in the dark, and there'll be more people out and about to give us cover."

He turned off the stove and pulled the pot off the burner. Nadia's stomach gave a lurch when she took a quick glance at the contents. Some artificial chicken flavoring packets had turned the water a shade of yellow not seen in nature, and there were chunks of pink-tinted soy meat product and gray green beans floating in it.

"Dinner is served," Bishop said with an ironic flourish.

Nadia was sure she wasn't the only one whose appetite had retreated into a corner to hide, but they were all damn well going to eat what they were given.

until the moment that he, Kurt, and Agnes headed out into the night, Nate racked his brain in hopes that he could come up with a better plan. Splitting up seemed like a bad idea, and yet there was no good reason to risk letting Nadia, with her famous face and her so-so disguise, be seen out in public. Hell, there wasn't a whole lot of reason to risk *Nate* showing his face, except that he had put his foot down and insisted on coming along, disguised as his Basement alter ego, the Ghost. No one was going to recognize the Chairman Heir beneath the white wig, the bluish-white face powder, and the pale blue contact lenses. He needed to be *doing* something instead of sitting around thinking. His mind was too full of horrors, his heart too full of jumbled emotions. Besides, he was the rightful Chairman of Paxco. He needed Agnes to reassure her father she hadn't been kidnapped and to verify their crazy-sounding story, but if anyone was going to encourage a foreign power to invade his state, it was going to be him.

"Stay close," Kurt said unnecessarily as he and Nate and Agnes merged with the crowd that had started forming in the street the moment the sun went down.

Nate wished there were some way they could get in touch with Chairman Belinski without having to drag Agnes through the streets of the Basement. She was in disguise, of course, and the people of the Basement made a practice of minding their own business, but there was an aura of vulnerability about her that he feared might attract the wrong sort. But she had been adamant that she had to be the one to make the call, and it was hard to argue. He was certain that Belinski thought Nate had kidnapped his daughter, so there was no way he would listen to anything Nate had to say without Agnes there.

He and Kurt sandwiched Agnes, doing the best they could to shield her and make it obvious to any Basement predators that she was not unprotected, as they made their way toward the Basement's border. It was possible Dorothy had cut off phone service in the low-class Employee neighborhoods just beyond the Basement, but it seemed unlikely. Low-class those Employees might be, but they were still *Employees.* Dorothy could get away with shenanigans that only hurt Basement-dwellers, but she'd have a lot harder time justifying anything that might cause problems for Employees.

Hopefully, within a block or two after passing the Basement's border, they would be able to pick up a phone signal. Then they'd find somewhere as secluded as possible so that Agnes could make her phone call without being observed. And hope that they weren't caught on surveillance video and recognized before they could plan a strategy with Chairman Belinski.

"Something seems off," Kurt commented.

Nate shook himself out of his worries and looked around, trying to see what Kurt was talking about.

"What do you mean?" Agnes asked.

Kurt shook his head. "Not sure, really. Just feels . . . different out here."

As soon as Kurt pointed it out, Nate noticed it, too. Here in the "tourist" areas of the Basement, where Employees and Executives came to play, there was usually a palpable buzz of energy in the air. Lots of adrenaline-fueled excitement from the tourists, lots of predatory anticipation in the Basement-dwellers who planned to take advantage of them.

Tonight, the mood felt strangely subdued, even though there were just as many people on the streets as usual, and business was being transacted.

"I have a bad feeling about this," Nate muttered. But there was nothing to do but keep moving and hope it was all in their imagination.

Unfortunately, it wasn't.

When the street they were following neared the Basement's edge, the tension in the air reached such a level that even Agnes felt it, and they soon found out why.

A row of sawhorses had been set up at the border, crossing from sidewalk to sidewalk with only two small openings at the center. Each opening was manned by two uniformed security officers, and it appeared that anyone who wanted to cross the border in either direction was being required to show ID.

Worse, there was a giant video screen set up behind the barricade facing the Basement, its message blinking ostentatiously. Impossible to miss.

First, a picture of Nadia; then a picture of Nate; then WANTED DEAD OR ALIVE. And finally, most chilling of all: REWARD $100,000 AND EMPLOYEE STATUS.

Nate stopped in his tracks and swallowed hard. That would be a hell of a lot of money for a Basement-dweller even if it was being offered in *credits,* but in *dollars* . . .

Kurt uttered a string of curses, then took hold of both Nate's and Agnes's arms and steered them away in a hurry.

“No talking!” he snapped at them even though no one had tried to say anything. He glanced around him significantly. Nate got the message, and he presumed Agnes did, too. There were ears all around them, and if they said anything that suggested the roadblock was meant for them, someone would be sure to hear. They’d probably drawn enough attention to themselves by their abrupt about-face, although glancing over his shoulder Nate could see they weren’t the only ones doing it. There were plenty of people in the Basement who did not want to parade themselves in front of security officers.

Trying not to look overly furtive, they headed back toward Kurt’s apartment. It was time to come up with a plan B.

CHAPTER TWO

nadia hadn't considered that with Agnes, Nate, and Bishop all heading out to try to reach Chairman Belinski, she and Dante would be left alone together in Bishop's apartment.

There wasn't any furniture in his living room—unless you counted the smattering of mismatched, stained sofa cushions that were scattered around the floor. Nadia made herself comfortable by dragging one of those cushions to the edge of the room so she could use the wall as an impromptu backrest. Dante grabbed another cushion and came toward her.

"Scooch forward," he said, then tucked the cushion behind her when she obeyed. He grinned down at her. "Almost as comfy as your living room couch, no?"

She smiled at him as he joined her on the "couch," sitting shoulder to shoulder with her and stretching out his legs. "Depends on your definition of *almost*," she replied. She leaned into him, and he took the hint, draping his arm around her shoulders. She sighed and snuggled against him, closing her eyes and trying not to think.

They sat like that for a few minutes in companionable silence, just enjoying each other's company and the luxury of privacy. Then Dante kissed the top of her head, and the very air that surrounded them seemed to change. Nadia's pulse picked up its pace, and her hand somehow found its way to the center of Dante's nicely muscled chest. He sucked in a hurried breath, his heart kicking beneath her fingertips.

Such innocent touches, and yet they filled the room with an electric sense of anticipation. Nadia turned her face up to his, hardly able to believe the longing that coursed through her. They were sitting on the floor on stained cushions in an apartment that was about one step short of being condemned. They were on the run, their lives in constant danger. It was about as unromantic a situation as Nadia could imagine. But when Dante kissed her, it was as if the rest of the world just fell away.

A needy little sound escaped Nadia's throat, and she buried her fingers in Dante's hair, clinging to him as if she would never let go. Her skin felt hot and tingly all over, and the touch of his hands sent her heart racing. She wanted to know what his skin felt like next to hers, wanted to get their shirts out of the way so she could find out, and from Dante's greedy kisses, she could tell he wanted the same.

Her hands drifted down his back, tucking into the hem of his shirt and dragging it upward. He showed no inclination to protest as she dragged the hem up his back, all the way to his shoulders.

They had to break the kiss so Nadia could pull the shirt off over his head, but the sacrifice was worth it. Nadia admired the sculpted muscles of his chest with the tips of her fingers, loving how his skin peppered with goose bumps at her touch.

"We don't know how long the others will be gone," he reminded her breathlessly. But his hands were reaching for the bottom of her tattered and stained tunic top.

"We have at least a few minutes, surely," she said, lifting her arms over her head so that Dante could pull the tunic off.

"Definitely not enough time," he said.

Nadia was left in nothing but her bra and the shapeless pants she'd been issued at the retreat. Having never undressed in front of a guy before, she was surprised by the wave of self-consciousness that crashed over her as his eyes examined the expanse of flesh that had been revealed. Were her breasts too small for his liking? She'd never had many curves, and based on the rest of the women of her family, she was pretty sure she wouldn't be developing any. She had to fight the urge to cover herself with her arms, and her cheeks glowed with heat. And yet for all her nerves, she couldn't deny the thrill of excitement that coursed through her.

"You're so beautiful," he whispered, reaching out to touch her shoulders in a gesture that was almost reverent.

"You, too," she managed to choke out, then realized what she'd said and felt the glow in her cheeks grow hotter.

Dante's eyes twinkled with a mixture of desire and humor, his lips turned up in a tempting smile. He was clearly not insulted. His fingers traced down the edges of her collarbone, drifting lower.

Nadia made an appreciative, encouraging sound in her throat and saw how he swallowed hard, his eyes huge and dark.

They both stiffened in a hurry when they heard the sound

of footsteps pounding in the hall outside. Nadia let out a little gasp and lunged for her tunic, while Dante cursed under his breath and pulled on his T-shirt. Inside out.

Nadia struggled into the tunic, and as she tugged it into place, the footsteps kept right on pounding—all the way past the door. She and Dante both let out little laughs of relief, and he fixed his T-shirt. There was no way they could start back up where they'd left off—they'd both have half their attention focused on the hallway outside, listening for a sign that their friends were about to walk in on them.

"It's kinda hot in here," Nadia said, fanning her face. She knew perfectly well the heat was coming from inside her, but she climbed to her feet anyway. "Let's open a window."

"Sure," Dante said, sounding resigned. "Only let me kill the lights first so no one can see your face."

She grimaced, realizing she'd been about to do something stupid and careless. Standing in front of a window with the lights on and showing her face to anyone who cared to look up was not the best plan for someone who was supposed to be in hiding. She waited until Dante flipped the lights off, then opened the window.

The air that wafted in from the open window probably wasn't any cooler than the air inside the apartment, but there was a pleasant breeze blowing. She propped her forearms on the windowsill and gazed out at the teeming streets of the Basement. At first, all she saw was a sea of color, the denizens of the Basement vying with each other to be the most eye-catching. Then she started noticing individuals, the women dressed in clothes that left little to the imagination, the drug dealers peddling their wares out in the open because laws weren't enforced here, the thieves and pick-pockets trolling the "tourists" for easy prey.

"I used to think my life sucked," Dante said, joining her at the window and looking down at the crowd. "There's not a lot of perks to being the son of a couple of sanitation workers. I've been to the Basement before, but it wasn't until lately that I realized how good I had it growing up."

Nadia nodded, but made no comment. She had often envied Employees the freedom of their lives—the freedom to choose their own careers and their own spouses—but she had never felt that way about Basement-dwellers. Their choices were limited at best from the moment of their birth, just like Executives, and yet they didn't have the safe and comfortable living conditions to make up for it. All of the downsides of being an Executive, with none of the perks.

The sound of a loudspeaker, distant enough that she couldn't make out any words, caught Nadia's attention, and she glanced around looking for its source. She didn't see anything, but Dante nudged her arm with his elbow and pointed upward.

A blimp was hovering above the Basement, and on its side was a huge video screen. The voice Nadia had heard was Dorothy, gazing sternly out from the screen as she spoke into a bank of microphones. It was some kind of press conference, but it appeared to be finishing up. The scene quickly shifted to slightly grainy surveillance footage. Footage that showed Nate pointing a gun at his father's head and calmly pulling the trigger while Dorothy lay unconscious on the floor and Nadia stood by, a gun in her hand and a smirk on her face.

"Christ!" Dante said beside her, and he held tighter to her hand. "That looks completely real."

"It isn't," Nadia said, a little too emphatically. She knew Dante believed her and Nate's version of the story, but she knew she herself would have doubts if she hadn't been there to see what really happened in person. The video was a complete fabrication. Nadia supposed that if Thea was able to create perfect Replicas of human beings in the flesh, it wasn't hard to imagine she could create digital images of them, complete with voices.

The scene shifted again as the blimp made its lazy way through the sky, this time showing Paxco's new chief of security offering a reward for information leading to Nate and Nadia's capture. The scene shifted one more time, and Nadia clapped her hand over her mouth to try to contain a cry of dismay.

A mob of reporters, snapping pictures and shouting questions, were being held back by security officers as Gerald and Esmeralda Lake, Nadia's parents, were dragged out of the Lake Towers in handcuffs. Her father's face was white, his eyes glazed with shock, and her mother was openly sobbing. As if that weren't bad enough, Gerri's husband was being dragged along right behind them. He must have gone over to their apartment to share in their grief over Gerri's death, thereby making it easy for Dorothy to round up everyone together. Gerri's two kids, Corinne and Rory, were both howling with tears as members of Child Protective Services carried them out of the building.

"No," Nadia gasped, shaking her head as if she could make the horrifying images go away. She had tried so hard to protect her family, especially her little niece and nephew. Thanks to Nadia's decisions, Gerri was dead. Now their parents and Gerri's husband were in custody, and her children about to disappear into the foster care system. It was more than Nadia could take.

Dante wrapped his arms around her and held her tight. Nadia's eyes remained dry, but her heart was hammering and she could hardly draw in a full breath. Her skin felt cold and clammy, and the floor beneath her seemed to be moving. A detached part of her mind wondered if she was having a full-fledged panic attack. As scared as she was for herself and her friends, it couldn't compare to the fear she felt for her family, who had no idea what was going on and who were helpless to defend themselves against Thea's cruelty.

Dante slammed the window shut with more force than necessary while Nadia stood paralyzed by mute horror. He gently guided her away from the window and toward their makeshift sofa.

"SO to sum up," Nate said, when he, Kurt, and Agnes returned to the apartment after their failed attempt to get a phone signal, "we can't get out of the Basement. We can't call anyone. Some number of Basement-dwellers will be eager to turn us in because they hate us for being Execs or they just want the reward money. And we don't have enough money to keep a roof over our heads and food in our mouths for more than about a week."

As bad as everything about their situation seemed, it was that last part that was the most immediate concern. Money didn't solve all the world's problems, but it sure could be helpful.

"There are ways we can earn money," Kurt said tentatively, watching closely for Nate's reaction. Nate might not even have realized what he was suggesting if it weren't for the way he was looking at him.

"No," Nate said, proud of himself for keeping his voice calm and level, even if his blood pressure did go through the roof. "You are not working ever again. Period."

Agnes blushed a deep, dark red when she figured out the implications of the exchange, and even Dante looked uncomfortable, pointedly looking away. Only Nadia seemed unfazed by Kurt's suggestion.

"I agree with Nate," she said. "You're taking enough risks for us as it is."

"And if it's the only way we can get money?" Kurt challenged.

"Maybe it isn't," Nadia said. "I know the resistance doesn't want to help us or shelter us or anything like that. But maybe they'd be willing to pay us for information."

Kurt scowled at her. "You mean information like the stuff I already know about Dorothy and Thea? Stuff I would tell them for free? You know I *am* still a member of the resistance, least as far as I know. I haven't disobeyed any orders."

"Only because you haven't talked to anyone yet," Dante countered. "You know they're going to order you to stay away from Nate and Nadia the second you check in. You're going to have to choose between their resistance and ours." His glance flicked quickly to Nate and back. "I'm going to take a wild guess and say you'll choose ours. And if that's the case, getting them to pay us for information is a good idea."

Kurt did not look at all happy with the idea, and Nate couldn't blame him. He supposed in Kurt's shoes, he'd feel pretty disloyal if he tried to squeeze money out of a resistance movement he'd been involved with for so long. But all indications were that the resistance had money, and using some of it to fund a new auxiliary resistance movement didn't seem like it was that bad an idea to him.

"They're not going to like it," Kurt said.

"We'll put the money to good use," Nate said. "They might not want anything to do with us, but it seems to me having a second resistance movement in place could be to their advantage. We'll be attracting a lot of attention from Dorothy and from the security department, and who knows what the resistance will be able to accomplish while the government's attention is focused elsewhere."

Nate was making things up as he went along, but he actually thought his argument made pretty good sense. Maybe calling five teenagers hiding out in the Basement a "resistance movement" was overstating things a bit, but the longer they all stayed alive and free, the longer Dorothy would be distracted by them.

"I'll take it to my cell leader," Kurt said. "It'll be up to him."

It was after midnight by the time Bishop returned from his meeting with his cell leader, and Nadia was still sunk deep in her pool of misery. She knew Thea was broadcasting the footage of her family's arrest because she hoped Nadia would give herself up to save them. Nadia had put aside her conscience and her personal safety on more than one occasion to protect her family, and she ached to do that now. The thought that her parents were now in Rikers Island and that Corinne and Rory had been robbed of both of their parents and relegated to the foster care system, all because of Nadia's actions, made her want to throw up.

If she'd had any reason to hope Thea would release her family, Nadia might have considered giving herself up. But with Thea's callous disregard for human life, it was possible the only reason Nadia's family were still alive was because of their potential usefulness as hostages. If Nadia turned herself in, her parents and brother-in-law would most likely be found guilty of some trumped-up treason charge and executed. And Nadia would be tortured until she told Thea everything she knew about the resistance and the location of her friends.

So logic told her keeping hidden was the right thing to do. But logic couldn't soothe her guilt every time the blimp passed near enough for her to hear the broadcast. She wondered if it was going to hover over the Basement all night and dreamed of arming herself with a rocket launcher to bring it down.

Nadia dragged herself away from her brooding thoughts when Bishop finally returned. Nate, who had been pacing across the living room and generally driving everyone crazy, came to a stop and let out a dramatic sigh of relief as Bishop closed the door and worked his way through all the locks.

"I was beginning to worry about you," Nate said, and Nadia smiled ruefully to herself. Nate had started worrying the second Bishop had set foot outside the building, and he hadn't let up in the hours since.

Because it was an unseasonably warm night and everyone appreciated the fresh air, they had left the living room window open and kept the lights off inside, so no one got a good look at Bishop until he'd turned away from the door and taken a couple of limping steps in their direction. Then Nate let out a gasp of dismay and quickly crossed the distance between them, and Nadia jumped to her feet. Dante cursed, and Agnes covered her mouth to stifle a gasp.

"Don't panic," Bishop said, putting his arms in front of him to stop Nate from hugging him. "I'm fine."

"The hell you are!" Nate shouted.

Nadia had to agree with him. Bishop's left eye was blackened and swollen, and he had a fat lip that had obviously bled on him, leaving dark blotches on the lime-green mesh shirt he wore to show off his tattoos. And then there was that limp.

"What happened?" Nadia asked, wondering if everyone she knew was going to get hurt before this whole nightmare was over.

"I got knocked around a little," Bishop said, still holding Nate off. "Can't tell you how many times I've had worse. Believe me, I'm fine." He gave Nate's shoulders a little shake for emphasis.

"I guess Razor wasn't too happy with your defection," Dante said. Nadia realized it was the first time either of the former resistance members had said the cell leader's name and wondered if that meant there had been some lingering distrust. If there was, it was obviously gone now.

"Not so much," Bishop said. "But the shit didn't hit the fan until he kicked me up the food chain. Mind if we sit down while we talk? I banged my knee pretty good during the fun and games."

Nate's jaw muscles worked busily as he draped one of Bishop's arms over his shoulders and helped him to one of the cushions. Bishop sat with a heavy sigh, stretching one leg out in front of him while tucking the other close to his body.

"Do you need any ice?" Dante asked, then frowned. "Do you *have* any ice?"

"Yes, and no," Bishop responded. "But I do have that frozen dinner."

Dante went into the kitchen to fetch it, and Nate somehow managed to contain his impatience until the thing was awkwardly perched on Bishop's sore knee. Nadia thought it might do more good on bare skin, but Bishop's pants were way too tight to roll up, and she certainly wasn't going to be the one to suggest he take them off.

"All right," Bishop began. "So like I said, Razor wasn't too happy with me and ordered me to tell him everything I knew. I said no, and he was even more unhappy with me."

"I'm going to kill this guy," Nate growled, and he looked fierce enough to do it with his bare hands.

"Told you—he didn't do this. He decided to call in his boss, and that's when things got a little intense."

"Who's his boss?" Dante asked, head cocked to the side. The resistance tried to be as compartmentalized as possible so that a captured member couldn't name all his fellow resistance members under torture, so neither Dante nor Bishop would have known the name of anyone who outranked their cell leader.

"No one you know," Bishop said, then turned a shrewd gaze to Nate. "But *you* know her. Better than you'd like."

Nate's eyes widened. "Angel!"

Bishop nodded. Nadia had never met Angel of Mercy, and she never wanted to. The woman owned a seedy club in the Basement, and she'd had her bouncers beat the hell out of Nate a couple of weeks ago to try to keep him from finding Bishop.

"Before you ask," Bishop said, "no, I didn't know she was with the resistance. Not until today. But it makes perfect sense. Wanna know how she got the name Angel of Mercy?"

"I assumed it was because she was the exact opposite," Nate said. He clenched his fists so hard the knuckles cracked.

"Besides her club, she has a side business, called the Pipeline. She helps people get out of Paxco—for profit, of course. You pay her with money or services, and she'll smuggle you to wherever you want to go. Usually somewhere that has way more opportunities for Basement-dwellers than Paxco does. Chances to get jobs—and better subsidized housing, food, and health care. A lot of her whores are working for her to get a chance at going through the Pipeline. I'm sure her unique skills have come in handy for the resistance."

"Yeah, I'm sure she's a real saint."

Bishop snorted. "I didn't say that. And she was way pissed at me. Called me a profiteer for trying to sell the information. She sorta had a point, so I've got no problem with her considering beating the info out of me."

"She obviously did more than consider it," Nate growled.

The look on Bishop's face said he was genuinely unconcerned about what had happened. "I'm fine. And I managed to guilt her out of going any further. Pointed out that beating the intel out of me was the kind of thing Paxco security would do. I also told her that our new Chairman is an impostor and that if she wanted the whole story, she had to pay for it. She's still not happy about it, but she's agreed to meet with us for an information exchange."

"When?" Nate asked. "And where?"

"Nine o'clock tomorrow night at her club. Here's the thing, though: we can't all go. I don't think she's going to double-cross us, but I can't be sure. She might think it's better for the resistance to bleed us for the information, then kill us to make sure we don't get caught and do a bunch of talking. I think we should send me and either Nate or Nadia while the rest of you stay put. She's not going to believe the intel unless it comes from an Exec, or I'd deal with her by myself."

"Obviously it's going to have to be me," Nate said.

He glanced sidelong at Nadia, perhaps sensing the way she'd bristled at his words. He was getting better at being aware of people's feelings, because usually he would have been oblivious to it. "Not because you're not up to it," he hastened to clarify. "Just because I have more information to trade. I can give her access codes to places like the Fortress and Headquarters on top of information about Thea."

Nadia narrowed her eyes at him. Although Thea was probably even more arrogant than Chairman Hayes had been, there was no way she hadn't thought to change all the access codes since she let Nate go. If he thought offering this "logical" explanation of his objection was making him sound less arrogant and bossy, he was sorely mistaken.

"If you think outdated codes would be helpful, then give them to me," she said. "But *I'm* the one who's going to meet with Angel." She raised her hand to stave off Nate's knee-jerk protest and was pleasantly surprised when his mouth snapped shut. "I'm a better negotiator than you are, and I don't have a personal history with Angel like you do."

Nate's jaw clenched in a familiar, mulish way. "I'm not—"

"—going to lose your temper?" she asked with a raise of

her eyebrow. What Angel had done to him—on Bishop's orders—hadn't been anything personal as far as she knew, but that didn't mean Nate hadn't taken it personally. He was already simmering just *thinking* about Angel; Nadia doubted he'd be able to keep his cool while talking to her.

Nate took a deep breath and lowered his voice to a normal speaking level. "I'm the rightful Chairman of Paxco. Doing stuff like this is part of my job description now. It's certainly not part of yours."

"Is this because I'm a girl?" Nadia asked, and realized immediately that yes, indeed, it was. "You think it's part of your job description to protect the helpless damsel in distress?" Her own temper bubbled to the surface and she glared at him.

Nate met her glare with one of his own, leaning forward as if to intimidate her with his greater size. "I'm sure as hell not sending a sixteen-year-old Executive girl into a Basement bar and sex club to do something I should be doing myself!" He turned to Dante. "She's *your* girlfriend! How 'bout a little backup here?"

Nadia blinked in surprise. Somehow, she hadn't allowed herself to think of Dante as her boyfriend, but she supposed that's what he was. The thought lit an inappropriate glow of warmth in her chest, and the little grin Dante sent Nate's way turned up the heat.

"You've been engaged to her *how* long?" Dante asked. "Twelve years or something? And you don't know better than to think she's going to take orders from you?"

In all fairness, for most of those twelve years Nadia had been too much of a slave to propriety and societal expectations to stand up to Nate as much as she should have, but she didn't feel inclined to rush to his defense.

"You'll do whatever gives us the best chance of staying alive," Nadia told Nate firmly. "And that's sending *me* to talk to Angel, whether you like it or not. Think with your head, not with your—" Nadia cut herself off, wondering if she'd been listening to Bishop and his foul mouth for too long. "Uh, you know." She felt the blood rising to her cheeks and wished she could will it away.

"You can't even mention my 'you know' without blushing," Nate said with a smirk. "How do you think you'll do in a club full of strippers?"

"The club won't be open yet at nine," Bishop pointed out. "There might be strippers hanging around getting ready, but they'll have their clothes on."

"Nadia should go," Agnes said, startling everyone. She was usually painfully quiet and shy, but both Nate and Nadia had seen evidence that she had a sharp mind and a good head for strategy. She looked at Bishop. "You said you don't quite trust this Angel person. If you think Angel might double-cross you, it's best not to send the only people who know her personally and know what she looks like right into her den. She won't want to antagonize us by hurting our delegation if she thinks we might be able to hurt her."

Nadia smiled faintly at the thought of her and Bishop being a "delegation," but she had to agree Agnes had a point. Nadia didn't exactly *want* to venture out into the streets of the Basement, and the idea of setting foot in Angel's club gave her the shivers, but she could do it.

"Think about everything I've faced in the last couple of

weeks," she urged Nate. "Then ask yourself if I'm going to swoon if I see a bunch of strippers."

"It's not the strippers I'm worried about," Nate grumbled, but she could tell he was starting to run out of steam.

"I won't let anyone hurt her," Bishop said, giving Nate's thigh a squeeze.

"You couldn't stop anyone from hurting *you,*" Nate quipped back.

Bishop grinned. "Ever think I might have brought it on myself? On purpose?"

"Why the hell would you do that?"

"Hey, Agnes," Bishop said, startling the girl's eyes wide. "You've got a head for this sorta thing. Any idea why I might have goaded Angel?"

Agnes's brows drew together, but she didn't have to think very long before she came up with an answer. "Because then you could compare her to the enemy and make her feel guilty."

Bishop nodded and turned to Nate. "I know my way around these kinds of people. I can keep Nadia safe. And Angel'll be more likely to cooperate with Nadia than with you."

"I still don't like it," Nate said, crossing his arms over his chest. But he was out of arguments.

CHAPTER THREE

nadia's stomach quivered with nerves as she and Bishop stepped out of the relative safety of his apartment building and onto the streets of the Basement. If she allowed herself to think too much about any of Nate's dire warnings or his graphic descriptions of the depravities of the Basement, she would run screaming back into the building. So instead of thinking, she held her head up high and focused on projecting an aura of ease and confidence.

She was dressed in her now-familiar Basement costume of a formfitting catsuit, a neon-pink wig, and a band of black face paint over her eyes. Her gait was mincing and wobbly, thanks to the four-inch stiletto heels and platform soles of her boots, which made it rather harder to project the proper image, but added yet another subtle layer to her disguise. A lot of things about tonight's adventure worried her, but being recognized wasn't one of them.

Nadia couldn't help glancing over her shoulder right before she and Bishop turned the corner. It was hard to pick out his apartment windows from all the bland, identical ones around it, especially since they'd left the lights off when they left, but she thought she could see the shadowed forms of Nate and Dante standing there watching her progress. She hoped the two of them would be able to keep their dislike for one another under control without her there to act as peacemaker.

She looked resolutely forward as she and Bishop left everything that was familiar behind her.

It was early by Basement standards, so there wasn't a whole lot of foot traffic, but there was enough to make Nadia jittery, and everyone looked so exotic it was hard not to stare.

"Don't make eye contact with anyone," Bishop warned, taking her arm as if to guide her around something and then not letting go. "Pretend like we're alone on the street. And stick real close."

Like she had any choice when he had his hand on her arm. Not that she felt inclined to complain. Bishop wasn't particularly large or burly—not like Dante, who exuded strength—but he nonetheless looked scary enough to keep predators at a distance. He wasn't as exotically colorful as most of the Basement-dwellers, the only color on him being a thin, many-times-ripped chartreuse T-shirt that displayed more than it hid of his heavily tattooed torso. But there were obvious wiry muscles under those tattoos, and his kohl-lined eyes were a particular piercing shade of blue and projected an instant aura of menace. The facial piercings and the currently ultra-short mohawk he was growing put the finishing touches on his look, and she knew it would be a rare Basement-dweller indeed who would choose to mess with him.

The walk to Angel's club seemed to take forever. Partly because the ridiculous boots with their torturous heels were killing Nadia's feet, and partly because of her hyperactive threat radar. Avoiding eye contact turned out to be harder than she'd expected. Her eyes kept wanting to scope out her surroundings, take a second look at anyone who might be a predator on the hunt. But keeping an eye on their surroundings was Bishop's job. Hers was to not attract attention.

Eventually, they stopped in front of a high-rise that looked like all the others around it, except the word ANGEL'S was spray-painted over the entrance. Nadia could hardly wait to get behind a closed door, even though she knew the hard part of her mission hadn't yet begun. She tried to hurry her steps, but Bishop still had hold of her arm, and he came to a stop, forcing her to stop with him.

"What is it?" she asked, her pulse pounding in her throat.

"They're gonna search you when we go in," he warned.

Nadia looked down at herself and blinked. "Where do they think I would hide a weapon in this outfit?" she asked. The catsuit was so tight you could probably see the slightly raised birthmark on her left shoulder blade.

"It's not really about weapons," he said. "Think of it as a kind of dominance display. They want us to know who's in charge—and it ain't us."

"Okay," she said slowly, though the look in his eyes told her there was more to come.

"They'll probably be assholes about it. The less you react, the better. If you make it obvious it's bothering you, they'll get off on it and make it worse."

Nadia swallowed hard. "Funny how you didn't mention any of this when we were talking things over with Nate and Dante." She could just imagine how the two of them would react to the thought of her being manhandled. Not that she was doing so great with the idea herself.

Bishop shrugged. "What Dante doesn't know won't hurt him. And Nate's kinda being Nate. He's been felt up here a million times, but it hasn't occurred to him that they'll do the same to you. If he knew, we'd probably have to tie him up and have Dante sit on him to keep him from coming along and pitching a fit."

Nadia smiled faintly at the image. "Guess it's a good thing he didn't fully think it through, then."

"Yup." He met her eyes, and she thought she saw genuine sympathy in his gaze. He'd never much liked her—and the feeling had been mutual—but she thought they were well on their way to reaching a level of mutual respect. "Sorry to spring it on you, but I didn't think telling you earlier would help. If I'm right and you're not going to go all girlie on me and run away."

She'd have been irritated at his sexist comment if she didn't see through it so easily. "You don't have to provoke me to get me to do this. There's too much at stake."

He gave her a sharp-edged grin. "Thought it wouldn't hurt for you to go in there pissed off."

"Are we going in, or are we standing here in the street *discussing* going in for the next hour and a half?"

Bishop answered by rapping on the door. There was a long moment of silence, then a male voice shouted without opening the door.

"We're closed!"

"Angel's expecting us," Bishop shouted back.

There was another long silence, then the sound of locks clicking open. Nadia sucked in a deep breath, hoping to calm the racing of her pulse. She was dreading the search Bishop had described and wasn't sure how she was going to contain her reaction. She was fairly certain she was going to be touched in places she'd never been touched by a man before, and this was not at all how she wanted those first touches to be.

"Hang in there," Bishop muttered under his breath as the door swung open, revealing a dimly lit interior.

Gritting her teeth and raising her chin, Nadia followed Bishop through the door. When she got her first look at the man whose voice had shouted at them on the doorstep, it was all Nadia could do to keep her feet moving forward. The guy had to be over three hundred pounds, and he was painted solid blue from head to toe. Which Nadia could tell because he was wearing nothing but a pair of skintight bicycle shorts. The paint job was so thorough she had no idea what his natural skin color might be. His eyes gave her no clue, as he was wearing disturbing-looking orange contact lenses, and his hair was buzzed down to little more than stubble.

"Hands up, face the wall," the Blue Giant commanded. He looked like he was hoping they would disobey so he could slam them against the wall.

Bishop turned to the wall and put the palms of his hands against it, his legs slightly spread. Sweat beading her skin, Nadia followed his lead.

The giant searched Bishop first, giving Nadia a preview of what she was in for. She knew from the little sidelong glances the blue man gave her that he was hoping for an entertaining reaction, and she tried not to give him one. Her insides shriveled at the way he handled Bishop's groin and butt. If it bothered Bishop, he was very good at hiding it, his face looking almost bored. Then again, he couldn't have survived his previous profession if being touched there made him squirm.

When the blue man turned to her, Nadia's pulse was

pounding and her breath was coming short. She kept herself in place by sheer force of will, but she knew she was doing a terrible job of hiding her fear and disgust. The blue man smiled at her, and she saw a spark of excitement in his orange eyes as he crossed to her. She quickly looked away and met Bishop's eyes. He lent her what moral support he could, but she still couldn't suppress a little jump when the blue man's hands landed on her shoulders and started slowly making their way down her back.

Nadia was sweating, and her knees trembled under the strain of holding still. Everything Nate had told her about Angel had already given her a healthy dislike of the woman, but that dislike was turning into something more virulent. This search was completely unnecessary, an intimidation tactic that served no purpose when Nadia was here to negotiate a mutually beneficial deal.

But maybe it served a purpose after all. What better way was there to establish that you were negotiating from a position of power than to unsettle and humiliate your opponent before you even began?

The blue man's hands slid down to Nadia's bottom, and instead of cringing at the violation, Nadia itched to turn around and knee the Blue Molester in the groin. Anger fired her blood, masking some of the fear.

"My price just went up twenty percent," she said, sure Angel was watching, measuring her. "He touches anything else he shouldn't, it goes up again."

The corner of Bishop's mouth lifted in a hint of a grin, and he gave her a faint nod of approval. The blue man had paused with his hands on her butt. Awaiting orders, perhaps.

From somewhere behind her, hidden by the blue man's massive body, there came the sound of a dark, low chuckle.

"That's enough, Djinni," a woman's voice said.

The blue man gave Nadia's rump what under other circumstances she might call a playful pat, then backed off. She dropped her arms and turned around, letting her simmering anger rebuild her sense of dignity.

Nadia got her first good look at Angel's club, and the idea that people actually paid money to come in—that *Executives* who thought they were taking a walk on the wild side paid to come in—made no sense whatsoever. To call the place a dump was too kind.

Angel had apparently had all the apartments torn out of the first couple floors of this building, creating a large, open space peppered with support pillars in odd places. The walls were covered with graffiti, the floor looked like it hadn't been mopped in eighteen years, and the only light came from bare bulbs hanging from the ceiling on long wires. There were plywood tables and plastic chairs—none of which matched each other—and the bar appeared to have been cobbled together with cinder blocks and scrap wood.

The only even mildly decorative feature was a huge mural on one wall depicting a woman with a gray mohawk fingering a knife and glaring out over the room.

The real-life version of that woman stood in one of the shadowy areas behind a support pillar, her arms folded and a cigarette hanging from her lips. She came forward with a sinewy, hip-rolling walk, though Nadia couldn't imagine how the woman thought of herself as sexy. The gray mohawk was at least six inches high, and though her face was smooth and unlined, there were wattles under the spiked collar around her neck that suggested she was considerably older than the image she tried to project. When she got closer, Nadia wrinkled her nose at the scent that emanated from the cigarette. She didn't know what it was, except that it wasn't tobacco.

When Angel got close enough to invade Nadia's personal space, she looked Nadia up and down and she took a drag on her cigarette. Guessing what was coming, Nadia held her breath just before Angel exhaled smoke directly into her face. The smoke stung her eyes, and even holding her breath she could taste something bitter in the back of her throat, but at least she didn't cough.

"I was expecting the Ghost," Angel said, smoke leaking from her nostrils as she spoke.

Nadia would have to take a breath to respond, but Bishop answered for her.

"Well, you got the Honey Badger instead."

Nadia turned to frown at him, taking in a sip of smoky air. "The Honey Badger?"

He grinned at her. "Congrats. You just earned your street name."

Nadia had almost forgotten that Basement-dwellers didn't use names the way Employees and Executives did. Given names were for children only, and adults went by whatever street name they had "earned." They probably should have come up with a fake street name for her before she set foot outside the apartment. Surely they could have come up with something better than Honey Badger. It sounded like a really bad stripper name, not a tough-as-nails street name.

"Honey Badger," Angel said speculatively. "I like it. Mind if I call you Honey for short?"

Yes, she minded. But she suspected Angel knew that. "If I say I mind, will you stop calling me that?"

Angel's eyes sparkled with amusement. She took another drag off her cigarette, but this time blew the smoke off to the side. "Nope."

"Then I don't mind a bit." The glare she sent Bishop's way belied her words, but he looked at least as amused as Angel.

"Good," Angel said with an approving nod. "Let's have a seat and chat, shall we?"

Without waiting for an answer, she turned and headed for the far corner of the club, leaving Bishop and Nadia to follow or not, as they chose. Although Djinni was now between them and the door, Nadia doubted he would take well to them trying to leave.

"Honey Badger?" Nadia said again as she and Bishop followed Angel across the club. "Where the hell did *that* come from? And how do I get rid of it?"

Bishop still looked amused and maybe even a little proud of himself. "Honey badgers are these small animals that look kinda harmless and cute but are really fierce and fearless. You gotta admit, it fits."

"No, I don't have to admit anything," she grumped, but she realized Bishop meant the name as a compliment. She couldn't remember ever receiving one from him before, and she liked the idea of being thought fierce and fearless. Not that she was going to tell him that.

"How does someone who grew up in the Basement know what a honey badger is?" she asked. There weren't even any schools in the Basement. Schools cost money, and the government of Paxco wasn't about to provide anything that wasn't a survival necessity for its poorest and most powerless citizens. "I've never even heard of it before."

"Saw it on a nature show."

Nadia's eyebrows climbed and she looked at him in amazement. "*You* watch nature shows?" It was not something she would ever associate with a pierced, tattooed tough-guy street kid.

"When I went to work for Nate, I had free time on my hands for the first time in my life. I watched all kinds of weird shit just because I could."

Nadia hadn't realized until now how little she knew about Bishop. She had never really thought of him as an individual before, had always thought about him in terms of his relationship with and influence on Nate. She'd always told herself she didn't have the typical Executive feeling of superiority over the Basement-dwellers, but perhaps she'd been lying to herself.

"I wish you'd come up with something that couldn't be shortened to Honey," she grumbled. "And is there anyone else in the Basement who'd have any idea what the name means?"

"Doesn't matter. That's not how names work here."

"Huh?"

Bishop came to a stop, letting Angel get ahead of them. "Don't take anything at face value. Street names often don't mean what it sounds like they mean. The leader of the Red Death gang is called the Maiden, but it ain't because there's anything girlie about him. No one's gonna hear the name Honey and assume it's a put-down of some kind. Trust me."

Angel had reached a makeshift booth in the corner

and was staring at them impatiently. Nadia nodded her acceptance—she would definitely trust Bishop about all things Basement—and they started forward again.

"So why is the Red Death leader called the Maiden?" she asked.

"'Cause he owns a collection of iron maidens and ain't afraid to use 'em."

Charming, Nadia thought as she and Bishop slid into the booth across from Angel. She supposed being named after a fierce animal was better than being named after a medieval torture device. Only a happy accident of birth had kept Nadia from being faced with a life like the one Bishop had known, and never had she been more aware of it than now, as she folded her hands on top of the sticky, pitted table and met Angel's cool, assessing gaze.

"I could make a lot of money turning you in," Angel said. An opening salvo, looking for a weakness in Nadia's defenses.

"You could," Nadia agreed. "And then I'd start talking before they even got around to *threatening* to torture me. I know some things you'd probably rather I didn't share."

Angel laughed, deep and throaty. "Who said anything about turning you in *alive*?"

"Yeah that wouldn't go so well for you," Bishop said as Nadia weathered the unpleasant shock of Angel's words. "Nate and Dante would be kinda annoyed if something happened to Honey or me, and they might start feeling talkative themselves."

Nadia recovered her composure—after everything she'd been through, she shouldn't have let a little thing like a death threat throw her off her stride—and decided that no matter how complimentary it might be, she really loathed being called Honey.

"You might also find that the information I can give you is more valuable than whatever money Paxco may be offering for a reward," Nadia said. "I don't know how deeply your resistance has infiltrated the government, but I'm quite sure they aren't deep enough to know the things that I know. I don't think you're a poor woman." According to Nate, Angel, with her highly successful club and her array of profitable side businesses, was one of the richest people in all of the Basement. "You need information more than you need money."

Angel thought that over, tapping sharpened, bloodred fingernails on the table. Nadia should have just let her think, but nerves prompted her to keep talking.

"Try to imagine the magnitude of what we must know to make the Chairman Heir turn against the government of Paxco. And imagine what it means that Paxco's so desperate to find us. Desperate enough to set up roadblocks and cut off phone service and fly a blimp overhead all night. They do *not* want us telling anyone what we know."

Angel nodded slowly. "Can't pretend I'm not curious as hell. But for all I know, you're government spies sent in here to learn about the resistance."

Bishop rolled his eyes. "Oh for Christ's sake, Angel. Can we just skip all this tap dancing and get on with things. You don't think the Chairman Heir and his fiancée were sent into the Basement as spies. You're just playing hard to get because you don't know any other way."

Angel's eyes narrowed for a moment, and Nadia feared Bishop had jeopardized their negotiations by pissing her off. But of course Bishop was too street-smart to do something stupid like that, and unlike Nadia, he had previous experience with Angel. Angel's glare slowly transformed into a grin, and she spread her hands in a gesture of surrender.

"Guilty as charged," she admitted, then turned to Nadia. "You give me good information, I give you good money. And then you and the rest of your little kiddie gang don't get within five blocks of my club or me again. I'm taking one hell of a risk even talking to you."

Not as much of a risk as we're *taking,* Nadia thought. But she and the rest of the new resistance were at risk no matter what they did, and at least dealing with Angel meant they could take care of their immediate financial needs.

"Let me start by telling you that that video on the blimp is a complete fabrication," Nadia said, and was rewarded by a glint of interest in Angel's eyes. "Now tell me how much you'll pay to find out what really happened to our dear departed Chairman Hayes."

CHAPTER FOUR

nate paced the living room for about five minutes after he lost sight of Nadia and Kurt, but he quickly discovered pacing wasn't enough to defuse his nervous tension, so he unilaterally decided he and Dante and Agnes should change into their Basement disguises even though they weren't planning to leave the apartment. Not only would it give them something to do while they waited, it would make it easier to launch a rescue mission the moment he decided Nadia and Kurt had been gone too long. Knowing Nadia was plunging headfirst into danger while he was safe and secure in Kurt's apartment was a blow to his ego, and it was making him so crazy he wanted to chew the scenery.

Neither Dante nor Agnes argued Nate's decision, though Agnes made no bones about how much she hated her disguise. She was used to wearing frumpy, poufy clothes in an attempt to camouflage her bottom-heavy figure, and the formfitting, eye-searing blue bodysuit provided no camouflage whatsoever. She put it on, but she kept her ugly pink opera gown wrapped around her like a shield.

"I'll drop it if we have to go out," she assured Nate when he frowned at her. "It's chilly in here." She wrapped the gown more tightly around her shoulders and tried to look like she was cold.

"You don't have to hide," he told her. "You look fantastic in that outfit."

It was true, although he was rather surprised at himself for saying it. He had despised Agnes from the moment he'd first met her. Not for any fault of her own, but because his father was going to force him to marry her and ruin Nadia. He'd treated her abysmally, and though Nadia had shamed him into being more fair, he'd been convinced he could never do more than tolerate the girl.

Agnes was as startled by his words as he, and she continued to huddle under the cover of her pink flounces. "I look ridiculous. You don't have to try to flatter me." Her face practically glowed with her familiar mottled blush.

"I'm not flattering you," he said, feeling bad for all the times he'd sneered at her. He didn't think he'd ever said anything derogatory about her appearance to her face, but he'd certainly had unflattering thoughts. Agnes would never be beautiful, but she would be a hell of a lot more attractive if she'd just stop being so self-conscious about her looks. Every attempt she made to hide her flaws just made them more obvious—like her insistence on pleated pants and poufy skirts. "You look awesome in that outfit. Sexy."

Her blush deepened, but there was a spark of anger in her eyes, too. She was seriously resistant to taking a compliment. "Is it even possible for a girl to look sexy to you?"

Reminding Nate once again of just how many ways he had mistreated her during their brief unofficial engagement. He had been fully prepared to let her sign the marriage agreement without revealing the truth about his sexual preferences. He'd been protecting himself from the horrors of being sent to "reprogramming" to correct what his father termed his "sexual deviance," but that hadn't made his silence any more fair to Agnes.

"You know when a girl looks sexy even if you're not attracted to girls, don't you?" he asked.

She looked like she wanted to argue, then sighed and nodded. "Yeah. I guess I do. But I still think you're full of it."

Thinking about the marriage arrangement made Nate suddenly remember something. "My father planned for you to sign the marriage agreement today," he said. Nate had already been coerced into signing it, and Agnes was meant to sign it at 12:01 on the day of her eighteenth birthday, making the agreement legally binding for all involved. "Happy birthday."

Agnes looked around the squalid little room and shook her head. "This isn't quite what I had planned for the big one-eight," she said quietly. There was a haunted look in her eyes that made Nate squirm on the inside. He was responsible for all the crazy changes in her life, and he wished he could do something to cheer her up. Unfortunately, he didn't see any birthday cake or big parties in her near future.

"I'm not complaining," Agnes said. "Ask me how much I love big, formal birthday parties where I'm supposed to be the star of the show." She shuddered delicately.

No, Nate was sure she wasn't a big fan of those parties; however, he doubted she found hiding out in the Basement under threat of death to be a great improvement. Maybe when Kurt and Nadia came back, they could whip up some small improvised imitation of a party. Or at least sing "Happy Birthday."

It was too soon to expect Nadia and Kurt back yet, but

that didn't stop him from scanning the growing crowd outside in search of two familiar figures.

He didn't see them. But what he *did* see made him go cold all over.

"I think we may have a big problem," he said, gesturing Dante and Agnes over and pointing.

A group of five uniformed security officers were making their way down the street with purposeful strides. All the laws of Paxco officially applied to the Basement as well as to the rest of society, but there was no such thing as enforcement here, and security officers didn't set foot in the place unless they were on the hunt for a fugitive.

"Damn it," Dante said as he followed Nate's pointing finger. "What are the chances they're here for someone else?"

Nate snorted. "What are the chances something would actually go right for us for once?"

"They couldn't possibly know where we are," Agnes said. "Could they?"

"Until we all went on the lam," Dante said, "Bishop wasn't in hiding. I'm sure there are Basement-dwellers who know where he lives and that security can find a way to convince them to talk."

Nate uttered a curse that would have done Bishop proud. The officers *did* look like they had a specific destination in mind, and that destination *did* seem to be this apartment building. "We need to get out of here. Fast." The officers were already too close for comfort, and Nate didn't think they had much chance of getting out without being seen.

"And go where?" Agnes asked in a small voice.

"Angel's," Nate responded instantly. "We have to meet up with Bishop and Nadia anyway."

He tore himself away from the window and began pawing through his meager pile of belongings to find the gun he'd had hidden on his person when he and Nadia had confronted Dorothy. Dorothy had confiscated their other weapons, but she'd never known about the extra gun. Hardly an expert with guns, Nate had no idea how many bullets were in this one, but he doubted it was enough to get them through a shootout with a security squad. Didn't mean he was going to leave it behind, though.

"They're definitely coming here," Dante announced, backing away from the window. "Let's move it." He saw what Nate was doing and wordlessly reached out his hand.

Nate swallowed his ego and handed the gun over to someone who knew how to use it. Agnes let go of her evening gown/security blanket with obvious reluctance as the three of them rushed to the door.

"How are we going to get past the security squad without being seen?" Nate asked, hoping Dante, as a professional spy, might have some clever tactic in mind. But it was Agnes who answered.

"We walk right past them as if we have nothing to hide."

Nate stared at her in astonishment.

"Our disguises are good," Agnes said, "and they're expecting us to be holed up in the apartment. They *certainly* won't be expecting us to come right out in the open like that. I'll bet they barely give us a passing glance if we pass them on the stairs."

"She has a point," Dante agreed as they darted out into the hallway and closed the door behind them. Kurt had the keys, so they weren't able to lock the door, but the security squad was probably going to bash it down anyway. "They'd expect us to run or sneak away, not walk right by them. Besides, I don't know if we have any other choice. If there's a back way out of here, I don't know about it, and they probably have a couple of men watching it anyway."

"For the record," Nate said as they hurried down the hallway to the stairs, "I hate this plan." Unfortunately, he didn't have an alternative suggestion.

"Just act cool and natural," Dante said. He put his hand on the door to the stairwell. "Walk at a normal pace, don't act like you're trying to hide your face, and ignore them like they're no business of yours whatsoever."

Agnes's face looked pale and frightened, and though her disguise was good, Nate worried that it wasn't enough. Her face was almost as famous as his, and her disguise was more superficial, having been cobbled together in a hurry. Nate's had been built over a period of months, and included details like contact lenses and cheek pouches. He'd be shocked if anyone recognized him, but Agnes . . . He put his arm around Agnes's shoulders and tucked her against his side.

"I'll keep between you and them when we pass," he said in response to her startled look.

"Don't try to hide!" Dante reminded them brusquely.

"I'm not talking about hiding her," Nate snapped. "I'm just going to give her a little extra cover."

"We don't have time for arguing," Agnes said, slipping her arm around Nate's waist as if it were the most natural thing in the world. "Let's just go."

They went, but Nate still had an uneasy feeling in his

stomach about Agnes's disguise. They should have put some face paint or something on her to draw attention away from her features. The bright blue gunk that plastered her hair to her scalp certainly drew the eye, but if anyone took a second look . . .

Since the building's elevator didn't work, there was a fair amount of traffic on the stairs, which could work to their advantage. It was still a little early for Debasement's permanent street fair to be in full swing, but the early birds were already heading out.

With Dante leading the way, they headed down the stairs, quickly catching up with three women who were most likely prostitutes on their way to work. One of the women had enormous boobs that were barely contained by a red lace bra top, and Nate hoped the display would distract a member or two of the security squad. He could hear one of the officers from below barking at people to get out of the way, his voice echoing up the stairwell. He sounded like a hard-ass, and if he wasn't careful, he was going to get his whole squad killed. Basement-dwellers weren't fond of security officers at the best of times, and despite their training and superior weaponry, the security squad was badly outnumbered.

Dante looked over his shoulder with a concerned expression. "At the first sign of trouble, we get out of the stairwell immediately."

Nate wondered if they shouldn't do that anyway until the squad had passed them by, but they were currently between floors, and by the time they reached the next floor, the squad would be able to see them. Trying not to hold his breath, Nate tightened his arm around Agnes's shoulders and continued downward.

They reached the third-floor landing just as the security squad did, and Nate saw it was a good thing they hadn't ducked into a hallway until the squad passed. One of the men stuck some kind of metallic rod into the door mechanism, jamming it shut, keeping the residents of that floor trapped. They were also taking close looks at everyone who passed them on the stairs. The three hookers started strutting their stuff as if they thought the officers were on the hunt for an on-the-job quickie, and Nate hoped that would give him and his friends the distraction they needed to slip by unnoticed, but Captain Tight-ass of the barked orders suggested he might do something unpleasant with his night stick if the hookers didn't move along.

There was nothing to do but walk on by as planned.

Dante hit the landing and continued walking at a steady pace. The officers each took a close look as he went by, but the chances of *him* being recognized were slim. Then it was Nate and Agnes's turn. They stepped onto the landing, and Nate was painfully aware of all those eyes scanning his face, and, more alarmingly, Agnes's.

Under normal circumstances, Agnes had approximately zero self-confidence. The kind of girl you'd expect to cower in the corner or hide under the bed at the first sign of trouble. But Nate had already seen what a different person she became when under fire, and he shouldn't have been surprised that she improvised a new plan in the blink of an eye.

When the officers started looking her over, Agnes affected a sexy pout and stuck out her chest to make the most of her modest assets.

"I gotta date for the next hour," she said, running her

hand seductively over Nate's chest, "but I'm sure I can fit you boys in afterward if you want."

She had put an unfamiliar rasp into her voice and lowered it by about an octave. Usually, she sounded like a little girl, but tonight she sounded like a world-weary adult with a serious smoking habit. She made a face that was probably supposed to look like a leer, but looked more like a grimace of fear to Nate's eyes.

Good thing for them Nate wasn't the one she had to convince.

Captain Tight-ass gave Agnes an icy glare as he shouted up the stairwell. "Next whore that propositions me or my men is gonna get more than she bargained for!"

And then he dismissed both Nate and Agnes from his attention and ordered his men up the steps.

nate was almost giddy with relief over their narrow escape from the security squad, but they were still in deep trouble and they all knew it. Kurt no doubt had money hidden somewhere in that apartment of his, but Nate didn't know where and hadn't had time to search for it. Which meant the three of them were completely broke, no dollars, no credits, nothing. Being broke in the Basement was all kinds of dangerous.

After the brave show she'd put on in the stairwell, Agnes had lost some of her starch, and she clung to Nate's hand as he led the way to Angel's. The streets were getting progressively more crowded, and he prayed Agnes's case of nerves didn't attract any predators. Vulnerability was quite an aphrodisiac to a certain kind of Basement-dweller, and though Nate knew Agnes was trying her best to hide hers, she wasn't doing a very good job of it. At least they were on the Basement's outer edges, which were safe and tame in comparison to the neighborhoods at its heart.

By the time they reached Angel's, they'd been solicited by prostitutes of both sexes, drug dealers, black marketeers, and sundry others who were too stoned to make it clear what they were offering. Nate also had the feeling that they were being followed, though perhaps that was just paranoia. He looked over his shoulder a couple of times, but no one stood out. Or, considering this was the Basement, it might be more accurate to say that everyone stood out equally.

"We have a tail," Dante said, and Nate kind of wished he'd voiced his own suspicion. Then he mentally rolled his eyes at himself for his constant need to play games of one-upmanship with Dante. Especially since he always came out the loser. He resisted the urge to take another look back over his shoulder.

"Is it security?" Agnes asked, biting her lip.

Dante shook his head. "Don't think so. There are undercover agents in the Basement, but if this guy were one of them he'd have sicced the squad on us."

"Maybe he couldn't," Nate suggested. "No phone service, remember?"

"They'll have walkies. Everyone knows phone service is unreliable here."

Nate didn't know what a "walkie" was, but he wasn't going to reveal his ignorance by asking. The security department wasn't the military, but it was pretty clear Dante had had some kind of military training before he'd joined up as a spy, and he liked to lord it over Nate in this sneaky kind of way.

Nate took a deep breath and let it out slowly, trying to let his irritation with Dante seep out with it. He should have been *grateful* for Dante's skills and competence. Especially when his physique advertised them so plainly—Nate was sure some of the people who'd solicited them would have been more aggressive about it if Dante weren't imposing enough to make them back off.

"As long as it's not security, I don't think it matters right now," Nate said. He jerked his chin in the direction of Angel's club, which was just opening for the night as indicated by the pair of bouncers who exited and then stationed themselves by the door. "We're here."

His heart was thumping in his chest, and a cold sweat broke out over his body as he eyed the bouncers and wondered if they had been among the goons Angel had ordered to beat the crap out of him. The goons had been wearing masks, so he didn't know who they were, except that they were the kind of big, burly men Angel liked to use as bouncers.

Maybe coming here hadn't been such a great idea. While the beating hadn't caused any serious injury, Nate's body remembered the ordeal and was telling him in no uncertain terms that he was not setting foot in that club. Even if they *did* have some Basement predator on their tail, waiting for the first sign of weakness.

A dense, jostling crowd converged on the entrance to Angel's in the Basement-dweller version of queuing up. Elbows were thrown and curses uttered as the would-be club-goers waited impatiently for their turn to be felt up by the bouncers. And then the problem with Nate's plan to meet up with Kurt and Nadia here slapped him in the face.

"We don't have money to pay the cover charge," he said, cursing himself for not thinking of it sooner. Not that thinking of it sooner would have done them any good. It wasn't like there was any chance of them getting hold of any money, not unless and until Nadia had managed to squeeze it out of Angel.

Embarrassingly, there was a part of him that was relieved at the idea that he couldn't go in. He kept trying to shake off the memory of that horrible night, but he wasn't having a lot of success, and nerves were making his gut churn.

"I guess we just have to wait until they come out," Dante said, his face set in grim lines. He might not be a Basement-dweller himself, but he obviously knew how bad an idea it was to stand around in the street, especially when they knew someone was following them. His Basement costume included a flamboyant ankle-length duster, and he slipped his hand into its front pocket, no doubt fingering the gun.

"Can't we just ask one of the bouncers to tell Angel we're here?" Agnes asked.

Nate shook his head. "Those guys are not the helpful type. And if we tried to cut ahead in line, it would get real ugly."

"So let's get in the back of the line," she suggested. "We're going to draw attention if we just stand around here with no purpose."

It was as good a plan as any, and their tail didn't seem inclined to emerge from the crowd and confront them—not yet, at least—so they shuffled their way to the back of the line, and all three of them stared at the door, willing Nadia and Kurt to make a swift appearance.

CHAPTER FIVE

nadia could hardly say she was surprised by the increasingly skeptical expression on Angel's face as she recounted what happened on the day she and Nate confronted Chairman Hayes at the Paxco Headquarters Building. It did sound pretty ridiculous when you came right down to it.

"So what you're telling me," Angel said slowly, her eyes narrowed in a glare that was probably supposed to intimidate the "real" truth out of Nadia, "is that our new Chairman isn't really a human being at all. Do I have that right?"

"I wouldn't put it quite that way," Nadia said. "I think Dorothy probably technically qualifies as human, it's just that her *mind* isn't human. Think of her as a kind of robot housed in human flesh."

Angel glanced over at Bishop. "She been dipping into the happy pills lately? 'Cause this all sounds more like a bad trip than reality."

"I'll vouch for Ghost and Honey both," he said. "If they say that's what's going on, I believe 'em."

"But *you* haven't confirmed any of this bullshit story."

"I can confirm that Ghost and I overheard the Chairman talking to Mosely about Thea and that when the Chairman found out we had heard him he ordered Mosely to stab his own son to death. Saw that part with my own two eyes. The story isn't bullshit."

Nadia had the suspicion it wasn't so much that Angel didn't believe the story, it was that she wanted to get out of paying for it. If the upper echelons of the official resistance consisted of people like Angel, then Nadia was just as glad they weren't interested in joining forces. Just because they were opposed to Paxco's current oppressive regime didn't mean they were the good guys.

"Dorothy is going to make the late Chairman Hayes seem like a saint by comparison," Nadia said. "He had a lot of flaws, but he did at least have some level of concern over the well-being of his state and some rudimentary respect for human life. Dorothy doesn't have even that. When I threatened to go public with what I knew, Chairman Hayes wanted to protect his legacy, but he also wanted to protect the people of Paxco. He knew if it went public, there would be riots at the very least, a civil war at worst, and he knew thousands of people would probably die. Dorothy killed him because he wasn't willing to take that risk—and she was. Because to her, thousands of people dying is not a big deal as long as she comes out on top."

Angel rocked back in her chair and crossed her arms over her chest. The sound system came roaring to life, blasting out the kind of heavy, rhythmic music that made Nadia's teeth vibrate. Nadia could see the front door opening as the club's staff emerged from the shadows, ready to service their clientele.

"You know the information's good," Bishop shouted over the music. "Why don't you just pay us and let us get the hell out of here."

Angel leaned forward again. "Because this all sounds like a plot to a B-movie, and I still haven't taken the idea of killing you off the table."

"Remember what I said about Ghost and the others," Bishop said, sounding not in the least bit intimidated by the threat. "They can cause you a shitload of trouble if anything happens to me or Honey."

Angel grinned broadly. "Yeah, well here's the thing: my bouncer just spotted the Ghost loitering around on the sidewalk outside the club."

Nadia almost gasped at the news. It wasn't until that moment that she noticed the discreet rubber earpiece Angel was wearing. The last Nadia had checked, phone service was still down, so whatever communication system Angel was using didn't utilize phone frequencies.

Bishop laughed. "Now who's spouting bullshit stories? The Ghost sure as hell wouldn't come *here*."

"No?" Angel asked with a confident smirk. "So my bouncer is lying when he says the Ghost is outside my door with some blue-haired chick and a guy with a multicolored duster."

Bishop sobered quickly and Nadia swallowed hard. There was no way Angel would know anything about Agnes's and Dante's Basement disguises—unless she was telling the truth. But Angel's death threats aside, there had to be something seriously wrong for Nate and the others to have left the apartment and come to the club.

Nadia hastily stood up, almost knocking her chair over. There was a steady stream of Basement-dwellers pouring in through the front door, to the point that getting out might be a challenge.

"Sit down, Honey," Angel commanded. "We're not finished here." She then spoke into what Nadia presumed was a microphone, although it was so well hidden it was invisible. "Bring them in. If they give you any trouble, go for the girl. That'll be their weakness."

Nadia looked at Bishop. He was the expert in surviving in the Basement and was more likely to know if this situation called for an escape attempt or more negotiation. He was still seated, and when she met his eyes, he nodded.

Slowly, Nadia sank back into her chair.

when one of the bouncers left his post by the front door and started making his way along the line—if that's what you'd call the jumbled crowd of Basement-dwellers and tourists vying for a place in the unruly mob waiting to get in—it didn't immediately occur to Nate that the huge blue-painted man was coming for him and his friends. Nate had encountered the blue man before in his trips to Angel's, back when he'd been one of the privileged assholes who came here for fun. He went by the name Djinni, and he seemed to take great pleasure in patting people down, trying to provoke a reaction by being unduly rough or invasive.

Djinni was enough of a bruiser that even hardened Basement veterans moved aside for him as he made his way toward the back of the pack. His eyes scanned the entire crowd without ever pausing on anyone in particular, so Nate figured he could be excused for not seeing the man's purpose until it was too late.

Nate turned his face slightly away, but it wasn't like that would stop Djinni from recognizing him. Not that Djinni had any idea who the Ghost really was, but Nate

to himself that he didn't take any satisfaction in the fact that the superspy didn't see it coming and that Djinni had divested him of his weapon before he knew what hit him.

"No guns allowed in the club." Djinni smirked as he popped the clip out of the gun and checked to make sure the chamber was empty. He tucked the gun into the back of his shorts.

Dante glared at the bouncer. "You could have just asked." He straightened the duster with an air of offended dignity.

Nate worried that he and Dante—and more alarmingly, Agnes—might be searched more thoroughly, seeing as that was the club's standard procedure, but it seemed Djinni was through with the fun and games.

"This way," he said, leading them across the room. The club wasn't crowded yet—too many people were still waiting outside—so they didn't really need him to lead them to Angel. Nate could see her sitting at a table in the far corner. He let out a little breath of relief to see that Nadia and Bishop were also seated at that table, although even from a distance he could read the body language and see the tension. Maybe negotiations were going badly and showing up here had been a big mistake. But it wasn't like they'd had a lot of choices.

Djinni didn't let go of Agnes's arm until they were practically on top of the table, and even then, he stood in such a way as to block her retreat—and keep Nate and Dante from getting to her.

Angel leaned back in her chair, lacing her hands over her stomach, showing them how completely relaxed and in control she was.

"Why Ghost," she said in a slow drawl, "what a pleasant

surprise. I had no idea you had so much fun the last time you visited. Back for more?"

Nate was sweating, unable to suppress his body's visceral memory of what Angel had done to him. He tried to project an image of nonchalance, but he was probably failing, and there was no way he could scrape up the words for a witty comeback.

He was an utter coward. Timid little Agnes did a better job of standing up to bullies than he did. His face flushed with shame, and he hoped the layers of white powder he wore to make his complexion ghostly were thick enough to hide it.

"Leave him alone, Angel," Kurt said, pushing back his chair and rising to his feet.

Nate's cheeks flamed hotter. Bad enough that he was showing his fear in front of everyone, but to have Kurt have to jump to his rescue . . . He was being a total wuss about this. Yeah, the beating had hurt like hell, but Angel and her merry men hadn't done any actual *damage.* In the grand scheme of things, it wasn't that big a deal. At least that's what he tried to tell himself.

Kurt interrupted Nate's shame-spiral by clapping a hand on his shoulder and squeezing. "What are you doing here?" he asked.

The simple touch of Kurt's hand helped steady and balance him, chasing the shadows away. He cleared his throat quietly to make sure his voice didn't come out sounding weak and thready.

"A security squad showed up to search the building," he answered. "We had to get out of there. This seemed the only logical place to go."

He wanted to ask what was going on, how the negotiations were going—if they were indeed still going—but Kurt wasn't in a position to give him an honest answer with Angel hanging on his every word, so there was no point.

"Are you sure they were looking for us?" Nadia asked, biting her lip, but then she shook her head. "Never mind. Stupid question."

Angel snorted. "As if I needed another reminder that the lot of you are too hot to handle."

"We're not asking you to 'handle' us," Nadia snapped. "We're asking you to pay us what you owe us and let us go."

Angel narrowed her eyes. "Go where, exactly?"

"That's none of your business."

"If you're gonna get caught and interrogated then yeah, it is very much my business," Angel said. "The more I think about it, the more I like the idea of putting a permanent end to that problem."

Putting the clues together, Nate deduced that Nadia had already sold Angel the true story about Dorothy and Thea, but that Angel was leaning toward killing them all instead of paying them. Which meant that showing up here with Agnes and Dante in tow was about the worst thing he could have done, making it easier for Angel to tie up all the loose ends at once.

Nate had never fantasized about hitting a woman before, but he was seriously considering making an exception for Angel. She was supposed to be a resistance leader, for God's sake!

Outrage overtook the last of his fear, and Nate leaned forward, putting his hands on the table so he could glare at Angel at eye level.

"Let me get this straight," he said, his voice just loud enough to be heard over the music. "You're a leader in the resistance movement that wants to overthrow the government of Paxco, and yet you think it's a good idea to kill us all, which is exactly what said government wants. Isn't giving aid and comfort to the enemy supposed to be a bad thing?"

To his surprise, Angel broke the stare first. It was a small victory, though Angel made as if she were just taking a moment to survey the activity in the club.

"We are not the enemy," he continued, hoping to hammer home his point. "As long as we're alive, we will be a constant thorn in Dorothy's side. She's going to expend lots of time and energy and money trying to hunt us down. Won't that make it easier for you and your people to do . . . whatever it is you do?"

It was a rather weak ending to his speech, but he still wasn't terribly clear on what the resistance saw its endgame to be. And at the moment, he didn't care.

"That sounds very reasonable and all," Angel said, "but my problem is that as long as you're out there alive and being hunted, there's an unacceptable risk of you being captured and running your mouths. You know too fucking much."

Nate didn't think they knew all that much about the resistance—not enough to be worth murdering five people over, at least. But if Angel thought there was, he doubted he'd be able to talk her into seeing it differently.

"Dorothy doesn't want us alive," Nadia said. "That was the whole point of letting Nate and me go in the first place. She wants us dead, and she wants it done unofficially. Her best-case scenario would be for us to be killed by Basement-dwellers so there's no possible way she can be linked to it. And if we can be killed without anyone even knowing for sure whether we're alive or dead, well that would just be icing on the cake. She doesn't want any chance that we can be used as symbols or martyrs or rallying cries."

"If that's the case," Angel quickly countered, "then why did she send a security squad to the apartment you were hiding in? And why is she offering a reward for you?"

With a start, Nate remembered that both he and Dante had been under the impression they were being followed in the streets of the Basement.

"She wasn't trying to capture us," he said. "She was trying to flush us out. Somewhere between the apartment and here, we picked up a tail. Why would some random Basement-dweller decide to tail the three of us? We sure don't look like people who would be rolling in money. And what self-respecting Basement-dweller is going to think we look like a tempting target when we have Captain Studly on our side?" He made a sweeping gesture at Dante, who looked kind of puny next to someone like Djinni but who was definitely big and imposing compared to normal people.

"Dorothy wants us on the move," he concluded, "with nowhere safe to hide. She's got some gun-for-hire following us, waiting for the perfect moment of privacy when he can kill us all without any witnesses. And ten to one he'll make it so that no one will ever find the bodies."

"Don't do Dorothy's work for her," Nadia said. "Don't make it easier for her to get what she wants. Especially when what she wants includes snatching people from the Basement and dissecting their brains for her sick idea of research."

Angel looked each of them in the face for a long moment,

her eyes shining with calculation and cunning. But however reprehensible a person she might be, she wouldn't have joined up with the resistance if she didn't think the poor and disenfranchised people of Paxco were getting a raw deal—and if she didn't want to do something about it. Helping Thea in any way, even indirectly, would trample all over her cause.

After what felt like about an hour of staring at them and thinking, Angel finally nodded.

"I'm not sure I one hundred percent buy your story," she said. "But I'm willing to admit our new Chairman Hayes is bad news."

"Her name is Dorothy," Nate corrected, his stomach feeling queasy. "Chairman Hayes was my father, and Dorothy is no relation, no matter what she claims." Since he'd awakened as a Replica, he'd often thought he wanted his father dead. But that didn't mean he wasn't now struggling with a tangle of mixed emotions after seeing the man shot to death before his eyes. He knew everyone would naturally refer to Dorothy as Chairman Hayes now that she had supposedly succeeded Nate's father, but he was never going to be able to hear that title without cringing.

Angel raised an eyebrow at him, so he knew she'd heard him, but she continued talking as if she hadn't. "There's something fishy about a woman who appears out of nowhere claiming to be the late Chairman's daughter—just in time to conveniently take over the Chairmanship when the Chairman Heir murders his father and the Replica program is 'on hiatus.' Whatever her game is, I doubt I'm going to like it, so I guess I'll give you children a helping hand after all."

"You mean you'll give us the money you already agreed you would pay us?" Nadia asked pointedly.

Angel laughed. "Bishop's right: Honey Badger is the perfect street name for you."

Honey Badger? When did Nadia acquire a street name? And what the hell was a honey badger?

"I could give you the money like we agreed," Angel continued, "but even with Bishop's help, I don't know how you kids could find a safe place to hole up before you got yourselves killed. So I'm going to do you one better." She pushed back her chair and stood up. "Wait here. Make yourselves at home. This may take a while."

"*What* may take a while?" Nate asked, but Angel walked away with no answer but a smirk.

Djinni hovered menacingly, making it clear that Angel wasn't *inviting* them to stay so much as *ordering* them to. And since Nate was far from eager to head back out to the street where their tail was waiting for them—assuming his guesses about the guy were true—he took a seat beside Bishop and resigned himself to waiting.

CHAPTER SIX

There were no clocks at Angel's, and Nadia wasn't wearing a watch, but she knew she and her friends had been sitting here at this corner table, waiting for whatever Angel had in store for them, for hours. It had to be well past midnight by now, and Nadia hadn't caught so much as a glimpse of their hostess since she'd left the table. Djinni the Blue Giant, however, hovered constantly, always watching them.

Talking over the music was hard—and inadvisable with Djinni hanging on their every word—so they mostly just sat in brooding silence. Which gave Nadia little else to do but to look around and see what kind of a place this really was.

Angel's was packed to the gills with people of all kinds. Lots of Basement-dwellers, of course, but a startling number of Employees and Executives as well. Some of them people Nate and Nadia knew personally, although luckily no one seemed to recognize them through their Basement disguises. Nadia knew that going to the Basement with a pack of buddies to take a walk on the wild side was something like a rite of passage for teenage boys, but most of the Employees and Executives in the club were a long way from being teenagers. They still traveled in packs, some even with bodyguards, and Angel's staff fawned on them, said fawning often involving the removal of clothes.

There were strippers everywhere, some of them dressed like the Basement-dwellers they were, some wearing outfits that mimicked Executive attire. Every few minutes, one of them would climb onto the bar or a table and start doing a bump-and-grind to the music, and men would flock to that area to stuff bills in garters. Usually, the strippers were women—though some were young enough that Nadia thought the term "girls" might be more appropriate—but there was the occasional man as well. Nadia had squirmed uncomfortably when the first female stripper started her act, but when the first man climbed up on a table only a few feet away, her face went hot and she hurriedly looked away. Beside her, Agnes was staring at the show with a look on her face that was somewhere between horror and fascination.

Nadia glanced over at Nate, who sat shoulder to shoulder with Bishop. They each took a moment to admire the stripper, but they were far more into each other than the show. It looked like they were holding hands under the table. They had grown increasingly less wary of revealing their relationship in public, a kind of openness she knew Nate had been longing for ever since he'd figured out his sexual preference.

"I can't believe Nate actually *likes* this place," Dante said, practically shouting in her ear to be heard. He was looking at the stripper with his nose wrinkled in distaste. To his credit, he'd looked at the female strippers with a similar expression. Nadia knew because she hadn't been able to resist glancing at him to check out his reaction.

"I don't think he does anymore," Nadia said. "And I

think what he really liked was being able to be with Bishop without having to hide it."

Which wasn't the whole truth—she knew Nate had enjoyed the club because coming here had made him feel wild and rebellious. Once upon a time, he'd been blind to the ugliness of Angel's and of life in the Basement itself. Cheerfully oblivious. He had changed over the last few weeks, and though he'd been her best friend for as long as she could remember, she liked him a hell of a lot better now than she had before.

One of the club's servers came over to their table and laid out five glasses of something bright pink in color. "Compliments of the house," the server said, then darted away.

The crush of so many bodies gave Angel's club the sultry atmosphere of a tropical greenhouse, and Nadia became acutely aware of how dry her mouth was. And yet all five of them stared at the glasses with evident distrust.

Bishop was the first to reach for a glass, but he held it up to his nose and sniffed before daring to drink. Apparently it didn't smell like poison, so he took a tentative sip while the rest of them watched. He swished it around his mouth, and Nadia found herself holding her breath. Then he swallowed, shaking his head and smiling wryly.

"It's fucking fruit punch," he announced, then drained the rest of his glass in a few gulps.

"Fruit punch?" Nate said incredulously. "Angel serves *fruit punch*?"

Dante snorted and reached for a glass. "I think it's supposed to be an insult. You know, fruit punch for the kiddies."

"Ya think?" Bishop said. "Best to wait a coupla minutes before anyone else drinks it. Just in case."

"If you weren't sure it was safe, why did you drink it?" Nate asked anxiously.

Bishop shrugged. "I was thirsty. I don't think Angel would try to drug us, but it never hurts to be too careful."

When ten minutes later Bishop didn't show any sign of being drugged, he gave the okay, and everyone else picked up a glass. Nadia took a sip and wrinkled her nose. The stuff was fruit-punch-flavored, but she doubted there was any actual fruit in it, and it was sickeningly sweet. Still, it was wet, so she drank it.

When she put down her glass, she saw Angel wending her way through the crowd toward them, a man following close in her wake. He was of medium height and build, in his early twenties or maybe late teens, with dark skin and curly, neon-orange hair cropped close to his skull. The orange was just the right shade to clash with the crimson muscle shirt and wine-red leather pants he wore. Still not completely used to the Basement mode of dress, Nadia's first thought was that the guy looked like a clown, but then she noticed the nervous glances Angel's clientele shot in his direction, the way they hurried to get out of his way, and he didn't look so clownish anymore.

Bishop made a little groaning sound and rubbed his eyes. "I shoulda known," he said, then pushed to his feet, holding out a hand to indicate that the rest of them should stay sitting down. "Let me handle this."

Handle *what?* Nadia wondered, sharing a mystified gaze with Nate. Nate shrugged.

The man caught sight of Bishop and his face broke out in a grin, flashing a gold front tooth. There was no irony in that smile, and Nadia swore there was genuine warmth in those eyes, making Bishop's reaction even more puzzling. Angel stepped aside, inviting the man to pass her, which he did. Bishop returned the smile, stepping forward and holding out his hand. The two of them clasped hands and bumped shoulders.

Bishop was still smiling as he turned to the rest of them, but there was a warning in his eyes. "Everyone, this is my friend Shrimp. Shrimp, this is everyone."

Shrimp? It was obviously a street name, but Nadia had no clue how the guy had earned it. She'd expect someone named Shrimp to be either very big or very small.

"Yo," Shrimp said in greeting, touching his fingers to his forehead as if tipping a cap.

"Pull up a chair," Bishop invited, and Shrimp obliged him.

"I'll leave you to get reacquainted," Angel said before wandering off into the crowd.

Shrimp turned the chair around and straddled it, resting his forearms on the back as his keenly intelligent eyes scanned over them one by one before returning to Bishop.

"So, Angel tells me y'all need a place to hide. Again." He rolled his eyes and shook his head in apparent exasperation.

Nadia had a sudden realization of who Shrimp might be—or at least whom he might represent. He obviously knew about Bishop's time in hiding with the Red Death. And he was ostentatiously wearing red. And the locals were clearly wary of him, despite his average build and friendly demeanor.

"Yeah," Bishop said. "Can't seem to keep outta trouble."

"I hear ya. But we're always there for you, bro."

"Uh-huh," Bishop responded. "As long as there's money involved."

Shrimp grinned, unrepentant. "What'd ya expect? Charity?"

Bishop looked pointedly from Nate, to Agnes, to Nadia before meeting Shrimp's gaze again. "Angel tell you who they are?"

"Yep," Shrimp confirmed. "Said she'd take care of room and board for all five of you."

"For how long?"

"Till she gets tired of paying, I reckon."

Nadia supposed it was as good a use of their money as any, though she would have much preferred to hold the purse strings herself. She didn't like the idea of Angel holding their future in her hands.

"Or till Maiden decides he can get more by turning us in?" Bishop challenged.

Nadia shivered. Bishop had mentioned the leader of the Red Death was called Maiden because he collected—and used—iron maidens. Not exactly the kind of person she was eager to cast in a "protector" role.

Shrimp's expression hardened. "I know I didn't just hear you insult my brother while you're sitting here asking for help."

Bishop raised his hands in a gesture of surrender. "I'm just sayin' . . . He's not one to stick his neck out, and we're pretty hot right now."

"Oh, don't worry. We'll be well paid for our trouble." He broke into his easy smile once again. "Besides, can you see Maiden making friendly with security?"

"No, I suppose not," Bishop said, but he still looked

uneasy. He gave Agnes and Nadia another furtive glance. "Be straight with me. Are my girls gonna be safe?"

Nadia thought it a telling detail that Shrimp had bristled at the possibility that his brother might turn them in for the reward money but took the question about the girls' safety with no sign of offense. She had to bite her tongue to stop herself from making some comment about taking care of herself. She certainly didn't like Bishop referring to her and Agnes as "my girls."

Shrimp gave both Nadia and Agnes a closer look, then nodded at Bishop.

"I'll personally guarantee it," Shrimp said. "But to be extra safe, they should stay at my place. No one's gonna mess with them there."

"Even Maiden?" Bishop pressed.

"Yeah. Even my bro don't wanna get on Angel's bad side. She's payin' us to keep you safe. All of you. So that's what we're gonna do. Unless my word ain't good enough for you." He turned off the smile once again and fixed Bishop with a cold, challenging look.

Nadia expected a macho showdown of some sort, but Bishop's shoulders sagged, and he looked suddenly weary.

"Can we skip this shit and just get outta here?" he asked.

Shrimp shook his head. "Skip it? No. But we can do the short version." He looked at each person at the table one by one, his gaze now positively menacing. "The minute you set foot in Red Death territory, you're ours," he said. "You do what you're told. You don't make waves. You keep your heads down and your mouths shut. If anyone has a problem with that, stay here. Got it?"

Nadia could see how Nate bristled at Shrimp's tone. She

could also see the pointed look Bishop shot him. It looked like it physically hurt Nate to do so, but he nodded his agreement to Shrimp's terms. The others all followed suit, and Shrimp dropped the glare like it had been a mask, once again looking genial and friendly.

"Good deal. *Now* we can get outta here."

It came as no great surprise that Angel's had a secret exit. In fact, Nadia wouldn't have been surprised if there was more than one. She was similarly unsurprised to see the exit manned by one of Angel's bouncers. The cashbox on the floor beside him suggested that ordinarily, there was a charge—no doubt a hefty one—for going out the back way.

They were in a dim hallway behind the main body of the club. Nadia could still feel the pulsing beat of the music beneath her feet, but at least the noise level was reduced. Shrimp stopped them and had them gather around before they set foot outside the exit.

"We got a long walk coming," he warned. "There's a lotta people on the street, but we gotta stay together. We'll do it by buddy system." He looked over them all, one by one. "I'll take the lead; Bishop'll take the rear. Honey Badger, you're with me."

He flashed Nadia a gold-toothed grin, and she let out an internal sigh of defeat. Looked like she was now officially stuck with the name. Thanks to Angel, no doubt—certainly Nadia hadn't introduced herself that way.

"Ghost, you're with Bishop," Shrimp continued. "Captain Studly and the girl with no name stay in the middle."

"Oh no," Dante protested. "You are *not* calling me Captain Studly." He looked only briefly at Shrimp, then fixed his glare on Nate, who apparently had given him his street name, unbeknown to either of them. Nadia had to suppress a smile, because Dante was actually *blushing* at the name.

Shrimp's cheerful grin remained firmly in place. "Sorry, man. Street names are hard to shake once they've stuck to you. I should know."

"Well this one hasn't stuck!" Dante insisted.

"That's what you think."

"Whatever. But Nadia—I mean Honey Badger—stays with me."

Nadia could almost smell the testosterone building in the air. She'd have thought as an agent of the security department, Dante would have had to learn to follow orders, but he never seemed to be very good at it. He was puffing himself up, ready to lock horns with Shrimp in some stupid male power game, but Shrimp derailed the whole thing before it got started.

"Fine," he said. "I guess the girl with no name's with me then."

"My name is Agnes," Agnes said with a raise of her chin.

"Not here it ain't," Shrimp responded, but he said it kindly. "But hey, at least you ain't stuck with something like Captain Studly."

Dante groaned, and Agnes tried a tentative smile.

"Let's hit the road," Shrimp said, surprising them all by holding out his elbow to Agnes like an Executive gentleman.

"Layin' it on a little thick, aren't you?" Bishop asked, but he was smiling.

walking through the crowded Basement streets with Kurt at his side wasn't a new experience for Nate, and yet tonight's venture felt utterly foreign. The crowd felt more oppressive, the smells more overwhelming, the sense of danger way past the harmless fun stage. Staying together was a challenge, but Shrimp was a good and conscientious guide. He seemed to be chatting amiably with Agnes, which was something of a miracle, considering her usual reticence. People made way for him with surprising ease, and he probably could have covered the distance in half the time if he weren't constantly having to wait for the rest of them to catch up.

"Why is everyone so scared of him?" Nate asked Kurt as they jostled and bumped their way around. "He doesn't exactly look scary to me. I guess it's all an act, but he kinda seems like a nice guy."

His experience with Basement-dwellers was fairly limited, but it was rare for one of them to give off a nice-guy vibe. Even Kurt, when Nate had first met him, had given off a sense of sexy and dangerous, rather than *nice*.

"It's not an act," Kurt said. "Shrimp's a good guy. His brother, on the other hand . . . Shrimp's the only guy I know who isn't scared shitless of Maiden."

Nate made a face. How scared could you be of a gang lord who called himself the Maiden?

"Maiden is about as far from a nice guy as it's possible to get," Kurt continued. "He takes good care of his people, and he'd gut anyone who so much as laid a finger on Shrimp, but that's about it for redeeming features. He'll be able to hide us from security, and probably from whoever Dorothy's sent after us, but don't ever forget that we will *not* be safe in his territory."

"I think the safety boat sailed a long time ago," Nate

said, suddenly feeling tired. How had he gone so fast from being the carefree Chairman Heir of the richest, most powerful state in the world to being a fugitive taking shelter with a notoriously evil gangster?

The contrast between the teeming streets of the Basement's free territory and the streets of its gang-controlled heart was striking. There was still pedestrian traffic, and there were still obvious business transactions being carried out right in the open, but the crowd was a lot thinner and the mood more subdued and wary.

With fewer people around—and no "tourists" to entice—it was easier to see the Basement for the seedy slum it was. The pavement was many times cracked and never repaired, as evidenced by the weeds and grass that had taken root in every crevice. Litter blew in the breeze, little slips of paper, glassine packets, torn plastic wrappers. Broken glass and crushed cans gathered in the gutters, some of which were so thoroughly blocked that little algae-filled ponds of rainwater had formed in them like rancid tide pools.

There was no missing it when you crossed into Red Death territory. Red spray paint marked every building, sometimes in pictures, sometimes in indecipherable script. Every man, woman, and child who walked the streets wore something red, the moving river of people making it look like the city was bleeding.

Unlike in the free territories, there were actually a few cars and motorcycles parked by the side of the road in Red Death land. All of them red, of course. A dingy red convertible cruised slowly by, music blaring. The driver sat alone in the front seat, and in the back were a couple of scowling men, holding machine guns and scanning the crowd. No one met their eyes—except for Shrimp, who gave them a thumbs-up—and Nate could practically feel the increased tension in the air, tension that wasn't released until the car reached the next intersection and turned.

"Maiden's enforcers patrol the streets twenty-four/seven," Kurt said. "Nothing happens in his territory that he doesn't know about."

Shrimp led them to a corner building that looked just like all the others, except instead of being marked with red gang tags, it was painted entirely red. The paint job was patchy and amateurish, with about a hundred different shades of red, but the fact that the Basement-dwellers had been able to paint an entire high-rise without the benefit of cranes and scaffolding was pretty damned impressive.

If the red paint job wasn't enough to clue you in that this place was Red Death Central, the pair of thugs standing one on each side of the door with machine guns slung over their shoulders would definitely do it.

"Home sweet home," Shrimp said, waving cheerfully at the guards, who barely acknowledged his presence.

It wasn't until Nate had passed the guards to follow Shrimp and the others through the door that he noticed the two transparent shields that had been cemented into the pavement and covered the guards from head to toe. There were several openings in the shields—like arrow slits in a castle—and Nate wondered how these guys got hold of military supplies. Bulletproof glass and machine guns were not easily accessible to civilians, even on the black market.

Unlike Kurt's building, this one had a working elevator, which was a good thing, Nate thought to himself when they all packed themselves in and Shrimp hit the button for eighteen. That would have been a lot of stairs to climb.

"I'm on nineteen," Shrimp said as the elevator began to climb. "I'm putting y'all in a vacant unit we've got on eighteen. You need anything, you come right on up."

The elevator dinged, and they piled out into a hallway that theoretically should have looked exactly the same as the ones in Kurt's building. It didn't. The walls were painted a muted beige with not a stain or scuff mark to be seen. Instead of peeling linoleum flooring, there was plush wall-to-wall carpeting, and light was provided by decorative wall sconces instead of overhead fluorescents. If Nate had been transported here without seeing the neighborhood, he might have thought the building was meant to house mid- to high-level Employees, not Basement-dwellers. He wondered if any of the other buildings in the area were as nicely appointed, but quickly answered his own question. This building was in such good shape because it housed VIPs, and Nate would eat his wig if the rank-and-file Red Death members lived as well.

Shrimp led them to a door at the end of the hall and let them into a pleasant little apartment that again looked nothing like Kurt's. The layout was the same, but it was furnished and clean, with updated fixtures and an aura of homeyness.

"There's two bedrooms," Shrimp said, laying the key on the kitchen counter, "but only one bed in each. I'm guessing if I take the girls upstairs to my place, you boys can work out the sleeping arrangements." He waggled his brows at Kurt.

Shrimp seemed friendly enough, and Kurt seemed to

trust him, but Nate didn't like the idea of being separated from the girls. He must have been wearing his doubts on his face, because Kurt gave him a pat on the back.

"They'll be safe with Shrimp," he said. "And I don't know about you, but I don't want to share a bed with Captain Studly, which is what we'll have to do if the girls stay here."

"I'm beginning to hate you almost as much as I hate *him,*" Dante said, jerking his thumb toward Nate.

The lights suddenly went out. Nate thought at first it was only in the apartment, but the curtains over the living room window were open, and when he looked out, he saw nothing but a sea of darkness.

The lights went back on before anyone had a chance to react. There was a moment of tense silence as they all waited for the power to die a second time, but it didn't.

"Weird," Shrimp commented. "Not like it's stormy out or nothing."

Nate and Nadia shared a look, and he suspected they were wondering the same thing: Had that blackout been some kind of technical glitch? Or was it the power drain of Thea creating a new Replica?

Probably paranoia to think the latter. But that didn't stop him from thinking it.

"Think we'll take the stairs to my place," Shrimp said. "Just in case." He looked back and forth between Nate and Dante. "Swear to God they'll be safe with me."

"And will the boys be safe down here *without* you?" Nadia asked. Nate knew her well enough to see how she was bristling over the whole idea of needing special protection, but she managed to keep it out of her voice, and Shrimp probably had no idea how irritated she was.

"Maiden's not into boys," Shrimp responded. "They'll be fine down here, and you'll be fine with me 'cause he wouldn't mess with you in front of me."

This Maiden guy was obviously a real prince.

"Rest up while you can," Shrimp continued. "Maiden'll want to meet you tomorrow. Probably for dinner. I'll come get you when it's time. Just to be safe, don't leave the apartment before then, unless it's to come to my place, 'kay?"

Fantastic. This Maiden was some sadistic gang lord who couldn't be trusted around Nadia and Agnes, and it was beginning to look like they were going to become prisoners here. Which was better than dead, but it was hardly an auspicious position from which to start building their new resistance movement.

Maybe the whole resistance thing was a pipe dream, and the best they could hope for was survival.

CHAPTER SEVEN

The apartment the boys were staying in was nice and comfortable, but Shrimp's was a cut or two above. The furniture was good quality, if not particularly special, but Nadia imagined the wall of electronics that took up one whole side of the living room cost in the tens of thousands of dollars. Laid on the floor, the video screen would be big enough to serve as a bed, and with the number of speakers Shrimp had, he could probably play music loud enough to cause an earthquake. The kitchen was fitted with state-of-the-art appliances, and when Shrimp opened the fridge to offer Nadia and Agnes something to drink, she saw that it was well stocked with food and drink that most definitely did not come from a soup kitchen. No powdered soup or soy "ham" for him.

The guest bedroom had an air of neglect to it—Nadia figured there wasn't much occasion for guests in Red Death territory—but it was clean, and there was an inviting queen-sized bed. Nadia looked forward to sleeping on something other than a sofa cushion. Sheets and pillows had become a luxury, and sleep pulled at her the moment she stepped through the door.

"Bathroom's across the hall," Shrimp said, pointing. "I can give you some old clothes to wear to bed if you want to change into something more comfortable. And feel free to use the shower. We got a tankless water heater so you don't have to do one of those rush jobs."

The expression on Agnes's face turned to something almost like lust, and Nadia suspected her own expression was similar. The hot water in Bishop's place lasted for all of about three minutes, and there was no way all five of them could have hot showers one after the other. Nadia hadn't had a good, hot shower since she'd fled the Preston Sanctuary.

Shrimp grinned knowingly. "My favorite pickup line is 'Hey, baby, wanna hot shower?' Works every time."

Somehow, Nadia didn't think Shrimp needed any lines to pick up women. He wasn't classically handsome, especially with the orange hair and gold tooth, but his face had character, and he had more than enough charm to make up for his unspectacular appearance. Not to mention his status as brother of one of the most powerful people in all of the Basement.

"Why do they call you Shrimp?" Nadia asked, hoping the question wasn't a violation of what passed for etiquette here.

He rolled his eyes hugely. "'Cause back when I was like fourteen, we found out the hard way I was allergic to shellfish. I puffed up like a balloon. I didn't die, so everyone decided it was funny and started calling me Shrimp. I tried to fight it, 'cause, you know, it's not that cool. But like I said, names stick to you here." He gave Agnes a solemn look. "You might want to come up with a name before someone does it for you. Can't guarantee it'll stick if you give it to yourself, but at least it'll have a shot. Otherwise, you'll probably end up being Princess 'cause you're the daughter of a Chairman."

Agnes wrinkled her nose. "Ugh. Are you sure you can't just call me Agnes?"

Shrimp shook his head. "Calling you by your birth name would be an insult. It says you're a little kid. You don't want people using your birth name."

"We'll think of something," Nadia said. "*After* we've had our showers."

with the Basement lifestyle being largely nocturnal, Nadia was trying to get used to sleeping during the day, but she wasn't quite there yet and hadn't slept for more than a couple of hours at a time since arriving. However, it turned out Shrimp's guest room had blackout drapes over the windows. There was still a little light leaking in around the edges, but the room itself was blessedly dark, and Nadia groaned with relief as she slid between the covers. The bed was comfortably soft, the sheets smelled fresh, and Nadia was finally clean after a long scrub in the shower. For once, Agnes wasn't the only one who dropped off into an instant slumber.

When Nadia next awoke, the light around the curtains had a reddish-orange hue that spoke of sunset. She had to blink a few times before she could remember where she was and what was going on. Agnes was sitting up in bed beside her, arms wrapped around her knees.

"Oh good," Agnes said, "you're awake." She reached over and snapped on the bedside lamp.

Nadia winced in the sudden light, then sat up and squinted as she waited for her eyes to adjust. "How long have you been up?"

"Not long," Agnes replied. "I thought I heard voices outside. Then I realized it was the TV."

That's a surprise, Nadia thought as she rubbed her eyes. As far as she knew, phone service and net access used the same signal, so if one was down, both should be. Was it possible yesterday's phone outage really was an accident and not a deliberate plot by Dorothy to cut off contact with the Basement?

"We still don't have a phone signal," Agnes said, and for the first time Nadia noticed she was holding her phone in her hand. She held it up so Nadia could see the NO SIGNAL message.

Nadia listened to the faint sound of voices coming through the walls, and knew Agnes was right: it was the TV. She couldn't make out any words, but the cadence was all wrong for it to be a bunch of Basement-dwellers gathered in the apartment.

"Apparently Shrimp has some way of getting a net signal even when the phones are out," Nadia said.

"Seems that way."

Neither Nadia nor Agnes had any interest in putting on their dirty Basement disguises, so by mutual agreement, they padded out into the living room together wearing the oversized T-shirts and cutoff sweatpants Shrimp had given them. The pair of them had to look pretty ridiculous, barefoot and swimming in men's clothes. The gel Agnes used on her hair for her Basement disguise was supposed to wash out completely, but it didn't, leaving her hair tinted baby blue. Shrimp didn't keep conditioner in his bathroom, so Nadia's long blond hair was dry and frizzy, but at least it wasn't blue.

Shrimp was reclining on his leather sofa, bare feet propped on the coffee table, a steaming mug in his hand.

On the wall, the huge video screen showed an image of Dorothy standing before a podium of microphones at what was obviously a press conference. Thea's puppet had flaunted her youthful beauty in the past, but now she seemed to have adopted a more subdued look. Her gray suit was perfectly fitted, but nondescript, and though she was no doubt wearing plenty of makeup, the shades were all so natural you couldn't even tell. Perhaps she worried people wouldn't take her seriously if she looked too young and beautiful.

Shrimp muted the sound before Nadia had a chance to hear more than a couple of words. She couldn't decide whether that was a good thing or a bad thing, but the crease between his brows didn't bode well. Or maybe he just wasn't a "morning" person.

Shrimp put his mug down and jumped to his feet. He was wearing a plain black T-shirt and ordinary-looking blue jeans. If it weren't for the orange hair, he could have passed for a respectable Employee on his day off. Apparently, Basement-dwellers only dressed in their colorful regalia when they went out. Nadia couldn't blame them, considering how many of the outfits she'd seen looked torturously uncomfortable.

"Morning, ladies," he said. "Want some coffee? I got good stuff."

"I'd *love* some coffee," Agnes said, her eyes practically glowing.

Nadia wasn't ordinarily a big coffee drinker, but considering the quantity and quality of the food and drink she'd had since entering the Basement, it suddenly sounded like heaven. If only that giant image of Dorothy weren't looming there, speaking into the microphones with a combination of sternness and concern on her phony face.

"How come you get a TV signal when the phone lines are down?" Nadia asked Shrimp as he went to the kitchen and poured two mugs of coffee.

"Used to be most TV signals came through cables," he answered. "They tore down all the aboveground stuff when they built the Basement, but there are still old underground cables left in places. Maiden's got a contact on the outside who splices the signal into the cable. Doesn't help with the phone sitch, but at least we're not completely cut off when the lines are down."

"Can we use these cables to make phone calls?" Agnes asked with barely repressed excitement in her voice. Nadia supposed she still had visions of her father smuggling the five of them out of Paxco and into Synchrony, back into a life that was safe and familiar.

Shrimp gave Agnes a wary look as he handed her a mug of tar-black coffee. Agnes took it with reverence, but Nadia looked around for the cream and sugar.

"It's possible," Shrimp said. "But you'd have to get Maiden's okay, and he ain't gonna give it."

"Why not?" Agnes asked.

He raised an eyebrow at her. "Who you gonna call?"

Agnes pressed her lips together, as if somehow not answering the question out loud might make it so Shrimp didn't know the answer.

"You think no one's gonna notice if a call comes in to your dad over a landline in Debasement?" He shook his head. "You call out, they can trace it like this." He snapped his fingers.

"We signed up to hide you, not protect you." The look on his face was as apologetic as it was implacable.

Agnes nodded grimly and took a sip of her coffee. She sighed with contentment at the first taste, as if the coffee had washed away her every care. But Nadia was sure her agile mind was still mulling over the problem, trying to find a way to reach out to her father without betraying their location to Dorothy.

Nadia filled her mug to the rim with milk, but that only managed to make the coffee a couple of shades lighter. She added in three teaspoons of sugar, but even then the stuff was too strong for her taste. She couldn't imagine how Agnes was drinking it—and *enjoying* it—black. Still, despite everything that had happened, Nadia refused to abandon her manners, so she sipped at the toxic brew and made sure her face betrayed none of her distaste.

"What is Dorothy going on about?" she asked, jerking her chin toward the TV. Dorothy's press conference was still in progress—or more likely at this hour, was being played over and over again.

Shrimp shrugged and frowned. "Some shit about stock prices. Nothing important."

Shrimp might not think stock prices were important—and usually they weren't, to Basement-dwellers—but Paxco's stock had dipped over rumors that the Replica program was defunct, and Nadia knew the assassination of Chairman Hayes had halted any recovery those stocks might have been making. The fact that Dorothy had taken over as Chairman rather than creating a Replica of the late Chairman Hayes must have made the public even more convinced that the official story—that the Replica program was not defunct and was merely in a hiatus due to technical difficulties—was a fabrication. Dorothy wouldn't be giving a press conference about it if things were going well, and if stocks dropped low enough and there was belt-tightening to be done, you could be sure it wasn't the Executives whose belts would be affected.

"Mind if I give a listen anyway?" Nadia asked.

"Suit yourself," Shrimp said, making a sweeping gesture toward the living room.

Nadia expected Agnes to follow her out of the kitchen, but she stayed behind to refill her coffee cup instead. Shrimp, leaning against the kitchen counter, said something that Nadia didn't catch, and Agnes laughed. Nadia practically tripped over her feet in surprise. Agnes, in that kitchen, talking to a gang lord's younger brother in the heart of the Basement, looked almost . . . relaxed. Nadia wondered if that was because of Shrimp's easygoing personality, or whether it was just because she was outside the view of Executive society and didn't have to worry that her every word and gesture would be scrutinized. There was a certain sense of freedom to leaving all of that behind.

Forcing herself to take another sip of coffee, Nadia sat on the couch and turned the sound on. Dorothy's voice instantly filled the room, and Nadia found her gut muscles clenching at the sound of it. Images of Dorothy shooting Nate's father filled her head.

Her Pavlovian reaction to Dorothy's voice kept Nadia from immediately absorbing what she was hearing, but she shook herself out of it and forced herself to listen to the words, rather than the voice. What she heard was far from comforting.

"This is a difficult time for all the Employees and Executives of Paxco," Dorothy said, and she knew how to mimic earnestness to perfection. "The economic downturn resulting from the brutal murder of our late Chairman is an undeniable source of alarm, and I cannot blame investors for being wary of us in this time of unrest."

Nadia snorted and shook her head. Of *course* investors were wary. Just a few weeks ago, no one had ever heard of Dorothy, had never had any indication that Chairman Hayes had an illegitimate daughter. Surely there were people who found it suspicious that she had come out of nowhere and then succeeded to the Chairmanship so quickly.

"Rest assured that I and your board of directors and the Paxco security department are working tirelessly to repair the damage done to our state by the Replica of Nathaniel Hayes. He will not remain at large for long, and when he is captured, our scientists will be able to examine him closely to determine what went wrong with the Replication process."

Nadia gaped at the TV. She should have known Dorothy would pull something like this. Even before Dorothy had made an appearance, the press had been spreading rumors that Nate's Replica was somehow flawed, that it had violent tendencies the original Nate hadn't had. All this based on one brief loss of temper when Nate had shoved a reporter out of the way with more force than necessary. It made sense that Dorothy would take advantage of the ridiculous rumor to continue degrading Nate's image.

"I want to reassure our customers that there are no known issues with our backup storage or scanners. We will continue to process scans and to store backup data, but we will not create another Replica until we are certain we understand what went wrong with the Replica of Nathaniel Hayes. Safety must always be our first priority."

Dorothy sounded firm and confident, and her gaze as she stared into the cameras before her was regal. She looked every bit like a Chairman, in control of her state and with a bright future ahead of her. But though she had successfully seized the Chairmanship, her own Replica program had backed her into a corner. As long as she continued to claim it was on hiatus, Paxco's stock crisis would continue to worsen. But the moment she admitted it was up and running, people would expect her to create a Replica of Chairman Hayes and put him back in power. If she didn't—if she, for example, claimed that the Chairman's backup data was damaged—people couldn't help but begin to suspect her of foul play.

"Our state is strong and resilient," Dorothy said, holding her chin at just the right angle to communicate pride. "There will likely be some dark times ahead. We may be forced to introduce certain austerity measures to preserve and protect our economy." Her voice rose, filling with power and purpose. "But we will not allow these troubles to defeat us. We will show the world how resilient the people of Paxco can be! We will overcome all obstacles, and we will be great again!" She pumped a fist to emphasize her point, and everyone in the room burst into applause.

Nadia had never heard applause like that at a press conference before, but she thought it had been started by a handful of board members who were standing in the background behind Dorothy. They were cheering loudly and enthusiastically, and their excitement seemed to be contagious. Nadia had the cynical suspicion that Dorothy and those board members had choreographed the scene in advance, trying to make the news sound exciting and promising when in fact Dorothy was telling people things were going to suck for a while.

The image went still and was reduced to a small box in the upper right corner of the screen while a serious-faced reporter behind a desk looked into the camera and said, "That was the scene earlier at Paxco Headquarters." No doubt he would soon begin an ad nauseam analysis of everything Dorothy had just said. The picture from the press conference/pep rally remained in the upper part of the screen, Dorothy's triumphant smile immortalized. Fearing she might throw something at the TV if the reporter started rhapsodizing about Dorothy's speech, Nadia turned the sound off once more.

CHAPTER EIGHT

nadia wasn't entirely sure what she'd expected of her time hiding in the Basement, but it wasn't boredom. Shrimp informed everyone in no uncertain terms that they were not to set foot outside the building until they'd been introduced to Maiden and received his approval, but Maiden was clearly in no hurry to talk to them. He was supposedly planning to invite them to dinner at his place, but as the days passed one by one and no dinner invitation was forthcoming, Nadia began to feel more like a prisoner than a paying "guest." The boys were having an even harder time, thanks to Dante feeling like a third wheel and thanks to his and Nate's mutual dislike. They generally came up to Shrimp's apartment shortly after sunset each night, though sometimes Nate and Bishop appeared noticeably later.

At least it was a comfortable captivity. Maiden might not have extended an invitation to dinner, but Shrimp did so every night. And, although it was a skill Nadia never would have expected from the brother of a notorious Basement gang lord, cooking was apparently one of Shrimp's favorite hobbies. Every evening, Nadia and Agnes would awaken to an array of mouth-watering scents wafting from the kitchen. Nadia let Agnes have dibs on the shower, and invariably when Nadia was all dressed and ready, she'd enter the living room to find Agnes had joined Shrimp in the kitchen. She wasn't just being social, either—it appeared Shrimp was teaching her how to cook, and that she was having fun.

Nadia enjoyed the nice meals as much as her friends, but she couldn't help feeling a twinge of guilt. Shrimp always had the best ingredients—no doubt thanks to the thriving black market trade the Red Death engaged in—but she couldn't help remembering the sights and sounds and smells of the Basement streets when he'd guided them to this building. He and the other Red Death bigwigs had a comfortable home and high-end food and extravagances like the huge TV, while their less powerful fellows lived in squalor and sold themselves body and soul to survive—and were no doubt forced to give a high percentage of their hard-earned money to Maiden's enforcers.

Every night after dinner, Shrimp would head out to conduct Red Death "business." No one asked him what that business might be, probably because no one really wanted to know. They would then have to face a long night in their apartments with *nothing* to do except talk or watch TV. Talking almost invariably led to bickering—they had all spent way too much time in each other's company—so usually they watched TV instead.

As depressing as it was, Nadia couldn't help checking the news every night. She hoped against hope to hear that her parents had been released, but of course Dorothy had no intention of letting them go, or she wouldn't have had them arrested in the first place.

Phone service was not restored, and Dorothy's press secretary informed the public that it had been cut off in an effort to quell unrest within the Basement. Nadia wasn't sure how cutting off phone service was supposed to quell unrest, but then obviously Dorothy didn't have much regard for the truth. After all, any unrest that might be occurring had happened *after* phone service had been cut off, not before.

The decline in Paxco's stock had slowed, but not stopped, and by the weekend, Dorothy held yet another press conference.

"Thanks to the generous support of investors and foreign allies, I am happy to announce that we have begun the process of rebuilding the Paxco economy," she said, smiling at the cameras. This time, she was wearing a conservative navy blue suit and had added a pair of glasses she surely didn't need. For someone who wasn't really a human being and hadn't had to choose outfits until recently, she was doing a good job of building up an aura of authority and competence. "However, our state will not be restored to its former glory overnight, and we must do all we can to hurry that restoration along. To that end, certain nonessential services to the Basement will be temporarily halted."

Since the government provided only food, shelter, power, and rudimentary health care to its poorest citizens, Nadia wondered what those "nonessential services" might be.

"Let me assure the working people of Paxco that these austerity measures will not affect you. You are the backbone of our society, and together, we will weather this storm and come out the other end stronger for it."

"If you've made so much progress," Nadia muttered at the TV, "then why is there a storm still to be weathered?"

But if any of the reporters at the press conference thought

to question Dorothy's assertions, those questions and answers didn't make the news. And it soon became apparent that Dorothy considered the stupid blimps "essential," because there was always one or two of them hovering over the Basement at night, blaring out messages.

Power outages were becoming annoyingly common. Usually they lasted only a few minutes, and Nadia wondered if Dorothy was actively ordering the outages to save money, or whether she was saving money by willfully neglecting maintenance issues. One thing she was certain of: the outages were Dorothy's doing, not random acts of nature. And they were happening only in the Basement, not in the "respectable" parts of the city.

The news never spent much time covering anything that happened in the Basement, and they probably wouldn't have even mentioned the phone service if it weren't for the fact that Executives were being inconvenienced by their inability to call their black market contacts. Anything Nadia learned about the doings in the Basement came from the recaps Shrimp delivered every morning when he returned from his outings.

The news Shrimp had to share was as ominous as what they heard on the TV. Predictably, Basement-dwellers were starting to get cranky about the phone and power outages. Tempers were running short, and more than one Employee or Executive tourist had found out the hard way that despite the money they spent in the Basement, they weren't well liked there.

"There hasn't been anything serious," Shrimp said. "Bumps and bruises, is all. But security is getting uptight about it. They've beefed up those checkpoints around the border.

Enough to scare off customers. Even Angel's is half empty these days, and cuttin' off the money ain't gonna go over too well, if you know what I mean."

If Dorothy was hoping to provoke rioting in the Basement, then she was on the right track. Someday, probably in the near future, some Employee or Executive was going to be in the wrong place at the wrong time with the wrong people and was going to get killed. And that would give Dorothy just the excuse she needed to take even more drastic measures.

one week after arriving in Red Death territory, Nadia arose in the evening to find that Shrimp wasn't bustling around the kitchen as usual, and Agnes said he hadn't been around when she'd emerged from the shower earlier. His absence made both of them vaguely uneasy, and when the boys joined them at the time when Shrimp ordinarily served dinner, he still wasn't around.

Shrimp showed up before they had a chance to imagine too many worst-case scenarios, arriving at the apartment with three garment bags draped over his arm.

"Maiden wants to see you," he announced.

"So you keep telling us," Nate said irritably. "It's not like we're hard to find."

Bishop shot him a warning look, but Shrimp was a hard man to annoy—which was a good thing, considering the state of everyone's temper after the long period of inactivity.

"For real this time," Shrimp assured them. "Dinner at his place tonight, eight o'clock. Just the Execs, though," he said with an apologetic shrug toward Bishop and Dante.

Nate shot up from the sofa he'd been sitting on beside

Bishop, a belligerent scowl on his face. "No way. We all go, or nobody goes." Of all of them, Nate seemed to be struggling most with their maddening captivity.

Shrimp met the scowl with one of his own. "Bishop, put a leash on your boy before he gets himself in trouble."

Apparently, it wasn't that hard to annoy Shrimp after all. Not for Nate, at least.

Bishop grabbed Nate's arm and yanked him back down to the sofa so abruptly Nate let out a little grunt of surprise.

"If Maiden says Dante and me stay here, we stay here," Bishop said in response to Nate's shocked expression. "And you need to think over anything you want to say at least three times before word one leaves your mouth tonight. You do *not* want to piss him off."

Maybe having Nate and Maiden in the same room was a bad idea, though Nadia didn't suppose they had any choice in the matter. Nate had never been any good at guarding his words. To be fair, he'd never had to be, never been as vulnerable as someone like Nadia, who didn't have the cloak of near invincibility that came with being the Chairman Heir.

But Nate wasn't the Chairman Heir anymore, was no longer anywhere near the top of the food chain, and he couldn't afford to let his mouth get away from him.

Nate nodded his acceptance of Bishop's warning while still managing to look mutinous. If Maiden were to act deliberately provoking, Nadia had no idea if Nate would be able to control his temper. Bishop leaned over and whispered something in Nate's ear that coaxed a reluctant smile out of Nate—and made him blush to the roots of his hair. Nadia was perfectly happy not to know what Bishop had said.

"Good decision," Shrimp said, but there was still an

unaccustomed tension in his shoulders. Bishop had said Shrimp was the one person who wasn't afraid of Maiden, but Nadia wondered if that was wholly true. Or maybe he was just worried that Nate would run his mouth at dinner and someone would get hurt.

"Will you be coming with us?" Nadia asked Shrimp. She doubted he could or would help them if they got into trouble with his brother, but she had a feeling things would go more smoothly if they had a Basement ally with them to help keep things on an even keel.

"I'll be there," he confirmed. He brushed at his orange hair, suddenly looking uncomfortable. "And, uh, I brought you some stuff to wear. Maiden likes his dinner guests to dress up. I know shit about sizes, so I had to guess."

Nadia shared a grimace with Agnes. They'd both gotten used to wearing Shrimp's roomy, comfortable castoffs, and changing into elaborate Basement regalia held no appeal. Not that Nadia had any intention of defying Maiden's wishes when he held her life and the lives of all her friends in his hands.

Shrimp distributed the three garment bags, and Nadia and Agnes returned to their bedroom to change, both expecting the worst. Basement outfits were not the kind of thing you ordinarily carried around in garment bags, so Nadia had no idea what they would find when they opened those zippers.

"How bad can it be?" Agnes asked with a little smile, then dropped her garment bag on the bed and yanked down the zipper. She was clearly braced to see something hideously flamboyant, and her mouth dropped open in shock when the opening revealed a length of scarlet silk chiffon.

Nadia crept closer as Agnes reached in and pulled out a padded hanger, carefully extracting the silk from the bag and revealing a knee-length cocktail dress with a beaded bodice and short, fluttery sleeves. The skirt was a layer of diaphanous chiffon over a closely fit sheath with a slit that reached to mid-thigh.

It was not at all something Agnes would usually wear, based on Nadia's admittedly limited experience with the girl. Agnes tended to favor muted pastel colors or basic black, with skirts or pants that were very loosely fitted, most likely in an attempt to camouflage her bottom-heavy figure. She probably couldn't have picked a more unflattering wardrobe if she'd tried. But the dress she was still holding up and gaping at was exactly the kind of thing Nadia would have chosen for her.

"Well," Nadia said, "that's a step up from what I was expecting."

Agnes let out a little huff of laughter. "More like several staircases up." She shook her head. "But I think Shrimp must have mixed up the bags. He must have meant this one for you. You'd look so beautiful in it!"

No, she wouldn't, Nadia knew. The red was far too bright for her pale complexion and blond hair, and she wasn't curvy enough to do the fitted skirt justice. Shrimp had known exactly what he was doing when he picked the dress for Agnes.

Agnes tried to hold the hanger out to her, but Nadia pretended not to notice as she unzipped her own bag.

Nadia's dress was lovely, but nowhere near as striking as Agnes's. It was the kind of dress a woman wore when she wanted to disappear into the sea of little black dresses at a cocktail party, although the panels of deep red lace around the edges of the flaring hem added a spot of color and interest. Nadia had to suppress a smile as she realized that Shrimp had chosen the perfect showstopper for Agnes while picking something much more ordinary for Nadia. The two of them did seem to be getting along awfully well as Agnes grew more proficient in the kitchen and Shrimp trusted her with more challenging tasks.

"That one must be meant for me," Agnes said, looking at the black dress longingly.

Nadia smiled at her. "I don't think so."

"But I can't wear this!" Agnes wailed, eyes wide.

"You're freaking out over a red cocktail dress after walking around the Basement wearing nothing but a bodysuit and boots?"

Agnes's face turned a shade of red that was a nice match for her dress. "But that outfit was practically invisible out there," she protested, waving a hand in the direction of the window. "No one gave me a second look." She swallowed hard and tried again to hand her dress to Nadia. "I'm sure this was meant for you."

Despite their differences in body type, Nadia suspected she could fit into Agnes's dress and vice versa, but there might be one way she could prove beyond a shadow of a doubt that the red dress was meant for Agnes.

Laying her own dress down on the bed, Nadia reached into the garment bag once again and felt around the bottom. Sure enough, the outfit came with shoes. A pair of black velvet pumps that fit Nadia's small feet perfectly.

With a groan, Agnes pulled out the shoes that came with the red dress and found a pair of strappy red heels that were two sizes larger than the ones Nadia had on.

Nadia grinned at her. "The shoes fit, Cinderella."

"I could wear these shoes with that dress," Agnes said, staring longingly at the black.

Nadia shook her head. "The lace panels would clash. And I suspect Shrimp would be insulted. I'm afraid you're stuck being stunning tonight."

Agnes gave her a dirty look. "Maybe it won't fit," she said hopefully, but they both knew it would.

"Who'd have thought we'd have to wear cocktail dresses to have dinner with a gang lord?" Nadia said as she took her dress off the hanger and started to change. She had a feeling it was time to set aside all her preconceived notions of what a gang lord would be like. Except for the part about him being dangerous. *That* he couldn't change with a hundred beautiful dresses or fancy manners—assuming he had the latter, which considering the dresses seemed like a good bet. A wolf in sheep's clothing was still a wolf.

CHAPTER NINE

Tonight was far from the first time Nate had had another guy choose his outfit for him—he'd had a valet for as long as he could remember—but he'd never been dressed in borrowed clothes before, and so far, he was not enjoying the experience. The charcoal gray suit Shrimp had provided was expensive and well cut, but its shoulders were too broad for him, and the sleeves came all the way down over the ball of his thumbs. The thing would probably fit Dante's muscular form just right, but Nate felt like a skinny kid wearing his father's clothes. At least the pants fit better, though he had to cinch the belt tight to hold them up.

If he were dressing for a business meeting or a media event, Nate would undoubtedly have skipped the bland red tie and pocket square that came with the outfit, but tonight was not the time to show his usual attitude, so he put on the tie and stuffed the pocket square into its proper place, then examined himself in the bathroom mirror. Except for the imperfect fit of the suit, he wouldn't have looked out of place stepping into a boardroom. Not at all the look he'd have chosen when going to meet a Basement gang lord who was named after his favorite torture device.

Nate stopped dead in his tracks when he stepped out of the bathroom and got a look at the girls, who were waiting in the hallway for him. Nadia looked like her old, elegant self in a conservative black cocktail dress accented with red lace, though she wore no makeup, and her hair was styled in a simple bun that cried out for a dose of hair spray.

Agnes, however, looked like a different person in a look-at-me red dress that accented her figure perfectly. The skirt's slit revealed a generous glimpse of thigh, and the red heels made her legs look long and sexy. The mousy brown hair with baby blue highlights detracted slightly from the look, as did her guarded, closed-off body language. This was not her usual camouflage attire, and she wasn't exactly wearing it with confidence.

"You look amazing," he told her, triggering one of her easy blushes.

"Hot enough to burn," Shrimp agreed, emerging from the bedroom at the end of the hall. His suit was a tailored pinstripe, under which he was wearing a red tuxedo shirt that was a good match to Agnes's dress. Nate wondered if that was by accident or by design.

Agnes was no good at taking compliments—Nate had the impression she hadn't received a whole lot of them during her life. Instead of answering, she just stood there and blushed, her gaze fixed on the floor. He wanted to say something to put her at ease—not that he'd ever had much success with that before—but Shrimp brushed by him before he could think of anything.

"Let's not keep Maiden waiting," Shrimp said, holding out his elbow to Agnes. Nate wondered if he practiced these gentlemanly manners with the women of Red Death, or whether this was something special for Agnes. He suspected the latter.

Nate held his elbow out for Nadia, and together they followed Shrimp and Agnes to the door, where Dante and Bishop were waiting to see them off.

"Be good," Bishop reminded him, only half joking.

Nate wished everyone would stop treating him like some out-of-control hothead determined to run his mouth no matter what the consequences. He understood *why* they saw him that way, but that didn't mean it didn't sting. And it sure as hell got under his skin that no one seemed to have noticed how much he had changed. He would never be as quiet as Agnes or as cautious as Nadia, but he wasn't about to put everyone in danger by antagonizing Maiden.

They took the stairs to the top floor, because no one wanted to risk having a power outage while they were in the elevator.

As soon as they stepped out of the stairwell, it was obvious that Maiden had done a massive renovation of the whole floor. The kind of renovation that required knocking down walls and ripping out appliances and wiring.

The stairwell opened out into what in an office building Nate would have called a reception area. The reception here, however, was far from warm and friendly. Four guards with machine guns and body armor were stationed around the room, and their first reaction when the door had opened was to train their guns on it. Shrimp took it completely in stride, no doubt used to the reception, and the machine guns lowered.

"This way," he prompted, giving Agnes's arm a little tug when she initially stayed rooted to the floor. Unlike Nate and Nadia, this was almost certainly the first time she'd had a gun pointed at her, and Nate couldn't blame her for being unsettled.

Shrimp led them toward a long hallway, and Agnes balked again. Nate and Nadia moved forward, and that was when Nate saw the reason for Agnes's hesitation.

Lining the hallway on both sides was a grisly array of coffin-like metal cases, their insides bristling with spikes. The iron maidens for which Maiden was named. Some were rusted, corroded antiques, and some were polished and shiny as if made yesterday, but all of them had vicious teeth. A couple of them had teeth so long that it was obviously impossible for anyone to survive if they were closed, but most were short enough that it seemed possible their victims could survive and suffer for a long time.

"You're safe with me," Nate heard Shrimp tell Agnes in a soothing voice, and then the two of them stepped into the hallway.

Nate shared a long look with Nadia. Her hand tightened on his arm, but by silent mutual agreement, they moved forward. The iron maidens had obviously been put there specifically for their intimidation factor. Nate glared at the back of Shrimp's head.

"He could have warned us," Nate muttered under his breath to Nadia.

"Yes, he could have," she agreed with a grim set to her jaw.

Maybe Shrimp wasn't as nice and easygoing as he seemed. He *was* a member of the Red Death, after all. Or maybe he just wanted to make absolutely certain they knew how dangerous his brother was.

Nate forced himself to keep moving, even when he noticed what looked suspiciously like dried blood on the spikes of the first iron maiden they passed. And he worked really hard to avoid speculating when they passed one in the middle that was closed.

If the hall of iron maidens was meant to scare the crap out of you, then the spacious living room into which it led was meant to trigger drop-jawed awe. The floor was of red marble, with several marble faux pillars set into the walls. The walls were papered in what looked like raw silk fabric in a warm golden hue that matched the velvet drapes. A marble fireplace big enough to double as a walk-in closet was the focal point of the room, and there were lamps and vases and various knickknacks everywhere—all antique, all gold or crystal or shiny red lacquer. A fussy antique sofa and love seat fronted the fireplace, and when Nate glanced upward, he saw that the edges of the ceiling were covered in gold leaf, and the center contained a bad imitation of the Sistine Chapel painting of God reaching out to Adam.

Perhaps the room succeeded in inspiring awe in Basement-dwellers who were used to small, squalid apartments decorated with Dumpster finds, but Nate had to bite the inside of his cheek to keep himself from laughing. He'd been in the homes of some of the richest people in the entire Corporate States—had in fact grown up in his father's mansion, which cost more than the gross national product of certain small countries—but he had never seen anything as ridiculously over-the-top as Maiden's home base. Clearly, being a gang lord paid well, and thanks to the black market—of which Maiden no doubt owned a large portion—any extravagance Maiden might desire was within easy reach.

"Do you like my home?" a voice asked from behind them, and Nate couldn't help his jerk of surprise.

Maiden obviously had a flair for the dramatic, first parading them through his hall of horrors, then dazzling them with his gaudy eyesore of a living room, then sneaking up on them from behind. If Nate hadn't learned to contain his temper, he might have lost it right then and there.

Turning around, he saw a tall, handsome black man in his thirties wearing a red suit as gaudy as his living room. A huge diamond sparkled in his earlobe, and his tie clasp was a skull and crossbones composed of diamonds and rubies. Several of his fingers sported diamond and/or ruby rings, and his watch sparkled ostentatiously as it poked out from under his cuff. Subtlety was obviously not one of his virtues, and Nate wondered if he ventured out into the streets with all that bling. Then he thought about the iron maidens and wondered who in the Basement would be stupid enough to even think about stealing from him.

"I've never seen anything like it," Nadia answered.

It should have come out as sarcasm worthy of Nate, and he knew that's exactly how Nadia meant it, but she had said it in such a breathless tone that Maiden took it as the compliment he'd been expecting and beamed. Nate swallowed hard, reminding himself of the blood on the spikes in the hallway in hopes it would quell his urge to laugh. He very much doubted Maiden would take that well, especially when he realized what Nate was laughing at.

Maiden approached them with a predatory grace, intelligent eyes looking them each up and down with thinly veiled calculation. He stopped in front of Nate, just a hair closer than was comfortable. Nate didn't appreciate the invasion of his personal space, but he knew better than to take a step back. Running away from predators was almost never a good thing to do.

"You must be Nathaniel," Maiden said, holding out his hand to shake. "I am the Maiden."

Nate knew he was about to be subjected to a crushing handshake, the kind of handshake meant to establish dominance, but he took Maiden's hand anyway. He wondered if he should insist that Maiden call him Ghost, since that was his Basement name. Was Maiden calling him by his real name as a subtle put-down, suggesting he considered Nate a child? Or was it just another affectation, a lowlife trying to act like he had genteel Executive manners and was greeting an equal?

"Pleased to meet you," Nate lied, then tried to keep his face from giving anything away when Maiden gave him the expected vise-grip squeeze. He decided against making an issue of his name.

"Yes, a pleasure," Maiden said, finally letting go of Nate's hand. Nate wondered if he'd be able to create replicas of Maiden's rings from the impressions they'd left in his flesh.

Maiden turned his oily smile to Nadia, who kept her right hand firmly in the crook of Nate's elbow.

"And Nadia," Maiden said. "You are even more lovely in person than you are on television."

"You're too kind," she replied with a modest smile, once again smoothly hiding the sarcasm behind her words. Nate was going to end up with strained abdominal muscles from trying to restrain his urge to laugh. Nadia was treating Maiden with just the kind of barbed courtesy she used to reserve for the Terrible Trio. And Maiden apparently thought that not using contractions made him sound upper class.

Maiden raised an eyebrow when he saw that not only was Agnes's hand tucked into Shrimp's elbow, but Shrimp had also covered her hand with his own as if to make sure Maiden didn't shake it. Or, worse, try to kiss it. Maiden was pretentious enough that Nate wouldn't put it past him.

"And our esteemed visitor from Synchrony," Maiden said, inclining his head regally.

Agnes mirrored his gesture but kept her mouth shut. Over the course of the past week, she had seemed to be coming out of her shell, relaxing as she adjusted to the relief of being out of the public eye, but it seemed now all of her defenses had sprung back up.

"Your timing is impeccable," Maiden said. "Dinner is almost ready. Please join me."

He waved his hand toward an arched doorway at the far side of the room, and they obediently filed into a dining room every bit as overdone as the living room, complete with a crystal chandelier, a fancy flower arrangement, a candelabra, and antique silver utensils. Two places were set on each side of the table, with one place at the head and one place at the foot. Nate wondered if someone else would be joining them. He automatically pulled back Nadia's chair, and the two of them shared another look as they sat. For all of Maiden's fancy fake manners, he didn't know which side of the plate the forks were supposed to go on.

Maiden stood behind his chair at the head of the table, looking over the tableau with a gleam of satisfaction in his eyes. Maybe he thought this was how Executives dined every night. Admittedly, there had been many a formal dinner in Nate's past, but rarely with such a small group. Formal dinners were nine-tenths theater, and what good was theater without a large and appreciative audience?

Maiden still didn't sit down, and Nate wondered what he was waiting for. Until he heard the click of high heels approaching from the far hall. Maiden stood up a little straighter. Preening?

A proper Executive man would rise to his feet to greet a woman, but Nate noticed Shrimp remained seated. Eschewing Executive manners even in this false setting made Nate squirm, but he judged that following Shrimp's lead would be the wiser move, so he resisted the urge to push back his chair.

The woman who soon appeared in the doorway was completely stunning, the kind of woman he'd expect to see gracing the covers of fashion magazines. Tall, slender, with honey-colored skin and lustrous blue-black hair, she wore a low-cut red silk gown that clung enticingly to her every curve. Maiden smiled, but the expression held too much lust and greed to be anything resembling pleasant.

"Turn around," he said in a low purr. "Let us see the whole package."

The woman raised her chin and did as she was told, revealing that the dress was completely backless, dipping so low it showed the first swell of her butt and clinging so tightly you could see every contour of the rest. The tiny spaghetti straps were barely holding the front of the dress up, and one wrong move would have her flashing the room. As stunning as she was, she didn't exactly seem comfortable in the outfit, nor did she seem to be looking forward to a wonderful dinner. In fact, she looked like she'd rather be anywhere else, and she watched Maiden with wary eyes.

"Beautiful," Maiden declared with a satisfied, possessive sigh. "This is my girl, Kitty," he said to no one in particular, and that was the only introduction he made. Nate had the impression Maiden considered Kitty just one more beautiful object to show off, and it made him angry on the girl's behalf.

Kitty took her place at the foot of the table, moving gingerly and sitting up painfully straight in order to keep the dress in place. When she sat, Nate noticed the bands of tattoos that circled her wrists and her throat. Her skin was just dark enough—and her dress just distracting enough—that he hadn't at first seen the lines of red skull and crossbones that marked her in a disturbingly permanent way as one of the Red Death.

Not long after Kitty entered the room, another woman appeared, but this one was dressed in a plain white shirt tucked into a microscopic miniskirt that revealed a set of red garters. Maiden looked her up and down with evident appreciation, the look in his eyes making Nate want to squirm in his seat.

The woman carried a bottle of wine, and said not a word as she poured for each of them in turn. It was red wine, and she was pouring it into glasses meant for white—another false note in Maiden's attempt to ape a formal dinner. Nate wondered why he was bothering with the charade. Maybe he expected them to be awed by the grandeur, but you'd think if that had been his aim he'd have done a little research to get the details right. And the parade of beautiful women who were obviously scared of him overshadowed any other impression he wished to make.

"Has my little brother been taking good care of you?" Maiden asked, swirling his ruby red wine around in its narrow white-wine glass.

"He's been great," Nadia answered for them. Short, but sweet.

"I am glad to hear that," Maiden said. He sniffed his wine, then swirled it around a little more.

Nate had to resist the urge to roll his eyes at the pretension. He reached for his own glass and took a sip without any of the swirling and sniffing. The sharp look Maiden gave him said he'd sensed the disrespect. Under the table, Nadia stepped on his foot in warning.

Maiden put his glass down without having tasted the wine. "You should know I have certain . . . concerns about hosting you in my territory."

Another woman, dressed in the same miniskirt-and-garters outfit as the last, entered the room with a tray of salad plates. She, too, bore the tattoos. She also bore a black eye and had angry red ligature marks marring the bands on her wrists. It was now abundantly clear to Nate why Kurt had been concerned about the girls' safety around Maiden. He had the nasty feeling those tattoos weren't meant to be decorative, that they were Maiden's version of a brand, marking those women as belonging to him.

Nate's temper stirred, but he tamped it down. Now was not the time to play the heroic defender of women, especially not given Maiden's words.

"I was under the impression Angel is paying you well

enough to overlook those concerns," Nate said in an even tone of voice.

Maiden smirked and indicated the room with a sweep of his hand. "Does it look to you like I need the money?"

"No," Nate admitted, "but presumably you *want* the money, or you wouldn't have agreed to take us in the first place."

"True. But the price on your head keeps going up. Perhaps I can reduce my risk and maximize my profit by turning you in."

The lights suddenly went out, and Maiden uttered a foul curse. Thanks to the candles, it wasn't completely dark in the room, and Nate could see the way Kitty shrank in on herself in the face of Maiden's anger. Considering how banged up the "waitress" had been, Nate couldn't blame her. Maiden seemed like the kind of man who always looked for an outlet for his anger, even if that outlet was an innocent bystander.

"You don't want to turn us in," Nadia said smoothly, as if she hadn't even noticed the lights going out—or Maiden's outburst.

Maiden turned to her and cocked his head. "Oh no?"

"No. Right now, Dorothy has no idea where we are or who has us. If you turn us in for the reward, she'll know we were with you. She's after us because we know secrets and she's afraid we'll tell people. If she finds out you have us, she'll assume we've told you our secrets and she'll come after you."

Maiden laughed. "Am I supposed to believe that?"

Nate found it interesting that Maiden hadn't asked what the big secret was. Did he not care? Or did he already know?

It was possible Angel could have told him when she arranged this whole thing, though she hardly seemed the type to volunteer information.

"You wouldn't be where you are if you weren't smart," Nadia said. "Tell me, when an offer sounds too good to be true, is it a good idea to take it?"

"Don't condescend to me, little girl," he growled.

"But she's right, Maiden," Shrimp said, neatly deflecting Maiden's attention. "And why should they make good on their promise anyway? They couldn't stiff an Employee or Exec without getting into trouble, but a Basement-dweller . . ." He snorted. "Since when do they give a shit about us? They can't even be bothered to fix the fucking lights." He glared up at the chandelier, which remained stubbornly dark, then shook his head.

"Nothing good can happen if we turn them over," Shrimp concluded. "And a whole lotta bad could."

Maiden gave a noncommittal grunt and turned his attention to his salad, stabbing with his fork in a way that suggested he was still simmering over Nadia's "condescension." Who would have thought it was *Nadia* who'd end up pissing off their host? Though obviously it didn't take much to piss him off.

Following Maiden's lead, Nate picked up the fork closest to his plate, even though it wasn't a salad fork. And was on the wrong side. He noticed that Nadia and Agnes did the same. Nate wondered if the small errors weren't errors after all. Maybe Maiden was getting a kick out of watching them follow his lead. It would be just the kind of petty power play people like him would enjoy.

For a while, they all munched quietly. All but Kitty, that

is. She stirred the salad around her plate and took the occasional nibble, but she seemed much more interested in the contents of her wineglass. Nate didn't know who she was or how she had ended up in this position, but he felt sorry for her.

"I won't turn you in," Maiden announced as the salad plates were being cleared. "As long as the money keeps flowing and you don't cause any trouble, you can stay. But trust me when I say you do not want to get on my bad side. I don't care who you were before you came into my territory, but as long as you are here, you are Red Death property. You will not make any waves, and you will not do anything that might draw unwanted attention to me or my people." He turned his menacing gaze on Agnes, who hadn't uttered a peep so far.

"My brother tells me you wanted to use our signal hookup to make a phone call. If you even *think* of doing something like that, I will do things to you that your genteel Executive mind cannot even begin to comprehend. Is that quite clear?"

Agnes blanched, and Nate wanted to leap to her defense, or at least beat Maiden senseless for being a coldhearted bully. But this was one of those times when he had to control his temper, to think about anything he might say at least three times before speaking, and so far, he hadn't come up with anything to say that wouldn't make the situation worse.

"I told you I already warned them about that, bro," Shrimp said. "There's no need to be such a hard-ass about it." He met Maiden's eyes with his own fearless gaze and put his arm protectively around Agnes's shoulders. She jumped a little at the touch, but otherwise made no objection.

"You warn them your way," Maiden said, "I'll warn them

mine. And if they bring Paxco security forces into our territory, I will hold you personally responsible." He didn't raise his voice, but his ice-cold stare made it very clear how serious he was. "Just because I won't let anyone else hurt you doesn't mean *I* won't."

Shrimp showed no sign of being rattled by his brother's threat. Neither his face, nor his voice, nor his body language betrayed anything Nate could label as fear or even anger. He merely accepted it with a slight nod.

"Understood."

Maiden's stare lingered on him a moment longer before turning to Agnes. "And you, Agnes Belinski? Do you understand?"

"I understand," she responded quietly, her eyes demurely lowered, her naturally high-pitched voice making her sound innocent and childlike.

Maiden's self-satisfied smile said it was exactly what he wanted to hear.

CHAPTER TEN

The lights didn't come back on.

Dinner was a quiet, tense affair, with no one except Maiden doing much talking. Considering the man's delusions of grandeur, the food was probably good quality, but Nadia barely tasted it. The whole past week, she and the others had been in wait-and-see mode, waiting for their audience with Maiden, waiting for his permission to leave the building, waiting to see if he was going to follow through with the shelter Angel had paid him to provide.

Now, the wait was over. As if he were granting some kind of special blessing, Maiden gave them permission to leave the building at will, provided they stayed within Red Death territory and always wore something red whenever they were in public. Wearing red would mark them as honorary members of the Red Death, and that meant that none of his people would dare lay a finger on them. (Unless, of course, he gave them permission to do so.)

Their immediate future was taken care of—as long as Angel kept the money flowing, of course. But they were no closer to stopping Dorothy than they had been the day they'd fled Paxco Headquarters. Maiden had expressly forbidden them to make contact with the outside world, and if the power remained out, they wouldn't even know what

Dorothy was up to. Nadia had never realized before just how cut off the Basement-dwellers were from the rest of society.

Taking the candles from the dinner table to light their way, they returned to Shrimp's apartment. He dug out a couple of flashlights, then headed out into the night.

"I'm gonna get more candles and flashlights," he said. "Think we're gonna need 'em. And I'll see if I can find out what's up with the power."

"Austerity measures," Nate and Nadia said together, and neither one of them cracked a smile at their unison.

Shrimp frowned. "You think she'd really just leave us all in the dark for good?"

"Hard to believe the board of directors would let her get away with it," Nadia said, wondering just how Dorothy had managed to twist their arms so thoroughly. It was true that most Executives looked upon Basement-dwellers as little better than leeches, useless parasites who sucked out the lifeblood of society. But even the hardest-nosed of them would at least make a show of wanting to take care of the poor, and cutting all power to the Basement seemed extreme.

"And yet the power is still out," Nate said. "With Dorothy, I'm always going to assume the worst until proven wrong."

Shrimp headed for the door, but paused before opening it. "I know Maiden gave you the okay to go out, but you might not wanna risk it when the lights are out. The dark brings out the worst in people."

Nadia suppressed a shudder. She did *not* want to see the worst of the people of the Red Death. She felt she'd done an admirable job of maintaining her poise during dinner, but Maiden reminded her disturbingly of Dirk Mosely, Paxco's late chief of security, who had murdered the original Nate and threatened Nadia as well as her young niece and nephew with torture. At least Mosely had done it all under a veneer of patriotism; Maiden made no apology for his blatant evil. She felt like she needed a shower after spending so much time in his company.

And yet Maiden was the one Nadia and all her friends were counting on to keep them safe. Shutting out her inner voice, which kept telling her this couldn't end well, was the only way she could cope with what she'd learned about their host this evening.

After Shrimp left for his nightly rounds, Bishop announced that he and Nate were going back to the boys' apartment to take advantage of the "romantic" darkness. It went without saying that Dante was staying at Shrimp's until someone gave him the all clear. Even in the candlelight, Nadia could see how Nate blushed at Bishop's none-too-subtle proposition. There were still times when the Executive taboo made Nate uncomfortable about being out of the closet, but even prim Agnes hardly batted an eyelash at it anymore.

Nate and Bishop's exit left Nadia, Dante, and Agnes alone in Shrimp's living room, but about five minutes later, Agnes looked meaningfully back and forth between Nadia and Dante and then claimed she had a headache and wanted to go to bed early.

"You don't have to go running off," Nadia said. The idea of spending some quality time with Dante in the candlelit dark was unquestionably appealing, but sending Agnes into what amounted to solitary confinement just seemed wrong.

Agnes forced a yawn and pinched the bridge of her nose. "No, really. I need to lie down for a bit. I didn't sleep well last night, and I need some time to decompress after that dinner anyway."

Nadia bit her lip. Now that Agnes had made an issue of it, it would probably be awkward for her to stay anyway, but still . . .

"Are you sure?"

Agnes nodded and smiled faintly. "Introverts need alone time every once in a while, and I haven't had any in forever. Don't worry about me."

Agnes's departure left a strangely uncomfortable silence in its wake. Dante was sitting on the sofa, his legs stretched out in front of him, and Nadia was standing by the coffee table, wondering if she should just sit down or if she should snuggle up against Dante's side. Or on his lap, for that matter. It wasn't like she'd never been alone with him before, but somehow Agnes's obvious assumption that they were going to fool around made things feel . . . unnatural.

Dante smiled and reached out a hand to her, a hand she gratefully took. He gently guided her down to the couch beside him, fingers intertwined with hers.

"We don't have to make out just because Agnes thinks we're going to," he said as he slipped his arm around her shoulders.

Nadia laughed nervously and laid her head against him, closing her eyes and savoring the feel of him. "Are you saying you don't want to?" she teased.

He snorted. "I'm a guy. Of course I want to. I just don't want you to feel awkward about it."

She opened her eyes and tilted her face up to his. The candles cast flickering shadows across his face, their flames reflecting in his eyes. She reached up to stroke his cheek, loving how he shivered at the brush of her fingertips over his skin. No other guy had ever come close to making her feel the way Dante made her feel.

For years, she had tried hard not to think about what her future would bring, knowing she was fated to marry someone who could never be attracted to her. She had never allowed herself the romantic dreams and fantasies that girls were supposed to have. But if she *had* allowed herself such dreams, they would have starred someone just like Dante. Someone kind, and gentle, and brave, and, let's face it, just plain *hot*.

Maybe she was *living* that dream right now, though it was peppered with pockets of nightmare. She should be eagerly taking advantage of every one of these stolen moments with Dante, because one day she was sure to wake up. If she didn't die first, of course.

"You look like you're thinking too much." Dante smiled at her and cupped her cheek in his hand.

"Occupational hazard," she said, shaking off her momentary gloom.

"Maybe I can help you with that," he said, moving in for a kiss.

Nadia made a humming sound of agreement in the back of her throat while his lips feathered over hers—lightly at first, but that restraint didn't last. She buried one hand in his hair and wrapped her other arm around him, holding on tight and reveling in the sweet sensations.

The sensual brush of his lips against hers. The incendiary strokes of his tongue. The silky texture of his hair between her fingertips. The faint scent of the sandalwood soap Shrimp provided them all with. The quickening of his breath and heartbeats.

Nadia ran her hands over him, feeling the subtle play of the muscles in his back as he laid her down on the couch, his body leaning over her as he tried to balance and not crush her. Without breaking the kiss, Nadia felt around her until she found the edge of the sofa's back cushion and yanked it out of the way, making more room. Dante followed her lead, and soon they were lying side to side, the position still a tad precarious, but reasonably stable.

Dante broke the kiss to stare into her eyes as he stroked her hair reverently. "Someday, we're gonna do this in complete privacy, where we can both lie down comfortably, and when our lives aren't in danger."

"Making out in the woods in the cold rain, or on the floor of a ratty Basement apartment, or in the living room of a gang lord's little brother's place not romantic enough for you?" she asked. She wished that someday could be *now,* but with their luck, as soon as clothes started coming off, Shrimp would bring some of his enforcer buddies home for a drink. She really envied Nate and Bishop with their own apartment and their own bedroom.

"Any time you're with me, it's plenty romantic," Dante said, kissing her again.

The words practically melted her heart, and she clung to him ever more tightly. All the cares and troubles of her world seemed to disappear when Dante kissed her. Her brain stopped whirring with plans and ideas and fears, and all she could do was *feel*.

In Dante's arms, it felt like all was right with her world. And even though a little part of her knew that was an illusion, it was an illusion she was more than happy to lose herself to for a little while.

nadia stayed on the sofa with Dante for hours. They kissed and cuddled and explored each other's bodies as much as they could while staying fully clothed. If Shrimp walked in on them, he'd be able to tell what they'd been up to, but at least he wouldn't be getting a peep show.

When it was nearing dawn, Bishop knocked on the door and let Dante know that it was now safe for him to return to the boys' apartment, and he and Nadia reluctantly parted.

Much as she had enjoyed those stolen hours, Nadia found herself strangely melancholy when she tiptoed into the bedroom she shared with Agnes. There were a lot of things she missed about her old life, she thought as she snuggled into the covers. She missed being able to go outside whenever she felt like it. She missed thinking the worst thing that could happen to her was some kind of petty scandal. She missed reading and studying, being able to focus her mind on something other than the struggle to survive.

The list of things she *didn't* miss, however, was also surprisingly long. She didn't miss being photographed every two seconds, or having the press and their talking heads scrutinizing her every move, her every outfit, her every word. She didn't miss the barbed jealousy of her peers, who were all polite to her face while secretly hoping something dreadful would happen and she'd be socially ruined. Nor did she miss the endless party circuit wherein Executive families constantly strove to one-up each other with the elegance and pointless extravagance of their hospitality. That life seemed so foreign and distant these days.

As was inevitable whenever she allowed herself to think of her old life, Nadia couldn't help wondering if her parents were all right.

Well, no. Of *course* they weren't all right. They were both locked up in Rikers Island, and who knew what horrors they had to face inside that infamous prison. But she hoped they were at least alive. That they hadn't been tortured. That they hadn't been broken.

The heat of her little make-out session with Dante was long gone, replaced by guilt that she'd been indulging herself while her parents were locked up in Rikers because of her. Tears dribbled down Nadia's cheeks and dripped on her pillow. Thinking about what her parents were going through made her miserable; and yet *not* thinking about it made her feel like the worst, most uncaring daughter ever. There was no winning. In the direct aftermath of Dorothy's murder of Chairman Hayes, Nadia had bolstered herself with the image of her and Nate gathering and leading a new resistance movement, one that would somehow topple the government and bring Thea to justice. Now, it turned out their great resistance activities consisted of hiding out in a gang lord's apartment and doing absolutely nothing.

"Are you awake?" Agnes whispered.

Nadia drew in a shaky breath. She was pretty sure her tears had been quiet—and that Agnes wouldn't scorn her for them if she knew—but she surreptitiously brushed at her face and rubbed her eyes in hopes of erasing all traces.

"Yeah," she admitted. "It's hard to sleep knowing what kind of monster we're trusting our lives to." Not that that had anything to do with the little pity party that had been keeping Nadia awake.

The bed shook and creaked as Agnes turned over. Nadia wiped her face with her hand one more time before turning over to face her in the darkness. The blackout drapes were effective enough that she could barely see the other girl's form.

"I can't sleep because I can't stand the thought that we're letting her win," Agnes said.

Nadia groaned softly. "I hate it, too. I wish we could at least do *something,* even something tiny, to help bring her down. But I think Maiden made it pretty clear that he won't put up with anything that might cause trouble."

Beside her, Agnes propped her head on her hand, and though Nadia couldn't see the expression on her face, she could almost feel her intensity. "So maybe Maiden isn't who we need to talk to."

There was only one other person Agnes could have in mind. "I'll admit Shrimp seems pretty decent, but I can't see him helping us behind his brother's back. He does a good job of fronting, but I'm pretty sure Maiden scares him almost as much as he scares the rest of us."

Agnes let out a frustrated huff. "He does," she confirmed. "Evan's told me some stories that make my blood run cold."

"Evan?"

"That's Shrimp's birth name. I like it a lot better than 'Shrimp,' don't you?"

Nadia smiled at the hint of smugness in Agnes's voice. It seemed that she and Shrimp were getting on even better than Nadia had thought.

"Absolutely," Nadia agreed. "But somehow I don't think he'd be too happy if *I* called him that."

She would bet everything she owned—which, granted, was almost nothing—that Agnes was blushing.

"Probably not. And, uh, it's probably best if you don't let him know I told you."

"I won't. Promise."

"Anyway, you're right that he's kind of scared of Maiden, but he has a heart. And he can see the bigger picture." Propping her head on her hand was apparently no longer enough, because Agnes sat up and crossed her legs. Once again, Nadia could feel the intensity wafting from her. "We all know Thea's not going to let up anytime soon. Maiden can sit up there in his gaudy tower room with his slave girls and live like he thinks a king should, but if Thea keeps escalating, a lot of people are going to die. Maiden might not care as long as they're not *his* people, but Evan does. And Evan knows it's only a matter of time before Red Death people start getting hurt anyway."

Nadia sat up, too, putting her back against the headboard and wrapping her arms around her knees. "And yet you don't see him volunteering to help us. I think he was pretty clear that he wanted us to be good little children and do nothing."

"That's what he thinks is *safest* for us to do. But how long do you think Dorothy can keep the lights out before her 'austerity measures' start causing riots? And how do you think she's going to proceed once those riots start?"

Nadia grimaced, because she could see the future that was creeping up on them all too clearly.

"If we sit here quietly and do what Maiden wants," Agnes continued, "then a whole lot of people are going to die."

"You don't have to convince *me,*" Nadia said. "I'm totally with you. It's just that we can't do it without help, and Shrimp has already said no."

"And that means we should stop asking?"

"Well, no. I guess it doesn't." She smiled at Agnes, not sure the other girl could pick out her expression. "And if you're the one doing the asking, I suppose it's always possible he'll have a change of heart."

Agnes hesitated a beat before speaking. "We do sort of get along well."

Nadia tilted her head to one side. "You make kind of an odd couple, you know."

Agnes waved a hand vaguely. "We're not a couple. We just like each other is all. And even if we were, we're not any odder than you and Dante."

It was true that Dante and Nadia came from very different worlds, and she supposed that made them something of an unlikely couple. "Nate was the only Executive boy I ever met who I genuinely liked," she said. "The others were all too pompous, or too ambitious, or too phony. Dante's as genuine as they come, and he's not the kind of guy who sits on the sidelines critiquing someone's outfit while people are being oppressed. He's everything those Executive boys weren't, so I'm not sure we're really all that odd a couple after all."

"Evan's the only guy I've ever met who hasn't seen me as

a chess piece on his game board," Agnes said. "I've never seen that look in his eye that says he's putting my looks on one side of the scale and my status as a Chairman's daughter on the other and trying to figure out if they balance. He never nags me to talk when I don't have anything to say, never expects me to be witty and entertaining." She sighed heavily. "Add to that that he's funny, and kind, and goodhearted, and, well . . ."

Nadia nodded. "I can see that," she said, though she wondered how Agnes managed to ignore his status as a gang member. He was a whole lot nicer than Nadia would ever have expected someone like him to be, but she couldn't help speculating about what it was he did while he was out all night. He often came back with satchels of money or goods, and Nadia wasn't sure she wanted to know what he did to get them.

"What do you suppose is going to happen to us when this is all over?" Agnes asked.

Nadia lay back down with a sigh. "To tell you the truth, I never put a lot of thought into it." Partly because of her pessimistic view of their chances of being alive when all was said and done, but also because she had trouble imagining ever returning to her old life. It seemed impossible that she might once again find herself standing around at some stuffy Executive cocktail party making small talk with VIPs while fending off the backhanded compliments and outright insults of the Terrible Trio.

Agnes lay down also, rolling onto her stomach and hugging her pillow to her chin. "I think about it all the time," she said. "Even if we get out of this alive, we're both of us damaged goods."

Nadia made a face, but she couldn't argue the point. She'd already been socially ruined herself, and that was *before* she'd supposedly been an accomplice to murder and fled to the Basement. As far as the public knew, Agnes was a victim of kidnapping, and if it ever came out that she had gone with Nate voluntarily and spent weeks unchaperoned in a Basement-dweller's apartment, she would quickly acquire a label less appealing than "victim." No matter how unfair that might be.

"Ten to one we both spend the rest of our lives hidden away in some Executive retreat where our families can pretend we don't exist," Agnes continued glumly. "And that's the best-case scenario. So, you know, if I want to spend time with someone like Evan—and *you* want to spend time with someone like Dante—seems to me it can't make our situation any worse."

"I am *not* going back into a retreat," Nadia said with conviction. "And you'd better not let them do that to *you*, either. If our families are embarrassed by us, then that's *their* problem, not ours."

Agnes's silence said she was unconvinced. Maybe she was right, and there was no way either of them could return to Executive society after hiding out in the Basement. Nadia had allowed herself to be locked up in a retreat once before, but she was never going to do it again. And though Agnes was shy and timid, Nadia thought their time spent on the run had gone a long way toward giving her a backbone.

No. If they emerged from the Basement alive, Nadia refused to accept any disgrace society might want to foist on her. She had awakened her inner honey badger, and unless she was very much mistaken, so had Agnes. Their lives might never be the same if they survived, but they were going to carve out their own places. If society didn't like it, well, that was just too damn bad.

AS usual, Shrimp was already up and cooking by the time Nadia was dressed and ready to meet the day. And as usual, Agnes was in the kitchen with him. Nadia didn't mean to eavesdrop, but she found herself stopping in the hallway, watching the two of them for a moment without announcing her presence. The way they moved around the small kitchen with such careless, familiar ease reminded Nadia almost of a dance, especially when you added in the way Agnes kind of lit up from the inside.

She looked genuinely happy, and more relaxed than Nadia could ever remember seeing her before. And the person who made her look that way was a gang member, someone who had lived all his life in the squalor and crime of the Basement.

Shrimp said something that made Agnes giggle, and she laid her hand on his shoulder in a way that would have scandalized Executive society. And the warmth in Shrimp's eyes when he looked at her said that the touch was more than welcome. Nadia decided she'd better announce her presence before things got uncomfortable.

Trying to make a little extra noise as she walked, Nadia sailed into the living room and tried not to notice how Agnes and Shrimp jumped apart.

"Good morning," Nadia said cheerfully, though of course it was way closer to sunset than to dawn.

Thanks to the power outage, Shrimp had to do some

serious improvising in the kitchen—the stove required electricity—but he'd done a pretty good job of it. He'd created a makeshift grill out of a large soup pot, and he was preparing steaks he'd kept cold in a cooler packed with ice.

"This'll probably be our last fresh food for a while," he commented as he and Agnes toted the makeshift grill and the food over toward a table near the window. "The ice is pretty much history, so from now on, it's gonna be canned everything."

Agnes opened the window to let the smoke out while Shrimp lit the charcoal in his grill. Even with the window open, the room would fill with smoke, so Nadia picked up a pillow from the sofa and started fanning the smoke in the direction of the window. Shrimp nodded his thanks, then retrieved a beer from the fridge. Nadia doubted it was even vaguely cool after all this time, and she shook her head when he offered her one. She couldn't abide beer even when it was cold.

Nate, Bishop, and Dante had a knack for showing up in plenty of time for dinner. Shrimp was keeping a close eye on the grill when they knocked, so Nadia let them in, and they joined the little campfire circle that was forming.

"Do we still have to stay inside tonight?" Nate asked. "I'm going out of my mind being cooped up like this."

Anyone who knew him could see he was going stir-crazy without him having to say it. Nadia had never seen him so fidgety, constantly in motion.

Shrimp shrugged. "Nothin' stopping you from going out. 'Cept common sense."

Nate grimaced. "Can you at least give us some idea what's going on out there?" He nodded toward the open window.

"You're out in it every night, and without the TV we're completely blind."

"It's getting ugly," Shrimp replied. "Lotsa people on the street who shouldn't be. Tempers even shorter than usual. I cruised into the free territory last night, out near Angel's. Some dumb-asses lit a bonfire in the middle of the street, and people were gathered around it, throwing shit in." Another swig of beer. "If they don't turn the lights back on soon, it's gonna go from ugly to the kind of dangerous where people die.

"That ain't the worst of it," Shrimp continued. "I went to see if the checkpoints were still up—I mean, you'd think if the government was so hard up for cash they'd have better things to do with their money than park Employees all the way around the Basement twenty-four hours a day."

Nate shook his head in disgust. "But they were still there."

"Worse than that. There were *more* of them. They've put up sawhorses across the streets and sidewalks, and they're not letting anyone in or out, even with ID."

Grim news indeed, Nadia thought, wondering if she should have accepted that beer after all. Shrimp seemed to have the same idea, finishing off his beer with a few quick chugs, then grabbing the whole six-pack from the fridge and bringing it into the living room.

The flames in the "grill" had died down, and most of the smoke was now obediently making its way out the window, but Shrimp pronounced that the charcoal wasn't ready yet. Nate and Bishop sat on the couch, leaving just enough room for Nadia and Dante to squeeze in beside them. Agnes sat in the armchair, and Shrimp plopped down onto the floor, sitting cross-legged.

"You don't have to sit on the floor," Agnes said. She moved over and patted the seat of the armchair she was sitting on. It was a seat meant for one, but two could probably squeeze in if they didn't mind sitting real close.

Shrimp flashed her his gold-toothed grin. "Floor's fine for now. I don't wanna squish you."

Agnes tried with no success to hide the crestfallen look on her face, taking Shrimp's refusal as a rejection. Nadia was pretty sure he hadn't meant it that way, but even so, she was pleasantly surprised when Shrimp took one look at Agnes's face and scooted over to lean his back against the leg of her chair.

"Could use a backrest, though, if that's okay with you," he said, settling in comfortably with his arm and shoulder touching her leg. Then he gave Nate an apologetic look. "I know y'all're goin' nuts, but it ain't safe for you out in the streets."

"Even when we're supposedly under Maiden's protection?" Nate challenged. "I thought everyone was supposed to be terrified of him and do what he says."

Shrimp shook his head. "Morons who fuck with Maiden don't live long 'round here. But there's a new one born every day, and the dark is gonna give people ideas. You wanna risk it, fine by me. But I ain't babysitting you out there."

Nate scowled and shoved an errant strand of hair away from his face. He was in need of a haircut, or at least some hair product, and it looked like it was one more thing that was driving him crazy.

"So we're all going to sit back and do nothing while conditions get worse and worse?" Agnes said, an unmistakable challenge in her voice.

Nadia had expected Agnes to talk to Shrimp about the

need to fight Dorothy sometime when they had privacy, rather than when everyone was gathered together. That's what Nadia would have done, anyway. She worried that Shrimp would get extra defensive with an audience, but of course Agnes knew him better than Nadia did.

Shrimp made a face and groaned. "Not this again." He twisted around so he could look up at Agnes, the twinkle gone from his usually lively eyes. "Maiden ain't gonna help you fight the government. Thought you *got* that."

Agnes nodded. "I do. I'm not asking Maiden to help. I'm asking *you*."

Shrimp's eyes went almost comically wide, and at first all he could do was gaze at Agnes in speechless shock. Like it had never occurred to him that he could do something independent of his brother. He rose slowly to his feet, looking down at her.

"Are you shittin' me?" he finally asked. "D'you have any idea what Maiden would do to you if he found out you were tryin' to recruit me?"

Shrimp spoke right over her attempted protest. "There's only room for one chief 'round here, and that's Maiden. You start trying to get people to join your little resistance, Maiden'll see it as a challenge to his authority. You don't wanna see what happens to people who challenge his authority."

"Do some of them end up with tattoos around their wrists and throat?" Agnes challenged, looking him straight in the eye.

"Only the really lucky ones," he fired back. "Though you ask any of his girls if they feel lucky, they might tell you a different story." He squatted down in front of Agnes. "I can protect you," he said, then swept his gaze over the rest of them as if he just remembered they were there. "*All* of you. But not if you try to steal his people."

"We wouldn't—"

"That's how he'd see it," Shrimp said firmly. "I know my brother. Know how he thinks. I'm as much his property as anyone else in the Red Death, and you're trying to recruit me behind his back."

"So he'd be okay with letting Thea win? You think the Basement is hell now? Wait till you see what it's like when Thea *really* gets going."

He shook his head in frustration. "Maiden is in charge, and I'm tellin' you, he only cares about money, and territory. We can hide and protect you here. But the Red Death is not going to become your personal army of righteousness. End of story."

CHAPTER ELEVEN

one thing Nate would give Agnes: she was persistent. Shrimp had seemed pretty implacable when she'd attempted to recruit him on Tuesday, but that didn't stop her from trying again on Wednesday, and yet again on Thursday. With similar results, naturally. Shrimp was certain his brother wasn't civic-minded enough to take any action unless directly threatened, and having met the guy, Nate was inclined to agree. The frustration of sitting around in hiding like frightened children was getting to all of them, and bickering became a favorite pastime as they gathered in Shrimp's apartment every night to do nothing.

On Thursday night, Nate decided that if he spent one more hour in Dante's presence the two of them were going to kill each other, so after dinner, he suggested that Kurt come down to their apartment with him, leaving the girls and Dante upstairs at Shrimp's place. He figured perhaps a little alone time with Kurt might help smooth over some of the sharp edges on his temper, and he didn't care that everyone would know what the two of them were up to.

They headed down to their apartment at the same time that Shrimp left for his nightly rounds, but when they reached the eighteenth-floor landing, Shrimp blocked the door with his hand.

"You can play later," he said. "First, I wanna show you something."

Nate frowned at him. "Show us what?"

"You'll see. Now come on."

Nate glanced at Kurt to see if he had any idea what was going on, but Kurt just shrugged and said, "Only one way to find out."

Nate would much have preferred to stick to the original plan, but he doubted Shrimp's request could be counted as optional. Not to mention that the thought of venturing outside and getting some fresh air was extremely appealing.

The thought lost some of its appeal as the three of them descended the seemingly endless stairs, and Nate tried not to think about how much fun it was going to be to climb back up. Under his breath, he cursed Dorothy for her Draconian decision to cut all power to the Basement and wondered how long she was going to keep this up. Surely, *surely* it wasn't going to be forever.

When they reached the ground floor, Shrimp pulled out some electronic gizmo that was clipped to his belt, and mumbled something cryptic into it. A man's voice emerged from the gizmo, his words indecipherable—to Nate at least—behind the crackle of static.

"Walkie-talkie," Kurt explained, seeing Nate's puzzled look. "Runs on batteries and uses different frequencies than phones. The range on 'em is real short, but it's better than nothing."

Shrimp nodded. "We lose phone service enough it's useful to keep some around, just in case. Though its never been out more than a few hours before, and we don't have all that many batteries."

Shrimp pushed open the door into the lobby, leading Nate and Kurt out the front entrance. The bodyguard bookends were still there, stationed behind their bulletproof glass, barely visible in the oppressive darkness of the blackout. Nate figured shining his flashlight on them to get a better look would be a really dumb idea, so he kept the beam pointed at his feet, though having armed men in the shadows at his back made the hairs on the back of his neck prickle.

"So, where're we going?" Kurt asked.

"Block and a half over," Shrimp replied, gesturing vaguely to the left and beckoning them to follow.

Granted, Nate hadn't been paying a whole lot of attention to his surroundings when Shrimp had originally guided them to the red tower, but the neighborhood seemed to have deteriorated since he'd last seen it. There had always been a generous layer of litter—once you got about fifty yards away from the red tower—but there was even more of it now, and the narrow alleys between the buildings were all overflowing with garbage bags. Nate shone his flashlight down one of those alleys as they passed, the beam catching a pair of glowing eyes staring out at him. He couldn't see the creature the eyes belonged to, but he hoped it was a cat.

"They stopped collecting trash when they put up the blockades," Shrimp said.

"Because trash collection is a 'nonessential service,'" Nate muttered, wondering if any of the assholes who'd approved Dorothy's decision had any idea what it was like to have garbage piling up in the street.

Nate certainly wasn't getting the "fresh air" he'd been fantasizing about. The garbage bags were full of rotting food people had had to throw away when their refrigerators died, and the gentle evening breeze carried that stink everywhere.

Despite the unpleasantness, there were still people on the street, transacting business as usual. Nate suspected the big drug money came from larger transactions than the petty sales in the street, but there was still a lot of money changing hands, and Nate guessed that recreational drugs were more popular than ever.

Of course, drugs weren't the only things being sold, and despite the piles of garbage, a couple of the alleys they passed on the way to wherever they were going echoed with moans and grunts. Nate shuddered and felt vaguely queasy. No way he was shining his flashlight down one of *those* alleys.

Eventually, they came to a stop in front of a high-rise that looked just like all the others. Nate momentarily wondered why they had stopped. But then Shrimp shone his flashlight on a figure huddled on the pavement at the side of the stoop.

It was a man, possibly of Hispanic origin, although it was hard to tell. His hair was a mass of mats and snarls—not neat, cultivated dreadlocks, but the kind of mats you'd expect on someone who'd been stranded on a desert island for three years. An equally ratty beard hid most of his face, except for the two hollow sockets where his eyes should have been.

"This is Handy," Shrimp said, the beam of his flashlight fixed on the man's face. "He used to be Maiden's right-hand man, back in the day."

Handy squirmed as if trying to make himself comfortable, and Nate heard the clink of metal on metal. That was when he realized for the first time that Handy was chained to the railing of the stoop. The beam of the flashlight moved away from his face down his chained arm, illuminating the rusty metal cuff around his wrist, and then the bent and twisted ruin of his hand. Nate's stomach turned over and played dead.

It looked like every one of Handy's fingers had been broken in multiple places and then allowed to heal while the bones were out of line. There was no way he'd be able to use those fingers to grasp anything, and when Shrimp moved the flashlight beam to his other hand, Nate saw that it was just as bad.

"Handy grew up with Maiden," Shrimp continued. "The two of them were tight. Right up until the time Handy put those hands on the wrong girl, one of Maiden's. Maiden doesn't share, and Handy knew that."

His flashlight beam moved again, this time shining on Handy's chest, which was clearly visible through a huge tear in his shirt—a tear that had obviously been put there so the message tattooed across Handy's chest was visible: DON'T FUCK WITH THE MAIDEN.

Nate swallowed hard, hoping he wasn't about to puke. He was going to see images of those empty eye sockets and ruined hands in his nightmares for the rest of his life.

Shrimp mercifully turned his flashlight away from the poor bastard.

"I don't wanna bring Agnes to see him," Shrimp said. "But I thought maybe you guys could tell her about this so she'll understand why I keep saying no to her."

"And you didn't just tell her yourself because you wanted us to look all green and pukey when we talked to her," Kurt said, and as hardened as he was by his life in the Basement, his voice came out a little shaky.

"Something like that."

The breeze shifted direction, bringing a whiff of Handy's body odor along with the scent of rotting garbage to Nate's nose, and he lost his battle to keep his gorge down. Turning away, he emptied his stomach out into the gutter. He heard the squawk of Shrimp's walkie-talkie, but he was too busy heaving to make out what was being said.

Until Shrimp practically shouted, "We gotta go. Fast!"

Nate wasn't sure he could have taken a step, despite the urgency in Shrimp's voice, if Kurt hadn't grabbed hold of his arm and given it a firm yank.

shrimp had been gone for about fifteen minutes when there was a knock on his front door.

Nadia had been standing at the window, staring absently out into the darkness of the Basement, occasionally glaring up at the blimp that continued to circle, displaying Dorothy's message over and over and over. She jumped when she heard the knock at the door, whirling around. Based on the way Dante also jumped at the sound, Nadia suspected he'd been at least halfway asleep. Agnes might have been, too, though perhaps she'd just been lost in thought. There really was *nothing* to do—Shrimp didn't have any books around they could read, and as long as they didn't dare recruit from among Maiden's people, they had nothing to talk about.

Nadia shared a puzzled look with Dante and Agnes. There hadn't been a single visitor to Shrimp's apartment since they'd arrived—probably because Shrimp was almost never around except when he was sleeping.

"Hello?" a woman's voice called from the hall outside. "Anyone home?"

Natural politeness had Nadia wanting to answer; natural caution urged her to stay silent. Caution won. Shrimp had promised nobody would mess with them at his place—but he'd also told them not to leave the building while the power was still out, so obviously they weren't as perfectly safe as he liked to pretend.

"It's Kitty," the woman continued, undaunted by the lack of response. "Maiden's girl?"

Dante and Agnes both looked at Nadia, putting the burden of decision on her. Kitty had to know they were here—there was enough light from the candles to be seen around the edges of the door when the hallway was dark. Maybe it wasn't a good idea to snub Maiden's girl. Even if he'd made it clear she wasn't important to him, that she was no more than a pretty trophy to trot out as a cautionary tale.

Still uncertain how to proceed, Nadia approached the door and glanced out the peephole, just to confirm their visitor's identity—and to make sure she was alone.

"Maiden wanted me to chat with you," Kitty said, a hint of a tremor entering her voice. "If I don't do what he says, he'll hurt me. Please let me in."

Through the peephole, Nadia saw that Kitty was carrying what appeared to be a bottle of wine, and that she was blinking quickly as if to stave off tears. If Maiden had ordered her to talk to them, Nadia had no trouble believing he'd mistreat her if she failed.

A floorboard creaked behind her, and Nadia saw that Dante had risen from the sofa. She also saw that he had a gun in his hand. It wasn't the big automatic Nate and Nadia had brought back after their disastrous confrontation with Dorothy. This was something smaller and easier to conceal. Shrimp must have given it to him, which again made Nadia wonder just how safe their host really thought they were.

Nadia checked out the peephole one more time, but Kitty was still the only person she saw. And she also saw by the flashlight Kitty held that her outfit was way too skimpy and formfitting to hide a weapon. She motioned for Dante to put the gun away, sure he would keep it in easy reach anyway, then opened the door.

Kitty smiled brightly, and there was an almost manic gleam in her eyes. Nadia wondered if she was high or if it was just the result of too much adrenaline. Kitty's life couldn't be an easy one, and Nadia wished she could help her somehow. But for tonight at least, the best she could do was open the door and let Kitty in. No doubt Maiden had sent her—hard to believe this was a social call—but Nadia had no idea what he might want.

"Come on in," she invited, making room.

Kitty took her up on the invitation, her eyes scanning the room. "Where are the rest of your crew?" she asked.

Nadia wasn't sure why the question made her uncomfortable, but it did, and she answered accordingly. "Not here."

Kitty blinked, surprised by the shortness of Nadia's response, but she didn't let it throw her for long. She held up the wine bottle again. Nadia noticed that the bottle was open, and that there was a smear of lipstick around its mouth. Lipstick that must have come from Kitty's overdone lips when she swigged directly from the bottle. Nadia sniffed the air, but she didn't smell any alcohol fumes coming off the woman, and the bottle was still mostly full.

"Somebody want to get some glasses?" she asked. "Maiden's being generous. This is the good stuff. He said it was like a hundred years old or something."

Agnes went to get the glasses as Nadia led the way into the living room. She noticed that Dante had tucked his gun into his belt, keeping it accessible—and visible. The slight narrowing of Kitty's eyes said she saw it, too, and recognized it for the warning it was. He remained on his feet and at a slight distance as Kitty and Nadia sat.

Agnes hurried in with four tumblers in her hands. "Shrimp doesn't seem to have wineglasses," she explained as she put the tumblers down on the coffee table.

Kitty smiled. "He thinks wine is for sissies. Real men drink the hard stuff. Course he'd never say that where Maiden could hear." She gave a nervous little laugh, then uncorked the bottle and poured them each a healthy dose of red wine. Her movements were just a tad hurried, betraying her nerves. Maiden might have sent her here for a friendly chat with his guests, and the thought that they might not let her in had obviously scared her, but that wasn't the only reason she was nervous, or she'd have calmed by now.

Nadia debated whether to come right out and ask Kitty why Maiden had sent her down here but decided against it. Kitty would get around to it eventually.

Kitty distributed the glasses of wine, leaving Dante's on the far end of the coffee table and then moving away. Obviously, she was aware that Dante was being very watchful and was unwilling to get too close to her. Nadia wondered if he suspected she might go for his gun. It was hard to see Kitty as much of a threat in general, much less as a threat to three people, but she couldn't fault Dante for keeping his guard up.

Even with the safe distance, Dante didn't pick up his glass. "I don't mean to be rude or anything," he said, "but Kitty, would you switch glasses with Nadia?"

Kitty gave another one of her nervous laughs. "You think I'm trying to poison you?"

"Probably not," he admitted. "But I'd hate to be wrong, so if you wouldn't mind . . ."

Nadia thought Dante might be taking his security concerns a bit far, but there seemed to be no harm in swapping glasses just to be safe. Unless Kitty told Maiden about it later and he held it against them.

Kitty shrugged, showing no sign that she was terribly insulted by Dante's implication. She exchanged glasses with Nadia with no further comment, quickly taking a big gulp.

When Kitty didn't keel over or start choking, Nadia took a more tentative sip of her own wine. If the bottle was as old as Kitty had said, they were already doing the stuff an injustice by drinking it out of tumblers. The least she could do was sip it with the respect it deserved.

One sip was all it took to tell Nadia that this really was the good stuff. She was hardly a wine expert—technically, she wasn't old enough to drink yet, but in preparation for her future life, her parents had started introducing her to fine wine when she was thirteen, never giving her enough to let her feel any but the mildest effects. It had taken a while to acquire a taste for it, but by now her palate was sophisticated enough to recognize quality of this level.

"This is wonderful," Agnes said, taking another sip and rolling it around her mouth before she swallowed. She looked over at Dante, whose glass still sat untouched on the table. "You should try it."

"Thanks, but no thanks," he said. "I'm more of a beer kind of guy. I'll leave the fine wine to people who can appreciate it."

For the first time, Kitty looked genuinely annoyed. "Maiden has sent you a gift. This wine probably costs more than your average Employee earns in a year."

Dante was unmoved. "I'm sure the gift was meant for Nate and Nadia and Agnes, not for me or Bishop. We weren't invited to Maiden's fancy dinner, remember?"

Kitty's eyes glittered, and she tried to stare him down. However, she wasn't very good at it, and she quickly looked away. "Fine," she muttered. "Have it your way and insult Maiden. Good idea." She finished the rest of her wine in one long swallow, then grabbed his glass. "You don't want it, I'll drink it for you."

Nadia wasn't entirely sure what was going on in Dante's head. Kitty had already demonstrated that the wine wasn't poisoned. Maybe he just didn't want to risk alcohol when he was on self-appointed guard duty.

Kitty took a sip from Dante's glass, then put it back down, pushing it away from her. "Whew," she said, fanning her face. "The good stuff really has a kick." She reached up and put her hands in her hair, pulling it up off the nape of her neck as if she was hot. Nadia felt no effects from the alcohol yet, but then she'd only been taking delicate sips from her glass—and she hadn't chugged straight from the bottle before entering the apartment, as Kitty had.

"It *is* rather . . . potent," Agnes agreed, having polished off her glass already. "But very good. Maybe just a little more." She leaned forward to put her glass down on the table. And missed. She gave a startled exclamation and tried to catch the tumbler before it hit the floor, but instead of grabbing the glass, she ended up banging her hand against the edge of the table.

Out of the corner of her eye, Nadia saw Kitty's lips turn up just the slightest bit. A chill raced through her body as she looked down at the wine in her hand. Strong it might be, but there was no way it was strong enough to make Agnes that uncoordinated after one glass.

A whole bunch of things happened at once then.

Agnes tried to stand up, and her knees buckled beneath her.

Dante shouted and drew his gun.

And Kitty grabbed for Nadia's throat. Nadia meant to leap to her feet, but her body reacted sluggishly. All she managed to do was drop her glass and spill the remains of her wine. Before she knew it, something was wrapped around her neck, biting into her skin.

"Put the fucking gun down," Kitty ordered, tightening whatever she had around Nadia's neck. Nadia tried to reach up and pull it away, but she couldn't feel her hands, and her arms flopped uselessly.

Dante's eyes were huge and startled in his shadow-darkened face. He was crouched in a shooter's stance, his arms rock-steady as he kept the gun trained on Kitty.

Unfortunately, they all knew he couldn't shoot, not with Nadia so close.

"You ever seen what a garrote can do, kid?" Kitty snarled. "I can take her head clean off with this thing. Put the gun down now, or I'll show you."

Nadia cursed herself for her lack of foresight. She'd seen how little Kitty was wearing and assumed that meant she couldn't hide a weapon, but she'd never considered the woman's long, lustrous hair as a potential hiding place. She wanted to tell Dante not to do what Kitty ordered, but whatever was in the wine had taken firm control of her body and she couldn't make her lips obey her. Her mind, however, stayed entirely clear. She shuddered to think what this drug was generally used for on the streets of Debasement.

Slowly, reluctantly, Dante lowered his gun.

"I said put it *down*!" Kitty shouted, tightening the garrote until Nadia felt a trickle of blood run down her throat.

Dante hastily dropped the gun, then kicked it away. "Please don't hurt her."

"That's better," she said with smug satisfaction. "Now drink your wine like a good boy. And don't even *think* of trying anything."

"Why didn't the wine affect you?" Dante asked, moving forward slowly, his hands raised. Nadia could practically see the way he was coming up with plans in his head, then rejecting them one by one.

"There's an antidote," she said. "I took it before I came in."

"What is it you want, exactly?" he asked, but Kitty wasn't about to let him stall.

"Drink the wine, and I'll tell you. Do it fast unless you like seeing her bleed."

Dante had no choice, and he knew it. The agony in his eyes made Nadia heartsick, but there was nothing she could do or say to comfort him when her mouth wouldn't move. She wanted to tell him it wasn't his fault. Wanted to point out that he'd done everything he could to protect her, even gone above and beyond what seemed reasonable.

Dante stared at the contents of his glass for a long moment, then forced himself to drink it down. He closed his eyes afterward, his throat working convulsively. Trying not to gag on something he knew was drugged, Nadia supposed.

Kitty's hold loosened slightly, but not enough for Dante to take advantage of it, and Nadia had all the fight of a rag doll. "I was never gonna get away from Maiden," Kitty said. "Once he put the slave bands on me, I was his for life. No one else would touch me, and anywhere I could go in Debasement, he would find me."

Moving carefully, though it was too soon for the drug to take effect yet, Dante lowered himself into the nearest armchair. "So you're going to turn her in for the reward?" he asked.

Nadia felt her nod. "Nothing personal, and for what it's worth, I'm sorry. But they're offering Employee status along with the money. They'll get me out of Debasement, out of Maiden's reach."

Nadia suspected Kitty was underestimating Maiden if she thought he couldn't get to her outside of the Basement. Gang lords tended to have long arms. Not to mention the fact that Dorothy didn't actually *want* Nate or Nadia to be captured. Nadia was damn sure that when Kitty tried to turn her in, something was going to go horribly wrong—by design—and Kitty was going to wind up dead. Just like Nadia.

"It won't work," Dante slurred. "You . . . Y . . ." His mouth stopped working and the words died in his throat. He had probably meant to explain the big flaw in Kitty's brilliant plan, but thanks to the drug, he couldn't do it. She probably wouldn't have believed him anyway.

Kitty waited a couple of minutes after Dante's last words before she finally unwound the garrote from around Nadia's neck.

CHAPTER TWELVE

nadia half expected Dante to leap out of his chair the moment Kitty released her, but unfortunately, he wasn't faking his paralysis. There was nothing he or Agnes could do to help, and Nadia was in no shape to help herself. So much for the safety they'd bought and paid for.

Kitty shoved Nadia down onto the couch and kept a wary eye on Dante as she retrieved his gun from the floor. She examined it quickly, then gave a nod of approval and stuffed it into the back of her miniskirt. Nadia wondered how the woman was planning to get her down all those flights of stairs, sneak her past Maiden's patrolling enforcers, and get her all the way to one of the checkpoints to turn her in. Nadia would be dead weight, and Kitty didn't look like the athletic type. Nadia wasn't even sure if the other woman could *lift* her, much less carry her all that way.

"You all just sit tight," Kitty said with a self-satisfied smile. She'd claimed she was sorry about what she was doing, but as far as Nadia could tell, she was enjoying herself quite a bit. Her eyes in the candlelight gleamed with excitement, though the perspiration that beaded on her upper lip said she was still scared under it all. She was far from home free, and she knew it.

With what felt like a Herculean effort, Nadia managed

to turn her head so she could keep an eye on Kitty. She hadn't drunk much of the wine, and she probably didn't have a full dose in her system. Unfortunately, the partial dose was more than enough.

Kitty's high heels clicked as she stepped off the living room rug and onto the hardwood floor of the entryway. The woman must have at least one accomplice, someone who could help transport Nadia out of the building and out of Red Death territory. Someone who had stayed well out of sight when Nadia was looking through the peephole and was patiently waiting for Kitty to let him in.

Kitty flung the door open, and Nadia's heart leapt up into her throat.

The man standing in the hallway, waiting for Kitty's signal, the man who was going to turn Nadia in to get the reward money . . . was Shrimp.

At least, that was Nadia's first thought when she saw him standing there. She made a choked sound of protest, but Kitty cried out in terror, her hand reaching frantically for the gun. Her fingers had barely even touched the butt before Shrimp's fist made solid contact with her face and sent her sprawling to the floor. He followed up with a kick to her belly that sent her curling into fetal position—making it easy for him to bend over and pluck the gun out of her skirt.

Behind Shrimp was one of Maiden's enforcers, dressed in body armor and carrying the customary machine gun, and behind *him* were Nate and Bishop. Kitty was still in no shape to protest when the enforcer hauled her arms behind her back and fastened her wrists together with a zip tie.

"Stupid bitch," Shrimp said, shaking his head as he stood over her. "It ever occur to you that I might have my place watched when I leave, just in case someone got any funny ideas about collecting the reward? When you bring an accomplice and he lurks in the stairwell, it's pretty much a dead giveaway."

Kitty moaned pitifully as Maiden's enforcer hauled her to her feet. Her lip was split and bleeding from Shrimp's blow, and her hair stuck to the blood and tear tracks on her face. The terror in her eyes struck pity into Nadia's heart, despite what the woman had just tried to do.

"Get her upstairs," Shrimp ordered the enforcer. "I'm sure Maiden's gonna be real anxious to talk to her."

"No!" Kitty screamed. She struggled against the enforcer's hold, twisting and kicking and shrieking. "Kill me now! Please!"

"No can do," Shrimp said, his face a frozen mask. He punched her again, knocking her out and stilling her struggles. The enforcer grunted something that may have been a thank-you and hauled her limp body over his shoulder.

Shrimp gestured Nate and Bishop inside, closed the door, and locked it after the enforcer carried Kitty away. Nate ran to Nadia's side and dropped to his knees, his face pale and strained.

"Nadia!" he cried, reaching out to grab her shoulders and looking even more wild-eyed when she failed to respond. "What's wrong?" He turned his head to Agnes and Dante, neither of whom had moved, naturally.

"They'll be okay," Bishop said, laying a hand on his shoulder to calm him. "Looks like there was something in the wine." He gestured toward the bottle on the coffee table.

Shrimp had disappeared into the bathroom and soon returned, carrying a small glass bottle with a dropper lid. "I know what she gave them," he said, gently lifting Agnes from the floor and putting her on the sofa. He sat beside her and unscrewed the lid of the little bottle. He drew a few drops into the dropper, then positioned its end between Agnes's lips.

"This stuff tastes like shit," he said, "but it'll counteract the roofie."

Agnes made a little sound that probably indicated acceptance, though she made a face when the antidote hit her tongue.

"Give it a minute," Shrimp said, then came over to Nadia.

Nadia didn't care what the antidote tasted like if it would allow her to move again. Shrimp had to help her open her mouth, and it wasn't easy to swallow the unbelievably bitter liquid he dropped onto her tongue. Her throat didn't want to work, and her floppy, out-of-control tongue didn't help, but eventually she got it down, and Shrimp administered the antidote to Dante. Nate took Nadia's hand in silent support. The color had not returned to his face, and there was a haunted look in his eyes. She wondered why he and Bishop had arrived at the apartment at the same time as Shrimp. Surely if Shrimp had gotten word about Kitty's attack, he wouldn't have stopped by the boys' apartment to roust them out of bed before coming to the rescue.

"Should I ask why you just happen to have that antidote sitting around your apartment, or is that one of those questions I won't like the answer to?" Nate asked Shrimp without turning.

Nadia winced internally—her face still wasn't up to creating the expression—at the undertone of hostility in Nate's voice. She wanted to give him a piece of her mind for yelling at the person who had just saved her life, but of course, she couldn't.

Since Nate hadn't turned his head, he didn't see the dirty look Shrimp cast his way while he poured the remainder of Kitty's wine down the drain in the kitchen.

"I've never dosed anyone with Dollbaby, if that's what you're asking," he said. "That's Maiden's kinda thing."

Nadia shuddered. *Dollbaby.* The drug was nasty and disturbing enough without the name.

"But because it's his kinda thing, I like to have antidote around. Sometimes I can help out one of his girls when he's through."

If Nadia had ever doubted that they were taking shelter with a monster, she didn't anymore.

Shrimp looked almost as unhappy as Nate did when he came back into the living room. "Looks like I took y'all out tonight for nothing," he said.

Nadia wished the antidote would hurry up and work so she could ask what he was talking about.

"Y'all are gonna get to see Maiden in action anyway," Shrimp continued.

From the look on his face, Nadia was quite certain that was not going to be a good thing.

"YOU are *not* making the girls witness a murder!" Nate told Shrimp the next evening, using the tone of command he was so used to having obeyed in his days as Chairman

Heir. He didn't even care that Nadia was giving him one of her most scathing looks. She probably thought he was being a paternalistic asshole, but that was just too bad.

"You don't have any say in it," Shrimp responded coolly. "Maiden wants you there, so you'll be there. All of you. The end."

Nate hoped that *someone* would be on his side in this discussion, but so far, he seemed to be the only one arguing. He and Nadia had witnessed two murders already in the past month or so, and he would happily go the rest of his life without seeing another. In his mind's eye, he saw his father's still form, lying on his office floor in a pool of blood as Dorothy gloated. He hadn't told anyone, not even Kurt, but more than once in the past week he had awakened with the vestiges of a nightmare clawing at the edges of his mind. After seeing how Maiden had punished Handy, Nate knew the "execution" wasn't going to be quick and neat, and his brain had enough nightmare fodder already.

"He's right, Nate," Kurt said, giving Nate's shoulder an encouraging squeeze. "Maiden'll never let us get out of this. He wants to make sure we're as scared of him as everyone else is, and this'll do the trick."

"Isn't it enough that we know he's going to kill them?" Nate asked, but he knew a lost cause when he saw one. Kitty and her accomplice, one of Maiden's drug dealers, were going to die for their attempt to kidnap Nadia and turn her in. Not, of course, because Maiden was doing his part in protecting Nadia, but because betrayal was a crime punishable by death. Nate supposed the two of them were lucky they weren't going to spend the rest of their lives chained outside with their eyes gone and their fingers bending the wrong way.

"For what it's worth, I tried to talk him out of it," Shrimp said with an apologetic shrug. "Sometimes he listens to me, but not this time. Trust me when I say you hafta go."

Nate's stomach felt queasy. He'd made it sound like he was trying to protect the girls from having to witness the execution, but deep down inside he knew he was more worried about himself. Nadia was made of steel, and Agnes had surprised him so many times that he couldn't assume she would faint at the sight of blood. His own nerves were much more questionable, and he worried about his ability to control himself. He'd seen people die before, but both times it had been a shocking surprise, over before he could even think to protest or do anything about it. This would be a different story, and he wasn't sure if he was more likely to puke, or do something stupid because he couldn't just stand by and watch.

"How long do we have?" Kurt asked.

Kitty and her accomplice—Nate didn't know the guy's name and didn't want to—had been in "custody" for almost twenty-four hours, and Nate doubted Maiden was planning to keep them alive much longer.

He was right.

"It's going down at midnight," Shrimp said.

Less than an hour. Shrimp had waited until *after* dinner to tell them, probably hoping not to spoil their appetites. Nate didn't think he was the only one who'd picked at his food anyway, and right now he regretted doing even that. He wasn't going to get much in the way of street cred if he puked in front of everyone.

• • •

nate had expected the "executions" to be ugly—as, he suspected, had everyone else—but it was still a shock to the system when he and his friends followed Shrimp down the endless stairs onto the street below and saw what fate awaited Nadia's would-be kidnappers.

The lights, of course, were still out, and the scene was illuminated by a circle of metal trash barrels serving as torches. In the center of that circle stood an iron maiden, its teeth so long and lethal there was no chance of anyone surviving their bite. Nate didn't know if this was part of Maiden's collection—if so, getting it down from the top floor without an elevator had to have been a bitch—or whether it came from some easier-to-access storage area, but it hardly mattered. His stomach rolled, and he closed his eyes, but that didn't help. In his mind's eye, he saw the bodies of Dirk Mosely and of his father, smelled the coppery tang of their blood, felt the brain-scrambling shock of recoil that had hit him when he realized they were dead.

A hand slipped into his, a firm grip on his sweaty palm. He opened his eyes to meet Kurt's solemn gaze. "You can't stop this," Kurt said. "Shit like this happens in Debasement all the time. You've seen the ugly side of Exec society and you survived. Now you'll see the ugliest side of ours, and you'll survive that, too."

Nate swallowed hard, hoping to keep his gorge down. *Shit like this happens in Debasement all the time.* Kurt was the only one who didn't look like the prospect of seeing a couple of people killed in front of his eyes was making him sick. Even Dante, the tough guy with military training, looked a little green. But to Kurt, who'd grown up in the Basement, this whole thing didn't have much shock value at all.

What would it be like to grow up in an environment where seeing someone "executed" in an iron maiden didn't register as something out of the ordinary?

Nate had thought he'd long ago come to terms with how oblivious he had been to the real world when he had been the Chairman Heir, but he'd been wrong. Right now, he wanted to go back in time and beat some sense into the original Nate Hayes, make him see the corruption and injustice all around him, make him at least *try* to do something about it instead of putting it off until his mythical future.

He felt the pressure of Kurt's eyes on him and knew his thoughts were written across his face, at least to someone who knew him so well.

"I coulda told you what Debasement was really like," Kurt said. "I chose not to."

"Because you knew I was too blind to see it even if you shoved it in my face," he responded bitterly.

"No, because I knew there was nothing you could do about it. There was no point rubbing your nose in it."

Nate shook his head. It didn't matter what Kurt said. He had brought Nate to Angel's and watched as Nate treated the Basement like some kind of playground, never bothering to give more than a passing thought to how the people trapped here lived. There had to have been moments when he had hated Nate, at least a little.

Right now, Nate hated himself enough for the both of them. Maybe he should consider bearing witness to the atrocity that was about to happen his penance for all those years of blindness.

Determination eased some of the turmoil in his stomach, and though he still desperately wished he could be anywhere but here, he knew he would not turn his head and look away, no matter how much it cost him.

Raising his head, he glanced around at the crowd that had gathered in the street. It was quite a mixed bag, consisting of Maiden's enforcers and gangbangers of all descriptions, but also of senior citizens who were well past the age of cruising the streets, as well as children too young to be more than errand runners. A couple of the women in the crowd even held babies. Giving them early exposure to the hell that was destined to be their lives, perhaps.

Many of the people in the crowd were looking at Nate and his friends with expressions of curiosity, or disdain, or even hatred. Outsiders were not well loved here in the Basement. Nate couldn't blame them for it, though he hoped Maiden and Shrimp would discourage any overt hostility.

Nate wasn't sure whether he expected Kitty and her accomplice to be brought kicking and screaming to their deaths, or whether he expected some form of resignation. What he hadn't expected was to see them both being *carried* out of the building, limp and unresisting. The crowd started to murmur, and Nate's stomach threatened to start acting up again.

Both the soon-to-be victims were naked, and when the enforcers carrying them dumped them unceremoniously on the street in front of the iron maiden, the firelight revealed bodies that were covered from head to foot with bruises and cuts and burns. Nate was glad Kurt was still holding his hand, because he needed that sense of connection. Especially when he saw that despite the fact that they had to be carried to their deaths and had obviously been tortured for who knew how long, both of them were conscious.

Kurt uttered something foul under his breath. "He gave them the same shit Kitty put in the wine," he said.

"Oh dear God," Nadia whispered, covering her mouth with her hand as if to hold in a gasp.

To Nate's horror, only he and his friends seemed even remotely bothered by what they saw. He saw some people whispering together and laughing. A couple of the men even shouted suggestions for what further tortures should be inflicted on the unfortunate duo before they died.

The crowd seemed to be gathering steam, the murmur of conversation growing louder. More people were emboldened by their neighbors and added their own suggestions, and someone started a rhythmic stomping that soon spread through the crowd like a drumbeat. It was like something out of an old historical movie, where unruly mobs gathered to view executions as entertainment. Come one, come all, bring the kiddies. What could be more fun?

When the stomping got loud enough, Maiden emerged from the red tower, dressed in full Executive regalia, though no Executive Nate had ever seen would wear that much jewelry. Still stomping, the crowd cheered his appearance, watching him with an expression somewhere between worship and terror.

It went without saying that Nate and his friends did not join in the stomping or cheering, though from what he could tell they were the only ones not participating. Even Shrimp was stomping one foot to the beat, though he was also saying something under his breath to Agnes, who stood nearest to him.

Maiden sauntered casually into the center of the circle, followed closely by two of his enforcers. He looked down at the motionless figures at his feet and smiled, the gleam in his eye proving how much he enjoyed flaunting his power.

"Ladies first, don't you think?" he asked the crowd, who responded with another resounding cheer.

One of the enforcers bent down and grabbed Kitty's arm, hauling her up and over his shoulder as if she weighed nothing. She didn't have enough control of her muscles to scream, but a piteous mewl of pain and terror escaped her.

"Remember one thing," Kurt whispered in Nate's ear. "This isn't the first time Maiden has done this, so Kitty knew exactly what she was risking."

"That doesn't make it right."

"Never said it did."

Somewhere amid all the spikes, there were restraints within the iron maiden, and Kitty was strapped in, unable to resist. The other enforcer grabbed her accomplice's arm and turned him so he was facing the iron maiden and could see the fate that awaited him.

Nate was shaking, and he held on to Kurt's hand so tight he hoped he wasn't hurting him. Nadia was clinging to Dante, but from the looks on their faces, Nate thought she was giving *him* support rather than the other way around. Agnes stood close to Shrimp, but he wasn't touching her. Nate surprised both of them by reaching out and grabbing her hand. She shouldn't be the only one of them to watch this without the comfort of another's touch. Her face didn't reveal much about what she felt, but her hand was ice cold and clammy.

Maiden put his hand on the lid of the iron maiden. There was a long, dramatic pause. And then he slammed it closed.

CHAPTER THIRTEEN

everyone was heartily sick of everyone else's company, but there was no bickering in Shrimp's apartment that night. They stayed together—except for Shrimp, who went out on his nightly reconnaissance mission—but no one felt much like talking. There was a lot of staring moodily into the flames of the flickering candles.

Nate had expected it would be the executions themselves that haunted him when it was all over, and to be sure, he would remember what he saw for the rest of his life. But he found the crowd of onlookers had chilled him more, with their stomping and cheering. There had been little old ladies and five-year-old kids out there, shaking their fists in the air and screaming for blood.

The Red Death might be providing Nate and his friends with safety and shelter, but they were definitely *not* the good guys. Nate was beginning to wonder if there *were* any good guys in this whole mess.

His faith in humanity slipped down another notch when Shrimp returned from his venture into the free territories and told them what he'd seen.

"The roadblocks are now semipermanent blockades," he said. "They're not letting anyone in or out, not even medical staff or delivery trucks. I missed the worst of it, but there was still some rioting going on when I passed through. Security ain't shooting to kill, but rubber bullets and tear gas ain't gonna calm things."

"No delivery trucks?" Bishop said, shaking his head. "You mean they're not even stocking the soup kitchens?"

Shrimp nodded. "That's what I mean."

No wonder there was rioting! The "grocers" had no doubt been stockpiling for a long while, but they were more likely to up their prices based on increased demand rather than start feeding the people who no longer had any access to food.

"How can she be getting away with this?" Nadia asked, and Nate had to wonder the same thing.

The Chairman of Paxco had more power than any three other Executives put together, but it was hard to imagine even the Chairman could withhold food and medicine from the unfortunates in the Basement. Surely *someone* on the board of directors would object and do something about it. Not even the most corrupt of the Executives Nate knew would condone starving people.

"What is happening out there?" Nate muttered to himself. If only they had access to the net! It was helpful to get Shrimp's reports of what he saw out in the Basement free territories, but with the lack of net access and the blockades, it was impossible to know what was going on in the rest of Paxco.

"Dorothy has no concept of conscience," Nadia said. "It doesn't matter to her if people die, as long as her own position is secure."

"Yeah, I think she's made that quite clear," Nate said with a hint of impatience.

"But real human beings aren't like that," she continued as if he hadn't spoken. "Even the most selfish, bigoted, uncaring despot would think twice about doing the things Dorothy is doing."

Unless, of course, Dorothy was spreading misinformation.

"Maybe that bit we saw on the news where Dorothy said she cut off phone service to calm unrest was just the tip of the iceberg," Nate suggested. "She created a video of me shooting my father. How hard do you think it would be for her to manufacture evidence that the situation here is getting dangerously unstable? That it's become too dangerous for Executives and Employees to set foot in the Basement? And with no phone service and no one able to get in or out of the Basement, who's going to be able to prove her wrong?"

"And now that she's provoked riots," Nadia said, "she'll have even more 'evidence' that the Basement's too dangerous for anyone to go into."

"And the board will be willing to condone even more drastic measures," Agnes added. "They can probably be convinced the Basement's on the brink of starting a full-scale revolution and marching Executives to the guillotine."

"She may not be all wrong," Shrimp said. "I didn't stick around to get the details, but Angel seems to be up to something. She closed down her club, but there're still lotsa people going in, and a lot of them are carrying boxes—the kind guns're packed in."

"That's the kind of thing *we* should be doing," Nate said. "Instead of sitting here like ducks in a pond waiting to be shot, we should be organizing, banding together against Dorothy."

"I hear you," Shrimp said. "And I'm glad Angel's trying to get people together. But Maiden still ain't gonna go for it."

"Do you have any idea how bad it's going to get here when the food starts running low?" Agnes asked. "Maybe he doesn't care about anyone but the Red Death, but surely—"

Shrimp shook his head and cut her off. "Have you guys listened to yourselves? You sound like nut jobs talking about this crazy computer trying to take over the world and replacing people with puppets. You wouldn't get half-way through your story before he'd laugh you out of the room."

There was no way Nate could deny that it sounded pretty crazy. Angel had had a hard enough time believing it, and her role in the resistance said she was far more civic-minded than Maiden.

"Do *you* believe us?" Nate asked.

Shrimp thought long and hard before answering. "Yeah, I guess I do. But it ain't gonna help. Even if he *did* believe you, Maiden wouldn't care. He's already announced that if anyone from the Red Death joins in the rioting, he'll personally shoot them dead. He figures as long as we keep out of it and mind our own business, we'll keep out of trouble."

"But—" Agnes tried to interrupt.

"The way he sees it, if other gangs get sucked into the fighting and start getting themselves killed, it'll be a great opportunity for us to get more territory."

"I don't understand," Agnes said as her eyes filled with tears. "How can someone see what's happening and not care?"

Shrimp's face hardened and he sat up straighter. "'Course you don't get it. You grew up with mansions and money and all that shit. Pokin' your nose in other people's business was a way of life. Well, it ain't like that in Debasement, and you'd better get used to it."

The angry words made Agnes flinch, but though Shrimp had to have noticed, he didn't take back what he'd said, nor did he look any less pissed. Always before, he'd seemed surprisingly accepting of his Executive guests, never showing that he felt the same kind of anger and resentment Basement-dwellers often displayed toward Executives—when they weren't trying to get money out of them, that is.

Shrimp pushed to his feet, scowling. "Don't forget this is all one big business transaction," he said. "You get exactly what you pay for, no more, no less. And you'll be lucky if Angel keeps paying for *anything* much longer."

With that, he stormed out of the living room. Moments later, his bedroom door slammed behind him, signaling how thoroughly finished he was with the conversation.

The next week was brutal. Shrimp still went out every night to check the pulse of the Basement, but every night his route became shorter and shorter as the food supplies started dwindling and the rioting worsened. By Tuesday, he didn't dare enter the free territories anymore because of the rioting, and Maiden's enforcers no longer cruised the streets, instead parking themselves around the borders of Red Death territory to defend their turf.

Nadia got used to hearing gunfire in the night. The violence was still mostly in the free territories, but according to Shrimp, it was spreading. If some of the most well-armed gangs got swept up in it, the Basement could turn into a bona fide war zone.

The news helicopters didn't show up at the scene until Thursday, which Nate and Nadia both agreed was evidence of how Dorothy was controlling the story, not letting reporters get any live pictures until the Basement was a full-on battleground. Footage was no doubt being shown all over the world, but instead of the story being about the drastic and immoral actions Dorothy was taking against the Basement, it would be about a beleaguered Chairman trying to restore order to her rioting slumlords.

The tanks made their appearance on Friday.

No one could safely leave Red Death territory anymore, so there were no firsthand accounts of what was going on. However, Maiden had a generator hookup in his apartment—one that he used only sparingly, because he had a limited supply of fuel—and Shrimp had watched some news coverage on his brother's hijacked cable feed. Aerial footage showed the tanks rolling into place behind the now solid barricades that cut off the Basement from the rest of the city. They weren't firing yet, but the news now described the violence in the Basement as a "revolt" rather than rioting—just as Agnes had predicted.

Every night, Agnes pleaded their case to Shrimp, persevering in the face of his snappish answers. She and Nadia agreed that his anger was *not* fueled by class friction, as Nate assumed, but was in fact a symptom of guilt. Shrimp *knew* they were right, but he was still convinced Maiden would have no interest in casting himself and the rest of the Red Death as heroes of any kind.

"What the hell is it you think we can do, anyway?" he asked one night in exasperation. "Sure, we have guns. But they have *tanks*."

"We can reach out to my father," Agnes answered quietly. Once she'd gotten over being hurt by his anger, she'd become a real pro at absorbing it without a blip of response. Even when he shouted, her voice and demeanor remained cool and controlled. "There's no way my father or anyone outside of Paxco knows what's really going on here. If they knew Dorothy provoked the rioting, the whole world would be putting pressure on her to stop it. Maybe even military pressure."

Nate and Nadia shared an uneasy look, but both kept their mouths shut. It went against everything in Nadia's upbringing to encourage a foreign power to invade Paxco, but how else could Dorothy possibly be removed from power? Even if Maiden and all his fellow gang lords could agree to work together for a higher cause, Shrimp was right and they'd be nearly helpless in the face of an organized military action.

"Your dad thinks it's worth getting his own people killed to help a bunch of drug dealers, whores, and gang lords?" Shrimp said, regarding Agnes doubtfully.

"Synchrony's Basement is nothing like Paxco's," she explained patiently. "My father *does* care about Basement-dwellers, a hell of a lot more than any of Paxco's Chairmen have. And don't forget, *I'm* here. He won't want me in the middle of a war zone. If the only way to stop that is to send in peacekeeping troops, he'll do it."

"You *have* to see where this is going," Nadia put in.

"They're parking tanks on the borders! How long do you think it'll be before those tanks are rolling down the streets of Red Death territory?"

Shrimp made an incoherent sound of frustration. "It's not *me* you gotta convince. It's Maiden. And Maiden ain't budging."

Agnes put her hands on her hips and glared. "So what you're telling me is that your brother would rather let Dorothy raze the Basement to the ground than let me use his fucking phone?"

Everyone did a double take at Agnes's language. What had happened to the timid, shy, painfully polite Executive she had once been?

Shrimp's Adam's apple bobbed as he swallowed hard, and after seeing what Maiden had done to Kitty and her accomplice, Nadia couldn't blame him for not wanting to cross his brother.

On the next night, a new and unexpected voice joined the chorus.

Angel, accompanied by three of her bouncers, had apparently come to talk to Maiden, but Maiden had refused to see her. She knocked on the door of Shrimp's apartment just before he was set to go out for his nightly patrol. He politely invited her in while insisting her goons wait outside. Angel obviously felt safe with him, because she didn't bat an eyelash before accepting his invitation.

"Nice to see you kids again," Angel said insincerely as she sauntered into the living room, looking them over one by one.

"Can't say the same," Nate grumbled, getting an elbow in the ribs from Bishop for his trouble.

"Remember who's paying for your upkeep," Angel snapped. "And I'm not exactly doing a lot of business these days, so I might have to cut back on my spending."

"We're on the same side," Nadia reminded the two of them. "We both want Dorothy stopped, and we both want out from under the 'austerity measures' and blockades. Let's not waste time fighting each other."

Angel flashed her teeth in something vaguely resembling a grin. "Honey, I'm trying to organize a resistance out of a bunch of junkies, whores, and gangbangers. They're not the most cooperative bunch."

Nadia shrugged, unimpressed. "Doesn't mean you have to pick fights."

"Whatever," Angel mumbled, then turned to Shrimp and acted like the two of them were alone in the room. "So, I was trying to see Maiden 'cause we sure could use some more warm bodies out in the free territories."

Angel launched into a surprisingly eloquent—and obviously well-practiced—appeal for the people of the Basement to band together to put an end to the tyranny. Thanks to her activities in the resistance, she had a core of devoted followers who were more than ready to take up arms against the state, but now that the resistance was no longer underground—and the Basement was under siege—she was eager to add to her ranks.

"I know Maiden doesn't want to get involved," she said. "Hell, practically no one in Debasement wants to lift a finger to help anyone unless there's something in it for them. So I'd basically like to 'rent' some of his enforcers to help with a little action I'm planning. Hard to bring him my offer, though, when he refuses to see me, so I thought I'd bring it to you. Maybe you can let him know it'd be worth his while."

Funny how she'd suggested paying the Red Death to shelter Nate and Nadia was causing her some kind of financial hardship when she'd come with an offer to throw more money at Maiden.

"He won't go for it," Shrimp said.

Angel arched her eyebrows. "He'd turn down money?"

Shrimp's expression turned uncharacteristically cold and hard. "How many people do you expect are gonna survive this 'little action' you're planning?"

Angel's eyes narrowed. "They aren't using rubber bullets out there anymore, so yeah, some people aren't gonna make it back. That's kinda how these things go."

"You mean *a lot* of people won't make it back," Shrimp countered. "You're going up against tanks with a bunch of, as you put it, junkies, whores, and gangbangers armed with whatever guns they happen to get their hands on."

"I have a plan for the tanks," Angel said vaguely. "Look, it'll be dangerous, but—"

Shrimp cut her off with a sharp hand gesture. "I'll tell Maiden you want to talk. And I'll tell him you have an offer. But he's hoping we'll be able to make a land grab when the smoke clears, and we'll need as many enforcers as we can get for that. If he's willing to give you any people at all, he'll be scraping from the bottom of the barrel, not giving you able-bodied enforcers."

Nadia felt a now-familiar surge of righteous indignation, but though Angel had just minutes ago been giving the hard sell, she nodded in weary acceptance. Maiden was probably not the first gang lord she'd approached, and it was likely she'd gotten similar responses.

"Well," Dante said, standing up, "I'm just one person, but I'm able-bodied, and I'm sick of sitting on the sidelines. Whatever you're planning, count me in."

Nadia choked on a cry of protest, her heart suddenly leaping into her throat. She wanted to do everything she could to help the resistance, but that didn't include putting Dante in front of a line of tanks.

"Me, too," Bishop said.

Nate stood up, and from the look on his face, Nadia guessed he was going to volunteer as well, but both Shrimp and Angel piped in with refusals before he could even speak.

"You made it clear when you met Maiden that you knew stuff that could turn the heat on Red Death," Shrimp said. "No way he's gonna risk any of you getting captured and spilling your guts."

"And I wouldn't take you anyway," Angel finished. "Thanks to the damned blimp, you two are known associates of our Executive friends here. They're more likely to lynch you than work with you."

Guilty relief flooded Nadia, and she suspected Nate felt much the same way. Bishop and Dante would not be facing down tanks. Instead, they would remain trapped in the red tower, powerless to do anything, while others lost their lives in what would doubtless be futile heroics.

"I'll take the offer to Maiden," Shrimp said again. "I know y'all are right and sitting on the sidelines ain't a good idea. I just wish I knew how to convince Maiden of that."

• • •

shrimp spent about three hours up in Maiden's apartment, and the only thing he had to show for it when he returned was a black eye. Apparently, he'd gotten a bit impassioned in his plea, and Maiden hadn't appreciated it.

"He ain't gonna budge," Shrimp announced to no one in particular. Angel had left long ago.

"So that's it?" Nate challenged, glaring. "We're just going to sit here and do nothing until the tanks are rolling down the streets in front of us and Thea collects as many human lab rats as she'd like while the rest of the Basement-dwellers are gunned down or starve to death?" He was frustrated enough that he wanted to hit something, maybe throw some furniture around.

"We can't do that," Agnes said with quiet dignity. "If we do nothing, Dorothy's eventually going to find us and kill us. If we're going to die anyway, I'd rather at least be *trying* to stop her. Angel might not particularly want to work with us, but she said she needed warm bodies. We're warm bodies."

"No!" Shrimp said sharply.

Agnes looked up at him with a serene expression very much at odds with what she was proposing. "We'll 'sneak' out sometime when you're on your rounds. As long as you're not here, Maiden won't expect you to stop us, right? So you shouldn't get in trouble or anything."

Shrimp gaped at her. "You think *that's* why I'm saying no?"

Nate didn't much like the idea of the five of them joining up with a bunch of Basement-dwellers who hated them in order to throw themselves against Dorothy's tanks, but maybe that was the best possible outcome for all of them. Agnes was right: there was a certain dignity to going down fighting. A hell of a lot more dignity than there was in dying while in hiding.

"There are five of us, and one of you," Nate said, although technically he couldn't be sure Nadia, Kurt, and Dante were on board. "If we're determined to leave, you can't stop us."

Shrimp's eyes glittered in the glow of the candles. "Tell me you didn't just threaten me."

Kurt came to stand shoulder to shoulder with Nate, and Dante joined him. Nate wasn't much of a fighter, but Kurt and Dante were both formidable. Between the three of them, they could take Shrimp down no matter how scrappy he might be.

"I know you understand better than you're letting on," Agnes said to Shrimp with a sad little smile. "Just go on out and do your thing, and we'll be gone when you get back."

"You'd never make it out of Red Death territory," Shrimp responded. "Too many enforcers out there keeping an eye on things. And Angel's blaze of glory crap ain't gonna do anyone any good."

"That doesn't m—"

"Yes, it does matter!" Shrimp growled. "If y'all have to be heroes and get yourselves killed, you might as well do it for something that has a chance of working."

Agnes cocked her head. "What do you have in mind?"

"I'll tell you as soon as you get your boys to sit down and shut up."

Agnes smiled pleasantly. "I'm sure that can be arranged," she said in a saccharine-sweet voice. "Isn't that right, boys?" She gave Nate, Kurt, and Dante each a pointed look.

Nate had never been a big fan of doing as he was told—or of backing down once he'd taken a stance—but just this once, he would make an exception. If Shrimp had an idea about how they could fight Dorothy without making a suicidal charge against the barricades, he was more than eager to hear it.

CHAPTER FOURTEEN

shrimp remained on his feet while everyone else sat down and looked up at him expectantly. His shoulders were tight with strain, his eyes a little wild-looking. Whatever he was about to suggest, Nadia didn't think he was exactly comfortable with it.

"Lookin' at what's going on now," he said, rubbing his hands together in a nervous gesture, "I don't see any way it's gonna end well. Even if Maiden gave the okay for all of us to join up with Angel, we're gonna get our asses kicked. And it don't seem to me that Dorothy's gonna back off anytime soon."

"She won't," Nate agreed. "At least not until she's sure that we are dead."

"And anyone she thinks we might have talked to," Nadia hastily added. The last thing she wanted to do was give Maiden any reason to think killing them and turning their bodies over to the authorities for the reward might be a good idea.

Shrimp waved off her obvious concern. "Don't worry. My brother can be a dickhead, but he ain't stupid. If he'd understood the level of heat you'd put on us, Angel couldn't've paid him enough to shelter you. But he's stuck with you now, and he knows it.

"Anyway, like I was saying, Dorothy ain't gonna stop on her own, and a bunch of Basement-dwellers with guns ain't enough to stop her. So I think Agnes was right all along, and the only way to take her down is with help from the outside."

Agnes's face lit with hope. "So you'll let me use Maiden's phone connection?"

Shrimp shook his head. "No way. The only access is in his place, and he ain't gonna let us in to use it."

"So what are you suggesting?" Agnes asked.

"You wanted to get outside of the Basement, where you could pick up a signal. I think I might know how we can do that."

"And you're willing to do it behind Maiden's back?"

He scrubbed at his bristly orange hair. "I don't see that we got a choice. I don't wanna end up like Kitty, but I don't wanna hold my breath and hope the monster'll go away, either. If Maiden won't listen, then we gotta go behind his back."

"But you could just let us go behind his back without you," Nadia suggested. "Tell us what you have in mind, and if it sounds like a good plan, we'll go ahead with our 'escape' and take care of it ourselves. You don't have to put yourself in the line of fire."

"Thanks," he said, with a sad little smile, "but if you pull this off, Maiden'll know it came from me anyway. So I might as well go with you. And hope that a showdown with Maiden is the worst thing in my future."

"So how do you propose we get out of the Basement and in range of a phone signal?" Agnes asked.

"A coupla blocks from here, there's some kinda sinkhole.

When they built the Basement, they built around it instead of fixing it, so it's kinda like a wasteland."

Nadia remembered when she and Nate had been brought to the Basement to meet with Bishop when he was first in hiding. They'd met at an abandoned overpass. Not familiar with the Basement at the time, Nadia hadn't realized how unusual it was to have so much empty space with no high-rises on it.

"Is it near that overpass where we met with Bishop?" she asked, then belatedly realized Shrimp might have no idea what she was talking about.

"Yep," he said, grinning. "I was there that night, you know. Keeping an eye on our boy here." He gave Bishop a friendly punch in the arm. "It's just on the other side of the overpass where y'all had your little reunion. Anyway, I used to play there when I was a kid, and I found a hole in the rubble. Couldn't see much 'cause it was dark down there, but went back one night with Maiden. Turns out it's an old subway tunnel, probably collapsed when they were tearing down the neighborhood to build the Basement.

"We never explored it too much—it's really nasty down there, and we weren't sure how stable it was—but we hid the opening just in case we ever needed a place to hide where no one could find us. I don't know how far it goes, and I don't know if the air's any good or even if there's any way out, but it might be worth taking a look."

"It's perfect!" Agnes declared, her face lighting up with hope.

Nadia wouldn't go that far. It had been patently obvious to those who had planned the Basement that public transportation would not be needed there. Basement-dwellers would have no reason to venture out into the wider world—at least that was the theory—and respectable citizens would know better than to set foot into the dangers of the slums. Nadia knew from her history lessons that there had once been subway lines running through the neighborhood, before it was torn down and made into the Basement. But just because Shrimp had found access to a stretch of tunnel didn't mean the system was navigable, especially not when they would have to travel so far to get past the barricade and get a signal. The idea of blundering around in a dark, dank, stinky tunnel system with questionable air wasn't terribly appealing.

Shrimp shrugged. "I wouldn't get my hopes up yet, but at least there's a shot."

"Power's been out what, two weeks now?" Bishop said. "Anyone's phone still have juice?"

That threw a wet blanket over everything. Getting under the barricades wouldn't help if they couldn't make the phone call.

No one was carrying their useless phones around anymore, so they took a few minutes to gather all the ones they had and dump them onto the coffee table. Several were already dead, but a few had a small amount of battery power left.

"We take all the ones that have any power at all," Shrimp said, "and we might have to make multiple calls to get the message out."

Nadia bit her lip. "And we have to go soon—before the last phone dies." She'd been thinking they could maybe take a couple of days to plan for the terrifying venture into the tunnels, and that she and Nate and Agnes would be able to rehearse what they were going to say to Chairman Belinski in order to get as much information out as fast as possible—without making him think they were lunatics.

"Probably a good idea anyway," Nate said. "We don't know how long Dorothy will hold off before she launches a full-scale attack. And if we give Angel time to launch her 'little action,' that could be just the excuse Dorothy needs to send the tanks in. If we're going to do this, we have to do it, like, now."

"No reason to wait," Shrimp agreed. "Y'all don't hafta get all dressed up or anything, 'cause we're gonna hafta get to the sinkhole without anyone seein' us, but you might want sleeves and long pants. Like I said, it's nasty down there, and we might get a little scraped up trying to get through the opening."

Agnes's relief at not having to go out in public in her Basement regalia was palpable, almost enough to make Nadia laugh despite her terror of what they were about to do.

The last time Nate had set foot outside the building had been for the execution. The eighteen flights of stairs discouraged casual meandering, as did the fact that there was nowhere to go and nothing to do. Any fresh air he'd gotten, he'd gotten by sticking his head out the window, and though he'd seen from there how changed the Basement had been since the blackout began, it was nothing like being out on those darkened streets himself.

Despite the Basement's usual nocturnal hours, there was hardly anyone out on the streets at night these days, at least not in Red Death territory. Nate assumed there were more people stationed around the borders, but he was perfectly happy not to see for himself, and the fact that the overpass and the sinkhole were firmly in the middle of Red Death turf—and that there was nothing of interest there to most people—heightened the chances that they would be able to explore without being seen and reported to Maiden.

It was oppressively dark out, the moon and stars hidden behind clouds. Here and there, candlelight flickered from windows, but it was too dim to illuminate the streets themselves. There was some ambient light thanks to the glow from the city, but it was slow going without flashlights, which they weren't going to use unless absolutely necessary. In this instance, darkness was their friend, even if it did mean they were constantly tripping over cracks in the sidewalk.

The weather was unseasonably warm, and Nate was sweating beneath the thick thermal shirt he'd put on under his tee. The smell of rotting garbage was strong in the air, and there was a faint hint of smoke, possibly from the bonfires burning in the free territories. It had rained a few days ago, but the gutters were so blocked with rubbish that there were still filthy puddles everywhere, adding to the overall ambience.

The now-familiar sound of distant gunfire made everyone hurry their footsteps. It occurred in sporadic bursts, but if Angel launched her all-out offensive, it was likely to intensify. And the tanks might start advancing. People were already dying, and with the barricades keeping everyone and everything trapped, the dead would most likely rot in the streets.

In short, as awful as the Basement seemed now, it could get a whole lot worse in the blink of an eye.

It didn't take long to reach the dilapidated area surrounding the abandoned overpass. With the high-rises not looming so close, it was possible to see over greater distances. Enough to see the glow and flashes of the fighting in the free territories. They all paused a moment to look.

"The blimps are gone," Nadia commented, and Nate could see she was right.

Shrimp followed their gaze. "Might not be safe for them anymore. Red Death doesn't do a whole lot of arms deals—we just supply our own people—but some of the other gangs have serious military-grade stuff. Kinda shit that'll take a blimp down."

Nate had already seen the kind of military-grade equipment the Red Death's enforcers had. That there were other gangs with deadlier weapons was not a comfortable thought.

"We're no match for them in the end," Shrimp continued, "but if those tanks start rolling, they're gonna be in for a rude surprise."

"Let's see if we can find a way to keep those tanks from rolling," Agnes said. "Where's this tunnel?"

Shrimp led them through the overpass and out the other side, where sure enough the pavement had collapsed. They played the beams of their flashlights over the sunken area, and all Nate could see were broken chunks of concrete and asphalt, along with litter and weeds.

"It's at the bottom," Shrimp said, moving cautiously toward the lip of the pit. "Watch your step and don't put your full weight on anything till you're sure it'll hold you."

For safety's sake, they scrambled down one at a time. More than once, Nate put his foot down on a piece of rubble that looked solid, only to have it rock precariously under his weight, but despite a couple of stumbles and near misses, they all made it to the bottom without incident.

When everyone was down, Shrimp laid his flashlight on the ground, pointing it at a section of rubble that looked just like all the rest. He shrugged off the backpack containing the phones and the rest of their supplies. Squatting, he began pulling pieces of rock away, throwing them carelessly aside, along with the layers of litter that had gathered over the years. Nate grimaced when he saw Shrimp toss aside a desiccated used condom and wondered who in their right mind thought this was a good location for a hookup.

Dante tried to help—which belatedly Nate realized he should have offered to do himself—but Shrimp waved him off. "I got it. Almost there."

Shrimp dug down to a warped, rotting piece of wood that looked like it might have been part of a crate in a former life. When he moved the wood aside, a hole appeared, just large enough for a person to fit through if he or she wasn't too big. Nate eyed Dante and wondered if those shoulders of his would make it.

They gathered 'round as Shrimp shone his flashlight into the hole.

There wasn't a lot to see. There was more rubble down there, and the air in the beam of the flashlight swam with dust. A dank, musty smell wafted out, and a pair of rats skittered away from the light with indignant squeaks of protest. Nate glanced over at Nadia and Agnes, wondering if the girls were now having second thoughts. Nadia wrinkled her nose in distaste, and Agnes looked grim, but neither of them showed any sign of screaming or fainting at the sight of a rodent.

"In we go," Shrimp said, then lay flat on his belly to crawl through the hole onto the slope of rubble directly below it.

When his feet were through, he wriggled around and stood up, edging his way carefully down to the bottom.

Nate wasn't looking forward to crawling facefirst into a dark tunnel filled with rats, but he was damned if he was going to show that reluctance in front of Dante, so he leaned into the opening.

"Hold up a minute!" Shrimp said, raising one hand in a stop sign. "Gimme the backpack first."

Nate didn't appreciate the delay when his nerves were so jittery, but he grabbed for the backpack anyway and tossed it down, meaning to follow it immediately.

"I said hold up!" Shrimp repeated irritably as he dug through the backpack and pulled out one of the candles they had brought. "Told ya I don't know 'bout the air down here. No sense both of us breathin' it till we know it's okay."

Nate rolled his eyes at the precaution. He didn't doubt that there could be bad air in the tunnel, but not this close to the surface, and not when there was a hole for fresh air to get through. But it had been Nadia's idea to use candles to test the air quality, so he waited impatiently while Shrimp lit the wick. When it caught and burned easily, Shrimp finally gave the go-ahead for everyone else to follow him in.

If the air that wafted out of the hole was dank, the air inside was a lot worse. When Nate stepped aside to make room for Nadia to come in, his foot came down in a scum-covered puddle that immediately soaked through his shoe. He turned on his own flashlight and shone it around, picking out more puddles. The stink in the air was probably mildew, although there were undertones that were even fouler. The scent of wet rat, maybe?

He decided not to think about it as he moved farther

from the hole and into the tunnel proper. By the look of it, the entire street above and the remnants of whatever building had been built on it had collapsed into the tunnel, completely blocking it off on one side. It wasn't until about twenty yards in that the rubble thinned enough to make out the ancient, rusted subway tracks on the floor, disappearing into the darkness beyond.

Nate had thought the city was oppressively dark with the power off, but that was nothing compared to the light-eating dark of the tunnel. The setting reminded him of something from a horror movie, and his lizard brain was telling him in no uncertain terms that he should turn around and get the hell out of here ASAP.

When everyone was through the hole and down to the tunnel floor, they took a moment to assess the situation, flashlight beams streaking all around as each of them examined their surroundings. More than one beam caught sets of glowing eyes.

"I can't imagine why you and your brother wouldn't want to explore this place for hours," Nate said to Shrimp, trying for something like dry humor to hide how creeped out he was feeling.

Shrimp snorted. "This's nothing. You think we don't got rats on the streets 'round here? Wait'll we get a little farther in. You'll see why Maiden and me decided not to keep going."

Not exactly the kind of statement that made Nate anxious to proceed, but there was no way he was going to act like a wuss in front of the girls and Dante.

Nadia designated herself as the candle bearer, and she and Shrimp led the way into the darkness of the tunnel. The combination of darkness, rubble, and subway rails made the footing treacherous, and it was slow going. The stink of mildew grew stronger, as did the mysterious something else Nate had noticed at the entrance. Cracks in the walls and ceiling made it feel like the tunnel might collapse on them at any moment. Patches of slimy green stuff Nate presumed was algae of some kind clung to the walls and lined the floor, making it slippery. Just ahead of Nate, Dante's foot found one of those patches, and he went down, twisting his ankle and breaking his flashlight.

"Are you okay?" Nadia cried, eyes wide with concern as she rushed to his side.

"Fine," Dante grumbled, wiping his slime-slicked palms on his already grimy pants before letting her and Shrimp give him a hand up. "Nothing injured but my pride."

Shrimp dug a spare flashlight out of his backpack and handed it to Dante. "Be more careful with this one, Captain Studly. We need all the light we can get."

Dante gave him a dirty look—shockingly, he had not yet warmed to his street name—but clicked on the flashlight without comment.

They continued on even more slowly, everyone aware of the precarious footing.

Nate was almost getting used to the mildew stink, but the other smell, the one that was getting steadily stronger, was another story.

"Gah!" he eventually exclaimed, trying to breathe through his mouth. "What *is* that?"

Shrimp, who had pulled his T-shirt up over his nose and mouth, turned around and said, "Beats me, and I never wanted to stick around long enough to find out."

"It's bat guano," Agnes said, surprising everyone.

Shrimp cocked his head at her and said, "What's 'guano'?" at the same time Nadia asked, "How on earth would you know that?"

"Bat shit," Agnes clarified, grinning at Shrimp. "One of my brothers is into caving, and I went with him a few times when I was a kid. It's not a smell you forget."

Great, Nate thought to himself. *Rats on the ground, and flying rats in the air.* "Hope we don't all need rabies shots when this is over," he muttered.

Shrimp didn't look much happier about it than Nate felt.

"Let's keep moving," Nadia said, starting forward once more. "If the worst thing we have to face today is bats, it'll be a good day."

Beside him, Kurt gave a low whistle of appreciation and put a hand on Nate's shoulder. "You were right about her, I was wrong," Kurt admitted. "Girl's got balls."

Nate elbowed him in the ribs, though he was glad Kurt was finally beginning to see Nadia the way he did. Her courage put him to shame, and he tried to ignore the way his skin crawled. And the way Kurt stuck extra close as they continued forward, like he was afraid Nate would burst into hysterics at any moment. Kurt knew him too well not to see that Nate was struggling to keep putting one foot in front of the other. He would have been fine with the critters alone, but add the dark, the stench, and the irrational fear that the tunnel was going to choose this particular moment to collapse, and his nerves were stretched taut as guitar strings. Was he the only one who was feeling it?

"Remember," Kurt murmured at his side, "Shrimp and Maiden turned back instead of exploring."

Nate looked at him sideways. "You a mind reader suddenly?"

Kurt shook his head. "Nope. Just know how you think these days."

Being self-conscious was definitely a new experience for Nate, but he'd been getting a lot of practice at it lately. Hard not to scrutinize his every action now that he'd woken up to how careless and oblivious he'd been in the old days. The old Nate had never had any reason to doubt himself, and he'd certainly never had reason to be afraid. How Kurt could have loved him back then, he'd never understand.

They'd been walking down the tunnel about twenty minutes when the rubble started getting thicker. Shrimp's flashlight beam roamed all around, and when he pointed it upward, Nadia saw a large fissure in the tunnel's ceiling. The stench of bat guano was overpowering, making her feel nauseous, and when other flashlight beams joined Shrimp's, the fissure practically erupted with squeaking protests and the flutter of wings.

Shrimp uttered a foul curse and dropped to his knees, covering his head, and everyone but Agnes ducked as a swooping cloud of bats surrounded them. Shrimp wasn't the only one cursing, and Nadia closed her eyes because if she got a good look at what was flying around them she'd probably run away screaming.

"They're not attacking us," Agnes said, no hint of fear in her voice. "They're running away from us. Everyone just stay calm."

Judging by the continued cursing, Agnes's words didn't have much effect, and Nadia's adrenal glands didn't seem convinced either. Her heart was racing, and she tried not to picture little furry bodies with leathery wings tangling themselves in her hair.

Eventually, the outraged swarm dwindled to a few stragglers darting here and there, and Nadia breathed a sigh of relief. The stench was making her eyes water, and she didn't want to imagine how much guano they'd be carrying on them when they escaped from bat territory.

"Everyone okay?" Shrimp asked, brushing at his clothing and running a hand through his hair as if to reassure himself there were no bats clinging to him. For a tough guy, he was looking pretty green.

"I feel like they're crawling all over me," Nate muttered, squirming where he stood.

Agnes laughed. "Don't be such babies. They're more scared of you than you are of them."

"Glad to know that," Nate snapped. "Now can we get the hell out of here before they come back?"

It wasn't much later that the tunnel opened up into the ruins of a station, the cavernous space making their every breath and footstep echo. It was hard to get a good look at the station from the well of the tracks, and getting up onto the platform might be something of a challenge, at least for Nadia and Agnes.

"Maybe we should just keep going," Nadia suggested, but Dante had already grabbed the edge of the platform and was dragging himself up. "We aren't here to explore—we're trying to get to a phone signal."

Dante dusted off his hands, squatting on the platform and staring down at them. "None of you has ever set foot in a subway station in your lives, have you?"

Nadia bit her lip and looked away, hearing the hint of reproach in his voice. Executives didn't travel by public transportation, so even though the vast majority of Paxco citizens relied on subways and buses to get around, Dante was right and the closest she'd ever been to a subway was seeing one on TV. The same was no doubt true of Nate and Agnes, and Bishop and Shrimp would never have had need of public transportation when living in the Basement.

"Didn't think so," Dante said. "If we're lucky, there'll be a map around here somewhere, and we can figure out where we are, and how to get past the Basement borders as fast as possible." He put his flashlight down and reached out with both hands. "Come on, I'll help you."

It made sense, so Nadia allowed Dante to help her up onto the platform, and the others followed, spreading out in search of a map. There was a lot of rubble, and everything was covered with a carpet of dust that made the air thick and hard to breathe when their footsteps stirred it up. On one end of the platform, Nadia found a set of tall metal turnstiles, behind which were stairs, which no doubt used to lead to the surface. When she shone her light up those stairs, however, she saw that they'd been solidly sealed off, with sturdy buttresses supporting whatever had been built on top of them.

There was a clatter and a thud behind her, and Dante called out a victorious "Got it!"

Nadia picked her way over to the center of the platform, where Dante had overturned a fallen piece of tile. Under the tile was a dusty, scratched-up sheet of Plexiglas, beneath which was a faded, water-stained map with writing so small she could barely read it.

"I think we're here," Dante said, pointing to a speck on the map. A water stain made it almost illegible, but she could see the station name started with a J, and she'd noticed a bit of broken signage that said JACKSON AVE. on it. Of course, the streets had all been renamed when the Basement was built, so Jackson Avenue no longer existed and wasn't much use as a reference point.

Dante's finger traced over one of the lines on the map. "If we keep following this track here, it'll take us under the river and into Manhattan, and we should be able to get a signal."

Nadia eyed the line doubtfully. It was still a long way to go, and Nadia would be surprised if the city planners who'd designed the Basement hadn't blocked the subway tunnels off before they merged with those that were currently in use.

She was about to voice her concern when a muffled boom echoed through the tunnels, shaking the floor and causing a rain of dust to fall from above.

CHAPTER FIFTEEN

"What the fuck was that?" Bishop asked eloquently as he brushed dust and pebbles out of his mohawk.

There was another boom before anyone had a chance to answer, and Nadia's heart sank to the bottom of her stomach. They were too late. Dorothy had ordered the tanks to fire.

They all stood in stunned, horrified silence as the explosions continued, the platform shaking under their feet as more debris pattered down. The shaking was bad enough to knock something over with a loud crash, though in the darkness Nadia didn't know what it was. It was possible the station would collapse on top of them, and she tried not to think about being buried alive down here.

"Those explosions are too big to be just the tanks," Dante said, then yelped when a chunk of concrete from the ceiling hit him in the head.

"Dante!" Nadia cried, springing toward him, almost singeing him with the candle she still carried.

"I'm all right," he assured her, though there was blood running down the side of his face. "Let's get back in the tunnel where there's less open space."

Nadia wasn't sure the tunnel would be any more secure

than the station, but at least any debris from the ceiling wouldn't have as far to fall and might not hit as hard.

They scrambled toward the tracks and down. A louder, closer explosion echoed through the station just as Nadia's feet hit the tracks, the shaking so strong she lost her footing and went down with a thud.

"Those are bombs!" Dante shouted as he grabbed her arm and hauled her to her feet. His face was white, making the blood that streaked the side of it more stark.

Agnes screamed as one of the support pillars on the platform cracked. It didn't fall, but it wouldn't hold for long.

"Take cover!" Dante yelled, and they all sprinted for the nearest tunnel, which at that point was the one they'd come in from.

The booming and shaking made the footing even more treacherous than it had been before, and the sprint quickly turned to a staggering, lurching run. Nadia dropped her candle, the flame immediately snuffing out when it hit the ground. Luckily, the flashlights were enough to light the way as chunks of cement and tile dropped from the ceiling and crashed on the platform, filling the air with choking dust and flying debris.

Something caught the side of Nadia's face, leaving a stinging streak across her cheek, but she wasn't about to slow down and assess the damage.

Nate and Bishop were the first ones to reach the edge of the tunnel, though Nadia could barely see them through the cloud of dust. They both stopped just a few yards in, turning to urge the others to move faster.

Nadia was running as fast as she could, but she was

hardly a world-class sprinter. Dante had hold of her hand and was practically dragging her forward.

"Let go and run!" she screamed at him, knowing she was slowing him down. But of course he wouldn't do it.

The station was crumbling, the chunks of debris from the ceiling getting larger and more deadly. Nadia could hardly breathe, coughing and choking on the dust while her lungs screamed for more oxygen to fuel her run.

Nadia and Dante reached the edge of the tunnel just as an ominous groaning sounded from overhead. Dante tried to keep her moving, but Nadia stopped and squinted into the dusty darkness behind her, picking out the jerky beams of Shrimp's and Agnes's flashlights. Something big hit the edge of the platform right beside them and burst into a spray of debris, some of which hit Agnes, and she went down with a cry of pain.

Shrimp immediately stopped to help her, trying to pull her to her feet. When that didn't work, he dropped his flashlight and hauled her over his shoulder. Through the darkness and clouds of dust, Nadia could see little except the whites of his eyes and his gritted teeth.

A metal beam slammed to the floor, and the groaning grew louder. Shrimp continued to stagger forward, reaching the mouth of the tunnel just when the groan turned into a scream and the station's ceiling came crashing down.

Dante and Nadia both reached for Shrimp, helping him keep his balance as he struggled under Agnes's weight and the shaking ground. They hurried deeper into the tunnel, the cloud of dust from the collapsed station following them, making it nearly impossible to see even with the flashlights. Agnes lay limply over Shrimp's shoulder, not moving.

By mutual agreement, they stopped running when they reached a section of tunnel that seemed solid, the walls and ceiling showing no signs of cracking, no debris raining down. There were still the muffled sounds of explosions coming from the surface, and the dust carried the scent of smoke. Everyone was coughing and breathing hard, exhausted from exertion and adrenaline as they tried to get the dust out of their lungs.

Everyone except Agnes, that is.

Shrimp laid her down carefully on the smoothest spot he could find between the tracks. Her limbs flopped loosely, and her head lolled. The hair on one side of her head was matted with blood, and there was another bloody wound across her ribs on the same side.

"Is she breathing?" Nadia asked, dreading the answer.

"She's breathing," Shrimp reassured her hoarsely, turning to cough and spit. His eyes were shiny. "I shoulda been between her and the platform," he said. "I knew it was safer by the wall."

Nadia squatted beside him and put her hand on his shoulder. "Don't," she said. "None of us had time to think—we just ran. And if you'd been the one hit, Agnes wouldn't have been able to carry you to safety."

She didn't think Shrimp was much comforted, and indeed neither was she. Agnes was the most innocent of them all, the one who least deserved to be caught in the middle of this hell. So of course she was the one who got hurt.

Nadia settled in, sitting on the rail beside Agnes and holding the girl's hand. Dante sat beside her, draping his arm over her shoulders and holding her close. She looked at his bloody face and remembered that he, too, had been hurt.

"I'm all right," he said before she could ask.

"But—"

"Scalp wounds bleed a lot. Really, I'm fine."

She nodded, having no choice but to take his word for it.

Together, they sat silently in the dark and listened to the sounds of Dorothy bombing the people she, as Chairman, was supposed to protect.

The bombing went on for hours, with only the occasional respite. Not that Nate had much of a sense of time down here in the darkness.

They'd lost several flashlights over the course of their exploration and flight, so to conserve the batteries on the ones they had left, they lit a single candle as their only source of light. Agnes had regained consciousness, but it was obvious to everyone that she was in rough shape. She didn't seem to know where she was, and she groaned in pain whenever she tried to move. Shrimp was making her as comfortable as possible, keeping up a gentle murmur of dialog, both to keep her awake and to keep her from panicking.

Nate sat with his back against the tunnel wall, too numb and shocked to take much comfort in Kurt's arm around his shoulders. He'd thought the tanks were the worst Dorothy would bring to bear on the Basement, but he'd obviously been wrong.

How many people had died tonight? People who'd done nothing wrong, for there *were* innocents in the Basement, no matter how depraved the place might be. He was pretty sure tears were leaving tracks in the coating of dust on his face, and he didn't give a damn. His mind just couldn't encompass the evil that had been done this night. And he couldn't help feeling guilty that chance had led him to relative safety while the unfortunates above him were being slaughtered.

Nate wasn't sure how long they sat there, no one speaking, after the bombing let up. It was a long time, though, and it was Nadia who finally broke the silence.

"I guess we should see if we can get out of here," she said.

It showed something about how sluggishly Nate's mind was working that he hadn't even considered the possibility that they were trapped. But solid though the tunnel felt here, its walls and ceiling had already been compromised in other places along their route, and there could easily have been cave-ins.

"What do you think it's like out there?" Nate asked of no one in particular.

"Bad," Kurt said, and tough and thick-skinned though he was, Nate noticed there were tracks through the dust on *his* face, too. "Really, really bad."

Dante lowered his head into his hands. "God, I don't want to see it."

Nadia rose stiffly to her feet. "I don't want to see it, either, but it's better than the alternative. So let's go."

Agnes made a halfhearted attempt to stand, but Shrimp quickly scooped her up in his arms. There was no way she was walking, not in her condition.

"I can carry her for a while if you get tired," Nate said, and Kurt and Dante made similar offers.

"Nah, I got 'er," Shrimp said. "She don't weigh much."

Even in her pain and misery, Agnes managed a small smile.

And so, they picked their way forward, moving slowly by the light of a single flashlight. Nadia carried the candle once again, and Nate knew he wasn't the only one keeping an anxious eye on the flame. The heaviest dust particles had settled by now, but the air still felt thick and gritty, and they were all coughing occasionally. Nate hoped and prayed that whatever openings that had allowed air to get down here before were still intact.

There was a partial cave-in in the area where they'd encountered the bats. The crack in the ceiling had split open, spewing an impressive mound of rubble and dirt into the tunnel. One of the sides had also caved in, exposing another set of tracks on the other side of a thick wall. Nate was glad to see them, thinking now there was another potential way out of the tunnel if they found it blocked farther on.

Getting Agnes over the mound of debris was something of a challenge, but Nate supposed they should be glad the tunnel wasn't completely blocked—or still crumbling around them. The footing was treacherous, and the mound was high enough they had to crouch to avoid hitting their heads on the bent and twisted beams that had once supported the ceiling when they went over the top. The air still stank of guano, and Nate shuddered to see little hairy bodies interspersed with the rubble.

They managed to get Agnes over and through to the other side without getting her any more banged up than she already was, but Nate winced in sympathetic pain at her every whimper. He tried not to think about what kind of filth was getting ground into her wounds, or about the fact that she needed a doctor and there would be none available.

There were no more major blockages after that, but it was still slow going, and they had to stop and rest multiple times, their lungs straining in the dusty air. Nate's chest hurt from coughing, and he felt gritty inside and out. The hole they'd used to crawl into the tunnel in the first place had grown larger, but it was again going to be a challenge to get Agnes up the slope formed by the rubble.

Dante went up first, and they fashioned a crude sling out of his jacket and Kurt's, tied together. Dante lay down on his stomach, holding both ends of the makeshift sling as Shrimp settled Agnes on it and she held on as well as she could. With Dante pulling from the top and Shrimp pushing from beneath, they got her out of the tunnel and finally got their first look at the destruction Dorothy had wrought.

The Basement was alight with the glow of fire, the air thick with smoke. Nate was pleasantly surprised to see that most of the buildings in his immediate view were still standing and undamaged, and he guessed that most of the bombs had been directed at the riot-riddled free territories.

Most, but not all.

There was a gaping hole in the side of one of the highrises on the edge of the undeveloped area around the sinkhole, and another seemed to be missing its top few floors. Even with the glow of the distant firelight, it was too dark to see much, but Nate had the impression of shocked survivors stumbling around on the street or huddling together for comfort.

Shrimp was about ready to collapse from exhaustion,

and Dante finally convinced him to let him carry Agnes for a while. Staying close together, they made their way through the streets toward Shrimp's apartment.

In the grand scheme of things, there didn't appear to be that many buildings in the Red Death territory that were hit, but one bomb hitting a high-rise created unimaginable damage. They had to detour around a street that was completely blocked by the crumbled remains of a tower, and even in the darkness they could see the blood. Nate caught sight of a disembodied arm and almost threw up.

When they turned the next corner that should have brought them within sight of the red tower, there was another pile of rubble. The red tower, and all of the buildings around it, had been utterly destroyed.

Shrimp gave an incoherent cry of dismay and started running forward, stumbling over cracked pavement, twisted beams, and blocks of concrete. He flung himself onto one of the piles of rubble and started digging at it frantically with his hands, grabbing bricks and crumbles of plaster and twisted pieces of metal at random and throwing them out of the way. He shoved aside a block of red-painted concrete, and Nate understood: that was all that remained of the red tower. And chances were good Maiden had been inside it when it went down.

CHAPTER SIXTEEN

nate supposed they were lucky Dorothy hadn't flattened the entire Basement, though the fact that so many buildings around the red tower had been hit suggested she'd been targeting it. Although it was hard to see how security officers could penetrate this deep into Red Death territory, Dorothy obviously had enough spies to help her pick targets that would most destabilize the Basement survivors. He wondered how many other gangs would find themselves leaderless come morning.

Not that Maiden's death was a sure thing. It wouldn't exactly break Nate's heart if he was dead, but he joined in Shrimp's probably useless attempt to dig through the rubble. The man was evil through and through, but Nate knew exactly how much it hurt to lose family members, even when you loathed them.

Dante pitched in shortly after, and Kurt started snagging various wandering, shocked Red Death members and trying to get them to help. But they didn't know Kurt, and they were all too stunned and fearful to do anything.

Nate scrambled over the debris and gave Shrimp's shoulder a quick shake. "We need more help," he said. "They're not listening to Bishop, but maybe they'll listen to you."

Shrimp blinked as if he had no idea what Nate was talking about. His hands were already ragged and bleeding, and his desperate need to keep digging was written all over his face. Nate gestured at the street behind them, where survivors were milling around uselessly, many crying, some wounded.

"Get them organized," Nate urged, worried now that the shock might turn into violence. Nadia was sitting on the curb close by, Agnes laid out on the sidewalk with her head in Nadia's lap. If the survivors turned into an angry mob, Nadia and Agnes would be obvious and easy targets, as he would be himself.

Shrimp blinked some more, then closed his eyes and sucked in a deep breath. He did it again, then opened his eyes and looked more sane and stable. He didn't say anything to Nate, merely nodded, then dusted off his hands. He headed off toward the cluster of survivors, and Nate turned back to the rubble, grabbing a chunk of plaster and tossing it aside. He didn't think it likely there were any survivors under the debris, and even if there were, he doubted they'd be able to dig them out very effectively with nothing but bare hands. But he worked at it anyway, because it was the only halfway useful thing he could think of to do.

Shrimp had more success rallying the Red Death, and soon the rubble was swarming with people. Shrimp organized them into shifts, because the work was exhausting. And harrowing. And depressing as hell, especially when they started to find bodies.

When Shrimp called for a shift change, Nate grudgingly hauled himself to his feet and stepped away. He wanted to keep working, wanted desperately to find at least one survivor, but his limbs were trembling from exhaustion, and logic told him he had to at least take a break.

A swell of pride momentarily lifted his heart as Nate saw that Nadia was organizing the people who weren't digging, directing some to tend the wounded and getting a bunch of children to bring water to the diggers. A little girl no more than six, with wide, frightened-looking eyes, held a bottle of water out to Nate, and he accepted it.

"Thank you," he croaked, but she was already turning to someone else.

shrimp underwent a metamorphosis that awful night, and Nadia watched it happen before her eyes. At first, he was the shocked and grieving brother, mindless with his need to bury his grief in action. By the time the sun rose in the morning, it was clear that the Red Death had accepted him as their new leader. He had organized the digging effort so that they were now as efficient as it was possible to be when they were digging by hand, and had ordered some of his enforcers to help Nadia with other relief efforts.

There were a lot of wounded, and there was, of course, no medical aid available. With the help of the enforcers, Nadia cleared out the ground floor of several of the nearby towers. There was some grumbling by the owners of those apartments—but that was why Shrimp had sent the enforcers with her. She then had the most severely wounded—including Agnes—carried into those apartments, where fellow gang members did the best they could to tend the wounds. Mostly, this consisted of trying to clean them up and wrapping some bandages, but there were a few people who had experience sewing homemade stitches who went around closing up what they could.

Nadia knew the biggest danger was probably infection, especially when they were doing such an imperfect job of cleaning out the wounds, but it was the best they could do. Thanks to the black market, the Red Death had drugs stockpiled, and most of their supply had survived the bombing. Unfortunately, Nadia could find no one who had any medical expertise. Although she had access to boxes and boxes of drugs, the only ones anyone could positively identify were painkillers that were often sold for recreational use. She could be sitting on a mountain of badly needed antibiotics, and yet she didn't dare administer unknown drugs to the wounded. At least she could hand out painkillers.

When she was too tired to move anymore, Nadia plopped down onto the floor beside Agnes in the makeshift hospital. Someone had stitched up the wound on her head, shaving away a patch of her hair in the process. The cut was several inches long, but Nadia was more worried about whatever damage had been done to the inside of her head. The poor girl was so sick to her stomach she couldn't even keep water down, and she was too dizzy to sit up on her own. And then there was the wound at her ribs, which didn't look as serious, but which wasn't being helped by Agnes's constant need to heave. Seeing her like that and being unable to help was a form of torture.

Nadia managed a couple of hours of fitful sleep before she couldn't bear to sit still anymore. She woke Agnes, just to make sure the girl hadn't lapsed into a coma, then headed back outside.

It was her first time seeing the aftermath in broad daylight, and it was more horrible than she could have imagined. Shrimp still had people digging, but all they had found so far had been bodies and body parts, which were being laid out on the sidewalk, out of the way. Someone had thrown a tarp over them, but Nadia could see fingers and toes and hair peeking out from beneath. And there was blood everywhere.

She found Shrimp giving instructions to a squad of armed enforcers, who scattered when she approached.

"What was that all about?" she asked.

Shrimp's face was a dull gray color, and it wasn't just from the coating of dust. She doubted he'd slept at all, and he had to be exhausted. His hands were all scraped up from his own digging efforts, and she worried he was on the verge of collapse.

"Need to patrol our borders," Shrimp answered.

Nadia's mouth dropped open in outrage at the thought that he would be worried about territorial squabbles at a time like this, but he hastened to clarify.

"Just to make sure none of the bordering gangs decide this is a good time to stage a land grab. Last thing we need is a turf war, and if they see we're defended, they'll leave us alone."

Nadia nodded her acceptance. "Sorry. I shouldn't have jumped to conclusions."

"It's okay."

She turned her attention to the grim rescue efforts. "Have they found anyone alive?"

Shrimp pressed his lips together and shook his head. "Doubt they will, either, but it makes us all feel better to at least try." He brushed in vain at some of the dust and filth that clung to his clothes. "I shoulda made up my mind to help sooner," he said. "Maybe if we'd tried the tunnels a day earlier . . ."

"It's not your fault," Nadia said. "If you want to blame someone other than Dorothy for what happened, blame Maiden. If he'd agreed to help us in the first place, none of this would have happened."

It wasn't the most sensitive thing to say, not when they were standing amid the rubble that had once been the red tower. Ordinarily, Nadia thought carefully before she spoke, but today she was too tired—and too angry—to bother.

Shrimp's hands clenched into fists, and he grimaced as if he'd just been punched in the gut. Nadia regretted her harsh words, but knew taking them back wouldn't help. It was the thought behind the words that hurt, not the words themselves.

"They found Maiden a few hours ago," Shrimp said, and Nadia's heart broke for him just a little. "I always said the bastard was too mean to die. Guess I was wrong."

"I'm so sorry," Nadia said, and she meant it. Not that she was sorry Maiden was dead, per se. But she was sorry his death caused Shrimp pain, and sorry her own words had made it worse.

"That bitch Dorothy has made it personal now," he growled, and for just a moment, his expression was forbidding enough to remind Nadia of his brother. "I sent a coupla scouts out to the free territories—at least what's left of 'em. If Angel and her crew are still alive, Red Death is joining up, and we're gonna put a hurt on the fuckers who did this."

Nadia shook her head. "We already decided forming a

people's army wasn't going to be enough to stop Dorothy. That's why—"

"I don't give a shit!" Shrimp no longer looked like the amiable, easygoing guy who had puttered around the kitchen with Agnes. "I wanna make them pay!"

Anger, *fury,* radiated from him in palpable waves, and Nadia was sure the bombings had aroused similar feelings in survivors throughout the Basement—at least in those who weren't too terrified to think. Out of anger like this had atrocities been committed, and Nadia hoped Shrimp and the rest of the Red Death didn't suddenly remember she and Nate and Agnes were Executives and turn on them.

Not that she thought Shrimp would hurt Agnes, but this kind of anger had a way of boiling over and raging past anyone's command.

"Then make them pay by taking Dorothy down," she said, trying to keep her voice reasonable and soothing. "Our plan last night was a good one, and we didn't get to finish. Let's go back and see if we can get that signal."

Shrimp's Adam's apple bobbed, and he was shaking with his fury and grief. "I don't wanna make a fucking phone call. I wanna kill every motherfucking Exec who's eating caviar and sleeping soundly between silk sheets because they don't give a shit what happens to the rest of us."

"*I'm* an Exec. So is Nate. So is Agnes. There are good people out there who are being lied to, who are being shown faked footage of Basement-dwellers acting like savages because that's how Dorothy can get what she wants. Your problem isn't with Execs in general: it's with Dorothy. So let's take care of the problem instead of getting more people killed for nothing!"

Nadia wouldn't have blamed him if he'd refused to listen to her. She was all too familiar with the helpless anger he was feeling right now, with the desperate need to lash out.

"Look," she said as gently as possible, "Dorothy had my sister killed. She killed Nate's father right in front of our eyes. We both know exactly how you feel. But the best revenge isn't to die heroically. It's to *win*."

His shoulders loosened and the fire in his eyes cooled. The rage was still there, but it had been joined by reason. "I know you're right. And if the bombing didn't completely destroy the tunnels, we should go back out tonight as soon as it's too dark to keep digging. But if some of my people want to run off and join Angel, I ain't gonna stop 'em. And if we can't get through the tunnels or get a signal, then all bets are off."

"Fair enough," Nadia agreed.

If they couldn't get through the tunnels and put a call through to Chairman Belinski, then she didn't imagine they'd have anything better to do than join up with whoever was left and storm the barricades in an ultimately pointless show of resistance.

"YOU have to take me with you," Agnes insisted when Nadia and Shrimp told her they were going back into the tunnels.

"Honey, you're in no shape to be scrambling through tunnels," Nadia reminded her. Agnes's face was starkly pale, her eyes sunken.

"Then someone will have to carry me," she replied stubbornly. "As far as the outside world knows, you and Nate kidnapped me and murdered Chairman Hayes. You're not going to be able to convince my father or anyone else you're the good guys unless I'm there to verify it. We don't know how long the phones will last, so we need to be as quick and convincing as possible."

"No way, Agnes," Shrimp said, giving her the look of command he'd been giving the Red Death all day, the look that had even the toughest of them scurrying to obey. It wasn't that he looked particularly scary—just very much in charge. "We're not dragging a girl with a head injury into those tunnels. You could get brain damaged or something. Maybe even die."

Agnes was undaunted. "If we don't do this, I'm probably going to die anyway, as are all the rest of you. You think Dorothy's going to stop now? Think she's going to assume we're all dead so it's safe to let up on the Basement?"

Shrimp glared, but he'd already acknowledged the likelihood of more bombing.

Agnes pressed her point. "And where do you think I'll be safer? Out here in one of these buildings, or underground in the tunnels?"

Shrimp sat back on his heels and cursed under his breath. "Didn't think of that."

Nadia hadn't, either. The tunnels weren't exactly what she'd call safe, and she wasn't sure they'd hold up if a bomb burst directly above them. But when there were bombs being dropped, being underground sounded like a damn good idea.

"We should try to get as many people underground by nightfall as we can," she said, and Shrimp agreed.

"And hope she waits till night to start bombing again," he muttered.

"So it's settled," Agnes said. "You're taking me with you."

That Shrimp still didn't like it was etched into the lines of his face, but he grudgingly agreed.

shrimp called off the efforts to dig through the rubble, deeming that protecting the survivors they had was more important than spending the whole day hoping for a miracle. He directed his people to dig out the tunnel opening instead, creating a pathway so that people could walk in instead of having to drop down through the hole and scramble down an unstable slope.

When the entrance was relatively clear, Shrimp sent the men onward to try to clear the wreckage where the bats had been and to see if there was a way to get through the station. Meanwhile, Nadia organized the effort to transfer the wounded into the tunnel, using makeshift stretchers when necessary.

There wasn't a whole lot of room inside the narrow tunnels, but the good news was that the tunnels stretched for miles. One of Shrimp's digging teams reported that they had cleared the partial cave-in and that the hole in the wall gave them access to another set of tracks—and therefore more room.

In the afternoon, Nate was taking a break from the tunnels when he saw a helicopter in the distance. It was too far away to make out any words, but he could hear the sound of a loudspeaker. The helicopter was moving slowly, making a careful sweep over the Basement. Nate assumed the message was something to the effect of "be good little children and we'll stop beating the crap out of you." And it received exactly the kind of reception Nate would have expected.

For the first time since he'd gone into the tunnels last

night, he heard the distant sound of gunfire. The helicopter hastily gained altitude in an effort to get out of range, but that didn't discourage whoever was shooting. The helicopter got the message and turned around, moving considerably faster now, its loudspeaker silent.

From this distance, Nate wasn't sure how far away the Basement's border was, but he thought the helicopter was back into the Employee neighborhood on the border when there was a boom loud enough to rival the bombs. A trail of smoke rose into the sky, and something slammed into the fleeing helicopter. Another deafening boom, and the helicopter burst into flames, burning shrapnel falling from the sky, quickly followed by the helicopter itself.

Nate gaped in horror and hoped the burning helicopter wouldn't kill any innocent bystanders when it hit the ground.

"Told ya some of the other gangs are well armed," Shrimp said with a savage grin. Nate hadn't even realized the guy was beside him.

"Yeah," Nate agreed, "and in case Dorothy needed any more evidence that another bombing is justified, they just gave it to her." Which was probably why she'd ordered the helicopter to fly over the Basement with its message in the first place. Nate wondered if the pilot or crew had had any clue they were being sent on a suicide mission.

Shrimp's grin faded, but then he shrugged. "At least it buys us some time. She won't send her bombers in the daylight if she doesn't wanna lose some of them."

CHAPTER SEVENTEEN

It was getting perilously close to nightfall before they were ready to set out once again. Nadia found herself watching the sky anxiously, even though she knew Dorothy wouldn't send the bombers until it was dark.

It was tempting to just rush off into the darkness in search of help, but they had to see to the safety of the people of the Red Death first, get as many as possible into the safety of the tunnels. Shrimp had his enforcers doing door-to-door sweeps trying to make sure the towers were all empty, while Nate and Nadia organized the children, setting them to making sure everyone had food, blankets, and water. Nadia might have expected the kids to be terrified, but life in the streets of the Basement had hardened them, and they had been trained since birth to be good little soldiers.

Finally, they were ready to head out. Shrimp had spared a few men to check out the collapsed station, and the men reported that there was an opening in the wreckage that would allow them to pass through. How far they would get afterward was a big unknown.

Shrimp commanded a dozen of his people to make the trek with them, to help carry Agnes, to dig out if and when necessary, to act as scouts if the tunnel branched—and to protect their expedition, if it turned out the bombing had given other Basement-dwellers access to the tunnels. They were also better equipped than they had been the night before, Shrimp's men bringing shovels, pickaxes, and crowbars in case they were needed.

It was as dark and oppressive as ever in the tunnels, and even more stinky, since no one had had a chance to bathe after the day's exertions. Nadia was seriously worried about Agnes, who seemed to look paler and more wan as every hour ticked by. Worse, she seemed to be developing a fever, and Nadia didn't need a medical degree to know that was a bad sign.

There were piles of debris along the way, places where the shovels and crowbars came in handy, but once they got past the ruined station, the tunnels were relatively clear. After a tense and grueling trek, they came upon another station. This one had fared better than the last, and with a little scrambling—difficult when they were trying to be so careful with Agnes—they got through it.

It was when they reached the third abandoned station that things got tricky. It looked like the place might have taken a direct hit and collapsed in upon itself. There was no way to walk through it, but there were some small openings here and there. Shrimp sent his men to crawl into each one they could find and see if there was a way out on the other side.

And that was when the night's bombing started.

"Back into the tunnel!" Shrimp commanded, and everyone obeyed without thinking until they were out of the station's crumbling interior and in the relative safety of the tunnel. Everyone except the men who were looking for a way through, that is.

"Shouldn't we be helping them?" Agnes asked, though she wasn't in any shape to help anyone. "Or getting them out of there?"

Shrimp shook his head. "We don't have time to play it safe. If we wait till the bombing stops, it could be too late."

Nadia sidled over to Dante, slipping her hand into his, her heart racing as the floor beneath them shook. They were most likely under the free territories right now, where the bombing had been heaviest last night and probably would be again tonight. They could all die down here, buried in a pile of rubble, their bodies never to be found.

Dante squeezed her hand, and in the faint glow of the flashlights, she could see the look of grim determination on his face. He was scared—they all were—but he wasn't going to back down. And, more important, he wasn't going to go all guy-like and try to make her and Agnes stay in the tunnels where it was "safe."

A bomb hit somewhere too close for comfort, and the tunnel shook. A fine rain of dust and pebbles fell from the ceiling, and the rubble in the station gave a disquieting moan. One of Shrimp's men climbed out of the space he'd found, shaking his head.

"No way through," he declared before joining the rest of them in the tunnel.

They stood aside, breathless with nerves, waiting for Shrimp's other scouts to emerge. Nadia tried not to imagine what it was like crawling through the unstable rubble while the earth shook. The Red Death were ruthless gangsters, had cheered while people were put to death before their eyes, and yet in this moment they were showing themselves to be capable of bravery and heroism. She would see it as the triumph of the human spirit if she weren't so busy worrying that the roof was going to collapse.

Another scout emerged from the rubble without finding a way through, and Nadia prayed they weren't at a dead end. It might be possible to dig a passageway through to the other side with their shovels and pickaxes, but not only would the effort be risky in the extreme, it would take forever, and they didn't have that kind of time.

The bombs were exploding on a regular basis now, the ground continually vibrating under their feet. The rubble shifted ominously, and a small landslide began just as another bomb hit at what sounded like only a few yards away. Everyone ducked instinctively, but the ceiling held, and the landslide didn't seem to make much of a difference to the pile of rubble.

Shortly afterward, the third scout crawled back through the opening he'd explored, grinning and flashing a thumbs-up. He was filthy, and sporting tears in both his clothing and his skin, but he'd made it.

"Can we get Agnes through?" Shrimp asked when the scout rejoined them.

The scout shook his head. "Not on a stretcher."

"I can crawl if I have to," Agnes said. "You guys'll help me."

Shrimp put on his stubborn face. "You're not crawling with a fever and a head injury."

Nadia almost smiled as Agnes mirrored the stubborn face. "I'll do whatever it takes. I'm the only one my father will listen to, and that means we have to get me through there."

No one liked the idea—least of all, Shrimp—but it was hard to argue her point. The success or failure of this mission all depended on her. Nate, who had at one time treated

Agnes with contempt and casual cruelty, looked at her with something like awe.

"I think you've earned your street name," he told her. "I hereby dub thee 'Lionheart.'"

"Lionheart," Shrimp repeated, nodding. "I like it."

It was hard to tell in the patchy light of the flashlights, but Nadia was sure Agnes was blushing furiously, unused to praise.

"Great," Dante grumbled. "You get 'Lionheart,' and I get 'Captain Studly.' There is no justice in the universe."

There was no lifting the tension as they huddled in the dark tunnel with bombs bursting overhead, but Dante's quip did at least inspire a few smiles.

"Carry me over there, and we'll get going," Agnes said.

It was Shrimp, of course, who picked her up, and they all made their way over to the gap in the rubble that would eventually lead through to the other side. One of the men went over to the last remaining opening, shouting into it to let the scout know he could turn back.

There was no answer, and when they shone their flashlights into the opening, they could see that it was an opening no longer, the rubble having shifted about two or three body lengths in.

"Should I stay and try to dig him out?" one of Shrimp's men asked.

Shrimp frowned, then shook his head when the constant vibration of the bombs created another rain of pebbles and dust.

"Too dangerous," Shrimp said.

"We can't just leave him!" Agnes protested.

"I ain't risking more men if I don't know he's alive."

He yelled into the opening one more time, and they all listened intently for an answering voice, but there was nothing.

"Let's get moving before this whole place comes down on our heads."

nate wasn't sure how long it took to crawl through that opening in the wreckage, but it seemed like at least a week. And if it seemed like a week to him, it must have felt like a year to Agnes.

Nate wanted to go back in time and take back every unkind word he had ever said about the girl. She was dizzy, disoriented, feverish, and weak, and yet she refused to quit, even though she had to take a break to puke a couple of times. Taking rest breaks when you were in the middle of a pile of shifting rubble that could crush you at any moment was about as unnerving an experience as he had ever had.

The bombing continued throughout the long crawl, although it seemed to be concentrated farther away, at least for the time being. Perhaps the entirety of the free territories had been bombed into rubble by now and Dorothy was starting on the gang territories.

Toward the end, Agnes got so disoriented she couldn't remember what she was doing or where she was going. Shrimp, who was in front of her, and Nate, who was behind, had to push, pull, and drag to keep her moving forward. He prayed that all the jostling and bumping wouldn't cause her condition to deteriorate any more than it already had. He was afraid they might be killing her, but he also knew she would want them to do anything and everything possible to get her through.

Eventually, they popped through to the other side of the rubble and were able to make their way into the continuation of the train tunnel. Agnes lost consciousness almost immediately, but they kept going, Shrimp cradling her tenderly against his shoulder.

The bombing grew more and more distant, and soon they were in a stretch of tunnel that didn't look like it had seen any damage at all. There were a lot more rats in this section—they seemed to have realized this was the safest place to be during the bombing—but they squeaked and scattered whenever someone shone a light on them, and Nate much preferred them to the bombs.

According to the old subway map Dante had seen in the first station, they were probably now traveling under the Harlem River, which meant they were officially out of the Basement, into one of the fringe neighborhoods that were close enough to the Basement to be considered undesirable. Unfortunately, being under the river also meant that there was no way they could pick up a phone signal, so they had to press forward.

It was too much to ask that the tunnel from the Basement could simply merge with the active tunnels and give them an easy way to get close enough to the surface to get a phone signal. Nate couldn't say he was surprised when they came upon a solid brick wall sealing off the tunnel, but it made his heart sink just that much lower. Agnes needed medical attention *now,* and she wasn't going to get it.

Shrimp laid Agnes on the ground, using some of the scant supply of water they'd brought with them to clean some of the grime from her face. Her eyelashes fluttered, but she didn't wake up. Meanwhile, his men started to work on the wall, taking turns with the pickaxes. Nate powered up one of the phones they'd brought with them on the off chance it would get a signal, but of course it didn't. They were just going to have to wait for the brick to give way.

Everyone was exhausted. They'd gotten little to no sleep in the last forty-eight hours, and they'd all spent a lot of time doing hard physical labor—and that was before the difficult and nerve-racking scramble through the debris. Swinging pickaxes under the circumstances was far from easy, and Nate was glad Shrimp had had the foresight to bring enough men that they could work in shifts. Despite feeling like he had jelly in his limbs, Nate offered to take a turn, but Shrimp turned him down.

"No offense, but it'll go faster without you."

The old Nate would probably have been insulted enough to make an issue of it, his pride stung. But though he didn't like admitting it, he knew Shrimp was right. He wasn't accustomed to manual labor, and though he didn't think he was particularly weak, he wasn't particularly strong, either. Several of Shrimp's men—and Dante—definitely *were* strong, and they made steady progress on the wall, hacking away at the brick while everyone else stayed out of reach of the flying chips.

By the time there was a hole in the wall big enough for everyone to get through, Nate couldn't hear any more bombs going off. He didn't know if that meant the bombing had stopped, or if it had now moved far enough away for the sound not to carry through all the earth and water above.

Once again, Shrimp picked Agnes up, and they continued down the long, abandoned tunnel. After walking what felt like about five more miles, they found their way blocked once more, this time by a metal fence with a padlocked door. The tunnel they'd been following had begun a gradual curve a little while back, and when Nate shone his flashlight into the darkness beyond the fence, his heart gave a leap of hope.

"More tracks!" he said excitedly.

The rusty, disused rails that they'd been following through the abandoned tunnels merged just a little way ahead with another set of rails—ones that weren't rusted.

All flashlight beams focused on the new set of tracks. They weren't exactly shiny and new, and the spaces between them were as damp and nasty as the rest of the tracks they'd been following. But why would there be a fence here unless this was the border between the used and the unused tunnels?

Nate tried a cell phone again while Dante grabbed one of the pickaxes and started hacking at the padlock. For a brief moment, Nate picked up a feeble phone signal, but it quickly winked out. They were outside of Dorothy's phone blockade, but still too far underground to get a reliable signal.

The padlock broke, and the door in the fence creaked open. Everyone took a hurried step forward, seeing the proverbial light at the end of the tunnel, but Dante blocked the way and raised the hand not holding the pickax.

"Wait up," he said. "If those are real, live tracks up there, then we've got to be careful."

Nate had gotten a glance at the time when he'd checked for a phone signal. "It's three A.M. Subways don't run at this hour, do they?" Not that he was any kind of an expert on public transportation.

"Not in this neighborhood they don't," Dante said with a scowl. "This near the Basement, it's all unskilled laborers.

You know, no one Paxco thinks it's worth providing twenty-four-hour service for. But that's not what I'm worried about. Any of you guys know what the third rail is?" They all exchanged baffled glances, and Dante shone his flashlight on the tracks beneath their feet. "These two rails are harmless," he said, his beam moving back and forth between the rails on each side of the ties. "This one isn't." His flashlight illuminated a third rail, one Nate had never particularly noticed except for when it got in the way of his footing.

"In the live tunnels," Dante continued, "there will be one hell of an electric charge running through the third rail. One touch could kill you, so make sure you don't step on it."

Nate glared at him. "You didn't think to mention that when we first came down here? I've probably stepped on that damned rail a million times already!"

Dante rolled his eyes. "Like Paxco's going to waste the money to run electricity through the rails it's not using."

"It still would have been nice to know." Nate sounded sullen to his own ears, but he didn't like that Dante had made a blithe assumption that could have gotten any one of them killed. However, he seemed to be the only one getting pissed off, and both Kurt and Nadia gave him reproachful looks. He couldn't honestly say he felt jealous of Dante anymore, but that didn't mean he'd grown to like the guy.

"Well, we know now," Kurt said soothingly. "So let's all be real careful and keep moving. We do *not* want to be in these tunnels when the trains start running."

And so they walked on, now in single file, as far away from the third rail as they could get. Nate was sure he wasn't the only one placing his feet with exaggerated care, trying to avoid all chances of tripping.

It didn't take long before they started seeing signs that these tunnels were still in use—mostly in the form of litter scattered along the tracks, no doubt dragged there from the platforms by the trains. There might have been ancient litter in the disused tunnels, but if so, it had decomposed into unrecognizable gunk.

Luckily, it turned out they didn't have that far to travel before they literally saw a light at the end of the tunnel. Light that was no doubt coming from a station—which would have access to the surface, where they ought to be able to get a phone signal.

CHAPTER EIGHTEEN

The station was dimly lit, many banks of fluorescent bulbs turned off for the night. There were multiple platforms, and in the dim light Nadia could see ad posters plastered to the wall as well as darkened video screens. There was a little litter around the tracks, but the platform was spotless and the air about a hundred times fresher than in the tunnels.

"Everyone wait here," Dante said, when they all went to rush the platforms. "We don't want to go parading in front of security cameras and announcing to the world that we're here."

"Security cameras," Shrimp said, then cursed.

"Don't worry," Dante said, pulling out his gun. "There are always blind spots. And I have a good feel for where the cameras might be. I'll take care of them."

"Not with that you won't," Shrimp said, nodding at the gun. "Firing a nine mil in an enclosed space ain't exactly sneaky." He gestured at his men, who huddled together and then produced a small silver gun and a silencer, which they handed over. Shrimp screwed the silencer onto the end of the gun and presented it to Dante.

Dante looked at the gun—and at Shrimp—with genuine respect. "Nice," he said. "Guess I shouldn't be surprised you came prepared. It'll be a lot quieter than the nine, but still . . . Maybe this isn't the best idea after all. I wasn't thinking about the noise."

Shrimp shrugged. "We either walk in front of the cameras or we shoot 'em out. Which one draws less attention?"

"They're both risky," Dante admitted. "But I think we're better off not having our faces caught on camera."

Shrimp agreed, and Dante boosted himself up onto the platform. "Be ready to react if security comes running. And don't shoot unless you have to. Anyone patrolling the station is just doing his job. Okay?"

Shrimp nodded, but Nadia didn't think any security officer who stumbled upon them would stand much of a chance. She remembered the fanatical gleam that had come into Shrimp's eyes earlier and knew he was poised for violence.

A few seconds later, Nadia jumped at a loud bang, about like the sound a hardback book would make if you dropped it on the platform. She held her breath and crossed her fingers, noticing that Shrimp and all of his men now had guns in their hands. They couldn't afford to get into a shootout, and she prayed that no one was patrolling the station.

There were no shouts, and no sound of pounding footsteps, but no one relaxed as Dante took out the rest of the security cameras one by one before coming back and giving them the all clear. Getting Agnes up onto the platform was a delicate affair, but they managed it.

The phone signal was present but iffy on the platform, and so with Shrimp's gunmen leading the way, they headed for a set of stairs at the far end. Nadia wondered if they could just keep climbing until they reached the surface, fantasizing about what it would be like to walk through the streets of the respectable Employee section of the city above them. Would it look different to her now that she'd spent several weeks living in the squalor of the Basement?

Sounds of a sudden scuffle and a cry of alarm from above broke Nadia out of her brief moment of reverie. Everyone except Shrimp, who was still carrying Agnes, though his arms must have been about to fall off from fatigue, hurried to climb to the landing above.

Nadia skidded to a halt when she saw one of Shrimp's men riding a uniformed security officer to the floor, his forearm lodged firmly against the officer's throat, cutting off all sound. The officer struggled, trying to get to his sidearm, but the enforcer probably outweighed him by a good fifty pounds. Nadia put both hands over her mouth to stifle a scream when one of Shrimp's other men knelt on the floor beside the struggling pair and drove a long, sharp knife into the officer's ribs.

The man's eyes went wide, and his mouth gaped open in a silent scream, still pinned under the enforcer's weight. His struggles weakened as blood poured from the wound.

Nadia's eyes burned, and she found she wasn't as numb as she'd thought. The security officer had done nothing to deserve this, had just been doing his usually dull-as-dirt job of patrolling the closed station. And he was dying, even as Nadia looked on—and made no protest, despite her tumultuous feelings.

Dorothy had turned this into a war the moment she'd let loose that first bomb, and innocent Basement-dwellers, including children, had already died by the thousands. Nadia and her companions were trying to prevent many more thousands of deaths, and if one unlucky security officer had to die to protect their mission, then that was just the way of the world. It didn't mean she had to like it, though.

The security officer's eyes slowly glazed over, his struggles slowing even more and then stopping completely. The enforcer kept up his stranglehold a little longer, just to be safe, while his partner in crime wiped the blade of his knife on the officer's shirt and then hit a button that retracted the blade with a metallic snick. He locked gazes with Nadia, silently challenging her to condemn him for committing cold-blooded murder in front of her. Seeing as he was an adult male member of the Red Death, this probably wasn't the first murder he'd committed, and it was certainly for the most noble cause. That didn't make it sit easy on Nadia's conscience, and she was the first to look away.

Dante had come up beside her, and he gripped her hand. His jaw stood out in stark relief against his cheeks as he clenched his teeth, and his hand was squeezing tight enough to be uncomfortable. Nadia leaned her head against his shoulder, not because she was in need of comfort but because she suspected *he* was. As sad a commentary as it might be for a girl who was raised as a top Executive, she was becoming eerily familiar with murder and death, and though it upset her, it was hardly the kind of shock that would unravel her. She glanced over at Nate, who was holding hands with Bishop and had a look on his face that she suspected was very like the one on her own.

With the brief struggle obviously over, Shrimp climbed the final few steps, angling his body so that Agnes couldn't see the dead officer.

"Hide the body," he ordered his men. "Don't leave any traces. We don't know if he's the only one."

There was a line of vending machines against one of the walls, and Shrimp carried Agnes to the far side of those machines, gently putting her down with her back against the wall—where the machines would block her view of the enforcers picking up the body and cleaning up the blood.

"Are you getting a signal yet?" Nadia asked Nate, who was holding one of the phones in his hand. There was one more flight of stairs between them and what Nadia presumed was the street level, but it would be better if they could make the call where there was no chance of someone on the street hearing voices in a closed subway station.

"Yeah," Nate said, then blew out a bracing breath. "I guess it's time." He crouched in front of Agnes, who was nestled against Shrimp's side, her eyes half-closed. "Agnes?" he asked in an overly gentle tone.

"Lionheart," Shrimp corrected, and that made Agnes smile and open her eyes.

Agnes's eyes looked disturbingly glassy, and there was a sheen of sweat on her skin although it wasn't hot in the station. Nadia crouched on Agnes's other side and touched the girl's forehead, not surprised to find that she was burning with fever.

Agnes licked her lips and tried to sit up straighter, lifting her hand and gesturing feebly. "Phone," she said, and Nate handed over the one that had the most charge.

Shrimp frowned at the phone and called out to one of his men. "Bring us the guard's phone," he commanded, and Nadia wanted to smack herself on the forehead for not thinking of it first. She doubted any of the dying phones in their collection would last more than a couple of minutes, and it was going to take more than that to convey their message to Chairman Belinski.

Agnes took a shuddering breath, then laid the back of her head against the tile wall. "We'll have to use video to prove it's me," she said, reaching out to pat Shrimp's leg. "You shouldn't be in the picture."

Agnes closed her eyes, so she didn't see the way Shrimp recoiled at her words. Nadia suspected he'd allowed himself to forget that she was an Executive, and though Chairman Belinski would no doubt be grateful to Shrimp for taking such good care of his daughter, he would probably have a stroke at the thought that she was cozying up to a Basement-dweller.

"If you think that's best," Shrimp said stiffly, but though he was obviously hurt, Nadia noticed how gently he extracted his arm from behind Agnes and moved away, careful not to jar her head or let her slump over. In some ways, he was more of a gentleman than many of the Executive men Nadia had met, and he was certainly a better person at heart. However, even though she had never met Chairman Belinski, Nadia doubted he'd be able to see beyond Shrimp's status and upbringing, doubted he would even think to try.

When Agnes had the dead security officer's phone in her hands, Nate and Nadia sat on each side of her, huddling close both so that they could all be in the picture and also so that they could keep her upright.

Moving slowly and with exaggerated care because of her dizziness, Agnes pecked out a number on the phone.

"Calling Dad's bodyguard," she said. "Less likely Thea will be paying attention to his phone."

Nadia met Nate's eyes, and they shook their heads

simultaneously. Agnes was sick and suffering from a head wound, and she still had the presence of mind to realize her call with her father might be intercepted. Neither of them had even considered the possibility, too focused on the seemingly impossible task of making the phone call in the first place. They were all lucky Agnes was with them, though Nadia doubted Agnes felt quite so lucky herself.

Agnes held the phone away from herself so that they could all see its screen—and so that they could all appear in its picture. At Shrimp's command, the Red Death shone their flashlights on them to make an impromptu spotlight. The brightness made Agnes wince in pain, but she didn't protest.

A man answered the phone after three rings, not bothering with video though the phone would have indicated video was being used.

"Who is this?" the man barked in a sleep-roughened voice. Nadia had almost forgotten what time it was and that most of respectable society would be asleep at this hour.

"Marco," Agnes said, her voice sounding worse than the bodyguard's. "It's me, Agnes. I need to talk to Daddy right now. Hurry!"

"Agnes?" Marco said, suddenly sounding much more awake—and very suspicious. He turned on the video feed and Nadia saw a square-jawed bruiser with a military buzz cut and sharply intelligent eyes. Eyes that widened almost comically when he took in the image his phone was presenting.

Nadia hated to think about what the three of them looked like, dressed in ill-fitting castoffs with dirt ground into their skin and hair and clothes. Nate's face was getting bristly with stubble, his filthy hair hanging in his eyes. Nadia's face bore a bloody scratch from the debris that had struck her last night, and her blond hair formed greasy, dirt-grayed locks around her face. And poor Agnes, missing a big swath of hair where someone had inexpertly stitched her skin closed with black thread. The flashlights illuminated the wound in their relentless glare, and Nadia saw how its edges were puffy and red.

"Please, Marco," Agnes said. "Get Daddy."

"Where are you?" Marco demanded, but Nadia could tell by the unsteadiness of the picture and the way his attention was divided that he was on the move.

Agnes's eyes glazed over then closed, her body listing sideways as her head landed on Nate's shoulder. Nadia grabbed the phone from her limp hand before it clattered to the floor.

"Agnes!" Marco cried in alarm, the picture on his end stabilizing as he came to a stop.

"Keep moving and get her father!" Nate snapped at the man. "She goes in and out. We'll wake her when she needs to talk."

Despite current circumstances, Nate had lived most of his life as the Chairman Heir and was used to being obeyed. The command in his voice was enough to get Marco moving again, and moments later, he was pounding on a door and yelling "Mr. Chairman!" over and over again.

Nadia had never personally met Chairman Belinski, but as a dutiful Executive, she knew the names and faces of all the top Executives throughout the Corporate States, so she recognized him when he took the phone from Marco's hand. He had obviously been roused from sleep, his gray hair disheveled, his face peppered with stubble, but there was no hint of sleep in his furious gaze or his sharp voice.

"What have you done to my daughter?" he demanded, dismissing Nadia with one quick glance and then glaring at Nate, the man who had supposedly kidnapped Agnes.

"She was injured when Dorothy bombed the Basement last night," Nate replied, his voice calm and steady. "I swear to you I did not kidnap her. There's a lot going on you don't know about, but Agnes needs medical attention immediately. I think her wound's infected."

In the background, Nadia could hear yelling and slamming doors. Marco was obviously rousing the household.

"Please be careful, Mr. Chairman," she warned. "Dorothy has eyes and ears everywhere, and none of us will survive for long if she finds out where we are."

Chairman Belinski frowned at her. "And who are you?"

No doubt he would recognize her if she were dressed in her Executive best and cleaned up. "I'm Nadia Lake. Dorothy wants all three of us dead because we know too much. It's absolutely critical that she not know we've gotten out of the Basement."

"Where are you?"

Agnes roused at that moment, and Nadia wondered how long she'd been conscious. "Don't answer yet," she murmured, and her father looked horrified.

"Agnes?"

She raised her head, the movement painfully slow. "Should be the last thing we say, when you're ready to come get us. In case she's listening. Tell your men to stay off the phones."

Belinski looked doubtful, but he shouted a few orders

over his shoulder anyway. The sounds of activity were louder now as the Belinski household prepared for what was at this moment at least a very nebulous rescue mission.

Agnes let out a soft sigh. "Too tired to explain," she said, and sagged again.

Belinski's face was etched in grim, worried lines. "Agnes? Sweetheart?"

Agnes was out, and neither Nate nor Nadia had the heart to try to revive her.

"Let her rest," Nate said. "We can answer whatever questions you have, and she can confirm what we're saying later. But seriously, she needs a doctor as fast as possible. And we need to get out of here without Dorothy knowing about it."

Which could pose something of a problem if Chairman Belinski sent his security team in force to come pick them up. It was probably quiet on the streets above at this time of night, but *probably* wasn't good enough. If anyone saw them and took enough notice to remark on it, there was a chance Dorothy would hear about it.

Belinski thought about it a moment. "If I send a car, can you get to it without being seen?"

"It depends on whether there are people out on the street or not," Nate replied. It was not the hour of night when you'd expect to find a lot of people on the street, but they *were* in Manhattan, and it was unlikely the streets would be completely deserted. "And we'd probably be caught on a surveillance camera somewhere."

"As would the car you sent for us," Nadia said. "I suspect it would stand out in this neighborhood—and that Dorothy has you under surveillance in case Agnes reached out to you."

Belinski waved off her concern. "I'm well aware that I'm

being watched. My security team can get around the surveillance if necessary. The car will be inconspicuous, and my men will disable any cameras in the area."

Nadia had been so fixated on the phone that she hadn't noticed Shrimp standing nearby, leaning on one of the vending machines and listening to the conversation. Until he spoke.

"That'll be suspicious all by itself," he said. "We already knocked out a bunch of cameras in here. Eventually, someone's gonna notice and wonder what's up."

"Who's with you?" Belinski asked, eyes narrowing in suspicion.

"Some friends of ours from the Basement," Nate answered. "We wouldn't have made it this far without them."

"We hafta give security a good explanation for what happened to the cameras," Shrimp continued. "And it can't be something that makes 'em suspect our Execs are involved. It's gotta look like a bunch of angry Basement-dwellers making trouble instead of an escape."

"What did you have in mind?" Nate asked.

"Me and my boys go out ahead of you. Shoot out the cameras, break glass, make a lotta noise. Any innocent bystanders will run away, and no one'll pay attention to the rest of you calmly and quietly sneaking away. We'll make sure to keep all eyes on us."

Nadia swallowed hard. "They'll arrest you—if you're lucky."

He nodded. "Our life expectancy ain't so hot anyway, not if you don't stop Dorothy."

"Bring my daughter to me," Belinski said, "and I'll do what I can to help your friends."

Belinski was a powerful man, with a powerful military at his fingertips; however, he was deep in enemy territory, whether he knew it or not, and there was no way he'd be able to help the Red Death—especially not if Dorothy's orders to her security forces were to shoot them on sight. The chances were high that anyone who participated in creating the diversion was going to die, either immediately, or later in custody.

There was a long silence as they all looked at one another, but Nadia soon found that both Shrimp and Nate were looking at her expectantly. Waiting for *her* to make the final decision. How did it become her responsibility to decide the fate of all these people? She was in the presence of the leader of the Red Death and the rightful Chairman of Paxco, and yet it was her they both looked to.

Nate met her eyes gravely. "Sorry to put this on you, Honey Badger," he said with a faint smile that quickly faded. "But this is our battle, not Shrimp's, and we both know you make better decisions than I do."

"It's my battle, too," Shrimp protested, "or I wouldn't be volunteering. But it's still y'all's decision."

Nadia looked up at the man who had kept them all safe from Maiden and had done so much to aid their efforts. Words couldn't express how much she hated the idea of risking his life like this, but without the diversion, she didn't like their chances of successfully meeting up with Chairman Belinski.

"You take only volunteers," she told him. "I don't want anyone forced into this."

Shrimp grinned, showing his gold tooth. "Take a good look at me, Honey. Do I look like I can force these guys to do anything?"

She shrugged. "All right, let's say *pressure* instead of *force*."

"I picked these guys to come with us for a reason. I won't need to pressure 'em. Dorothy's killing our people; we'll do whatever we have to, to stop her."

Nadia's throat felt tight and her eyes burned with suppressed tears. She was almost glad Agnes was unconscious and didn't have to know what Shrimp was planning to do.

"Sounds to me like you've already decided," Chairman Belinski said. Somehow he managed to look both sympathetic and impatient at the same time. "Tell me where you are. My team is ready to come get you."

"We're at the 125th Street subway station," Nadia responded.

Belinski spoke to someone over his shoulder, then nodded and turned back to the phone. "The car will be there in fifteen minutes. They'll text this number when it's time to start the diversion."

Nadia was afraid she'd start crying if she spoke, so she merely nodded.

"Take good care of Agnes," Belinski continued. His Adam's apple bobbed as he swallowed hard. "She means the world to me."

Nadia nodded again, and Belinski hung up.

CHAPTER NINETEEN

fifteen minutes wasn't a whole lot of time to plan much of anything, but Nate was perfectly happy to accept the limitation. The longer they hung around this station, the closer it came to the time for the place to open, the more danger they were all in. And Agnes had not regained consciousness since the talk with her father, not even when Nate had tried to rouse her. At least she was breathing, but the faster she got medical attention, the better.

Shrimp talked things over with his men, all of whom volunteered to be part of the diversion. Nate looked at the Red Death with new eyes, wondering how a gang of murderers and cutthroats had turned into unlikely heroes.

"Seeing your people bombed into oblivion will do that to people," Kurt said, and Nate jumped, not having heard him approach.

"Was I talking out loud without noticing?" Nate asked, though he knew he had not been.

Kurt grinned at him. "Your face is an open book."

Nate grinned back, though the expression was forced. "You can't read, remember?" Nate had been teaching him, so he supposed that was no longer technically true, but it made Kurt smile anyway.

"Only because you're such a lame-ass teacher."

Kurt surprised him by pulling him into a hug, holding him tight. Nate had no desire to object, though they were both filthy and stinky, covered in who-knew-what.

"You know I'm not coming with you, right?" Kurt whispered into his ear.

Nate's arms tightened convulsively, as if he could keep Kurt by his side if only he held on tight enough. "You have to," he croaked, though a part of him had known all along this was going to happen.

Kurt rubbed his back soothingly. "I can do a hell of a lot more good in the Basement than I can do up there." Nate felt him jerk his chin toward the stairs leading to the surface. "That's your territory. The Basement is mine."

Nate shook his head. "I can't do this without you."

Kurt drew away, despite Nate's attempt to hold on to him, but he didn't go far, cupping Nate's face between his hands and peering into his eyes. "Yes, you can. You just don't want to."

"Kurt—"

"It's gotta be this way. We're the new resistance, remember? That means we've all gotta do our part." He dropped his hands from Nate's face and gestured toward the far end of the room, where Nadia and Dante were locked in a desperate-looking embrace. "Betcha they're having the same conversation. The Red Death are gonna need all hands on deck after another night of bombing. You know it's true."

Nate did. He hoped getting as many people into the subway tunnels as possible had saved a lot of lives, but there would have been significant casualties nonetheless. There would be people who were trapped, people who were injured. Kurt could save some lives—assuming he could even get back, of course. And there was no guarantee Belinski would be willing to shelter Kurt or Dante anyway.

Nate nodded and tried to look stoically accepting. He suspected his expression was closer to scared and miserable. "Don't you dare get yourself killed," he said, his voice going hoarse. "I will so kick your ass if you do."

"I'll do my best if you promise you'll do the same."

"I'm not the one going back into the war zone."

Kurt gave him a knowing look. "Yeah, like walking outta here and into Thea's domain is sooo much safer."

Nate had to admit, Kurt had a point.

The phone dinged with an incoming message—the signal that it was time to launch the diversion. Nate seized Kurt by the back of the neck, hauling him close and giving him a hard, desperate kiss, hoping against hope it was a see-you-later kiss rather than a good-bye kiss.

"That our cue?" Shrimp asked as soon as the kiss ended.

Nate dragged his eyes away from Kurt and faced Shrimp. "Yeah, that was it."

Shrimp gestured his men forward, and eight of them stepped up. "I'm sending the others back with Bishop and Captain Studly," he said, sounding ridiculously cheerful for someone who was about to turn himself into a target. "Can't leave my peeps back home completely in the dark."

The eight Red Death members who were part of the diversion were all armed, and Nate hoped they weren't going to kill any innocent bystanders while they wreaked havoc above. One of them kept coming forward when the others stopped. Shrimp started to turn with a puzzled look on his face, but he didn't get all the way around before the butt of a gun made contact with the back of his head and he went down like a rock.

"Hey!" Nate yelled in protest, though he wasn't in any position to stop eight armed men.

The guy who'd hit Shrimp stuck his gun in his waistband while those who were going back to the Basement stepped forward to pick Shrimp up.

"No point him getting killed over this," the guy said. "We don't need him. The rest of the Red Death does."

"You could have just said that," Nadia said with a glare.

"He wouldn't have let us go without him." He and the other seven men of the diversionary party started toward the stairs to the ground level. "Let's have some fun!" he shouted, then charged forward.

There were gunshots even before the men reached the top of the stairs. Nate hoped that was just Shrimp's men making noise to draw attention. He picked up Agnes, who didn't even stir at his touch, and he and Nadia waited at the base of the stairs for the sounds of the diversion to move away from the entrance. He looked over his shoulder to see Dante, Kurt, and the other Red Death members making their way back down to the platform, carrying Shrimp. Kurt met his eyes briefly, then blew him a kiss and disappeared into the darkness below.

nadia waited with Nate and an unconscious Agnes at the base of the stairs, working hard to shut down all emotions so she could concentrate on the task at hand. She didn't dare let herself think that she might never see Dante again. If she thought about that, she'd lose it completely, because having him had been the only bright spot in her life since the day the original Nate Hayes had died.

There was a loud metallic crash from above, and a section of what looked like fencing came clattering down the stairs. The Red Death yelled and whooped and shot, making so much noise people could probably hear them from a mile away. Glass shattered, and a car alarm started screaming.

"When these guys create a diversion," Nate quipped, "they go all out."

"Do you think the car is here yet?" she asked.

"Only one way to find out. Let's hope our friends don't get carried away and crush it before we get there."

Cautiously, they started up the stairs. The Red Death had destroyed the fence blocking the subway's entrance with a combination of gunfire and one of the well-used crowbars. When Nadia peeked around the railing on one side of the stairs, she saw three of them beating cars—the one wielding the pickax doing an impressive amount of damage. It looked like the other five had found a convenience store and had broken through its front window to loot it. Which, considering Dorothy had shut off food deliveries to the Basement before she'd started bombing, seemed like an excellent way to make their actions have a logical explanation.

Already, there was the sound of approaching sirens, and any civilians who'd been on the street had fled indoors to avoid the mob. In the distance, Nadia saw a car start to turn down the street, but the driver got a look at what was going on and swiftly changed his mind. Which made the old-fashioned station wagon that calmly pulled up to the curb all the more obvious.

"That must be our ride," Nate said, then ducked reflexively as another gunshot split the night. The sirens were a lot closer already, and a couple of the Red Death were firing at a uniformed officer who must have been patrolling on foot. Hopefully, the officer was too busy trying to stay alive to notice Nate and Nadia as they hurried toward the station wagon, Agnes still unconscious in Nate's arms.

It was the station wagon's rear hatch that opened, rather than any of the passenger doors, but that was just fine with Nadia. She sprinted ahead, meaning to jump in and help Nate with Agnes, but Belinski's security team took charge with a vengeance. One man leapt out of the back and grabbed Nadia, practically throwing her into the car while another snatched Agnes from Nate's arms.

Nadia didn't see what happened next, because someone turned her over onto her stomach and sat on her, grinding her face into the carpeted floor of the station wagon and fastening a zip tie around her wrists behind her back. Her every instinct urged her to struggle, but she forced herself to lie still and unresisting. There was no reason for Belinski to trust her or Nate with only the information they'd provided so far. Agnes hadn't been conscious enough to fully vouch for them, and as far as he knew Nate had kidnapped his daughter and assassinated the previous Chairman of Paxco. Nadia wasn't the least bit surprised that they were being treated like criminals, even if the injustice of it stung like hell.

Nate was not so resigned, and when he was shoved into the back of the wagon, he tried to kick out at the man who jumped in behind him and pulled the hatch closed. The car took off with a lurch, and Nate's kick missed. He fought and cursed foully as the man who'd secured Nadia's wrists got off her and went to help his buddy secure Nate. Nate managed to get him in the shin with one flailing leg, but the kick didn't have enough leverage to do any damage—except to the man's temper.

"Stop it, Nate!" Nadia ordered, worried Belinski's security team was going to get pissed off enough to hurt him. "You're not helping anything."

"Listen to the young lady," one of the men advised, grabbing a fistful of Nate's hair and using that grip to pin his head down.

Ordinarily, Nate was too stubborn and hotheaded to take such rational advice, but either he realized the futility of his efforts or he was just too exhausted to keep fighting. He went limp and allowed his wrists to be secured behind him. Unlike with Nadia, the men secured Nate's ankles as well—payback because he'd given them so much trouble, perhaps.

"We just smuggled Agnes out of the Basement at great personal risk," Nate grated, "and this is how you treat us?"

No one had any comment on that.

"Is it okay if I sit up?" Nadia asked. The men were probably on a hair trigger thanks to Nate, so she didn't want to make any move without permission first. However, lying facedown in a moving car was far from comfortable, especially when they went around turns. She was going to have rug burns on the side of her face.

Belinski's men didn't answer out loud, but one of them helped her into a sitting position, her back braced against the side of the car.

The station wagon ordinarily would have had three rows of seats, but one set of seats was folded down to make it roomier in the back. That's where Nate and Nadia and the two bodyguards were. Agnes had been laid out across the second row of seats, and a man wearing latex gloves was kneeling on the floorboards in front of her, frowning fiercely at the obviously infected wound on the side of her head.

"Damned savages," she heard him mutter under his breath as he reached into the bag beside him and pulled out a small pair of scissors.

"The health-care plan in the Basement consists of dropping bombs on their heads," Nadia informed him, glaring. "They did the best they could under the circumstances."

The doctor or medic or whatever he was curled his lip in scorn. "By sealing up a dirty wound? Yeah, that was real helpful."

"It would have been so much better to leave it open and bleeding," she agreed, taking a thorough dislike to the man already. But Agnes needed him, and it did no one any good for Nadia to waste time arguing with him, so she refrained from any other smart remarks. "She's also got a wound on her ribs on the right and almost certainly has a concussion."

The medic rolled his eyes. "That your professional opinion?" He turned his attention back to Agnes, carefully picking out the clumsy stitches.

Nadia refused to rise to the bait and gave Nate a precautionary look in case he was about to snap. He was clearly grinding his teeth, but he kept quiet.

"I'm assuming it's useful for you to know her symptoms," Nadia said, "since she's not awake to tell you herself. She was dizzy and disoriented and she threw up a lot."

The medic didn't respond, instead talking to the driver. "Crack the windows, would you? It reeks back here."

Nadia's cheeks flushed with embarrassment. They had to stink, of course, but she'd gotten used to the smell and didn't much appreciate having it pointed out.

The man who had helped Nadia sit up flashed her a rueful smile. "His bedside manner reeks almost as much as you guys do, but believe it or not he's good at what he does."

"And luckily most of his patients are unconscious when he works on them," the other member of Belinski's team muttered under his breath.

Nadia didn't have it in her to laugh, or even smile. Instead, she laid her head back and closed her eyes while trying to convince herself she was safe now.

nadia didn't know where Belinski's men were taking them—they weren't exactly a communicative bunch—but it was somewhere out of the city, and for that she was grateful. There was too much surveillance within the city limits, and much less of it out in the suburbs and the countryside.

They drove for what Nadia guessed was the better part of an hour, the dangers of Manhattan disappearing behind them as the sun rose and the steel and concrete of the city morphed into rolling farmland and quaint small towns.

Eventually, the car pulled into a winding gravel drive that led to a picturesque farmhouse with no visible neighbors. The bonds around Nate's ankles were cut so he could walk, and he and Nadia were hustled in through a side door. They passed a pair of men carrying a stretcher, which was presumably for Agnes, who had remained unconscious throughout the medic's ministrations and the rest of the drive. Nadia had met with nothing but a glare when she asked how Agnes was doing, and she worried that the girl needed to be in a hospital instead of being furtively treated in someone's country home. Not that she had any say in the matter.

Nate and Nadia were directed to a small but comfortable bedroom featuring a queen-sized bed covered in a patchwork quilt Nadia suspected was handmade. The nightstands and dresser had a rustic whitewash finish, and the walls were covered in blue- and white-striped wallpaper, all of which lent the room a homey feeling very much at odds with the heavy-duty electronic locks on the door and the surveillance cameras in the ceiling.

"The windows are locked and the glass is bulletproof," the head of the security detail, who'd introduced himself as Mr. Parker, informed them. "Don't get any funny ideas."

"We're not planning to go anywhere," Nadia assured him. "When can we see Chairman Belinski?"

Mr. Parker shrugged. "When he feels like it. Now hold still."

Mr. Parker's hands were coolly professional enough that Nadia didn't feel violated by his perfunctory pat-down, though she could tell by the high color in his face and the glitter in his eye that Nate was seething. For once, however, he managed to keep his mouth shut and endure in silence. Mr. Parker had already divested him of the gun when he'd first been shoved into the car, and he had no other weapons on him.

Mr. Parker looked at his hands when he was done and scowled. "What the hell do you have all over you?" he asked, rubbing his palms together in a futile attempt to remove the grime.

"Probably best you don't know," Nadia said. "Let's just say you'll want to wash your hands as soon as possible." Her eyes darted sideways to the open door of the en-suite bathroom, thinking that a long hot shower had never sounded so good.

"No kidding?" Mr. Parker mumbled, then took out a blunt-tipped cutting tool and freed Nate's and Nadia's wrists.

The bonds hadn't been inordinately tight, but they'd been on for a long time, and Nate and Nadia both had angry red marks on their skin. The look on Nate's face grew even more forbidding, and Nadia was afraid he was about to lose his temper. He'd been doing a really good job of holding it all in, for the most part, but surely there was an explosion to come.

"You might want to get cleaned up while you wait," Parker suggested. "There's likely something in the dresser that'll fit you, so you can dump what you're wearing in the trash." He turned to leave.

"Wait!" Nadia said, reaching out toward his arm, though she stopped short of touching him. "Any chance we can get some food if we've got a long wait ahead of us? We haven't eaten a real meal since the bombing began." Just the mention of food made her mouth flood with saliva, and her stomach rumbled loudly to emphasize her point.

The look on Mr. Parker's face softened to something almost like sympathy, and he nodded. "I'll see what I can do," he promised, and then he was gone, and the door closed with a solid thunk and a high-pitched beep.

CHAPTER TWENTY

The drawers of the dresser held sets of hospital-green scrubs, wrapped in plastic packaging with the size printed on white labels. Since they were unisex, Nadia picked out the smallest she could find while Nate picked large. The bottom drawer held underwear, also neatly packaged in plastic, though not unisex. Obviously it was not unusual for people who stayed in this room not to have any belongings with them.

"This must be some kind of a safe house," Nate muttered as he looked at his package of scrubs in distaste. "I'm trying real hard not to be creeped out at the idea that Belinski has a safe house here in Paxco."

Nadia agreed with him, wondering how long this house had been here. It certainly hadn't sprung up in the scant time since Agnes's disappearance—Nadia didn't have much experience with the spy business, but she was pretty sure a good, secure safe house took a while to build, even if you were just modifying an existing structure.

Nate insisted Nadia get first dibs on the shower, and she felt too filthy to argue. The hot water felt as wonderful as she had imagined it would. She had to wash her hair three times before the rinse water finally ran clear, and there were patches of ground-in dirt on her hands, elbows, and knees that would require a loofah to get rid of completely. Even so, she felt immeasurably better when she stepped out of the shower and put on the clean clothes. She couldn't say she felt quite like herself in the shapeless scrubs, with her hair still damp and tangled and no makeup on her face, but she no longer felt like a refugee.

Getting clean herself had the disadvantage that it cleared her nose, and the moment she opened the bathroom door and stepped back out into the room with Nate, the stench hit her, and she felt abruptly sorry for the men who had had to ride in the car with them for more than an hour.

"Don't worry," Nate said when he caught a look at her crinkled nose, "I didn't sit down or touch anything."

"Get in there," she replied, jerking her thumb toward the bathroom.

He complied with a tired grin, though the stink of the tunnels remained in the room after he'd left and she wished she could open the windows. Hard to believe that less than an hour ago, she'd been so inured to the smell that she had barely even noticed it.

While Nate was in the shower, Mr. Parker brought a tray with turkey sandwiches, a bowl of fruit, and a carafe of coffee. Nadia was so hungry she was tempted to tackle the man to the floor to get at the food. He stepped warily into the room, as if worried he might be attacked, and Nadia saw that another member of the security detail was stationed out in the hallway. These guys weren't taking any chances with their supposedly dangerous prisoners/guests.

Mr. Parker laid the tray on the foot of the bed—there wasn't a convenient table to hold it—then nodded at her and headed back out the door. He paused for a moment in the doorway.

"There's a doctor with Miss Belinski right now," he said. "She's getting IV fluids and antibiotics."

"Is she going to be okay?"

"Doc can't say for sure yet, but she thinks the prognosis is good. But she also says Miss Belinski would have died without treatment, so it looks like you kids saved her life. Assuming you weren't the ones who hurt her in the first place."

His voice held no hint of accusation, and though he was obviously proceeding with caution, Nadia felt sure he believed she and Nate were the good guys. She wished Mr. Parker would let them talk to Belinski immediately, but she understood that the Chairman's fear for his daughter was likely chasing all other concerns from his mind.

"Tell Chairman Belinski that our friends in the Basement started calling Agnes 'Lionheart' because of her courage. We never would have made it out of the Basement without her."

Mr. Parker raised his eyebrows, and Nadia suspected the Chairman would take the declaration with similar skepticism. They all knew the meek, shy, socially awkward Executive girl who had never quite fit in with others of her class. They had no idea what Agnes was really made of, and Nadia was going to do her best to make them see it.

"I'll tell him," Mr. Parker promised. "And if you really haven't eaten in two days, try not to gorge yourselves or you'll never keep it down."

The door closed, and Nadia turned to stare at the tray sitting on the foot of the bed, calling to her.

The polite thing to do was to wait for Nate to get out of

the shower before eating, but her willpower wasn't up to it, so she grabbed a sandwich and shoved it into her mouth, taking a bite so big she could barely chew.

The shower and the food had gone a long way toward making Nadia feel physically better. However, the hours she and Nate spent locked up in that comfortable bedroom with nothing to do but think and wait threatened to make her lose her mind.

Since the moment she'd first set foot in the subway tunnel two days ago, Nadia had been in constant motion, too busy trying to survive and tending to the victims of the bombing to think. When she'd fallen asleep, it had been because she was too exhausted to keep going, so there was no tossing and turning, no fear, no horror—only sweet oblivion.

After devouring his sandwich and several pieces of fruit, Nate had lain down on the bed and promptly retreated to that oblivion, asleep even before he closed his eyes. After everything the two of them had been through together, Nadia had no qualms about lying down beside him on the bed, but she knew sleep wouldn't claim her so easily. She kept watching the sun traveling across the sky, precious hours ticking by as Belinski kept them waiting.

Had Dante made it back to the Basement safely? Were the subway tunnels still reasonably intact and usable as shelters? And was Dorothy going to drop more bombs tonight?

Nadia's eyes burned with tears, and the idea that she was here in this comfortable little safe house in the middle of nowhere while Dante, Bishop, Shrimp, and the rest of the Red Death were hoping not to have bombs falling on their heads sent a wave of guilt washing over her. It was hard to feel like she was doing her part for their resistance here.

The other downside of being out of the Basement and back into somewhat more familiar territory was that it reminded Nadia that Dorothy had arrested her parents. Fighting for her life in the Basement—and being completely cut off from any news sources—Nadia had been able to keep her fear for them in the back of her mind, but it was out in the forefront now. There seemed to be no atrocity Thea wasn't capable of, and Nadia shuddered to think how her parents had fared in custody. Rikers Island was the ultimate nightmare even for ordinary citizens, and Executives, particularly famous ones like Nadia's parents, would attract the worst kind of attention from their fellow prisoners. She imagined her regal, strong-willed mother, dressed in a jumpsuit of prison orange, facing down a mob of hardened criminals who hated her just because she was born an Executive.

Nadia had sunk deep into her brooding, her arms wrapped around her knees as she stared into the middle distance, when the door to the bedroom made a soft beep and then opened. Beside her, Nate jerked awake at the sound, his eyes wide and startled, his breaths coming short, as if he'd just been awakened from a nightmare.

Chairman Belinski looked better than he had when they'd awakened him in the middle of the night. His stately gray hair was neatly combed, his face freshly shaved, his dark gray suit elegant and wrinkle-free. But there were still bags under his eyes, and the expression on his face was bewildered and haunted.

"How is Agnes?" Nadia asked, when the Chairman seemed at a momentary loss for words.

He blinked and swallowed, coming back to himself. "She's going to be all right," he said with obvious relief. "She'll have a scar, but the doctor said aside from that she should make a full recovery." He shook his head. "The doctor also assures me the concussion hasn't made her delusional, but . . ." His voice trailed off.

"But what Agnes told you when she woke up sounds completely nuts," Nate finished, rubbing at his eyes as if to force himself away from the brink of sleep.

"That's one way of putting it," Belinski said. He looked back and forth between Nate and Nadia, maybe hoping one of them would burst out with a confession that it was all some kind of dirty trick they'd played on his daughter. His gaze finally settled on Nate. "I've seen the video of you shooting your father. You certainly never made much of an attempt to hide your feelings for him in my presence. So why shouldn't I believe what my own eyes tell me?"

"Because it's not true," Nate answered simply. "The entire video is a fabrication."

Chairman Belinski didn't look any less skeptical.

"Look, I'm a Replica, right?" Nate said, making a sweeping arm gesture from head to foot. "I'm flesh and blood, and Thea created me out of nothing. If she can do that, why is it hard to believe she could create a completely false video that's really just a bunch of pixels?"

The Chairman lowered his head and pinched the bridge of his nose. Nadia didn't blame him for his doubts and uncertainty. She wasn't sure what *she* would believe in his position. After all, he hadn't seen Thea in action—and neither had Agnes, who had relayed the situation to him. Agnes was merely taking things on faith, so maybe she wasn't the most convincing spokesperson.

"Why don't you come on out to the living room," Belinski suggested, raising his head once more. "We'll have some coffee and you two can tell me your version of just what's going on."

Nate and Nadia followed the Chairman into a cheerfully sunny living room, the kind of room that looked just right in a modest-sized country farmhouse. Except for the security cameras and the electronic keypads set into every door.

The Chairman invited Nate and Nadia to sit on the floral-upholstered couch, while he chose a chenille-covered armchair that looked completely incongruous next to his tailored designer suit. One of his staff brought out a tray of tea and coffee. When the Chairman leaned forward to pour himself a cup of coffee, Nate and Nadia followed suit, although Nadia went for the tea. It was the first tea she had tasted in weeks, and she let out a sigh of contentment.

"Start from the beginning," Chairman Belinski said. "Tell me everything."

And so they did, starting on the day the original Nate Hayes was murdered.

It was a long story, and there were a lot of stops and starts along the way. Belinski listened in silence, sipping his coffee and keeping his thoughts to himself. They told him about their first encounter with Thea, and about how they'd blackmailed Nate's father into supposedly destroying her. They told him about Nate's first meeting with Dorothy, on the day of his mother's funeral, and how he had been convinced from the first moment that she was not really his sister.

Eventually, they told him about their last face-to-face confrontation with Dorothy and about what she was—just a flesh puppet, used by Thea to seize control of Paxco so that she no longer had to rely on any human being to look after her best interests. About how Dorothy had let them go so that they could not be turned into martyrs by rival factions who might want to seize the Chairmanship from someone so new and unknown. They talked about how Dorothy had sealed off the Basement and cut off the phone lines so that Nate and Nadia couldn't tell anyone who mattered about what they knew. And they explained the sequence of events that had led up to Dorothy trying to bomb the Basement into oblivion—a series of events that Belinski confirmed had been relayed to the public in a very different order.

"We don't know for sure what Thea's endgame is," Nadia finished, "but it can't be anything good. She's clearly demonstrated she has no concern for human life whatsoever. Right now, her aggression is all focused on the Basement, and I suppose there are certain segments of society who don't care all that much about the fate of Basement-dwellers, but I highly doubt she'll stop there."

Belinski poured himself a third cup of coffee, his face creased with thought.

"She has to be stopped, Mr. Chairman," Nate said, sitting on the edge of his seat and leaning forward. Nadia put a hand on his arm and shook her head subtly when he glanced her way.

Let him think, she mentally urged Nate, and to her surprise he seemed to get the message. He wasn't usually one for patience, but even he had to see that Chairman Belinski had a lot to absorb—assuming he wasn't ready to put them in straitjackets.

The Chairman sipped his coffee, frowning into the depths of his cup. Nate fidgeted, and Nadia kept an eye on him in case she'd have to remind him once again to be patient.

Finally, the Chairman put his cup down and faced them once more. "Your story is preposterous," he told them calmly, and Nadia preemptively grabbed on to Nate's arm. "But Agnes told me pretty close to the same thing. It's possible you were lying to her about Thea and Dorothy, since she didn't see any of that with her own eyes, but she *did* witness the escalation of hostilities in the Basement. If Dorothy is lying about that, then I have to assume she's lying about other things, too. I'm still having trouble believing some of the things you say are true, but I'm going to give you the benefit of the doubt because if I didn't and I was wrong, the results would be catastrophic."

"So what exactly does that mean?" Nate asked, unable to keep quiet any longer. "What are you going to do?"

The Chairman leaned back in his chair, one finger tapping restlessly against its arm. "That, son, is a very good question, and I don't have the answer yet."

Nadia was disappointed—if not surprised—when Chairman Belinski ended the conversation on that uncertain note. Despite everything she and Nate had been through, they were still kids in Belinski's eyes, and he was hardly likely to include them in any top-secret strategy meetings. Their mission had been to escape from the Basement and tell someone who had the power to make a difference the truth about Dorothy. They had succeeded, and despite the Chairman's doubts, he was going to act on their information—one way or another.

"You two must be exhausted from everything you've been through," Chairman Belinski said, rising to his feet. "There are a couple of guest rooms upstairs. Perhaps you'd like to get a little more rest. I was planning to go back to the city, but now I think I'll stay here tonight. I'll see you again at dinner and let you know what my team and I have come up with."

Nadia was pleased that Belinski meant to keep them in the loop at all, but Nate wasn't so easily mollified.

"Please, Mr. Chairman," he said. "We have friends and . . . loved ones still trapped in the Basement. Innocent people are dying in the thousands, and there's no sign that Dorothy's going to let up. We don't have time to—"

"I understand, son," Chairman Belinski interrupted. "I know it's urgent, and if I could snap my fingers and fix it all right now, I would. But going off half-cocked is only going to get more people killed. I have some of the best advisers in all of North America, and when we put our heads together, we can do amazing things."

"Military advisers?" Nadia asked, suddenly forming yet another unpleasant image in her mind. Synchrony was best known for its advanced military technology, and though it was far smaller and less wealthy than Paxco, its well-equipped, well-trained military was world famous. Had Nate and Nadia just tacitly given Belinski the okay to invade Paxco? The thought of a military invasion gave Nadia the shivers, although she was pretty sure being occupied by Synchrony would be the lesser evil to being ruled by Thea.

"Among others," Belinski said. "Considering Dorothy's use of force against her own people, it is possible a military intervention will be necessary. I'm sure you agree."

Nate raised his chin and squared his shoulders. "I am the rightful Chairman of Paxco," he said. "I didn't go through everything I've gone through to have you invade my state."

"A military intervention is not an invasion," Belinski countered. "You came to me because you needed an ally, one who had the power to do something about Thea. Don't tell me you didn't consider Synchrony's military one of my chief assets."

It was pointless to argue. Especially when Belinski was right. Dorothy had to be ousted from power, and Thea had to be destroyed. The chances that those things could happen without some kind of military support were almost nil. That didn't mean it was a comfortable situation to be in.

"Get a few more hours of rest," Belinski said. "We'll talk more at dinner." He looked at Nate. "Mr. Parker will show you to your room." He dismissed Nate and turned his gaze to Nadia. "If you would remain for a moment, Miss Lake, I'd like a private word with you first."

"This way, sir," Mr. Parker said to Nate, making a sweeping gesture toward the stairs in the foyer.

Nate raised a questioning eyebrow at Nadia.

"It's okay, Nate," she said, forcing a smile. "I'll be up soon."

Nate still didn't look happy about it—neither one of them was in much of a trusting frame of mind these days—but he allowed Mr. Parker to lead him up the stairs, leaving Nadia alone in the living room with Chairman Belinski, who looked at her with kindly, grave eyes.

"You indicated that you've had no access to the net or

telephone the last couple of weeks," he said, stepping closer to her and reaching out to put one hand on each of her shoulders.

Dread flooded Nadia's system as she registered the unmistakable signs of pity on Chairman Belinski's face and realized what his overly familiar gesture portended. She shook her head.

"No," she whispered. "Don't say anything. Please."

"I'm sorry, child," he said in a voice not much louder. "There was apparently a riot in Rikers Island over the weekend. Your father sustained only minor injuries, but your mother . . . I'm afraid she didn't make it."

CHAPTER TWENTY-ONE

nadia climbed the stairs, following Mr. Parker, in a glassy-eyed daze. When he gestured her toward a room, she walked in without question, closing the door behind her.

She wanted to cry, *needed* to cry, but somehow it all just hurt too much. She lay down on the bed, her body curling in upon itself as she clutched the pillow with both arms, willing the tears to start, desperately hoping for some release of the toxic emotions that swirled within her and made her chest ache.

Her sister was dead. Her mother was dead. Her father was injured and in prison. Dante was in the Basement where the bombs would no doubt continue to fall. In her head, she knew none of this was her fault. She'd always made the best choices she could, and she couldn't take the blame for the things that the late Chairman Hayes and Thea had done. But knowing that in her head did nothing to lessen the smothering blanket of guilt that made it so hard to breathe. Nor did it stop her mind from continually second-guessing every decision she'd made.

If she hadn't blackmailed Chairman Hayes into destroying the original Thea, would her mother and Gerri still be alive?

The worst, however, was the way her mind kept playing back the last time she had seen her parents, her final cruel words filling her with more shame and remorse than she could bear.

I never want to see either of you again.

She remembered how furious she had been at the time. Furious at her mother for sacrificing Nadia's happiness for the sake of social standing. Furious at her father for not fighting harder for her. Completely devastated by what felt like her parents' abandonment, Nadia had snarled those fateful words and had actually meant them. But only in the heat of the moment. Never in her wildest dreams had she considered the possibility that they would be the last words she ever spoke to her mother.

A choking sound rose from Nadia's throat, but still the tears wouldn't come, the pain and guilt and grief trapped in her body, making her want to escape from her own skin.

Would those spiteful words be the last she spoke to her father, too? For all Nadia knew, the "prison riot" had been engineered by Thea herself in an attempt to kill Nadia's parents without the inconvenience of a trial or conviction. If that was the case, then she would surely try again. And eventually, she would succeed.

The dam finally burst, and Nadia buried her face in the pillow while sobs racked her body.

nate slept until late in the afternoon, waking up only when Mr. Parker stopped by to deliver a shopping bag full of clothes and shoes so he had something to wear other than the scrubs. Nate took the bag gratefully.

"Miss Lake is asleep for the moment," Mr. Parker said,

"and it's probably best to let her get whatever rest she can. But I thought you should know she's had some very bad news."

Mr. Parker told Nate that Esmeralda Lake had been killed during a prison riot, and a black wave of fury rose from inside him. He wanted to kill Thea for putting Nadia's mother in that prison, and he was so pissed off at the universe in general for all the shit it had heaped on Nadia's shoulders—not to mention his own—that he had to fight the urge to kill the messenger. His whole body clenched up with the need to hit something, but he controlled it, pulling firmly on the reins of his temper, finding yet another occasion to practice his newfound self-control.

"Chairman Belinski had some flowers brought to her room," Mr. Parker said, as though he hadn't noticed Nate's fight against rage. "We kept an arrangement aside for you in case you'd like something to give her yourself."

All the belligerence drained from Nate's body, and he was surprised to feel a sudden prickle in his eyes. He blinked rapidly, hoping that somehow Mr. Parker had missed the sign of weakness. He had to clear his throat before he could talk.

"Thank you," was all he said, because if he said anything more, that one small gesture of kindness was going to start him bawling.

"I'll bring them up," Mr. Parker said. "The Chairman will be dining at eight, but he would understand completely if you and Miss Lake would prefer privacy in this difficult time."

"We'll be there," Nate said without hesitation. He knew Nadia would want to have a voice in whatever plan they came up with to defeat Thea, no matter how much pain she was in, and Nate, as the rightful Chairman of Paxco, had an obligation to be there as well.

"I'll tell the Chairman to expect you. There's a media room at the end of the hall," he said pointing. "The phone line and net access are both secure and untraceable, so feel free to make use of them however you'd like."

"Thank you," Nate said again. But there was no one he could imagine calling on the phone, and he couldn't stomach getting on the net and seeing Dorothy's version of current events.

nate stood outside the closed door to Nadia's room and had to swallow the aching lump in his throat. In his hand, he held the small flower arrangement Belinski's men had set aside for him, but he was having trouble convincing his free hand to knock on the door. Every time he caught the faint echo of Nadia's sobs, his own eyes teared up, and only copious deep breaths would bring back his sense of self-control.

He wanted to be strong for her, to be a solid and comforting presence in this time of grief, and bursting into sympathetic tears wasn't the way to accomplish that. He'd never much liked his would-be mother-in-law, had *hated* her when she'd sent Nadia away to that awful upstate retreat to hide her away like an embarrassment, but though Nadia had been just as angry, Nate knew how she felt right now. Knew it all too well.

"Damn it," he muttered between clenched teeth as his eyes tried to well up again. Kurt had told him that he still had a lot of grieving to do for his father, and Nate was beginning to think he was right. It certainly wasn't Esmeralda

Lake who was bringing tears to his eyes. Blinking rapidly and taking yet another deep breath, Nate gathered his courage and knocked softly on the door. Standing out here in the hall getting high on the overly sweet perfume of the lilies wasn't helping Nadia one bit, and it wasn't doing much for him, either.

"C-come in," Nadia stammered after a long pause. Her voice was hoarse, and though she'd gotten the sobs under control, he could still hear her sniffling. No doubt she was in there dabbing at her eyes, trying to control and hide her emotions—just as he'd been doing for the last five minutes. And maybe that was something they both needed to stop doing for a while. They were in a relatively safe place with no one trying to kill them right this moment, and maybe it was time to stop being so goddamned strong all the time.

Eyes stinging, throat tightening, Nate opened the door and ventured inside. If the best thing he could manage was to hold Nadia while they both cried, then that was what he was going to do.

nadia looked wan and tired when she and Nate headed downstairs for dinner, and he suspected he looked much the same way. The two of them had eventually fallen asleep cuddled together on her bed, holding on to each other for strength. Throughout their lives, they had always been there for each other, and never had they needed each other as much as they did on this terrible day. Especially when they were both painfully aware of the setting sun, of the horrors that would come as night fell. Assuming there was anything of the Basement left to bomb, of course.

Dinner was a quiet and somber affair, and five seconds

after each plate was cleared, Nate couldn't have said what had been on it, although he ate everything that was put in front of him.

There were only the three of them eating. Agnes wasn't well enough yet, and the rest of the household were staff. Agnes's mother, who suffered from severe chronic migraines, was back home in Synchrony.

After dinner, Chairman Belinski invited Nate and Nadia into a sleek, modern office that looked completely incongruous in the homey farmhouse. There was a small conference table on one side of the office, with a bank of video monitors on the wall at one end. The other side of the office held Belinski's desk with a couple of chairs facing it. The Chairman gestured Nate and Nadia into those chairs and then took his own seat.

"I've been on conference calls with my advisers most of the afternoon," he said. "We're all finding your story about Dorothy very hard to swallow."

The anger that Nate had been suppressing ever since he'd heard the news about Nadia's mother made his fists clench, and he opened his mouth to let all that anger spew out. But all it took was a significant look from Nadia to shut his mouth again.

"So you've decided you don't believe us?" she inquired, way calmer than Nate could hope to be.

"I didn't say that," Belinski answered. "I said it's hard to swallow. And the problem is if it's hard for *me* to swallow, it's going to be hard for anyone else to swallow, too."

"Where are you going with this?" Nadia asked.

"We need proof of what Dorothy is before we can act."

Nate shook his head in disgust. "You know perfectly

well Nadia and I can't provide proof. No one can, except Dorothy."

"Then that's who we'll have to get it from."

Nate blinked in surprise. "Come again?"

Belinski's lip twitched in the faintest of smiles. "You said that Thea communicates with Dorothy through some kind of receptor in Dorothy's brain. And that Dorothy is nonfunctional without Thea's input."

"That's what Dorothy told us," Nadia agreed. "I don't suppose she had any reason to lie at the time. I doubt she ever imagined we'd stay alive this long."

Belinski nodded. "Probably not. So we'll take it as a given that she was telling the truth. In which case we can prove she is not what she says she is by cutting off communication between Dorothy and Thea. We cut that communication, and Dorothy stops functioning. I suspect that would be very convincing evidence. Especially if it happens in front of witnesses."

"And how do you propose we do that?" Nadia asked.

"By use of a jamming device. Obviously we can't be sure exactly how Thea is communicating with Dorothy, but it's something wireless, which means it uses radio frequencies, which can be disrupted."

"And you have some kind of technology that will let us do that," Nate said.

"We'll have to improvise," Belinski said. "Most of our jamming devices target a limited range of frequencies, so that our own forces can use the free ones to communicate with each other. But we have no idea which frequencies Thea uses, so we'll have to jam them all. I have an engineer modifying one of our portable jammers as we speak."

"And is this going to knock out communications for the whole city?" Nate asked.

The Chairman shook his head. "There's no need for something so drastic. I've been invited to address the board of directors tomorrow afternoon. The new Chairman Hayes and I have been going over the existing trade agreements between Synchrony and Paxco, and we're planning to announce what we've come up with during the meeting. It's the perfect opportunity to tear the mask off Dorothy—in front of the board of directors, and captured on video, because all board meetings are recorded, even if the recordings are top secret. We can use a very localized signal jammer—one that's small enough to be carried in a pocket."

Nate imagined it would make quite a sensation if Dorothy suddenly collapsed in the middle of a board meeting, and once the board of directors found out what she was, she would not be Chairman anymore.

"Discrediting Dorothy isn't enough," Nate said. "The real enemy is Thea, and losing her puppet won't do her a whole lot of harm."

"True. But Thea is just a computer—an extraordinary one, to be sure, but a computer nonetheless. Without human beings to carry out her wishes, there's nothing to stop us from shutting her down—and this time we'll know enough to shut down the Replication tanks, too."

Nate shuddered, remembering what it was like when he and Nadia had faced Thea in the flesh. She was more than just a computer. She also had flesh and blood mixed in with her machinery, and shutting her down was not as simple as just flipping a switch. It would take guns, though no doubt Chairman Belinski had plenty of access to those as well.

"We'll be in the Fortress for the board meeting anyway," Belinski continued.

"In the Fortress?" Nate interrupted, surprised. "The board usually meets at Headquarters. I've never heard of them meeting in the Fortress."

"They've been meeting there ever since Dorothy took over," Belinski said. "According to her, it's a more secure location."

You couldn't get much more secure than the Fortress. It was in the Fortress's subbasement that Thea resided. But Paxco Headquarters was almost its equal, and it wasn't like Paxco was at war—except with the trapped denizens of the Basement. So why would Dorothy feel the need to have the board meet in a more secure location? Nate wondered if Thea's control of her puppet was better when Dorothy was nearby. Certainly she had better control of the building itself. Her original had been ensconced in that subbasement for years and had made unauthorized changes to some of its electronics. For instance, Nate's father claimed Thea had added listening devices where none had existed before by modifying whatever software she could connect to. Which no doubt made it easy for her to listen in on private conversations in rooms that were supposedly free of bugs—and thereby increase her power over the board members.

"Once we've proven that Dorothy isn't a real person," Belinski continued, "we can go down to the subbasement and take care of Thea right away, before she comes up with some other way to protect herself. With the entire board of directors as witnesses, I don't imagine we'll have too much trouble getting to her."

"You're assuming no one but Thea is going to resist,"

Nadia said. "Cutting Dorothy off from Thea might make the board acknowledge Nate is the true Chairman, but they won't necessarily all agree that Thea has to be destroyed. After all, Nate's father didn't see Thea for the monster that she was until way too late."

"That's why you and Nathaniel will be coming with me to the board meeting," Belinski said. "You're eyewitnesses to the things that Thea has done, and once we've shown them that you're telling the truth about Dorothy, the rest of the crazy story sounds a lot more plausible. I would be stunned if your board didn't agree Thea has to be put down after hearing everything."

Nate wondered if Belinski was giving the board too much credit, or whether he himself wasn't giving them enough. The last couple of months had turned him into a cynic, but the fact that the board had approved cutting off food and medical aid to the Basement and then bombing it didn't do much for his faith. Even if Dorothy had fabricated evidence that the Basement was in full revolt.

Apparently, Nadia was feeling equally cynical.

"You'll be asking them to give up the revenue from making backups and Replicas," she said. "They might be harder to convince than you think."

Belinski's eyes turned shrewd and cold. "If they won't listen to reason, then I'll have to resort to more drastic measures. If everything you've told me about Thea is true, then she has to be stopped. No matter what."

CHAPTER TWENTY-TWO

when Nadia returned to her comfortable little room after a brief visit with Agnes, she saw that someone had left a bottle of sleeping pills on her bedside table. She was so exhausted—both from a lack of sleep and from an excess of grief—that she didn't imagine she'd need any chemical aid, but almost as soon as she'd closed the bedroom door behind her, her mind turned on itself and the litany of recriminations began.

She took a pill, and was asleep within fifteen minutes.

She felt like she could sleep for a week, but a woman on Belinski's security team woke her up before the sun had risen. The board meeting was scheduled to begin at nine A.M., and there was a lot to do—plus an hour-long drive—before it began. Nadia soon found herself sitting in a chair surrounded by lights bright enough to make her head ache, while two other members of Belinski's household studied her with a focus and intensity that made her squirm.

"We'll need to change her hair, obviously," the female member of the duo said. They hadn't bothered to introduce themselves.

"Do that first," the man said, opening up a large black case and sifting through its contents.

The woman came at Nadia with a pair of scissors, and

she jumped out of the chair. "Wait a minute!" she said, glaring at the scissors. "What are you doing?"

The woman looked at her like she thought Nadia was a little slow in the head. "Disguising you, of course."

Nadia had known a disguise was part of the plan—it wasn't like she or Nate could just walk into the Fortress without anyone noticing—but she'd been envisioning wigs and makeup. Not having some stranger hacking at her hair with a pair of scissors.

"What's wrong with a wig?" Nadia asked, grabbing the end of her long braid protectively.

The woman crossed her arms and gave Nadia a stern look. "Wigs can come off, no matter how firmly you anchor them in place. And you'll be wearing this disguise for many hours. It's going to be uncomfortable enough without adding a wig into the mix. Your hair will grow back."

After everything she'd gone through, it seemed ridiculous for Nadia to be upset over getting her hair cut, but to her utter humiliation, there were tears gathering in her eyes.

The look on the woman's face softened with sympathy. "I'm sorry, Miss Lake. I'm being completely insensitive. My name is Andrea, and this is my partner, Roger." She indicated the man, who was still taking things out of his case. "I'm going to cut and color your hair, and Roger is going to do your face. When we're finished with you, you won't even be able to recognize yourself in the mirror."

Nadia swallowed hard and dabbed at her eyes. "I'm sorry for making such a big deal over my hair. It's so stupid, I know."

"I don't think it's your hair you're crying about," Andrea said gently, and Nadia practically lost it.

Of course, Andrea was right. Nadia still had a lot of crying left to do, but somehow she was going to have to shove it all down and put off her grief for later, after everything was over. She took a deep breath, then another. After the third, the grief receded to the back of her mind—still hovering, but not as overwhelming.

Nadia had had long hair all her life, but Andrea cut most of it off and dyed the remainder a deep chestnut brown, leaving her with a short, punky hairdo that required copious amounts of mousse and hair spray to hold in place. Already, she barely recognized herself, but then she sat in Roger's chair and the true transformation began.

Nadia had imagined Roger would disguise her by putting makeup on her with a trowel, but this disguise was more thorough than that. He wouldn't let her look in the mirror while he was working, but the stuff he was putting on her face looked more like putty than makeup, and she could feel it building up in places, especially around her nose and chin. Whatever the stuff was, it would be hell on her pores.

"Hold still," Roger snapped at her when she almost laughed at the absurdity of her thoughts.

After he'd finished with the putty, Roger went to work with a series of paintbrushes and mysterious metallic instruments that Nadia thought would fit in perfectly in a dentist's office. She was especially careful to hold still when he wielded those.

Eventually, he finished. Nadia's face felt strange and tight. Roger finally let her look in the mirror, and she couldn't suppress a gasp.

She looked nothing like Nadia Lake. Her nose was thicker and more sharply flared, her chin was pointier, her cheekbones were higher, her eyebrows had less of an arch, and somehow—Nadia had no clue how he'd done it—Roger had made her look older. With her new face, she could easily pass for twenty-five.

"Avoid touching it as much as you can for the next thirty minutes," Roger advised. "It's not entirely dry yet, but when it is, the adhesive will be strong enough to keep it in place even if you do, and nothing but the external makeup can get wiped off. I'll give you some towelettes with solvent on them. When you're ready to take the mask off, moisten the edge of it with the towelette, and then pull the rest off. It'll feel like peeling off a bandage, but I'm afraid that can't be helped."

Nadia blinked at herself in the mirror, hardly able to believe that it was her under that face. "Who are you?" she asked Roger, shaking her head in disbelief. "Do you work in the movies or something?"

He met her eyes in the mirror and smiled. "I do real life, not movies. Draw your own conclusions from that."

The fact that Synchrony had a safe house here within Paxco suggested that they had a pretty healthy and active spy network. Nadia supposed it wasn't surprising that someone in that network was good at creating disguises. She was anxious to see what Nate would look like when they were through with him.

"Thank you," she said to both Roger and Andrea. "You did amazing work."

"Good luck today," Roger said as Nadia slipped out of the chair and headed for the door.

Her disguise got its first test when she reached the stairs to the second floor. Nate was just coming down for his own transformation, and he passed her on the stairs, nodding an impersonal greeting. Nadia couldn't help laughing, and Nate paused on the stairs below her, looking at her with a puzzled frown. Which made her laugh harder. She hoped her watering eyes weren't damaging the mask.

"Nadia?" Nate asked wonderingly. "Is that you?"

"Took you long enough to recognize me," she teased, fighting off more laughter.

He shook his head. "I *still* don't recognize you. I would never have guessed if I hadn't recognized your laugh."

She nodded in satisfaction. "Then I very much doubt Dorothy or any of the board members will recognize us. At least not until we want them to."

"As long as we keep our mouths shut."

That, Nadia believed, they could do. It was everything else she had doubts about.

Belinski's team had turned Nate into a freckled redhead with pudgy cheeks and broad shoulders. There was no way anyone at the Fortress could recognize him or Nadia, but that didn't stop his heart from beating double time or his palms from sweating. Too many awful things had happened at the Fortress, too many images of the place haunted his nightmares.

He didn't want to set foot inside the building ever again. And though he mined his rage for strength, he had to admit that the thought of facing Dorothy again made his stomach curdle with fear. By walking into the lion's den, he and Nadia were putting a whole lot of faith into the small electronic device one of Belinski's bodyguards carried in the pocket of his suit jacket. It seemed only logical that

Thea was using radio waves to communicate with Dorothy and that disrupting those frequencies would cut off the communication. But they couldn't be *sure* that was how Thea was controlling her puppet. Thea's was a nonhuman intelligence. She had invented the Replica technology, and no human scientist had come close to figuring out how she'd done it. Who was to say she hadn't invented some new way to communicate without wires?

If that was the case, if Belinski's device couldn't cut the connection, then Nate and Nadia's story was going to sound like the ravings of a couple of lunatics. And, thanks to the fabricated video of Nate shooting his father, they would be *dangerous* lunatics. Belinski might still believe them if the plan failed, but Nate had no illusions about what would happen. With no proof that Thea existed and that Dorothy was her puppet, he would cut his losses and declare that he'd been duped. When Thea demanded he hand Nate and Nadia over to "face justice," he would likely do it.

Belinski's motorcade pulled up to the gates of the Fortress and was quickly motioned through. Nate sat in the rearmost car of the motorcade, while Nadia was in the car with Belinski. She was playing the part of a personal aide, and Nate was camouflaged as part of the security detail that accompanied the Chairman wherever he went.

Some of the security detail stayed with the cars when they arrived at the entrance, but Nate joined a group of four others and Marco, Belinski's chief bodyguard, all wearing bland dark suits and on obvious alert. He tried to mimic their posture and behavior, turning his head this way and that, scanning for danger as they approached the Chairman's car and opened the door for him.

The Chairman exited, accompanied by his entourage—including Nadia—and they all proceeded into the building and were guided to a large conference room on the fourth floor. The room wasn't large enough to host a board meeting, especially not with a visiting dignitary and his entourage attending. It was clear that extra chairs had been wedged in around the conference table, with only the chair at the very head—Dorothy's, no doubt—having any elbow room whatsoever.

About two thirds of the board members had already arrived, most of them with a couple of aides who were forced to stand with their backs against the wall—there wouldn't have been room to have chairs for all of them.

Getting Chairman Belinski to his seat at the foot of the table reminded Nate of trying to navigate a shopping mall during the Christmas season. A lot of squeezing and sidestepping, with the occasional inadvertent bump. It was similarly difficult for the Chairman's security detail and aides to make room for themselves against the back wall. Nate wondered again why Dorothy insisted on having board meetings here. The boardroom in the Paxco Headquarters Building was specifically designed for a gathering of this size, with ample seating at the table and a second row of seating behind for the aides and secretaries.

The rest of the board members trickled in one by one, and though Nate could hear the air conditioner going full blast, it wasn't powerful enough to cool a room this crowded. He longed to loosen his tie and take off his jacket, but of course such a thing was Not Done, at least not by members of a security detail. The board members were shedding their jackets as soon as they sat down, and Nate noticed more than one had brought fans with them, either the cheap paper kind or the tiny little battery-operated ones that could sit on the table. He'd have expected them to do more grumbling about the conditions, but perhaps they had gotten that out of their systems during the first couple of meetings here.

Nate's pulse soared when, fifteen minutes later, the door behind the head of the table opened and Dorothy's security detail filed in. Chairs rolled back cautiously—if they rolled back too far, they'd roll over toes—and everyone stood up. Nate's entire body went rigid, and he became vividly aware of the gun he wore in a shoulder holster. It was meant to be part of his disguise, but that didn't mean it wouldn't work.

Not that shooting Dorothy would accomplish anything, but it was a tempting fantasy. So tempting he clenched his hands into fists to remind himself not to do anything stupid. There was a breathless pause—for dramatic effect, no doubt—and then Dorothy entered the room.

The body she had created for herself was beautiful and bore just enough similarities to Nate and his father to make everyone believe she was a close relative. She wore a form-fitting shell pink skirt suit that managed to be business-appropriate and sexy at the same time, and she carried herself with all the pride and confidence of a woman used to being in charge.

Nate took a deep breath and forced himself not to stare at Dorothy and not to look at Nadia to see how she was handling seeing their nemesis in the flesh. His attention was supposed to be focused entirely on the task of guarding Belinski, though it wasn't like there was a whole lot to protect him from in this conference room.

Dorothy smiled brightly, her eyes sweeping over the assembly, passing over both Nate and Nadia with nary a flicker of recognition. She waited for one of her bodyguards to pull her chair back for her, forcing everyone else in the room to remain standing in the pettiest of power plays.

Finally, she sat, and everyone else did as well.

Like Nate's father, Dorothy seemed to take a special pleasure in asserting her authority with a multitude of small reminders. Discussing her business with a visiting head of state should have been the first item on her agenda if she were following any standards of courtesy. Then again, if she were following standards of courtesy, she and Belinski would have met before the meeting and entered the boardroom together. Instead, she had made him wait—and put him in the awkward position of having to stand when she entered or be the only person in the room who remained seated.

Nate was sure Dorothy had done it that way on purpose, and he wished Belinski had been a little less polite and stayed in his seat. Letting Dorothy win in even such a trivial matter felt like a mistake. Then again, Nate was incapable of thinking rationally while his mind kept replaying Dorothy's murder of his father.

Dorothy compounded the insult of her grand entrance by not immediately ceding Belinski the floor for his address. Instead, she spent a good ten minutes giving a speech about how well her campaign against the Basement was going and about how she predicted in the next two to three days, the "wannabe revolution" would be thoroughly crushed and order restored.

There was a round of applause when she'd finished, though Nate noticed some board members were more enthusiastic than others. A few of them seemed almost manic with glee, and Nate had to force himself to look away. He had always hated sycophants.

Although Chairman Belinski had stood when Dorothy entered the room, his excess of courtesy did not extend to applauding her litany of lies, and he crossed his arms and leaned back in his chair while the board members cheered, a couple of them even pounding on the table in their enthusiasm.

Dorothy noticed that Belinski did not join in the applause, her eyes and lips both narrowing in displeasure.

"I have just delivered excellent news," Dorothy said to him from across the length of the table when the noise level in the room lowered. "And yet you don't seem to share our spirit of celebration, Mr. Chairman. Are you not pleased that peace will soon return to Paxco? Surely you don't wish continued armed conflict within the borders of your closest ally."

Nate couldn't help staring at her, though since her attention was entirely focused on Chairman Belinski, she didn't notice.

What was the bitch up to? It was one thing to show the kinds of subtle disrespect she'd already shown, but challenging him on his lack of applause was a far bigger breach of etiquette. Some of the board members were made visibly uncomfortable by her words, but some of them clearly didn't care or were even pleased by the insult.

The hair on the back of Nate's neck rose. In his days as Chairman Heir, he had sat in on many a board meeting. He'd never made much of a show of paying attention, and he had always found them excruciatingly boring. Even so, he knew every one of the board members personally, and there was something decidedly off about the tone of this meeting. He was used to most of them being sycophants to some extent, but he was not used to the vocal minority keeping their mouths shut.

He looked closely at Directors Bull, Nielsen, and Riley, all three of whom had balls of steel—though Shana Nielsen might object to the description—and all three of whom were quietly nodding in agreement. Tom Bull was almost eighty years old and had the biggest stick up his ass of anyone Nate had ever known. The man could parse an insult out of even the most innocuous of statements and use it as an excuse to get up on his soapbox and pontificate. He'd even had the nerve to rebuke Nate's father a few times, using his advanced age to excuse his seeming disrespect. He should have been appalled at Dorothy's blatant lack of manners, not nodding in agreement.

Chairman Belinski stood up, his gaze traveling around the table, making eye contact with every member of the board of directors—at least those who weren't so embarrassed by Dorothy's rudeness that they were staring at the table or at their hands.

"Some very disturbing information has come my way," Belinski said. "Information that suggests you have not been entirely truthful about what has been happening in the Basement."

The board members looked variously intrigued, shocked, and outraged. Nate himself was surprised at Belinski's bluntness, but then considering the tone Dorothy had already set, perhaps it was only fitting.

Dorothy rose slowly to her feet, her eyes fixed on Belinski's, her face giving away nothing.

"I must say I resent your implications, Mr. Chairman," Dorothy said. "Perhaps we should continue this conversation in a more private setting rather than airing dirty laundry in public."

Belinski didn't budge. "I have nothing to hide, Madam Chairman. Can you say the same?"

"Are you calling me a liar? Right here in my own boardroom?"

There was an angry murmur among the board members, and several of them were glaring at Belinski so fiercely it looked like they were about to leap across the table and tackle him.

"According to my sources," Belinski said, his voice rising to be heard over the murmur, "you cut off phone service, then power, then food and medical supplies to the Basement—which caused them to riot, not surprisingly."

Dorothy snorted. "Your sources have it backward. Assuming these so-called sources even exist. Or are you trying to pick a fight in hopes of breaking our trade agreements without violating the letter of said agreements?"

Belinski's lips twitched in a small smile. "Believe me, Miss Hayes, if I wanted to get out of our trade agreements, I'd find a more subtle and tactful way than this to do it."

Dorothy's face flushed red, and several of the board members pushed back their chairs and stood up with shouts of outrage.

"You will address me as *Chairman* Hayes," Dorothy said, "or you can go back home to your pathetic little state and Paxco will have nothing more to do with you."

The board members who had stood up—there were

eight of them, Nate noticed—all voiced their agreement. Nate could hardly believe that Directors Bull, Nielsen, and Riley were all standing, all glaring at Belinski with almost identical looks of fury, as if he had personally insulted them. They should have been demanding answers from Dorothy, not blindly taking her side. Even if Dorothy had secured their loyalty through bribes or threats, they should have at least shown some interest in Belinski's claim.

"You are not the real Chairman Hayes," Belinski said, and Nate realized with a start that that was his cue.

Nate opened the moistened towelette the makeup artists had given him, using it to loosen the edges of his makeup/mask. Pulling the damned thing off was an exercise in torture—he wondered if he had any eyebrows when he was finished—but he managed it. Nadia, too, was removing her mask, pulling the false face off to reveal the familiar features beneath. It was a relief to be able to recognize her once again, and from the look they shared, he guessed she felt the same way.

The gasps that echoed around the room were gratifying enough that Nate couldn't help smiling, feeling like he'd pulled off a particularly clever magic trick.

Belinski was still staring across the table at Dorothy, who was looking back and forth between Nate and Nadia with openmouthed shock.

"Nathaniel Hayes and Nadia Lake have a very interesting story to tell," Belinski said.

"Guards!" Dorothy shouted. "Arrest them!"

Everyone was standing now, talking at once. Dorothy's security squad started forward, but the room was too crowded for them to move easily to where Nate and Nadia stood, and Belinski's own squad had positioned themselves to block the way.

"According to these young people," Belinski shouted over the noise, "you, Miss Hayes, are some kind of Replica, controlled remotely by an artificial intelligence named Thea."

The plan had been for Nate and Nadia to tell their whole story to the board, but no one had anticipated the level of chaos that would ensue as soon as the masks came off. Dorothy's security squad were drawing their weapons—something they should never have done in such a crowded room—shoving hapless aides and secretaries out of their way to get at Nate and Nadia.

Several of the board members who had so far been quiet were now clamoring for order—and shouting that they wanted to hear more.

And the other board members, the ones who'd been in such perfect agreement with Dorothy beyond all reason, were reaching into the pockets of the jackets they'd never removed despite the heat.

CHAPTER TWENTY-THREE

with an almost dreamlike sense of disbelief, Nadia saw Dorothy's security team drawing their guns. No one had imagined Dorothy would take Chairman Belinski's accusations gracefully, but in all the scenarios they'd hashed out in preparation for today's meeting, they hadn't discussed the possibility of a shoot-out in a conference room that was so overcrowded it was hard to move.

Everyone was shouting at once, and there were a few screams. The people closest to the door tried to open it and bolt, but the door opened inward, and the advancing security squad forced people to press their backs against the wall—and the door—to avoid being trampled.

Several of the board members did a quick risk assessment and then wisely ducked under the table, choosing its dubious protection over trying to force their way to the door.

There was empty space at the head of the table around Dorothy as her security squad forced everyone back from her, and she stood there rigidly, watching the chaos as if it were only marginally interesting to her. She didn't seem inclined to try to impose order.

The board members who'd been most vocal in their blind support of Dorothy all stood calmly in their places, none looking the least bit alarmed despite the drawn weapons and the panicking bystanders. Nadia's jaw dropped open when she saw all eight of them reach into their jacket pockets at exactly the same time, their synchronization too perfect to be coincidence.

"They're Replicas!" Nadia shouted, but her words were drowned out by more screams.

The Replicas, still moving in perfect unison, pulled guns from their pockets, each turning to the closest human board member—even if that board member was hiding under the table. Nadia's heart seized in terror as she realized that Thea was through with her charade of humanity. She had already replaced eight of the twenty board members with her special remote-controlled Replicas, and she was about to kill the rest. It was possible, even likely, that she had Replicas of them already prepared and ready to take their places. But no matter what, there was no way she was planning to leave surviving witnesses.

Nadia wanted to run to Belinski, to warn him what was happening, but his bodyguards had him surrounded, and one of the other members of his detail grabbed hold of her arm and yanked her backward so that she and Nate and Belinski were in a circle of heavily armed guards who had drawn their own weapons. The rest of his entourage, left outside the circle, joined the crowd fighting toward the exit.

But Chairman Belinski was far from an idiot, and even over the screams of the crowd Nadia heard him bellow, "Now!"

She held her breath, knowing that if their jamming device failed, every real human being in this room was going to die. Belinski's bodyguards were no doubt good, but between Dorothy's guards and the Replicas, they were badly outnumbered.

For a moment, nothing happened. The Replicas aimed at their targets, some of whom hadn't even noticed the threat yet because they were so stunned by everything that was happening. The ones who had noticed were frantically trying to scramble away, adding to the chaos.

And then suddenly, Dorothy and her eight Replica board members went down.

Most of the panicking people didn't notice, too frantic to reach the doors to see clearly or think rationally. A couple of the board members who'd been under the table popped up in the clear area where Dorothy had been standing and made for the door she had entered through. Her security guards were all well past them by now, so they made it to the door, yanking it open and bolting through. Those who weren't too panicked to think noticed the new exit and made for it, ducking under the table to crawl, or climbing on top of it.

Dorothy's security team *did* notice the board members and Dorothy going down. Some raced to her side, and others stopped in their tracks, looking confused. Alarms started blaring, adding to the noise and confusion.

With people finally exiting through Dorothy's entrance, the crowd in front of the main conference room entrance managed to get the door open and began streaming out. People trampled the bodies of the fallen Replicas with complete disregard, not noticing them unless they tripped. And even then, not caring, just struggling to their feet and continuing on their way.

"There are a lot more security officers in this building,"

Nate yelled at Belinski. "They won't know what's going on and will probably try to arrest everyone."

Which was not going to go over well when people were still in the grip of mindless panic. Nadia suspected the blaring alarms were making the situation worse, though at least the conference room was clearing out.

Several members of Dorothy's security team had made it to the head of the table. One of them scooped Dorothy's limp body into his arms, while the others stood in a protective circle, guns pointing outward. They might be confused about what was going on, but they *weren't* confused about their duty, which was to protect the Chairman. Nadia couldn't blame them for falling back on that duty when they didn't know what else to do.

"All I did was jam the radio frequencies so that Thea can't control her Replicas," Belinski shouted across the room at the confused guards. Despite the pandemonium around them, he remained calm and unruffled. "Dorothy is not a human being," he continued. "Your true Chairman is here with me." He nodded toward Nate.

Nadia thought they might buy it. After all, they had seen with their own eyes how Dorothy and the board members had mysteriously collapsed all at the same time. But Dorothy had gone on the offensive before Nate and Nadia had been able to recount the details of everything that had happened, details that would have helped their wild-sounding accusations make sense.

The rest of Dorothy's security team found purpose in protecting their fallen "leader," one of them carrying her out through the doorway while the others formed a human shield. There was no one left in the conference room except for them and Belinski's people, although there were plenty of shouts and screams still sounding from the hallway outside and the alarms were still filling the air with their earsplitting shrieks.

"Hand over the traitors!" one of Dorothy's security officers shouted over the background noise. Even from across the room, Nadia could see the man's eyes showed too much white, that he was overwhelmed and falling back on the only thing that made sense to him. Dorothy's last order had been to arrest Nate and Nadia, so that was what he was determined to do.

All of the guards who remained raised their guns, prompting Belinski's security team to do the same.

"Let's all try to calm down now," Belinski tried, though it was hard to be very calming when shouting over an alarm. "The crisis is over, and we can handle this like rational human beings."

But the leader of the security team had found his purpose, and he was sticking to it. He ignored Belinski and fixed his stare on Nate. "The building is in lock-down! There is no escape. Come out, get down on your knees, and put your hands behind your head!" He flicked a glance Nadia's way. "You, too!"

"Maybe we should just humor him," Nadia suggested, though the idea of letting Dorothy's people get their hands on her for even a minute made her quail. "We've proven our point, and the board members will back us up."

Belinski shook his head. "We'd be dead before the dust cleared. And for all we know, Thea's replacing the surviving board members as we speak. The jammer is too localized to reach throughout the building."

"I'm not asking again!" the officer yelled, his eyes blazing with fanaticism. "Hand them over, or I will shoot."

Under ordinary circumstances, that would no doubt have been an empty threat. Chairman Belinski was a foreign head of state, after all, and shooting at his people would be an act of war. But circumstances were far from ordinary.

Belinski took a step backward and went down to the floor, dragging Nate and Nadia with him. Nadia wasn't sure who fired first, but the room was soon filled with the roar of gunfire and more screams. Nadia covered her ringing ears and huddled on the floor with Nate and Belinski.

Two of Belinski's guards went down, the man with a hole in the middle of his forehead, the woman clasping her hands to her throat and making horrible choking sounds as she tried futilely to stanch the blood that poured from between her fingers.

There were a couple more shots, but then the room went quiet except for the constant blare of the alarm.

The woman who'd been shot in the throat bled out before anyone could even reach her. Shaking, Nadia uncurled from her protective ball and saw that all five of Dorothy's guards were down. The three surviving members of Belinski's team helped Nate, Nadia, and Belinski back up to their feet.

"What now, sir?" one of them asked. Unlike Dorothy's men, Belinski's team showed no sign of being rattled, each changing clips with cool aplomb.

It was a good question. The original plan to storm the subbasement to destroy Thea and the Replication tanks had been predicated on the idea that the board meeting finished in an orderly way, with the board recognizing Nate as the rightful Chairman. Under those circumstances, he could have used his authority to get to the subbasement with a small army of security officers to help him get through whatever obstacles Thea tried to put in his way.

Even if things had gone according to plan, the results would have been very much in question. But without any acknowledged authority—and without the aid of a rocket launcher—there was no way they could fight their way down to Thea.

"We need to find a way out of the building," Belinski said.

Nate shook his head. "If it's in lock-down, then there's no way we're getting out. This place isn't called the Fortress for nothing."

"Well, we're going to have to find a way out anyway," Belinski said grimly, and his tone sent a chill down Nadia's spine.

"Why is that, sir?" she asked, dreading the answer.

"Because I had a contingency plan I didn't tell you about," he replied. "I needed concrete proof before I could proceed, and you've given it to me. Thea cannot be allowed to survive, and if we can't get to her ourselves, then we have to find another way.

"The commander of my air force is awaiting my command to fire a barrage of missiles at this building."

"Thea's deep underground in the subbasement," Nate said doubtfully. "She should be protected even against an air strike when she's down that deep."

"In theory," Belinski agreed as he tapped a password into his phone. "But our military technology is the reason your father wanted to create an alliance between our states in the first place. I'm confident our missiles will reach all the way down to Thea's lair. But once they're fired, there's no calling them back." Belinski held his thumb hovering over one of the buttons on his phone as he looked back and forth between Nate and Nadia. "I can wait until we get out of the building before I make the call . . ." He let his voice trail off.

Nate grimaced. "But it's possible we won't be able to get out, and if we don't, you won't be able to order the missile strike."

Belinski nodded.

"How long will it take the missiles to get here?" Nadia asked.

"About twenty minutes."

She and Nate shared a long glance of silent communication.

"If we're not out of here in twenty minutes," Nate said, "then we're not getting out anyway."

Nadia swallowed hard and nodded her agreement. Belinski turned to Marco, who said, "I concur."

"Very well, then," Belinski said. "We'll have to turn the jammer off to get the signal."

Belinski gestured at the downed Replicas. Nadia didn't immediately recognize the order for what it was. Not until the three surviving members of Belinski's security team started shooting the Replicas in the head.

She put her hands over her mouth to stifle a scream, and beside her, Nate's face took on a sickly greenish color as the air filled with the scents of smoke and blood.

"They aren't people," Belinski reminded them. "No matter how much they may look like people, they're just empty shells."

Nadia took a shaky breath. She knew Belinski was right. These Replicas were nothing but empty shells with no sentience at all without Thea's input. But if they were to start receiving Thea's signal again, they would be an immediate threat. They had to die, no matter how wrong it seemed.

When the last Replica was shot, Marco turned off the jammer, and Belinski raised the phone to his ear.

CHAPTER TWENTY-FOUR

nate's pulse was hammering and his palms were clammy as he watched Belinski raise the phone to his ear. He had been in mortal danger more times than he could count over the past couple of months, had even experienced the terror of Dorothy's air strikes against the Basement, but that wasn't quite the same as ordering a missile strike on a building you were currently trapped in.

Despite his fear, Nate felt no temptation to ask Belinski to wait. The building was in lock-down, and two of Belinski's bodyguards were already dead. Missiles or not, there was a good chance they were all going to die soon. He didn't know how many armed security personnel were in the building, except that it was more than enough to leave Belinski's three surviving guards hopelessly outnumbered.

Belinski lowered the phone, shaking his head. "It appears Thea is blocking the phone signal."

Nate supposed it shouldn't have come as a surprise. It wasn't like Thea hadn't done it before. But if Nate had to die here in the Fortress, he much preferred to do it while taking Thea with him, rather than being gunned down by a bunch of security officers who didn't even know what they were fighting for.

"Apparently, we're going to have to get out of here after all," Belinski said.

Marco nodded and gestured for the two other guards to take the point as they headed for the conference room door.

"Do you know how to shoot that thing, son?" Belinski asked Nate, indicating the gun tucked in his shoulder holster.

Nate shook his head. "Not really."

Belinski held out his hand, and Nate handed over the gun with something akin to relief. He'd probably have shot his own foot off if he'd tried to fire the gun, and it hadn't been doing anyone any good in its holster.

"Coast is clear," one of the bodyguards said. He and his partner stepped out into the hallway back to back, guns at the ready.

"Which way?" Belinski asked Nate, the only one of them who knew the building well.

Nate glanced to the right, toward the central atrium where there were sets of stairs as well as the main bank of elevators. The usually bright atrium was dim, its windows and skylight no doubt covered by the sliding metal plates that came into play during lock-down. "Left," Nate said with feigned confidence. "There's a set of fire stairs at the end of the next hallway." In a normal building, the fire stairs would always be accessible, no matter what, but he suspected here in the Fortress, they would be locked. However, the elevators and the main stairs were out of the question.

With Marco taking the rear and the other two bodyguards moving forward, Nate, Nadia, and Belinski stepped into the hallway and started to the left.

"I'm not stupid," a disembodied female voice said, freezing them all in their tracks. "I have locked all doors, including the fire doors."

Belinski and his team looked around in frantic search of the body that went with the voice, but Nate and Nadia knew better.

"You will not escape this building," Thea's voice continued from whatever unseen speaker she was using.

"We have more chance of escaping it than you!" Nate taunted. "At least we have legs."

Belinski made an angry cutting motion across his throat—the universal sign for "shut up"—while glaring at Nate.

"I'm sure Thea was listening to us all along," Nadia said to Belinski, and Nate realized that Belinski still hadn't thoroughly grasped the scope of Thea's reach. He had thought Nate was giving away secrets with his taunt.

"Indeed," Thea confirmed. "It's very noble of you to be willing to sacrifice yourselves for what you see as the greater good. It is one of my goals to instill that spirit of self-sacrifice in my children. *All* of my children, not the few select noble ones."

Children? What the hell was Thea talking about? Nate had a feeling he really didn't want to know.

"Ignore her," Nate advised. "Let's just concentrate on proving her wrong."

Belinski nodded his agreement, and they moved cautiously toward the hallway that led to the fire stairs.

"If you lay down your weapons and surrender," Thea said, "I will be merciful and let you live."

Nate almost laughed at the absurdity of the suggestion.

"You were willing to kill thousands of innocents in the Basement to get to us, and now you want us to believe you're not going to kill us? Don't be ridiculous."

"One of the things that drove your father crazy about you was your assumption that everything that happened had to be about *you*," Thea said, and Nate had to clamp his jaws shut against a surge of fury that she would even *talk* about his father after murdering him. "I know you don't think very highly of me," she continued, "but surely you don't think I'm foolish enough to use bombs to swat flies."

Belinski's point men made it to the corner and peeked around. The point men gave the okay, and they all rounded the corner and headed toward the fire stairs and the heavy metal door that blocked them. One of the men gave the handle an experimental tug downward, but no one was surprised when it remained locked. There was a card reader and a keypad on the wall beside the door, but Thea could no doubt block that even if they had the proper card and code.

"Do you honestly think I bombed the Basement on the off chance that one of my bombs might hit you?" Thea asked, sounding incredulous.

Nate knew he should take his own advice and just ignore Thea's voice, but he found himself responding against his better judgment.

"If it wasn't about us, then what *was* it about?" he asked.

One of Belinski's men produced what looked like a tube of toothpaste from somewhere beneath his jacket. He squatted in front of the door and squeezed a line of off-white paste from the tube onto the area around the locking mechanism. He capped the tube while another of the men unspooled a length of wire so thin it was almost invisible, sticking one end into the paste and clipping it down to a length of about a foot.

"Do you have any idea how much money Paxco throws into the black hole you call the Basement?" Thea asked. "All to support people who are of no use to society, who are in fact *harmful* to society. They peddle drugs and contraband, they steal from legitimate citizens, they murder, they rape. The list goes on. And Paxco *pays* for the privilege of supporting them."

Nate fought a shudder as he and Nadia shared a horrified look. Bad enough to think that Thea was okay with causing massive collateral damage in an attempt to kill them, but to think that her ultimate goal had been to destroy the Basement entirely . . . that all those helpless people had been not collateral damage, but *targets*.

"Paxco will recoup the cost of the military strike in no time," Thea said with a hint of gloating in her voice, "and we will no longer have to spend our hard-earned money on supporting the dregs of society. We will reclaim the land, and I will have the funds I need to continue my work."

"We're going to want to stand around the corner," Belinski said. He sounded brisk and unruffled, but the look in his eyes said he was hearing everything Thea was saying with the same sense of mounting horror as Nate felt. If any of them had doubted before that destroying Thea was a goal worth risking their lives for, they didn't now.

"Does your security team always carry explosives when on bodyguard duty?" Nadia asked Belinski with an arch of her brow.

"Only when there's a possibility we might have to blast our way through doors," he answered. "I figured even in the best-case scenario, we might encounter immovable obstacles on our way down to the subbasement."

Everyone except for the man lighting the fuse took shelter, and when he came pelting around the corner, they all covered their ears.

A loud boom shook the hallway, followed by the metallic clink of debris raining down on the tile floor. The door had been blown open, and the stairwell beyond gaped enticingly.

They hurried down the hallway, their feet crunching on debris as they went. There was an acrid, burning smell in the air, and Nate had to stifle a cough. They slowed down when they neared the door, one of the guards taking point again and motioning for everyone else to wait.

His caution was well warranted. He was still five feet from the door when a shot rang out from somewhere above. The shot just missed. Belinski's man threw himself backward, but a second shot caught him before he was out of range. His colleague shot off a barrage of cover fire while Marco herded the rest of them back toward the corner.

"You didn't think it would be that easy, did you?" Thea's voice mocked. "Perhaps you'd like to reconsider your options. I'm sure we can reach some kind of mutually beneficial agreement, Mr. Chairman, if we sit down to talk, just the two of us."

"Somehow I doubt that," Belinski said.

The lights suddenly went out, leaving the hallway in utter darkness. In the event of a blackout, there should have been emergency lighting and illuminated exit signs, but there was nothing. The heavy protective shutters over the windows blocked out any hint of distant daylight.

"You had better *hope* we can reach an agreement," Thea said. "I don't foresee any positive outcomes on your horizon if you continue being so difficult."

Nate had slowed down when the lights went out, and Belinski's bodyguard had stopped shooting. It seemed like the darkness, while annoying and disorienting, would make it easier for them to stay hidden and escape. But Thea wouldn't have turned off the lights if she didn't think it was to her advantage.

"Keep moving," Marco growled under his breath, and there was an unmistakable sense of urgency in his tone.

With a chill of renewed alarm, Nate realized that just because *he* couldn't see his hand in front of his face didn't mean Thea's people had the same problem. They had access to the Fortress's arsenal, and there was enough gear in there to stage a small war.

"Hurry!" Nate shouted, sprinting for the corner he could no longer see and dragging Nadia stumbling behind him. "They can see!"

Nate put one hand on the wall so he would know when they reached the corner. Just as they did, the hallway lit with the white flashes of automatic weapon fire.

In those brief flashes, Nate saw men in full combat gear and wearing night vision goggles spilling out of the emergency stairwell. The last of Belinski's bodyguards was bringing up the rear, firing over his shoulder while Marco pushed Belinski in front of him, using his own body as a shield. But a handgun was no match for automatic weapons, and as Nate and Nadia careened around the corner, the gunfire stopped.

"Go!" Marco yelled, and for once Nate had no issue with

taking orders. In a manner of minutes, Thea had killed—or at least incapacitated—four of Belinski's five guards. The rest of them didn't stand a chance unless they could find some way to put a barrier between themselves and the security officers.

Apparently, Marco had the same thought, because he brought them all to a sudden halt, right around what Nate guessed was the conference room door.

"Inside!" the man ordered, just as their pursuers rounded the corner and started firing.

Nate dove through the door, dragging Nadia with him. The muzzle flashes were blinding, but in their glare, he saw Belinski standing in the doorway, gun firing into the darkness. Marco unceremoniously shoved Belinski through the door, pulling it shut with one hand while still shooting with the other hand.

Nate would have liked to open the door and pull Marco in, but the man had made his decision and was buying them what little time he could. There was no point in wasting it.

"Help me block the door!" Nadia said, and he could hear her shoving chairs out of the way so she could get to the conference table.

Nate tripped over the body of one of the dead Replicas in his haste to get to the table. There was a lock on the conference room door, but it wouldn't work with no power. That meant the only way to keep Thea's men out was to block it physically.

Together, he and Nadia toppled the table and manhandled it around until one end was shoved up under the handle of the door and the other was braced against the wall. The table was too big to fit in the room sideways, so the impromptu blockade was at an angle. It would slow down anyone trying to get into the room, but it wouldn't stop them.

The lights suddenly went on, blinding in their brilliance.

"I am becoming annoyed with you," Thea said.

Outside the door, the gunfire had ceased, which no doubt meant Marco was dead—and the rest of Thea's security squad would soon be at the door. Still blinking in the sudden light, Nate hastily hit the lock on the door. Its indicator light briefly flashed red, then flashed back to green again.

"The doors will obey *my* will, not yours," Thea said smugly.

Nate cursed, realizing they were trapped. He'd had hopes that they could block the main door, then exit through the door at the head of the table, but of course its red indicator light was on. Which explained why Thea had suddenly turned the power back on—she wanted them trapped in this room.

"Nate!" Nadia cried, and he turned to see her crouching beside Belinski, who sat on the floor with his back to the wall. There was a large patch of blood on his pants right above his knee.

Belinski's face was pale and sweaty as he put his hands over the wound and applied pressure. He closed his eyes and let out a strained breath. "It won't kill me," he said, pain evident in his voice. "But I won't be doing any more running."

"Perhaps now you will acknowledge your defeat," Thea said. "If you surrender now, I will spare your life, Mr. Chairman. Once you come to understand my vision for Paxco's future, I think you will find it is to our mutual advantage to work together."

Nate didn't have to tell Belinski that Thea was lying through her nonexistent teeth. She no doubt had a Replica of Belinski available, and once she took care of the real Belinski, she'd put her Replica in his place. Worst of all, Belinski had had a scan when he first arrived in Paxco—it had been part of the marriage agreement he and Nate's father had arranged—which probably meant Thea could extract all the Chairman's knowledge from his brain. No one would ever be able to prove the Replica wasn't really Belinski.

Whether Belinski realized all this or not, he evidently had no interest in cutting a deal. He took one hand off his wound to pull the gun out of his pocket. He swept his gaze around the room, fixating on the security camera discreetly located in the far corner.

"This is your last chance, Mr. Chairman," Thea's voice warned, and Nate realized it was coming from the security camera.

Belinski realized the same thing and smiled grimly. Then he raised his gun and fired one shot, and the camera exploded in a shower of glass shards.

"Any more generous offers you'd like to make?" Belinski asked, but this time Thea didn't answer. "I suspect her mike and speaker are in the camera housing," he said in a low voice, "but let's keep our voices down just in case."

Nate wasn't sure they had a whole lot to talk about. There was no way out. Unless . . .

Something banged into the door, making the conference table shudder. Belinski scooted over so that his back was now against the table, using his body weight to help hold it steady.

Nate glanced up at the ceiling. The white paneled ceiling. The kind that was used when there were things behind it maintenance workers might have to get to. Nadia and Belinski both followed his gaze.

"I don't think I'm up to acrobatics," Belinski said, then had to stop a moment to breathe through what looked like a wave of pain. "You two have to go on without me."

Nate and Nadia both let out sounds of protest, but Belinski spoke right over them.

"Find Colonel Bradford in my contacts, and send him the message I'm about to record," he said, pulling out his phone. "We *have* to get those missiles flying. It's the only way we can be sure she can't seize control of Synchrony—and its military—by Replicating me."

"Would your man really order a missile strike based on a recording?" Nate asked. Sending missiles against a foreign nation was surely something Bradford would be reluctant to do in the best of circumstances, and considering how easily recordings could be manipulated . . .

"We've known each other since we were kids," Belinski said as someone or something banged on the door again. The edge of the table slipped a tiny bit, despite Belinski's weight against it. Nate shoved it back into place with his shoulder.

"I'll make sure he knows it's from me. I can't guarantee he'll act on the orders, but I think he will."

Belinski opened his phone and pointed it at himself. He looked terrible, sweat beading on his almost gray skin, but there was no sign of fear or despair in his eyes. He looked to Nate like the kind of man people would obey without question.

Belinski identified himself and gave only the briefest explanation of the circumstances. "If any of the witnesses to the board meeting survive, they will be able to confirm my story," he said. "But even if you can't confirm what I've told you, rest assured that what I am doing is just and right."

He ordered Colonel Bradford to launch his missiles at the Fortress, giving a long authorization code that must have been a bear to memorize.

"I'll try to get out," Belinski finished, "but I don't like my chances. If I die, know that it's for a good cause." He smiled weakly. "And if I don't make it back, there's something I have to get off my chest: I was the one who sent Judy Perkins that valentine in your name when we were kids." The smile faded. "Good-bye, old friend," he said, then ended the recording.

Nadia cocked her head at Belinski, and his smile came back for a brief curtain call. "When we were ten," he explained, "there was this beautiful eleven-year-old we both admired. Neither one of us had the guts to talk to her. I made her a Valentine's Day card but chickened out at the last moment and signed Rob's name to it. He always thought his older brother did it to humiliate him, and I was too embarrassed by what I'd done to tell the truth. He'll know the message is genuine."

Nate took the phone from Belinski's hand, then gave it to Nadia. "You'll need my help to get up there," Nate said, "so you should go first. And whoever goes first should have the phone."

But he already knew there was no "first" here. He could probably get himself up through the ceiling without a boost by standing on one of the chairs, but that would mean leaving

Belinski here by himself. Thea might be keeping the door at the head of the table locked to ensure they didn't escape, but if they didn't do something about it, she could just line her men up outside that door and unlock it at her convenience.

Nadia gave him a knowing look, not fooled for a moment by his words. Tears swam in her eyes.

"You know you have to do it," he said. "And you know I have to stay. The longer we can keep them out, the longer before Thea knows you're not in the room." He nodded at the locked door. "I'm going to have to try to block that one." He suspected the best way to do that was to pile bodies in front of it, but he wasn't about to mention that part to Nadia. And he didn't much want to think about it himself.

Nadia shook her head doubtfully. "You think she doesn't know about the ceiling?"

"Probably," Nate admitted. "But it's that or we all sit here together and wait for them to blow the door—or come through the ceiling themselves. And assuming that camera was her only way to see in here, at least if you're up there, she won't be sure where you are."

"Just because I can get out of this room doesn't mean I can get out of the building."

"If you can get into the Chairman's office somehow, there will be an emergency escape route, just like the one in Headquarters. It'll take you straight outside." Once she somehow, miraculously, got out of this room and into the office.

The door shuddered under another impact, and this time Belinski couldn't hold back a cry of pain as he tried with all his might to keep the brace from slipping. The table scraped off some paint from the wall as it skidded over about half an inch. Once again, Nate set his shoulder to it and forced it back into place.

"We've got to hurry," he said. "I know you don't want to leave us here, but you have to."

Nadia swallowed hard, and a tear trickled down her cheek. But she dashed it away and nodded. "All right. I'll do it."

Her face set with fearsome determination, Nadia crouched beside one of the dead Replicas and took the gun he'd been about to draw when his link to Thea had been cut.

Keeping a nervous eye on the locked door's indicator light, Nate prepared to give Nadia the boost she needed.

CHAPTER TWENTY-FIVE

EVEN with Nate's help, getting up into the crawl space behind the ceiling was something of a challenge. Some of the panels were fixed in place, and the first one they managed to open had some kind of duct running over it so there was no room for Nadia to crawl through.

The whole time they were searching for a way up, Nadia was expecting the door to give way, or for Thea's men to resort to explosives, but when she finally hoisted herself up, both doors were still closed.

There was no time for an emotional parting from Nate. The moment she was up, he raced to the locked door. He hesitated, meeting her eyes as she watched from her perch. His gaze flicked toward the body of one of the dead Replicas, and her stomach turned over as she realized what he was about to do. Best not to watch, she decided.

Forcing herself not to think about anything except the present moment, Nadia put the ceiling tile back in place, then used Belinski's phone as a flashlight to look around her.

Unsurprisingly, the crawl space was low and claustrophobic. There were ducts and cables everywhere, and in the dim light of the phone she could only see a few feet ahead of herself. Pointing herself in the direction of the door at the head of the conference room, Nadia started to crawl.

Crawling while holding the phone was no easy feat, but Nadia needed the light. The ductwork and cables made the space into a maze, and it was impossible for her to move in a straight line. She didn't trust the ceiling panels to hold her weight, so she traveled along whatever beams and supports she could find.

There was, of course, no air conditioning in the crawl space, and within a couple of minutes, Nadia's whole body was soaked with sweat, and she was covered in dust and cobwebs. Maintenance workers might need access to the equipment on occasion, but it seemed they didn't take advantage of it very often—and they certainly didn't clean up when they did.

Nadia wasn't entirely sure what her plan was. She'd started out heading in the direction of Dorothy's entrance to the conference room on the assumption that it would lead toward the Chairman's office, but with all the dodging around she had to do, she had no idea if she was still heading in that direction. If only she had a map, something to help her orient herself.

Nadia had been crawling around for what felt like an eternity when she heard a much muffled bang from somewhere behind her, and the beam she was currently crawling over vibrated beneath her. Surely that had been the sound of the conference room door being blown open. She held her breath, waiting for the sound of renewed gunfire as Thea's men shot Nate and Belinski down, but it didn't come. Maybe Nate and Belinski had submitted without a struggle, and Thea's men hadn't had specific orders to kill them on sight. Not that Nadia thought the order would be long in coming.

She started forward again, only to freeze when she heard the rumble of hurried footsteps below her. Once more she held her breath, not daring to move an inch in case the men below might hear her.

"They've blown the door," she heard one of the men say. Then, after a few more steps, "The Lake girl isn't there. They think she's in the ceiling."

Someone responded to him, but as they were moving away, Nadia couldn't hear the response.

They knew she was up here. It was only a matter of time before someone found her. And she had no idea if she was any closer to the Chairman's office than she had been when she started.

Tears of fear and misery burned her eyes as she braced herself for the effort of continuing forward. She was prepared to fight until the moment all hope was irreparably lost, and no one had captured her yet. Her knees ached from their constant impacts against metal beams, and the heels of her hands weren't faring much better, but she would keep moving.

She crawled for maybe another five feet or so before a thought struck her so suddenly she almost cried out in surprise.

The guards she'd overheard had known what had happened in the conference room, had known Nadia wasn't in there. Even though they were nowhere near the conference room, as evidenced by the distant blast.

How were they communicating?

Nadia almost dropped the phone in her haste to check

its screen. Sure enough, the phone was receiving a signal. Her hands trembled as she brought up Colonel Bradford's contact and prepared to send the message from Belinski. But before she managed to attach the recording, the phone lost its connection again.

Nadia wanted to scream in frustration, but if the phone lines had been up once, they'd probably go up again if she just waited. She should have thought of this before! Thea couldn't control Dorothy if the phone lines were down, and she needed Dorothy to issue orders. No doubt she would keep the lines down as much as possible so no one could call out for help, but she was sure to need Dorothy again.

Tucking herself into the space formed by the juncture of two ducts and hunching over the phone to block its telltale light, Nadia made sure her message was ready to send at the tap of a finger and stared at the signal indicator, willing it to life. In the distance, she heard voices, voices that didn't seem to be muffled by the ceiling or walls. In all likelihood, it meant the security officers were now combing the crawl space for her. She had to fight a desperate desire to shake the phone, as if that would make the signal come back faster.

How long did she have? On the one hand, the crawl space had to be as much of a maze for the security officers as it had been for her. On the other hand, she'd probably left plenty of tracks in the dust.

Sweat dripped from her forehead onto the phone's screen. Or maybe it was tears. She had plenty of both. How many people would she be condemning to die if she managed to send her message? The lock-down meant that all the staff who regularly worked in the Fortress were trapped inside, along with all the extra staff who had come with Belinski and the board members.

But even though she didn't know what Thea's ultimate goal was, she was sure more people would die if Thea was allowed to live. So if the signal ever reappeared, Nadia knew what she had to do.

The signal indicator suddenly blinked on. Without giving herself even a fraction of a second to think about it, Nadia sent Belinski's message.

It occurred to her that if she was captured, someone might check her phone and see the message Belinski had recorded. The longer she could keep Thea in ignorance about the missile strike, the better, so Nadia turned the phone off and tucked it in the gap between a beam and an air duct.

Seconds later, a man in combat gear peeked around the edge of one of the ducts and saw her.

CHAPTER TWENTY-SIX

nadia could have gone for her purloined gun, but she wasn't about to shoot someone in cold blood even if she *had* just doomed him and herself to death. She had accomplished her mission, had sent out Chairman Belinski's message. Now all that was left to do was wait for the missiles to hit. She just wished there were some way she could get word to all the innocent bystanders in the building—including the security officers who were just following orders—so they could get out. But if Thea got wind of the approaching missile strike, she might be able to launch some kind of countermeasure, so Nadia held her tongue and hoped no one would find her phone.

"Don't move!" the officer said, pointing his gun.

Nadia held perfectly still as he crawled to her, his gun hand never wavering. She was glad Dorothy hadn't ordered her men to kill Nadia on sight, but it was hard to feel *too* relieved when the missiles were on their way.

Nadia made no protest when the officer grabbed her arm and forced her to lie on her stomach while he patted her down and confiscated her gun.

A second security officer opened a ceiling panel near where Nadia and her captor were crouching, and she was shoved unceremoniously through it. The man below tried to catch her, but he only softened her fall a bit.

Nadia hit the floor with a cry of pain, the wind momentarily knocked out of her. While she was trying to get her breath back, one of the officers hauled her to her feet and started dragging her down a hallway, his grip on her upper arm brutally tight. The second followed behind, gun in hand, although he didn't point it at her. She knew if she made one false move, he could aim and shoot in a heartbeat.

She didn't know where they were taking her, or what they were planning to do with her when they got there. She was trembling and sick to her stomach. Almost everyone she had ever loved—her parents, Gerri, Dante, even Nate—was either dead now or probably soon to be dead, as was she herself. She hoped her little niece and nephew were faring better in whatever foster home the state had sent them to.

The officers steered Nadia around yet another corner, and she saw an elegant reception area. She had never been in this part of the Fortress before, but the quality of the furnishings and the amount of electronics on the doors suggested they were entering VIP territory.

Sure enough, the guards marched her down one more short hallway, this one with a door at each end, and when they knocked on the far door, it was Dorothy's voice that answered.

"Enter," she said, and Nadia could hear the smile in her voice even though she couldn't see her.

Nadia took a deep breath and stood up as straight and tall as she could. There was nothing she could do about her disheveled appearance, or about her tear-streaked face, but she would face Thea's puppet with as much dignity as she could muster.

The dignity didn't last long.

Nadia couldn't help the little whimper that escaped her throat when she saw Nate sitting in a chair, and Dorothy standing beside him with a gun to his head. His hands had been bound behind him, and he was gagged. One of his eyes was blackened, and there was blood on his shirt as well as a couple of bloody handprints on his pants. Nadia couldn't see any wounds on him, so it was possible the blood was Belinski's. But he looked terrible anyway, and even though she'd already known he'd been captured, it was hard to bear seeing him like that. If Dorothy had ordered the two of them captured alive, it wasn't for any *good* reason.

Dorothy smiled ever more broadly as she soaked in Nadia's distress. Still smiling, she glanced up at the security officers.

"You may leave us now," she said.

Nadia couldn't look away from Nate's battered face, but she felt the start of surprise of the officer who was holding her.

"I don't think that would be a good idea, Madam Chairman," he said respectfully. "These two are dangerous criminals, and—"

Dorothy rolled her eyes and cut him off with an impatient gesture. "They are a pair of helpless children, and Miss Lake would never do anything to jeopardize Nathaniel's life. Would you dear?"

Dorothy was capable of an astonishing level of arrogance,

but Nadia doubted it was only overconfidence that made her dismiss the guards.

"What's the matter, Dorothy?" Nadia asked with a hard smile of her own. "Planning to say things you don't want your people to hear?"

Nadia had no doubt that Dorothy—or more accurately, Thea—had enlisted a core of loyal supporters who knew exactly what she was and supported her anyway, either for financial gain or for promises of power. But surely most of her people, most of the security officers who worked in this building under her command, would desert her in a heartbeat if they knew the truth.

"Don't be silly," Dorothy said. "Please, gentlemen, do stay. But close the door first, will you?"

Nadia heard the door swing shut behind her, and at the same moment saw Dorothy's hand moving—the hand with the gun in it.

"Watch out!" she screamed, but the warning came too late.

Dorothy fired off two shots, and both of Nadia's escorts crumpled to the floor. Nadia swallowed hard and willed herself to stop shaking. It didn't work.

"I'll blame that on you, naturally," Dorothy said to Nadia, the gun now aimed at Nate's head again.

"I guess you're through even pretending to care about human lives," Nadia said.

"Oh, I'll keep up the act a little longer," Dorothy assured her. "I still need just a little more time before my research is complete."

Thea's research was supposedly about gaining a perfect understanding of the mind/body connection. Her stated goal was to be able to create a young body from a backup scan, and then infuse that body with the knowledge and memories of its older self. To create artificial immortality. But her hunger for that particular brand of research made no sense when she treated human beings with all the care and compassion that a human scientist showed to lab rats.

"What research are you talking about?" Nadia asked.

Dorothy blinked at her. "I've told you all about it already."

"And I don't believe for a moment that you're selflessly trying to make mankind immortal."

Dorothy laughed. "Is that what you think I'm doing?"

"It's what you *said* you were doing."

"No, no, dear. I said I wanted to create a functioning mind in a body of my choosing. I never said that mind had to come from a human backup."

Nadia didn't completely understand what Dorothy was trying to say, but she knew it made her stomach feel queasy. "If the mind doesn't come from a backup, then where *does* it come from?"

"Why, I'll create it, of course." There was a gleam of eager fanaticism in her eyes. "I'm calling the project Humanity 2.0." She ran a hand absently through Nate's hair, and despite the threat of the gun, he jerked away from her touch. "Be still!" she snapped, her hand closing on his hair in what was obviously a painfully tight grip. He subsided.

The queasiness in Nadia's stomach grew worse. "What do you mean?" she asked, her voice little more than a whisper.

"Human beings are flawed creatures," Dorothy said, hand still twined in Nate's hair. "Greed, dishonesty, cruelty, disregard for the environment . . ." She shook her head. "Mankind could be so much better, so much nobler than it is.

"I believe I came into being for a reason. That I am here to save the world from mankind—and mankind from itself. I can create a body from scratch." She indicated herself with a sweep of her hand, letting go of Nate's hair to do so. "And I can create a mind from a model." She grabbed Nate's hair again.

"I am the closest thing mankind has ever seen to a real, live goddess."

Nadia couldn't help the way her mouth dropped open. Just before Dorothy had killed him, Nate's father had muttered some hint about Thea wanting to be a goddess, but Nadia had taken it as hyperbole.

"A goddess?" she repeated.

"What else would you call a being who can create an entirely new species of living, sentient creatures? Human beings who have all the positive traits of mankind, with none of the negatives. My children will be perfect. I will craft them myself, mold their DNA so they will breed true. Beautiful to look at. Pure of heart. Highly intelligent. Resistant to disease."

"And with the need to worship you built into them at a cellular level," Nadia finished for her.

Dorothy shrugged. "Naturally."

She frowned suddenly, her eyes narrowing, her jaw clenching. Her nostrils flared and she gave Nate's head a little shake, practically pulling his hair out.

"What have you done?" Dorothy said in a voice that was nearly a shriek.

Nadia could only presume she had just found out about the missiles. Now, more than ever, Nadia was convinced that calling for the strike had been the right thing to do, no matter how many innocents might be trapped inside this building. It wasn't hard to read between the lines of Dorothy's narrative. If she was planning to create a new race of human beings— Humanity 2.0, as she called them—then her plan also ultimately included wiping out the "legacy" humans.

No wonder she didn't care about bombing the Basement, or killing and replacing board members, or shooting a couple of her own men dead just because she didn't want them to hear her plans. She planned to kill them all eventually anyway.

"You stupid *child*!" Dorothy yelled, hauling Nate to his feet, the gun jammed into his ear. "You think I can't counter this little game of yours?"

Nadia crossed her arms over her chest, wondering how long they had until the missiles hit. Her sense of time was all askew; she had no idea how long ago she had made the call. Belinski had said it would take about twenty minutes, but that had been assuming he was on the phone in person with no possible question as to the validity of his orders.

"No," Nadia said. "I don't think you can."

"Perhaps if I make it clear to Synchrony's acting Chairman that I will launch a nuclear missile strike in retaliation if he doesn't cancel his own launch, he will see things my way." Her eyes filled with malice. "And if he doesn't, then I guess we'll have to see how many missiles I can launch before the end.

"I want you to move very slowly," she instructed Nadia. "Make sure I can see what you're doing at all times. I would like you to search my men and find some flex-cuffs and a gag. I'm sure they have some. Then we're all going to go downstairs to the situation room, and you can watch while I kill millions of people all because of your stupid, pointless heroics."

Moving slowly, as Dorothy had instructed, Nadia crouched down beside the fallen officers. If Thea had infiltrated the weapons systems, then there would be nothing Nadia could do to stop her from launching an attack against Synchrony, whether they gave in to her blackmail or not.

But unlike the phone system and the net, which Thea had so obviously infiltrated for her own use, the weapons systems would not be networked, and it might be difficult for her to weasel her way into every system she would need to launch a nuclear attack without human intervention. Not if she hadn't expected to have to use them anytime soon, at least.

"Tell me something, Dorothy," Nadia said while running her hands over a security officer's pockets and equipment belt. "Do you need to use retinal or fingerprint scans to access our nuclear missiles?"

Nadia's hand closed over the butt of the gun in the guard's shoulder holster.

"I know you and the Armed Forces Chief have to plug in a couple of keys," she continued, "but is that all?"

The spark of fury that lit in Dorothy's eyes answered Nadia's question, as did the way she tucked her own body more firmly behind Nate's.

"Don't move, or I swear, I'll blow his brains out!"

Nate's face was sweaty with fear, his eyes wide and pleading as Nadia drew the gun and rose to her feet. He started shaking his head, as much as he could with the muzzle of that gun up against it. It gave Nadia pause, but only for a moment.

"Why did you gag him, Dorothy?" Nadia asked, raising her gun despite Dorothy's threat. Her heart was thundering in her chest, everything within her recoiling.

"I said stop!" Dorothy screamed, poking the gun against Nate's skull.

Nadia swallowed hard. "I don't think that's Nate. I think it's one of your puppet Replicas."

Nate shook his head even more frantically, his mouth working around the gag as muffled protests rose from behind it. All of which was perfectly reasonable for someone who had a gun to his head. But Nate, *her* Nate, had been willing to sacrifice his life to stop Thea. He'd sent Nadia into the crawl space and stayed behind himself to help gain her more time. And if the person Dorothy was threatening were really Nate, he would be afraid, but he wouldn't be begging Nadia not to do it. He would agree with what she was doing, and he'd be communicating that agreement to her through his eyes and body language.

"Don't be a fool!" Dorothy said. "I don't need a Replica when I have the real thing. And I gagged him because I got tired of listening to him. Here, I'll take it off."

Nate was certainly more than capable of annoying someone enough to end up gagged. The sickening thought occurred to Nadia that even if this wasn't her Nate, Dorothy had the scan she needed to make another genuinely human Replica, one with all of Nate's memories up until the time of the last scan before his murder. That Nate would not have been through the last couple of months, which had tempered and changed him, made him a stronger, more courageous, more noble person. That Nate might not even know enough about what was going on to fully understand.

Dorothy was fumbling at the gag with one hand, careful to keep the gun menacingly close, but Nadia knew in her heart that it didn't matter. Thea could create another copy of Dorothy, but Nadia was damn sure she couldn't do it in time to get that Dorothy, with her retinas and fingerprints, down to the situation room to order the nuclear attack before Synchrony's missiles hit.

"I'm sorry, Nate," Nadia said. "But I can't let her nuke anyone."

Closing her eyes because she was too close to miss, Nadia pulled the trigger until the gun clicked empty.

CHAPTER TWENTY-SEVEN

nadia didn't want to open her eyes, didn't want to see what she'd done. The air stank of blood and smoke and her own fear-sweat, and her whole body was shaking. Droplets of hot liquid had splashed her face and hands, and she feared if she opened her eyes to confirm what it was, she might spend the next ten minutes retching in the corner.

But she might not even *have* ten minutes, so she couldn't spare the time to wallow in the horror. By bringing her to the Chairman's office, Dorothy might have inadvertently guided Nadia to the one and only way she could escape the locked-down building before the missiles hit.

Nadia pried her eyes open and forced herself to look, forced herself to make sure Dorothy was dead.

Through her eyes blurred with tears, Nadia saw that both Dorothy and her Nate-puppet were well and truly dead. There was so much blood . . .

Silently, Nadia prayed she had done the right thing, that she hadn't just killed the real Nate, *her* Nate. Or even a second duplicate of Nate. She hoped what she'd killed was just a mindless automaton, controlled by Thea. That, she could live with.

Letting out a shaking breath, Nadia lowered the gun, then dropped it altogether. She appropriated the other dead security officer's gun, knowing she was far from out of the woods, then examined the office, looking for the emergency exit Nate had told her would be there. The exit the Chairman could use to escape the building in case of attack.

In the Chairman's office in Paxco Headquarters, the exit had been behind an ornamental bookcase, so Nadia tried there, first. She pulled and pushed from all angles, but the bookcase remained firmly in place. At Headquarters, it had rolled smoothly out of the way, so she made an educated guess that the emergency exit here was not behind the bookcase. She moved on to the bar, set against the wall right next to the bookcase, but it showed no sign of being movable, either.

A low, feminine chuckle sounded from some unseen speaker.

"You had better hope I am able to bluff Synchrony into calling off that missile strike, little girl," Thea's voice gloated. "Because you're not getting out of this room. Not until you're in my custody once again."

Nadia's feet got tangled up and she almost tripped, unsettled by the realization that just because she had made it impossible for Thea to launch a nuclear attack before Synchrony's missiles hit didn't mean the threat had lost its teeth. Not with Thea's impressive ability to manipulate both video and audio.

Nadia forced herself to take a deep breath and *think*. Thea's voice was nothing but a distraction. The missiles would either come, or they wouldn't, and Nadia couldn't control that. All she could control was whether she was in the building when and if they hit.

"If you had just given yourself up when I asked you to oh-so-nicely," Thea continued, "I would have been merciful to you. I understand that in your own misguided way, you are doing what you think is best."

Nadia kept moving about the room, pressing and pulling and pushing on anything she could think of that might be masking a secret passageway. She almost laughed at the idea of Thea calling her "misguided," but there wasn't anything funny about the situation.

"But then, that's true of a great number of human beings who do terrible things, isn't it? My children will have a clear and universal definition of what is right and what is wrong, one they will all adhere to. There will be no more crime in the world, no more war, no more injustice, and all my children will truly be created equal, without regard to race or gender or financial status. I will create paradise on Earth."

"And that all these pseudo-people will bow down and worship you is nothing but a fringe benefit," Nadia said, chewing her lip as she looked around the room once more, searching for something she had missed. The emergency exit couldn't be *too* hard to access, or it wouldn't be much good in the face of a true emergency.

"You will not escape," Thea said, ignoring Nadia's gibe altogether. "I am even now in negotiation with Synchrony. I am showing them a very interesting video log, one that shows how you and Nathaniel coerced Chairman Belinski into sending that order. It shouldn't be long until the order is rescinded and you are recaptured. With four dead bodies arranged at your feet, I might add."

Don't listen to her, Nadia counseled herself. She had

seen ample evidence that Thea was a liar, and nothing she said could be trusted.

Frustration built as the minutes ticked by and Nadia found no sign of an emergency exit.

"I'm afraid there *is* no emergency exit from this room," Thea said. Nadia wished she could tell where the speaker was so she could shoot it, but there was no obvious security camera, and she didn't have time to go looking.

Nate had told her there was an exit, and therefore, there had to be an exit. He had even said the exit was "just like the one at Headquarters." Nadia eyed the bookcase again.

Thea gave a sigh of what sounded like satisfaction. "I've just received word that Synchrony has decided to set their missiles to self-destruct, pending further investigation."

Don't listen to her, don't listen to her, don't listen to her.

Nadia glared at the bookcase. In Headquarters, all it had taken to move the bookcase was a light push on the right side. Nadia tried pushing there again, but still with no results. Then, because she could think of nothing better to do, she put her back against the side of the bookcase and pushed hard with her legs.

There was resistance at first, then a sharp metallic screech. Then the bookcase flew out from behind her and she landed on the floor on her butt so hard, she bit her tongue.

She took a second to catch her breath and looked into the dark stairwell the bookcase had hidden. Just like the one in Headquarters, this bookcase was set upon rails. Only someone had put a twisted heavy-duty paper clip on these rails. It wasn't enough to stop the door from opening, but it was more than enough to make it take a much greater effort.

"Nice try, Thea," Nadia said as she rose to her feet and stepped into the stairwell. Dorothy must have put the paper clip there while she was waiting for Nadia to arrive, an extra safeguard in case Nadia called her bluff and went through her.

"You are too late!" Thea's voice shrieked through the speakers. "The missiles are here!"

Nadia wanted to point out that Thea's lies were contradicting each other, but just in case the latest *wasn't* a lie, she saved her breath and charged down the stairs. She was only on the fourth floor, but the stairs seemed to go on forever, and she was running so fast she practically pitched down them headfirst.

She made it to the bottom, where a dark concrete tunnel led off into the distance. Panting heavily, her ribs aching and her legs burning, she took off down the tunnel. Whether she was running from the missiles or from pursuers sent after her by Thea didn't matter. All that mattered was that she keep running.

She felt more than heard the first explosion, the tunnel vibrating under her feet, and she had a sudden flashback to her time in the subway tunnels. She hoped this one was sturdier—and that it would take no direct hits. She had no idea how far away she needed to get to be at a "safe" distance from a missile attack, but she was sure farther was better, so she kept running.

She reached the end of the tunnel, a small, square room with a metal ladder leading up to what looked like a manhole. She grabbed the ladder, then felt the world shake beneath her again.

She looked up at the manhole cover. She didn't know

what was above her: a building, a street, an empty lot. But at least down here, she was sure she had some cover. And if the missiles hit close enough to kill her down here, she wouldn't fare any better above.

And so, Nadia hunkered down in a corner, her arms wrapped around her knees, and listened to the barrage that she hoped against hope would destroy Thea once and for all.

The emergency lighting in Nadia's little shelter went out long before the explosions stopped. The air filled with dust and the scent of burning. She didn't think there was any actual smoke, but she stayed low to the ground anyway, just in case.

Even after the noise quieted and the ground stopped shaking, she remained huddled in thc relative safety of her little corner. Now that she wasn't running anymore, didn't have to *do* anything anymore, she was forced to face the heart-wrenching reality.

Nate was dead. Whether Nadia killed him herself, or whether he and Belinski were still stuck in that building somewhere when the missiles hit, he was gone. And this time, there would be no Replica.

Nadia sat in the darkness and sobbed until her throat was raw and her chest ached. There was part of her that almost wished she hadn't gotten out of that building after all, so she wouldn't have to live with yet another loss. Gerri. Her mother. Maybe Dante, though Nadia clung to the hope that he had survived Thea's continued assault on the Basement. And now Nate.

It was too much to bear. Too much for the universe to load onto her shoulders. It wasn't fucking *fair*!

Eventually, she cried herself out, at least for the time being. She scrubbed at her cheeks and eyes with her grubby, gritty hands, then forced herself to her feet and felt along the wall until she found the ladder. She gave it an experimental shake to make sure it was secure, then carefully climbed it, wishing she hadn't abandoned her phone so she could at least have its little glow of light.

Every few rungs, she reached above her, fingers searching for the manhole cover so she wouldn't bonk her head against it. When she found it, she gave it a push, but wasn't surprised when it didn't budge. She climbed higher up the ladder so she'd have more leverage and tried again, but still it didn't move.

Maybe it was locked somehow. She felt all the way around it, searching for a catch or a bolt or a button—any kind of identifiable locking mechanism. But she found nothing. Maybe the damn thing was just heavy. Maybe *too* heavy for a willowy Executive teenager to move.

Nadia pushed until she was so exhausted she worried she might fall down the ladder, but the manhole cover remained firmly in place. Screaming in frustration, she banged on the cover but only managed to bruise her hand. She was pretty sure she could hear sounds of movement outside, so she tried yelling for help. When that didn't work, she took off her shoe—a sturdy masculine loafer to fit her disguise as Belinski's aide—and banged its heel on the cover. The heel wasn't hard enough to make a satisfying bang, but she did manage a dull, metallic thud, which she kept up until her arms were so sore and tired she thought they might fall off and she might die down here after all.

The shoe slipped from Nadia's fingers and thumped on the floor below. She followed it down, knowing she had to rest before she tried again.

She had just regained her seat in the corner when there was a wrenching, metallic sound from above. Then there was something that sounded like a saw, followed by a clatter. And then the manhole was dragged out of the way and a shaft of blinding sunlight made Nadia shade her eyes with her forearm.

When her eyes could bear the light, she moved her arm and squinted against the brightness to see a woman in combat fatigues climbing down the ladder.

"Let me see your hands," the woman ordered, and Nadia noticed the muzzle of a rifle being pointed at her by someone on the surface.

Nadia held up her hands obediently. "My name is Nadia Lake," she said hoarsely, hoping the admission wouldn't get her immediately thrown in prison—or shot.

The woman nodded briskly, still keeping a safe distance and visually checking her out. "Are you injured?"

"No." Not except for bumps and bruises and aches, but she doubted the woman cared about that.

"There's a lot of blood on you."

Nadia's eyes teared up. "It's not mine."

It turned out the woman was a medic, and she gave Nadia a quick examination anyway, just to make sure she wasn't in shock and unaware of an injury. Afterward, she helped Nadia to her feet and then climbed up the ladder right behind her. When Nadia reached the top, a soldier bent down and grabbed her under the arms, easily hoisting her the rest of the way up and setting her down.

She was glad the soldier kept a hand on her arm, even though she suspected it was meant as a restraint rather than an act of comfort. The bombings she'd lived through in the Basement had not prepared her for the devastation left in the wake of a concentrated missile attack.

The Fortress was gone.

In its place was a gaping pit, one Nadia couldn't see the bottom of. The grounds between the building and its fence were littered with debris and crawling with soldiers. It appeared the Chairman's emergency exit had led to a small guardhouse near the fence, but the guardhouse had lost two of its walls. Nadia hadn't been able to get the manhole cover open because it had been buried in debris.

"Were there other survivors?" Nadia asked with little hope.

The soldier didn't answer her, instead urging her to come with him as he guided her through the field of debris. She was too exhausted and full of despair to ask again, or ask what was going to happen to her. She followed the soldier without protest as he led her to the Fortress's front gates, which were still intact, although they were now open so the soldiers and their equipment could pass through.

The area was teeming with vehicles, both military and civilian, and there were flashing lights everywhere. Nadia didn't see any sign of the press, so she presumed the soldiers had set up a perimeter somewhere well away from the blast site. There were also no news helicopters flying overhead.

The soldier and the medic loaded Nadia into the back of

a transport. A transport that contained two long benches with rails running along their backs. She balked, remembering her last ride in such a vehicle, when her hands had been cuffed behind her back and attached to an O ring high enough to practically dislocate her shoulders.

The medic patted her shoulder in an awkward gesture of sympathy. "We'll leave your hands free as long as you keep cooperating. Please, have a seat."

Nadia sank down onto one of the benches. The medic sat next to her, and the soldier across, making sure to position themselves between Nadia and the exit.

"Where are you taking me?" she asked, praying the answer wasn't Rikers Island.

"We're headed to Fort Hamilton," the medic answered, but that was all Nadia could get out of either of them.

Fort Hamilton was a high-security military base about thirty minutes from the Fortress. Before Paxco had bought out New York, Fort Hamilton had been an army base accessible to the public, but these days it was fenced in and heavily guarded. Nadia feared being taken there didn't bode well, but she was too numb and exhausted to spend much time speculating about her future. Instead, she closed her eyes and tried with every fiber of her being not to think.

CHAPTER TWENTY-EIGHT

It was getting dark by the time the transport arrived at Fort Hamilton. Nadia had nodded off once or twice during the ride, but the combination of the hard bench and the transport's poor suspension meant she couldn't get comfortable enough to do more than that.

The soldier, whose fatigues Nadia belatedly noticed had the name JENKINS sewn on the front, was surly and uncommunicative, his hand always on or near his gun. The medic, who introduced herself as Caroline, was considerably warmer and friendlier, but in the end she wasn't much more communicative than Jenkins. Apparently, they were not authorized to share any information with Nadia, and she was going to have to wait before she learned any details about the attack—like whether there were any survivors besides herself.

It was very likely that Paxco's Chairman—both the pretender and the rightful Chairman—and the entire board of directors had all been killed. Nadia couldn't imagine who would take charge under such circumstances, or how the government could manage to rebuild itself. And without a commander in chief to guide them, who knew how the military was reacting to what might well seem to them to be an attack against their state by a rival state?

Thea had had to be destroyed, no matter what the cost, but Nadia hoped Paxco hadn't just gotten itself tangled in a war against Synchrony.

At Fort Hamilton, Nadia was taken to a deserted wing of one of the barracks. She was given a room with a cot, and the smallest set of fatigues available. Caroline invited her to use the shower and promised someone would bring her some food. This wasn't exactly how Nadia expected prisoners to be treated, but it didn't seem like she was a guest, either.

"Am I free to walk around?" Nadia asked, although she had no real desire to do so, exhausted in body and soul.

Caroline smiled at her regretfully. "I'm afraid not. Not for now, at least. Perhaps tomorrow, when things are more . . . settled."

Nadia highly doubted things would be "more settled" so soon, not if the entire board of directors had been killed, but she nodded in something resembling agreement anyway.

nadia slept almost twelve hours straight, then spent the rest of the next day pacing her small room in the barracks with nothing to do. There were armed guards at each end of the hall, and though they weren't unkind to her, they wouldn't let her pass, and they wouldn't tell her anything.

Meals were brought to her room/cell, but Nadia had no appetite and barely nibbled at any of them. Sometimes she cried for all those she had lost and for her own uncertain future, and sometimes she was so numb she barely felt human.

The day felt endless, and she wondered how many more

she would spend in this state of suspended animation. She was pretty sure she'd go mad if it was much longer.

Nadia had just finished picking at her dinner tray when there was a commotion outside. She set the tray aside and rose to her feet, taking a deep breath and trying to look brave. This could be a firing squad coming to put her out of her misery, for all she knew, but she was in one of her numb phases, and the possibility barely raised her heart rate.

The door to her room was open, and she saw three armed men in off-the-rack business suits march down the hallway, looking right and left. A security detail if Nadia ever saw one, checking out the area before allowing an important dignitary to enter. She swallowed hard, some of the numbness fading away as she wondered who had risen to power to fill the sudden vacuum.

The security detail must have been satisfied, because she saw them pass by her room again, walking with brisk purpose. Nadia's heart was now beating like a trapped bird, and she was glad she'd eaten so little or it might have come back up.

More footsteps in the hall, coming toward her room. Nadia held her breath.

And let it out with an incoherent, wordless cry when Nate appeared in her doorway.

She flung herself at him, practically tackling him to the floor in her eagerness to touch him and reassure herself that he was real, that he was flesh and blood and not a figment of her imagination. Nate laughed and hugged her back just as eagerly.

They held each other somewhere between too long and not long enough, then by mutual agreement pulled apart.

There were shadows in Nate's eyes, though he seemed to be uninjured. Nadia's mind insisted on conjuring up the image of his body lying dead half on top of Dorothy's, blood pooling from multiple gunshot wounds, wounds Nadia had delivered. Her eyes burned with yet more tears, but she blinked them back.

"How did you get out?" she asked.

"We weren't the only people in that board meeting," he reminded her. "Not the only people who knew the truth about Thea and Dorothy. Everyone panicked and ran away when the guns came out, but since Thea wouldn't let them leave the building, they had time to calm down and regroup. Dorothy had given her men orders to detain everyone, but her men had a hard time carrying them out in the face of twelve angry board members. Especially when the board members started telling them what had happened.

"Belinski and I held the doors for as long as we could, but they eventually blasted their way in. We surrendered then, and they took us downstairs, meaning to lock us up with all the rest of the detainees, but by the time we got there, the board members were in charge. We told them the missile strike was coming, and except for a few of Dorothy's most stubborn men, we got the hell out of there."

His voice choked off and his eyes looked shiny. "I thought you were dead," he said. "I didn't know where the emergency exit let out, but I figured if you had made it, someone would have found you shortly after the attack ended. But they couldn't, so I assumed you were in the building. What happened to you?"

Nadia's story took a little longer to recount, so they both sat on the edge of the cot while she told him everything that had happened. There was a part of her that was tempted not to tell him about the Replica, not to tell him she'd shot that Replica dead even thinking it might be him, but in the end, she decided to tell him the whole truth.

"I'll never know whether that Replica was one of Dorothy's puppets or if it was really you. Sort of you." She sighed, because it was impossible to talk about Replicas without getting confused.

To her relief, Nate looked sad about what had happened, but not angry.

"You did the right thing," he said. "Even if that had really been me, it was the right thing to do. Jesus, Nadia, she was going to kill off the entire human race! Don't you dare feel guilty about what you had to do to stop her."

Just because it was the right thing to do didn't mean it didn't hurt like hell. Especially when she could never know if that Replica had had Nate's mind.

Nate reached over and took her hand, squeezing it hard. "It had to be one of her puppets," he assured her. "Why would she want an old copy of me running around when she could have one that looked just like me but did everything she told it to? The real me would have been a pain in her ass and might have resisted her even with a gun to its head. Much safer for her to use a puppet."

Nadia nodded, because the logic made sense. Too bad logic wasn't enough to create anything like a sense of certainty. And nothing Nate could say would heal the wound she had created in herself when she'd pulled that trigger, so she changed the subject.

"I take it Chairman Belinski and the board members made it out in time?"

Nate narrowed his eyes at her, knowing her too well not to see that she was still struggling, but he didn't push it. "Yes. All of them, and many of the security personnel. A couple of them even thought to grab one of the fake board members we shot so they could do an autopsy."

Nadia raised her eyebrows. "And did they? Do an autopsy, I mean?"

Nate nodded. "They were able to confirm that the brain wasn't a normal human brain and that there were a couple of microchips implanted. It's enough to prove we aren't raving lunatics.

"I'm sorry it took me so long to get to you," he continued. "At first, I didn't know you were alive, and then I was caught up in the whole 'who's in charge?' mess. The board members supported my claim to the Chairmanship, but the military wasn't too sure, so there was a lot of confusion. Proving our claim about Thea's puppets helped a lot, but my situation is a bit . . . precarious."

And the more information that leaked out to the general public about what had happened, what Thea had done and planned to do, the more precarious Nate's situation would become. He was a known Replica, and there had been people who'd held that against him *before* all of this mess.

"Have you . . . Have you been able to find Bishop or Dante?" she asked, terrified of the answer.

"Not yet," he said, squeezing her hand again. "As you can imagine, the Basement-dwellers who survived are pretty damn hostile right now, so for any of the rest of us to get in there is pretty much impossible unless we want there to be more killing. I've got people broadcasting the information that Dorothy has been removed from office and that there will be no further attacks on the Basement. I'm hoping that Kurt and Dante will hear the news and come out so we don't have to go in after them."

Nadia wanted to know *now,* as she was sure Nate did, but she understood the need to wait and be cautious. Even sending in humanitarian aid was going to be risky in the devastated region, and Nadia could hardly blame the surviving Basement-dwellers for adopting a "shoot first, ask questions later" attitude.

"What happens now?" she asked in a small voice, overwhelmed at even the thought of what Paxco would have to do to recover from everything Thea had done. She had to have practically drained Paxco dry to fund her "research" and her military campaigns and her board member replacements. And she had been their primary source of income ever since she had invented the Replication process. How were they going to rebuild the Basement with no money and no major source of income?

"For now, we just keep putting one foot in front of the other and see what happens next."

nate convinced the board of directors to overturn Gerald Lake's trumped-up treason conviction and set him free from Rikers Island. Nate wasn't there when Nadia and her father were reunited, but he talked to her on the phone, and she told him her father was not the same man she remembered. Nate didn't know what Mr. Lake had suffered at Rikers, but his injuries and the loss of his wife during the prison riot had broken his spirit. Nate could only hope for Nadia's sake that time really did heal all wounds. Nadia had suffered more than enough already, and she deserved to have her father back.

Freeing Gerald Lake had been the one bright spot in the truly dismal days after Nate became the Chairman of Paxco. Too much information about Thea and her puppet Replicas had leaked out into the public, and the backlash was bringing an already crippled economy to a standstill. Employees went on strike, and though that was technically illegal in Paxco, neither Nate nor the board had the heart to prosecute them.

More disturbing were the mounting calls for Nate's immediate resignation—or even his arrest and execution—because he was a Replica. He had never in his life been able to go anywhere without a security detail, but now he practically needed an army, and instead of traveling in a limo, he went by armored car. The unrest was ugly enough that Chairman Belinski offered to send a peacekeeping force to help keep order—and Nate was forced to accept, which didn't do much to improve his popularity.

The borders of the Basement were still closed because it wasn't safe for aid workers to go in. Nate further depleted the treasury by ordering food and water air-dropped into the ruins. When after three days there was still no word from Kurt or Dante, Nate bought a couple of cartons of cell phones with his own money and had them dropped with the food over what had once been Red Death territory. Phone service had been restored almost immediately, but the power had been out so long that it was unlikely anyone in the Basement had a charged phone to call out with—and power couldn't be restored until the survivors stopped shooting at people so utility workers could go in.

From the moment he knew the phones had been dropped, Nate had made sure he always had a phone in his hand or pocket, and he made doubly sure his staff knew that any personal calls were to be put directly through to him, no questions asked. Every time the damned phone rang, his heart leapt with hope, only to be disappointed time and time again.

Until Saturday night, when he returned to his apartment after yet another wearying day of bad news and public censure. He poured himself a drink and sat in front of his floor-to-ceiling windows, staring out at the city and ordering himself to stop at one, rather than drinking the whole bottle and sinking into oblivion as he longed to do.

He was midway through his second drink, which he swore would be his last, when the phone in his pocket buzzed. He'd had enough false alarms by now that he didn't get his hopes up, even when he glanced at the phone and didn't recognize the number.

"Hello?"

"So, do I have to call you Mr. Chairman now?" Kurt asked. And to his utter shock, Nate found himself bursting into tears.

He was not a crier, hadn't been even as a child. He'd shed some tears over the things he'd seen and experienced since he'd awakened as a Replica, but nothing like the maelstrom that shook him now.

"I'm all right," Kurt reassured him. "It took a while to hear the news this deep in, and I had no way to reach you until you dropped the phones."

Nate couldn't have talked if he'd wanted to. It felt like he had a basketball lodged in his throat.

"Is it true what I hear?" Kurt asked. "Is Thea dead?"

Nate tried to answer, but still couldn't manage it. Even drawing breath into his lungs was hard, but he kept trying. Kurt seemed to understand, waiting patiently on the other end of the line while Nate pulled the shreds of himself together.

"She's dead," Nate finally managed to croak out. Engineers had confirmed that the gaping crater that now existed where the Fortress had once stood was deep enough that even the subbasement had been taken out, the missile strike so precise that not a single building outside of the Fortress's gates had been damaged.

"You'll have to tell me the full story of what happened. Bet it's a good one."

It depended on your point of view, Nate supposed. "Is Dante okay?" he asked, surprised to find out he actually cared, and not just because he knew Nadia would. It was hard to have lived through everything they had together and keep up the spirit of cordial dislike.

"Mostly," Kurt confirmed. "He's got a broken arm, we think, but we splinted it up real good and he seems to be doing all right. Getting a doctor to look at him would be good, though, just in case. How about Nadia and Agnes?"

"They're both fine," Nate said. "I've only seen Agnes once since the missile strike, but she seems to have made a full recovery. Nadia wasn't hurt but . . . Well, she's gone through hell, and it's going to take a while before she's fully herself again. And Shrimp?"

"We almost lost him. He was trying to pull some kid out of the rubble, and the whole thing collapsed on him. I was there when it happened. Thought for sure he was dead. But he's tougher than he looks. We dug him out, and other than some nasty bruises, he was okay. Even saved the kid."

Nate smiled, all the good news lifting some of the gloom that had been hovering about him.

"We saved a lot of lives by getting people into those tunnels," Kurt continued, "but there are still a lot of dead." He sighed. "A *lot* of dead. Especially in what used to be the free territories. Haven't found anyone I used to know there still alive."

"Not even Angel?" Angel had seemed well-nigh indestructible to Nate, a tough-as-nails survivor.

"Nope. That little people's army she put together got wiped out when they tried to destroy one of the barricades. Good thing we didn't all join up or we'd probably be dead, too."

Nate didn't know what to say, especially while feeling guiltily glad that the people he cared most about had lived, so he changed the subject. "When can I see you? Will you come out of the Basement?"

"If you guarantee me the troops on the border aren't going to shoot me, I'll come out—and maybe we can talk about how to get some help in here, 'cause we sure as hell need it."

CHAPTER TWENTY-NINE

nadia was far too agitated to hold still, so instead of sitting demurely in the living room to await her guest, she paced the foyer of her apartment. The butler, Crane, kept giving her repressive looks meant to send her scurrying back to her proper place, but she no longer gave a damn about the fussy, antiquated etiquette that Executive girls were supposed to adhere to.

The expected knock on the door occurred, and Crane made his slow and stately way over to answer it. Having no patience with slow and stately, Nadia darted past him and yanked the door open so hard she was lucky it didn't fly off its hinges.

Standing in that doorway was the most beautiful sight Nadia had ever seen.

Dante had obviously stopped to get cleaned up—and to see a doctor, judging by the splint on his left arm—before coming to see her. She would have been just as glad to see him if he were covered from head to toe in dirt and stank like rotten cheese—and she would have been just as unladylike in her greeting.

"Dante!" she cried, throwing her arms around him and hugging him tight. She was well aware of Crane's disapproving frown, but she took her greeting one step further anyway, kissing Dante like her life depended on it.

Dante returned her kiss eagerly enough, but he pulled away sooner than she would have liked, giving Crane a self-conscious look.

She still didn't care what Crane thought, or what he might whisper to the other servants and her father. She was through with being a proper Executive, and if she wanted to kiss a low-level Employee right on the mouth, then that's what she would do.

Dante, however, was clearly not as comfortable with her newfound spirit of rebellion, so for his sake she reined herself in. She couldn't seem to let go of him, though, so she kept hold of his hand as she led him to the living room.

"We won't be needing anything," she told Crane, knowing he would pop in and ask in just a couple of minutes. "And we do not wish to be disturbed."

Crane's eyebrows reached for his hairline. "But, Miss Lake—"

Nadia made a dismissive gesture. "No arguments." If Crane knew how much time Nadia had spent unchaperoned in Dante's presence, he'd probably have heart failure. The idea that she had once worried so much about such things herself seemed almost impossible to believe. "Come on," she said, tugging on Dante's hand and ignoring the butler's second attempt at protest.

"Is he going to run off and tell your father?" Dante asked, worried.

Nadia shook her head. "My father's in no condition to play head-of-the-household right now, and Crane knows it."

There was a part of Nadia that was still deeply angry with her father for the way he had failed to stand up for her when she had needed him most. She suspected that was the kind of wound that never fully healed. And yet she couldn't help but feel sorry for him after everything he had suffered. He had survived Rikers Island, but he was far from unscathed. He had never been all that strong-willed in the first place, and he was no match for Nadia now.

Despite her request not to be disturbed, Nadia knew the living room was hardly a private place, so she refrained from sitting on Dante's lap and devouring his lips as she so wanted to do. Instead, she sat close beside him on the sofa and looked him over.

He had lost a bunch of weight, as evidenced by how loosely his clothing hung upon him. He'd also spent a lot of time out in the sun—no doubt trying to dig through the rubble—and the freckles on his nose had multiplied. He was in desperate need of a haircut, and his hands were covered in cuts and bruises and calluses. And yet the sight of him made her heart flutter, just as it always had.

"I was so worried about you," she said, fearing that she was going to burst into tears, as she'd done when he'd first called her from the Basement to tell her he was okay.

Dante grinned crookedly. "*You* were worried about *me?*" he said. "I wasn't the one who went waltzing into enemy territory and asked Synchrony to bomb the building *she was trapped in!*"

"It seemed like a good idea at the time."

He shook his head. "I'm glad I stayed somewhere safe, like the Basement."

Nadia could no longer hold herself back, and she practically lunged for Dante's mouth, wrapping her arms around him once more. He kissed her back with familiar passion, his tongue dancing with hers, his hands sneaking under the hem of her top and searing the skin of her lower back.

Once again, it was Dante who drew away first. His cheeks were pink beneath his tan, his eyes dark with desire, his breathing quickened.

"Maybe we should slow down," he said hoarsely, though every nuance of his body language said he didn't want to. "It's one thing for us to fool around in the Basement, when we don't even know if we're going to live through the night, but this is different."

Nadia knew he was right. Society was in too much of a state of upheaval right now to care much about her reputation, but that reprieve wouldn't last long. She had no idea what her fellow Executives would make of her time on the run, but it was possible they would ignore it, act as if nothing untoward could possibly have happened. After all, she had been far outside the public eye at the time, with no reporters capturing her every scandalous step for posterity. If Nadia was known to indulge in public displays of affection with an Employee *after* she'd been returned to society, it was likely to cause a scandal.

But the thing was, Nadia didn't give a crap about social politics anymore. Causing a scandal had once seemed like an unthinkable nightmare, and yet now she saw how truly unimportant such things were. She had escaped the Executive world, and though she was now nominally back in it, she was never going to fit herself back into its narrow-minded mold.

"You're right," she told Dante. "It *is* different. So maybe we should take this discussion somewhere more private."

The pink in Dante's cheeks deepened. He reached out and brushed a hand over her cheek, then ran his fingers through her hair. "Don't get me wrong," he said, leaning forward to feather his lips over hers. "I would love to." Another soft, feathery kiss. "But, um . . ."

His voice trailed off and he pulled away. "If we go somewhere more private," he mumbled, staring at the floor instead of looking at her, "things might get out of hand. And I'm not prepared for that, if you know what I mean."

Nadia let out a sigh and collapsed back into the cushions of the sofa. If she'd been thinking with her head instead of her hormones, she would have known that without being told. He could hardly have expected her to throw herself at him like this. What was she thinking? Her cheeks heated with a blush.

Dante smiled at her a little sheepishly. "Under the circumstances, I have to ask: is the engagement between you and Nate back on?"

She honestly hadn't given the idea any thought. Her present was way too chaotic and uncertain for her to spend much time thinking about her future. And yet the only reason her unofficial engagement to Nate had been broken was because Nate's father wanted to punish the two of them for blackmailing him. Nate was now Chairman himself, and, within reason, could marry whomever he wished. Nadia would still be a safe choice for him, someone who knew about Kurt and didn't object, someone who had been his friend since they were children.

But Paxco was in a very different situation now than it had been when their parents had first agreed to the arrangement, many years ago. Then, Paxco had been prosperous and stable, its position in the world of the Corporate States secure despite the corruption that lay in its heart. In such a position of power, Chairman Hayes hadn't needed to use Nate's marriage as a political bargaining chip, so he had chosen to marry Nate within the state.

"No," Nadia finally answered. "Paxco's going to need allies, badly. Nate's going to have to marry someone who will help stabilize our position, and that's not me. It might even still be Agnes. Paxco's vulnerable right now, and having Synchrony's military stay on our side would be a major advantage." Assuming their "peacekeeping" force wasn't already planning to overstay their welcome.

Dante shook his head ruefully. "After everything that's happened, we're no closer to being a democracy, are we? Still stuck back in the middle ages with this arranged marriage crap."

"We'll be closer with Nate in charge than we would be with Dorothy or with Nate's father." Nate had never been much of a revolutionary until very recently—certainly nothing like Dante and Bishop—but he had changed. And in time, he would change Paxco, she was sure of it.

"Nate might have to marry for political gain," Nadia continued "but *I* won't. I'm through with being an Executive. From now on, my life is my own, and I'm going to do what makes me happy, even if other people don't approve." Including dating an Employee who had once been a servant in her household.

Nadia could tell from the look in his eyes that Dante was still skeptical. He probably thought that once her world was restored to some semblance of order, she would drift away from him and they would each settle into their old, familiar places in society. She looked forward to proving him wrong.

Thanks to her concussion, the doctors had not cleared Agnes to travel yet, so instead of inviting her to his place and playing host, Nate visited her in the presidential suite of her hotel. She was waiting for him in the suite's living room when he was shown in, and he did a double take at the sight of her.

Gone was the mousy brown hair in its unflattering bob. She'd dyed it a rich auburn and had it cut in a fashionably asymmetric style—very short on one side to help camouflage the swath that had been shaved off to stitch her wound, and chin-length on the other. She'd also done away with her usual baggy wardrobe and was wearing a close-fitting camisole top and a pair of sleekly tailored pinstripe trousers that rode low on her hips.

When she saw the way he was looking at her, Agnes smiled and turned around, giving him the 360-degree view.

"Who are you, and what have you done with Agnes?" he asked, shaking his head.

"How do I look?" Her little-girl voice hadn't changed, and there was still an aura of shyness that clung to her, like she hadn't quite grown into her new look yet.

"Fantastic," he told her honestly.

Another thing that hadn't changed about her was her easy blush. But at least this time she was blushing because he'd said something *nice*. She reached up and patted her hair as if to remind herself what it looked like.

"I'm having a little trouble getting used to it," she admitted. "But everyone tells me I look better this way, so . . ." She shrugged. "But please, come on in. Sit down. Can I get you anything?"

"No, no," he said, taking a seat on the sofa and gesturing for her to do the same. "I'm fine. And you need to stay off your feet."

She rolled her eyes. "I keep telling everyone I feel fine, but no one seems to believe me."

"Concussions are nothing to mess with." As great as she looked, it was hard to miss the line of stitches the fuzz on her scalp wasn't yet long enough to hide.

"So they tell me," she said, finally accepting his invitation to sit down. "But if they don't give me the all clear soon, I'm staging an escape."

Nate raised an eyebrow at her. More than just her appearance had changed. Defiance of any kind had seemed impossible for her when he'd first met her.

"But you must have an impossibly busy schedule, Mr. Chairman," she said, "and I doubt you stopped by to trade small talk."

He made a face. "Please, Agnes. You don't have to call me that. Not after everything we've been through together."

"But you're here on official business, aren't you? If it's official business, then you should use your title even with your closest friends."

He thought about it a minute, then shook his head. "If we get around to talking anything that resembles business, then you can call me Mr. Chairman if you really want to. But right now it's just Nate talking to Agnes. Okay?"

Her expression turned faintly quizzical, and she cocked

her head at him. "Okay. So what is it you want to talk about that isn't strictly business?"

Nate sucked in a deep breath and let it out slowly before he started to speak. "First off, I want to apologize for the way I treated you when we first met. In all the drama, I don't know if I ever came right out and said that to you. I was a total dickhead, and I'm sorry."

Most Executive girls would have been offended by his language; but then most Executive girls hadn't spent time hanging around in the Basement. Agnes just smiled.

"You'll get no argument from me," she said, and Nate thought that perhaps now *he* might be blushing. "But we were both different people back then, and you had your reasons."

"That doesn't make what I did right."

"Maybe not, but it's still a thing of the past. In other words: apology accepted." She smiled at him again, and there was no hint of lingering anger or resentment in her eyes.

"Thank you."

"Now that that's over with, shall we talk about the elephant in the room?"

Nate blinked, not used to Agnes being so direct. But he should have known she would guess why he had come by to talk to her.

"Have you already spoken with my father?" she asked.

He shook his head. "No. Obviously I'll have to if you say yes, but you're a legal adult now, and you can make your own decision. As you and Nadia both pointed out to me, I wasn't such a prize catch before, and I'm even less of one now. But even though you never signed any paperwork, I'm willing to honor our fathers' agreement if you still think it's a good match."

The words weren't easy for him, and his pulse quickened with the first hints of panic. Not at the prospect of marrying Agnes, but of marrying *anyone*. His heart belonged to Kurt, and it always would. And though he'd been through a lot of changes recently and had finally come to accept the responsibilities that were his by birth, there was no way he was giving Kurt up. Which was not going to make for much of a happily ever after in the marriage department. However, a marriage of state was a business transaction, not a romance, and at least Agnes was someone he knew—and who already knew about his relationship with Kurt.

Not that there was any guarantee Chairman Belinski still wanted this arrangement. Marrying into Paxco in its current situation might be more of a gamble than Synchrony was willing to take, and it was possible Agnes could do considerably better.

Agnes peered closely at his face. "Is that what *you* want?"

"This isn't about me. It's about you."

Her smile held a tinge of irony. "We're talking about a marriage of state. It isn't about either one of us."

He let out a half-laugh, half-sigh. "True. But we are the ones who would have to live with each other." And produce an heir. The very thought of it made him shudder. Not because sex with a girl was completely repugnant to him—he'd managed it a couple of times in an effort to camouflage his true nature—but because of what it would inevitably do to his relationship with Kurt. But he was getting way ahead of himself.

"Well, my answer would be the same either way," Agnes

said. "I suspect my father would be happy to stick to the agreement. Paxco may be in turmoil, but one way or another it will recover, and if you and I marry, the next Chairman of Paxco will be my dad's grandchild. That's a pretty good deal."

"So it's on then?"

To his surprise, Agnes shook her head. "No. Believe me, it's nothing personal. And I haven't talked this over with my father yet, so I'd appreciate it if you don't say anything to him until I have a chance to."

Nate wasn't sure how he felt about the rejection—other than confused. "May I ask why not?"

Agnes licked her lips. "Because as you said, I'm a legal adult now, and I can make my own decisions. I like you, and after everything we've been through, I'll always consider you my friend. But I'm in love with Evan, and he's the one I want to be with."

"Evan?" Nate asked, wondering if Agnes's concussion was more severe than he'd realized. "Who the hell is Evan?"

She grinned at him. "You know him as Shrimp."

Nate opened his mouth to say something, but no words came out.

Shrimp? Really?

"When the doctors clear me, I'm going to join him in the Basement," Agnes said with quiet certainty. "We were constantly in danger, with the future looking so horribly grim it was hard to think about it, and yet I was happier there than I'd ever been in my life. No parties, no media, no gossip, no public speaking." She sighed wistfully. "I don't want my old life back."

Nate still didn't know what to say. It was true that Agnes had seemed more relaxed, more comfortable in her own skin, when they'd been in the Basement. And it had been impossible to miss the connection between her and Shrimp. But Nate had thought it was no more than a harmless flirtation. The scandal that would arise when the media found out was unthinkable.

"Your father's never going to let you do that," he finally said.

"Legal adult here. He can't stop me. Not if I don't care about not having any money."

It was true that withholding family funds was the most popular way for Executives to curb dependents who tried to stage rebellions. Now that Agnes was eighteen, Belinski would have no legal right to forbid her to do whatever she wanted.

"I know it will cause a big scandal," she continued, "and my father will be furious, at least at first. But in the Basement, I'll be out of the media's reach, so there's only so long they'll be able to keep the story going."

"Keep in mind that Shrimp's home and everything he owned went down with the red tower. If you go back to the Basement, it won't be to the comfortable apartment we spent time in."

"And the place is completely devastated," Agnes agreed. "Mostly ruins, with we don't yet know how many dead. It'll need a lot of rebuilding. I can help with that. I have an idea what I'll be facing thanks to the time we spent with Bishop. And I still think my life there will be better than my life here."

Nate felt humbled by her courage and conviction. Would *he* have had the courage to reject everything that was familiar and comfortable about his life, to throw himself into danger and deprivation for the sake of love? He honestly didn't know.

"If you and Shrimp ever need anything, you can call me," he said. "I'm doing a pretty good hatchet job on my personal funds already, but I owe you—*Paxco* owes you—more than we can ever repay. I'm going to do everything I can to make the Basement a better place when we rebuild it. And I suspect I won't be getting a whole lot of marriage offers in the near future, so if you change your mind, let me know. Odds are I'll still be available."

Agnes smiled and patted his hand. "Thank you. If I did have to do the whole marriage of state thing, you'd be an excellent choice. You are officially no longer a dickhead."

Nate couldn't do anything but laugh.

CHAPTER THIRTY

nate collapsed into bed, facedown and fully clothed, too tired and stressed and frustrated to bother with formalities like undressing or brushing his teeth, or even getting under the covers. Kurt, who had followed him into the bedroom, sat down on the edge of the bed and started prying off one of Nate's shoes. Nate mustered as much energy as he could find to jerk his foot out of reach.

"Stop it," he protested. "You're not really my valet, and I'll take off my own damn shoes in my own damn time."

With the level of hostility Nate was already facing from the public, he hadn't dared make his relationship with Kurt known, so he'd once again hired him on as a valet so they could have private time together. But just because he had to pretend to the outside world that Kurt was his servant didn't mean he would treat him as such, at least not in private.

"Another tough day at the office?" Kurt asked, unruffled by Nate's snappishness. He grabbed Nate's leg again. "I'll sit on you if I have to, so hold still."

Nate groaned but didn't have the energy to fight off Kurt's second attempt to remove his shoes.

"Wanna tell me about it?" Kurt asked, tossing first one shoe aside, then the other.

Nate turned over onto his back so he could see Kurt's

face, needing to look into a pair of sympathetic eyes. All day, he'd been faced with anger, and stubbornness, and condescension—even downright hatred—and he'd been fighting to keep himself contained, to project an aura of competence and control.

"I'm in over my head," he admitted, though in truth that was the least of his problems. "I don't know how to be Chairman even under *good* circumstances." Because he'd been the world's shittiest Chairman Heir, spending all his time and energy on petty rebellion and having fun instead of learning how to govern.

"Give it time," Kurt said, patting his leg absently.

"I *have* been giving it time!"

Kurt rolled his eyes. "What has it been? Ten days? I think it takes longer than that to learn to be Chairman."

Nate sighed and closed his eyes. It was true that ten days wasn't a lot of time, but as each of those days had passed, Nate had become more and more certain that he was not the right person to lead Paxco out of these dark times. And it wasn't just because of the learning curve, either.

"You've seen the news," Nate said. "The protests. The calls for my resignation. Or arrest. Or execution."

Nate wanted to tell Kurt the whole truth—that an attempt had been made on his life today, and that it hadn't been the first—but that would only make Kurt worry. Nate was already doing enough worrying for both of them. Two attempts in ten days was not a good sign, and if someone *competent* were to try it . . .

The bed dipped under Kurt's weight and he dragged Nate into his arms. Nate settled there with a sigh of relief.

"They hate me, Kurt. The public, the press—even the board members." The board had accepted him as Chairman in the immediate aftermath of Thea's death, but since then they'd been fighting him tooth and claw over every insignificant little decision. It wasn't completely unexpected, considering their first priority was to restore the status quo and Nate had no intention of letting that happen. And he was still legally underage, so he didn't yet have the full powers of the Chairmanship, which meant he couldn't throw his weight around like his father had. But what really bothered him was the way the board members eyed him with undisguised distrust and suspicion, as if he might turn out to be a maniacal robot taking orders from Thea after all.

Kurt snorted. "Don't those assholes know they'd all be dead if it weren't for you?"

It was true that if Nate and Nadia hadn't stepped in—and hadn't made their agreement with Belinski—Thea would no doubt have killed and replaced the entire board over time, but . . . "Somehow, Nadia seems to get all the credit for that," Nate said, hoping he didn't sound bitter or jealous. He didn't begrudge her the praise, or her growing reputation as a hero. She had, after all, been the one who had actually succeeded in calling for the missile strike at great personal risk. And once she was reunited with Dante and the surviving Basement-dwellers finally agreed to lay down their arms, she had spearheaded relief efforts that strengthened her public image even more. She deserved every ounce of the love she was getting.

Kurt hugged him tighter. "They're scared of you right

now," he said gently. "Gun-shy because of Dorothy. They'll get used to you."

That's what Nate had been telling himself, and maybe Kurt was right and he wasn't giving it enough time, but deep in his gut he feared the people of Paxco would never accept him. And it didn't look like the rest of the Corporate States were too eager to accept him, either. Not all of the scathing opinions he'd heard voiced had been from Paxco citizens, and there were several formerly allied states who were now refusing to trade with Paxco as long as their Chairman was a Replica.

"I don't think they will, Kurt," he said, feeling like he was being crushed under the weight of all that fear and hatred. "I'm afraid that Paxco will never be able to heal as long as I'm at the helm."

Kurt cupped Nate's face in one hand and leaned over to kiss him, the warmth of his lips enough to thaw a little of the ice in Nate's heart. Nate expected another pep talk, but Kurt surprised him, as he had a way of doing on a regular basis.

"So what's the alternative?"

"Huh?" Nate asked, his mind sluggish beneath the burdens he'd been dragging around.

"If you stepped down as Chairman, who'd take your place? Is it someone you think could fix the mess?"

Nate frowned, thinking about it for the first time. Since he didn't have kids, his heir would be whoever was his closest living relative on his father's side. He had a bunch of cousins scattered around Paxco, but they weren't first cousins, and he had no idea who his legal heir would be. He said as much to Kurt.

"Maybe you should look into it. See who's next in line."

Nate propped himself on one elbow and frowned at his boyfriend. "You *want* me to step down?" Kurt had been politically active enough that he'd been a member of the resistance movement. He was currently in prime position to influence Paxco's future by influencing Nate. It was more power than any Basement-born revolutionary could possibly hope to attain. And if Nate stepped down, he would lose it all.

"I want you to be happy," Kurt said. "I'd love to see you take control of Paxco and make it a better place. But not if it makes you miserable."

Nate's heart felt about three sizes too big for his chest. "That means a lot to me."

"So find out who would be Chairman if you stepped down. Chances are it'll be someone you can't stomach leaving in charge, but you can't be sure until you check."

"I'll get right on it," Nate promised.

"*Right* on it?" Kurt asked with a mischievous twinkle in his eye. "As in right this second?"

Nate smiled and was happy to discover that he could muster a little energy after all.

nadia snuggled contentedly into Dante's arms. Her nose was sunburned and her hands were roughened with calluses thanks to the work she'd been doing in the Basement. Not that it was anything dangerous or even particularly strenuous in comparison to what most of the aid workers were doing, but she spent a lot of time darting from tent to tent in the staging area, helping open and label boxes of food and clothing for the refugees left homeless by the bombing.

Dante's work was more brutal as he helped with the massive effort to clean up the wreckage, an effort that would take months, if not years, to complete. He promised her he was being careful with his left arm, which was still in a splint, so she tried not to worry. His face was peeling and his hands were a mess, dirt embedded so deep under his fingernails he couldn't get it out, but she didn't mind at all having those rough hands skimming over her body.

Dante bent to kiss her, and Nadia's heart fluttered pleasantly. She had shed the last vestiges of Executive constraint, and she didn't care who in her household knew that she was dating an Employee. If someone wanted to sell the story to the tabloids, she could live with the scandal. If Agnes was willing to leave the traditions of Executive society behind, then so was Nadia.

In fact, the only concession she made to propriety was to keep her bedroom door open, and really that had nothing to do with Executive class values at all. It was simply the line past which her father refused to be pushed. Gerald Lake might be a shadow of his former self, but about one thing he was adamant.

"You're only sixteen, Nadia," he'd told her. "I don't care what you may or may not have done with that boy when you were in hiding, but I will not have you alone with him behind closed doors. Not in my house!"

Nadia had given in because she knew it had nothing to do with Dante's class status—there was *no* boy he'd allow her to be behind closed doors with, as long as he had any say in the matter. It was a parent thing, not a class thing. But the more time she spent with Dante, the more desperately she wanted to close that door.

What could her father possibly do to her if she defied him? After the hell she'd been through, she felt practically invincible.

She wrapped her arms around Dante's neck, holding him close as she kissed his sun-chapped lips and felt the enticing play of muscles across his shoulders as he leaned over. His body was pressed against hers on the bed—on top of the covers, naturally—and the longing that thrummed through her veins was almost more than she could bear.

"Let's close the door," she whispered when Dante came up for air.

His dark eyes widened, and he pressed more tightly against her, letting her know how much he liked the suggestion. "But your father—"

"—doesn't get to tell me what to do anymore," Nadia finished firmly. "I'm taking charge of my own life, and I'm not letting him or anyone else get in my way."

Dante kissed her again, long and deep. "Are you sure this is what you want?" he whispered against her lips.

"Yes," she said, with absolute conviction. Over the last few days, she'd thought a lot about what she wanted. She had changed since the days of her engagement to Nate, but though she was no longer a slave to convention, she didn't think she'd ever shake her conservative, cautious center. Taking her relationship with Dante to the next level would entail risks, no matter how careful and conscientious they were, and it was not a step to be taken lightly. She wanted to take it anyway. "I want you."

She felt the tremor that rippled through him at those words and was glad to know this wasn't just some casual thing for him. She'd never questioned him about any past girlfriends, but considering he'd been a resistance spy working as an infiltrator in the Paxco security department, she seriously doubted he'd had much of a social life. She might not be his first—she was too chicken to ask—but she would not be one of many, either.

Dante swallowed hard. "Then next time I come over," he said breathlessly, "I'll come prepared. Unless you've been taking some pills I don't know about."

Nadia let out a frustrated groan. Apparently, he hadn't learned his lesson since the last time she'd tried to fling herself at him.

He smiled down at her. "It's better this way," he said, planting a light, teasing kiss on her lips. "Better to make a decision when we're not in the heat of the moment." His face sobered, and he brushed a strand of hair away from her face. "If we do this, you can't ever go back."

"I don't *want* to go back," she assured him. "Besides, people already assumed I was sleeping with Nate. I don't have much of a reputation left to protect."

Dante rolled off her, but didn't go far, cuddling her in his arms once more. "Executive society would eventually forgive you for sleeping with Nate. They won't be as forgiving about me."

"I don't care," Nadia said stubbornly. "I'm not going back to that life. Executive society can go to hell."

Footsteps sounded in the hallway outside, and despite her declaration, Nadia hastily sat up and put some distance between herself and Dante. Just because she was no longer terrified of scandal didn't mean she wanted to broadcast her private life to the world.

Crane appeared in the doorway and frowned mightily at what he saw. Nadia and Dante might have moved apart, but she suspected it wasn't hard for the butler to guess what they'd been up to moments before he'd arrived.

"Pardon the interruption, Miss Lake," he said, his voice dripping with disapproval, "but you have another visitor."

"Who?" she asked. She wasn't expecting anyone.

"Nathaniel. Excuse me, Chairman Hayes."

"Wonder what he wants?" Nadia asked with a frisson of unease. She talked to Nate on the phone regularly, but their paths hadn't crossed much in these early days of rebuilding Paxco.

"Shall I tell him you're indisposed?"

Nadia rolled her eyes. "No, no. Tell him I'll be right out."

Crane left with a haughty sniff, and Dante climbed off the bed. "I'm going to duck out the servants' entrance," he said.

"That's not necessary!" Nadia said. "It's not like Nate doesn't know about us."

Dante grinned sardonically. "Yeah, but there's knowing and there's *knowing,* if you know what I mean. And call me crazy, but I don't think dangling it in his face is a good idea."

Nadia sighed quietly. Dante was probably right. He and Nate would never be friends, and Nate would probably never get over the little hint of irrational jealousy he'd always felt. His temper was considerably better controlled these days, but there was no reason to tempt fate.

"All right," she said reluctantly.

Dante kissed her and smiled. "Just remember what we have planned for next time. Maybe that'll make you feel better."

He was right: it did.

CHAPTER THIRTY-ONE

On a Wednesday night, two weeks after Thea's death and two days after Nate's unexpected visit, Nadia allowed Crane to get the door while she waited in the small study where she had spent a lot of time doing schoolwork growing up. The living room just wouldn't do for this particular conversation—she needed a room with a door she could close, but she didn't want to send the wrong signal by using her bedroom. When she'd called to invite Dante over, he'd known immediately that something was wrong, though she'd refused to tell him about it on the phone. He probably wasn't expecting tonight to be the "big night" despite their earlier decision, but why take chances? This was going to be difficult enough already.

Her stomach churned with anxiety, and there was a dull throbbing behind her eyes that might very well turn into one hell of a headache soon. Dante must have seen the turmoil in her face the moment he set eyes on her, but he waited until Crane retreated before enveloping her in a hug.

"What is it?" he asked.

"Let's sit down for a bit," she said. "My answer's going to take a while." Assuming she could get herself to spit it out at all.

They sat down together on an overstuffed love seat that

ordinarily Nadia found very comfortable, a perfect spot to curl up and read. Tonight, though, she wanted to leap to her feet and pace the moment she sat down.

"You're worrying me," Dante said, his eyes full of gentle concern.

Nadia let out a grunt of frustration and ran her hand through her hair. It was an old habit that had worked fine with her long, silky hair, but not so much with her new heavily moussed 'do. She practically yanked her hair out by the roots when her fingers got stuck.

"Did you know that security has foiled two assassination plots against Nate already?" she asked, knowing that the question would seem to be coming out of left field.

Dante's brow furrowed in an expression that combined puzzlement and concern. "I haven't heard anything about it. Is he okay?"

"He's fine. Physically, at least. And they've managed to keep it out of the press so far."

"You're never going to convince me to *like* the bastard, but he doesn't deserve to be treated the way people are treating him. I don't get why they don't see the difference between him and one of Thea's puppets."

Nadia suspected it was a hell of a lot easier for people who knew Nate to accept him than it was for total strangers. Strangers who knew that the original Nate—the *real* Nate, in their opinion—had died more than two months ago. As his father's son and Thea's creation, he stood for all the oppression of his father's reign, and all the madness of Dorothy's, and though Nadia had refused to admit it out loud, she suspected he was right and the people would never be able to see past it.

"It doesn't matter why," she said sadly. "It just matters that they don't."

Dante nodded. "I know. I'm sure it sucks to be him—and if you'd asked me a few months ago if I'd ever say something like that about an Executive, I'd have laughed you out of the room."

Her lips twitched into a smile despite the heaviness in her heart. Dante had had one hell of a chip on his shoulder once upon a time. He still made disparaging comments about lazy, good-for-nothing Executives every once in a while, but at least he now acknowledged that there were exceptions to the rule.

"Don't take this the wrong way," Dante said. "If you have something you need to talk through, I'm always here for you. But why are we talking about Nate?"

Nadia rubbed her eyes, wishing she could rub away the headache that was forming between them. She didn't want to get to the point, because the more she thought about it, the more she knew what Dante was going to say—and the less she liked it. But putting it off wasn't going to make it any easier.

Nadia licked her lips, then recognized that she was still stalling and forced herself to talk. "Nate's thinking of stepping down," she said, though Nate had done more than just think about it. He'd made it clear when he'd come to see her that he was going to step down one way or another.

Dante looked momentarily surprised, then asked, "Who would be Chairman if he did?"

"Therein lies the rub," she muttered.

"Huh?"

"He doesn't have a clear heir. There are three cousins

who might legitimately have a claim, but they're all pretty distant relations, and Nate doesn't think any of them would be a big improvement over his father."

"Nadia, where are you going with this?"

"Nate consulted with some lawyers and the board of directors. It seems that in the absence of an undisputed heir, if Nate wants to step down, he can name his successor, as long as he picks someone the board approves of. Nate thinks they'd approve of just about *any* high-ranking Executive if it would mean getting rid of him."

"Ungrateful assholes," Dante contributed, and Nadia agreed with him. "So who is it he would name?" he asked, but she could see from the look in his eyes that he'd figured that out on his own. Not that she supposed it was that hard. Who else would Nate pick?

"Me," she said. A chill of panic ran down her spine, and the pain of her headache redoubled. Her skin felt clammy and cold, her ribs tight.

It wasn't the enormity of the job that scared her—she wouldn't have all the powers of the Chairmanship until she was twenty-one and would have to have one or more trustees vetting her decisions until then. She hadn't been her father's heir until Gerri had died, but she had received the same education in economics and political science. Being a more conscientious student than Nate, she probably knew more about running a government than he did, even though he was two years older.

Dante shook his head, looking disgusted. And hurt. "So much for giving Executive society the finger," he said with undisguised bitterness. "Guess you won't be needing *me* around anymore."

He tried to jump to his feet, but Nadia grabbed his arm and held on for dear life.

"I don't want to do it, Dante. I don't want to be Chairman." It was the exact opposite of everything she wanted for her life. "I told him no."

Dante stopped trying to get up, but his body was still alive with tension, his face still closed off. "But he talked you into it."

"No. I told him I wouldn't do it. I *can't*." In the past couple of weeks, when she'd stopped living her life based on what she was *supposed* to do and started basing it on what she *wanted* to do, she'd had her first real taste of freedom. How could she possibly give all of that up and go back to her old life in the fishbowl?

Dante frowned at her, cocking his head. "What do you mean you *can't*? I think you'd make a *great* Chairman."

Nadia blinked. "Wait. Now you want me to say yes?"

"No!" He rubbed his face, and when he met her gaze again, there was confusion in his eyes. "It's just . . ." He huffed out a frustrated sigh. "It's just that I'm being a selfish bastard. If you become Chairman, then you won't be able to afford being seen with me." His voice went hoarse. "I don't want to lose you."

Nadia's heart felt like a lump of lead in her chest. Dante was going through the same mental process she had herself: the quick, knee-jerk refusal, followed by the realization of how selfish that refusal was.

"I don't want to lose you, either," she said. "That's one of the many reasons I said no."

Dante groaned and rubbed his face again. "But one way or another, Nate's never going to be able to hold on to the

Chairmanship, or he wouldn't be thinking of stepping down. And if you don't take his place, then one of the cousins will, and everyone will do their best to make sure Paxco goes back to being just the way it was."

Nadia nodded. She already had a lot of burdens to live with thanks to all of the fateful decisions she'd been forced to make. How would she live with it if someone cut from the same cloth as the late Chairman Hayes came into power because she wasn't willing to sacrifice the little fantasy life she'd built for herself?

"So what it comes down to," Dante whispered, "is that we both know you have to say yes. No matter how much we both hate it."

Nadia fought off a shiver. "If I'm named Chairman, then I become property of Paxco for the rest of my life. Do you have any idea what that means?"

"It means you have to go back to caring what society thinks of you." He started, then looked a little queasy. "And it means you'll have to start working out a new marriage arrangement."

The thought made Nadia feel as queasy as Dante looked, but it was an inescapable truth. Forming a new alliance via a marriage arrangement might be the only way to get Paxco out of its current tailspin. Thanks to the economy and the recent unrest, there wouldn't exactly be a lot of attractive offers pouring in, but if her relationship with Dante—a low-level Employee who had once been a servant in her house—were to become public knowledge . . .

"We can still be friends," she said hoarsely, hating the cliché with a passion. "My reputation can withstand that. But we can't be alone together anymore, and we certainly can't risk being seen kissing or holding hands. If I say yes, that is."

"There's so much more wrong with our world than Thea and the late Chairman Hayes," Dante said. "So much more that needs to change." He swallowed hard. "I joined the resistance when I was fifteen, against my parents' wishes. I agreed to infiltrate Paxco security just before I turned seventeen. I was meant to be their inside man, to work for Dirk Mosely and gain his trust, over the course of years, before I would be able to do anything substantial for the resistance. And every minute I was there, I risked getting caught, and being tortured for information. I was willing to go through all of that and devote my life to trying to fix Paxco. What kind of a revolutionary would I be if I asked you not to take the Chairmanship because I'm in love with you?"

Nadia's throat now ached almost as much as her head. Her every instinct had told her what Dante would say, that he would nobly put the needs of his state before his own, as he always had. But there was a part of her that couldn't help wishing he would fight for her, wishing he would put *her* first instead. Just as she so desperately wanted to do herself.

"You can change the world, Nadia," he said in an almost reverent tone.

She gave a soft little snort. "Like anyone's really going to listen to me once the shine wears off. Then they'll remember that I'm just a kid. The Chairman isn't all powerful, and I'll be even less powerful than most as long as I'm still a minor."

"I didn't say you were going to change the world *tomorrow,*" Dante protested. "It'll take time. A lot of it. Just like it would have taken me a lot of time to be of use to the resistance once I infiltrated. But you won't be a minor forever.

And even as a minor, I think you've proven to the world that you're a force to be reckoned with." He forced a smile. "And just because you have to *arrange* a marriage soon doesn't actually mean you have to get *married* soon. You won't even be able to sign a legal agreement until you're eighteen. Maybe before anything gets more serious than a couple signatures on a piece of paper, the world'll loosen up a bit and you can get out of it. You wouldn't be the first person in history to use an engagement to political advantage without actually getting married."

It made a nice fantasy, but if Nadia was going to do this, she had to be prepared for the likely reality, which was that she would have to give up Dante and would one day have to marry a man she didn't love.

"You really think I should do it?"

The look in his eyes held equal parts sadness and determination. "Yeah, I think you should. I think you're Paxco's best hope of getting back on its feet and starting down the long road to democracy. I think Nate's heart is in the right place, but you're more suited to the Chairmanship than he is. And I think that even though it's not fair, the people will never truly accept a Replica as Chairman."

If only Nadia could argue those claims.

CHAPTER THIRTY-TWO

one month after Thea had been destroyed—and a mere three days after Nadia's seventeenth birthday—Nate formally stepped down as Chairman of Paxco, naming Nadia as his successor. She was sworn in at a small, private ceremony held within Paxco Headquarters. The swearing-in was usually performed outside Headquarters, with a substantial live audience, but with Nate having to formally renounce his position, security deemed it better to keep the ceremony private. Even after he'd announced his intention to step down, the hatred the press and public displayed toward him was unsettling, and he lived under constant threat.

After the understated ceremony was complete, there was the obligatory formal reception, attended by all of Paxco's top Executives as well as Chairman Belinski. Agnes was conspicuously absent, despite Nadia's invitation. She refused to attend without Shrimp, but she and Nadia both knew that even with a formal invitation, he would not be welcome in this crowd.

Nadia had hoped that passing the Chairmanship over to her would allow Nate to live a more normal life, but it was becoming increasingly obvious that he was a target and would remain so for the foreseeable future. Even at this highly secure reception, he was shadowed by bodyguards, and he'd confided to Nadia that they'd talked him into wearing a bulletproof vest whenever he was in public. There had been only two human Replicas created before Nate. One of them had died of old age a couple of years ago. But the other had recently been beaten to death by an angry mob who had stormed his house and overwhelmed his personal security.

Nadia put on her best Executive face as she mingled with the cream of the Paxco Executive crop. Everyone was eager to congratulate her and wish her well. Most were more than eager to offer their "services" should Nadia need any help as she faced the daunting task of rebuilding Paxco from the ashes Thea had left. She figured all of them were aware that she still had several dead board members to replace and wanted to get a head start on kissing up to her.

The party had been under way for about an hour when Nate caught her eye from across the room and gestured her toward him. She gladly cut off Jewel Howard—her onetime nemesis and suddenly wannabe best friend—in midsentence to make her way across the room toward Nate, whom the mingling Executives had shunned with determined glee. Several people tried to interject themselves into her path, but Nadia put them each off with a tight smile, her heart aching for her friend. Nate had once been well loved, at least by the younger crowd, and it had to hurt to be so thoroughly ignored by people who had once claimed to be his friends.

"Mind if we talk in private for a couple of minutes?" Nate asked when she was within earshot.

In all honesty, she'd have loved to quietly slip away from

the reception altogether, but that was not one of her options. The reception might be billed as a "party," but she was very aware that she was at work here.

"Sure," she said, gesturing toward the nearest doorway, "but you know I can't spend a lot of time at it."

He nodded. "Understood."

Nate's bodyguards checked the hallway before letting him out. Nadia's own security team followed close on their heels, and the only way she and Nate could find anything resembling privacy was to let themselves into one of the offices and close the door behind them. Even then, she was aware of how closely both sets of bodyguards hovered, so she kept her voice down.

"What is it you wanted to talk about?" she asked.

She expected it to be something of a political nature, some advice or a warning or a little bit of inside information, so what he said took her completely by surprise.

"I wanted to say good-bye."

Nadia felt like she'd been kicked in the chest as she looked up to meet his eyes in shock. "Good-bye? What?"

He heaved a sigh and sat down on the nearest desk. "I can't stay in Paxco," he said. "Even if the nut jobs don't get me eventually, this is no way to live."

Nadia couldn't argue. Nate was an extrovert if she'd ever seen one, and he would go crazy living a life of social isolation for very long. Already, the strain showed on his face, and he had lost enough weight to look almost fragile. Perhaps some of the stress would be relieved when the burden of the Chairmanship was off his shoulders, but if the way people were treating him at the reception was any indication, he was still going to be a social outcast.

"God, Nate," she said, shaking her head. "I'm so sorry. You don't deserve this."

He shrugged. "Deserve doesn't have much to do with it. As they say, it is what it is. I can't stay here, and I can't go anywhere else in the Corporate States. My face is too well known, and the public rage against Replicas is too entrenched."

Nadia blinked. "But . . . where will you go?"

"Chairman Belinski has some friends and family in Eastern Europe. He's offered to send me and Kurt there to start over. He and his people can create new identities for us, and my face isn't half so famous over there. I'll get a job and work for a living, like ordinary people do."

"Eastern Europe," Nadia murmured, then sat on the edge of another desk herself. All her life, Nate had been her best friend. The only person she could ever be truly honest with, the only person who really *saw* her, really *understood* her. And now that she had agreed to be Chairman of Paxco, to take this immense burden onto her shoulders, he was going to move halfway around the world under a new identity.

"I promise, I'll always be there if you need me," he said, his voice growing husky. "Just a phone call away."

"A phone call isn't quite the same," she protested, on the verge of panic. Dante swore he would always be her friend, even if their relationship had to turn platonic, but things were sure to be awkward between them. Especially when the marriage negotiations started. He would not be able to step into Nate's place. No one could. "I can't do this alone," she whispered.

Nate stood up, crossing the distance between them and taking both her hands. "You won't be alone. I'll be a phone call away, and Dante will be right here with you, and if he doesn't take good care of you I will come back just to kick his ass."

Nadia managed a weak little laugh. "I'd pay money to see that," she teased.

"And you've got Agnes, too," he said, smiling. "She's a pretty good friend to have around in a pinch."

Nadia nodded, her eyes misting over. Agnes had a good head on her shoulders and had a really good grasp of strategy and politics. Not only that, but her relationship with Shrimp made her capable of understanding Nadia's anguish over Dante. So Nate was right: she *wouldn't* be alone.

"When do you leave?" she asked.

"I'm heading straight to the plane from here."

"Oh. So soon."

"Didn't seem to be much point in sticking around and letting someone take another potshot at me."

"Good point." She rose from the desk and put her arms around him, still not quite believing that he was leaving. He'd been her presumed fiancé and her best friend since she was four years old. Not to have him nearby was almost unthinkable. "I'm going to miss you," she said, but it was a massive understatement.

"I'll miss you, too," he replied. He released her from the hug, dabbing surreptitiously at his eyes. "And I'd better get out of here before I make some big, embarrassing scene."

How she was going to go back to the stupid reception and play politics after this was a mystery. Then again, playing social politics when your emotions were a twisted mess was all part of being an Executive, and she'd been doing it all her life.

She and Nate both took a couple of deep breaths to steady themselves; then when she nodded that she was ready, he opened the door.

Both their security teams were waiting patiently for them, as was Bishop. Nadia almost didn't recognize him at first. Instead of wearing servant's livery or his flamboyant Basement regalia, he was dressed in a very ordinary-looking pair of jeans and a gray shirt. He'd done away with the mohawk and replaced it with a buzz cut. He still had the facial piercings and tattoos, and yet he managed to look almost respectable.

Once upon a time, Nadia hadn't much liked Bishop, and the feeling had been mutual. And though he wasn't dressed like a servant, everyone here knew who he was. Even the supposedly discreet bodyguards might be tempted to wag their tongues, but Nadia decided she didn't care and gave Bishop a hug—a gesture that clearly startled him, though he quickly returned it.

"You take good care of Nate, you hear me?" she said.

"Will do," he responded.

She stepped back, fighting down a surge of emotion.

"And you take good care of yourself," Bishop finished.

Nadia almost lost it right there, but a few deep breaths helped shore up her public face. She had a lot of practice storing up tears, waiting for moments of privacy to let them out, and she was very good at it.

"I'll call you as soon as we get settled," Nate promised. It looked like he might be storing up some tears himself.

"You'd better!"

They shared a last long look before Bishop slung his arm around Nate's shoulders.

"It ain't gonna get any easier," he said, turning Nate toward the elevators. "One foot in front of the other."

Nate allowed Bishop to steer him to the elevator, the bodyguards fanning out around them. Nadia took one last deep breath to steady herself before turning her back to them.

She had a lot of work to do. And today was just the beginning.